Kim,

You, alone are responsible for the presence of "good" dragons on Earth. Thanks!

Destiny Fulfilled

Book 3 of the Anandrian Series

Love,

Aunt Kathy

aka Kathryn Heaney

 FriesenPress

Suite 300 - 990 Fort St
Victoria, BC, Canada, V8V 3K2
www.friesenpress.com

All characters, organizations and events portrayed in this novel are either products of the
author's imagination or are used fictionally.

Cover illustration by:
Laura Heaney

ISBN
978-1-4602-6220-7 (Hardcover)
978-1-4602-6221-4 (Paperback)
978-1-4602-6222-1 (eBook)

1. Fiction, Dystopian

Distributed to the trade by The Ingram Book Company

A Note to the Reader

When I originally started writing the third book, *Destiny Fulfilled*, Lucifer had planned to stay at a spa in Arizona that was located next to a state park that contained natural caves. Here, he was to create a portal linking Earth and Anandria. And Mandy was a lackluster character – more zombie-like than the assertive woman I wanted her to be.

Unfortunately, even though I **was** about halfway through the story, it wasn't working! So, I scrapped the whole first draft and began again with the adage, "Write what you know," running through my head.

Where should Lucifer create a portal?

A light went off in my head when I began thinking about our family cottage on Salerno Lake. One portion of the shoreline consists of a jumble of rocks left behind by glaciers where, as a child, I had explored and found small "caves". There was even a porcupine in one – not sure who was more scared, the porcupine or me! So the setting I used, at our cottage on Salerno Lake, actually exists – and the hill behind the cottage is a killer to climb with all your vacation gear!

ACKNOWLEDGEMENTS

Lacey and Gavin were gracious enough to give up a morning and come to Ashbridges Bay Park, in Toronto, to model for the cover of *Destiny Fulfilled*. They represent the characters Kathryn and Raonull. And using the photos we got that morning, Laura Heaney has once again created an outstanding cover for *Destiny Fulfilled*. It has been drawn using pencil crayons, her medium of choice. Check out her work at **lauraheaney.com**

Another well deserved nod also goes out to Laura Heaney. She has acted as my critique and eagle eye, by reading through my drafts of *Destiny Fulfilled*. You can thank her for pointing out errors and inconsistencies that I missed – and for asking me to write her a story when she was a young girl. It's amazing what that request has resulted in.

And finally, to you the reader... I can't thank you enough for all the support and kind words I have received for the Anandrian Series. Thank you!

PROLOGUE

"Mom! It's time!"

Laura Evans cracked her eyelids, reluctant to leave the warmth of her bed. But she kicked her husband, startling him, and rolled out from beneath the covers. Her daughter, Diana, backlit by moonbeams streaming through the window, was hunched over clutching her distended belly and panting heavily. Vaaron automatically reached beneath the bed and came to his feet wielding an intimidating broadsword.

Diana sputtered out a guffaw at the sight of her naked father and growled between gritted teeth, "Dad, you won't need that unless you intend to cut the cord..." She gasped and waddled farther into the room.

Vaaron's sword clattered to the stone floor and he muttered, "Bloody hell!" as he pulled on pants. Now partially clothed, at a loss for words or action, he turned to his wife and stood gaping stupidly at her.

Laura rolled her eyes. "A little light and heat would be good, dear."

"Right!" Vaaron scrambled into action, conjuring magic on his fingertips to light the stones set in brackets on the walls about their bedchamber, before heating the rocks piled in the impressive stone hearth.

"Where's Manus?" Laura demanded as she approached Diana and draped an arm about her shoulders to lead her to the bed.

Vaaron tensed. "Aye, where is your husband?"

Diana groaned, toppled onto the bed, gasped again, and clutched at her rising belly. Finally she relaxed as the contraction released and she could talk again. "He's gone to feed Apona's baby. He had a nice piece of lamb he thought the little dragon would relish."

"He left you?" Vaaron bellowed.

Diana blew out a deep breath. Her belly was rising again. Through clenched teeth she muttered, "The contractions started *after* he left, Dad!"

"Oh, well... all right," Vaaron grumbled. "I will go fetch the lad." It was a lame excuse to leave his own bedchamber, but he ripped the door open in his haste to leave, flinched when it crashed against the wall, and dashed through the opening. Thank God, Manus had not been with Diana, otherwise he would not have made good his escape.

Mother and daughter locked gazes and burst into gales of laughter – somewhat strangled in Diana's case, since she was riding out her contraction. With a final gasp, Diana hissed, "I think it's probably a good thing Dad wasn't there for *our* births."

Laura nodded. "As much as I'd wished him to be there when I gave birth to you and your brother, I think Jeff made a better labour coach."

"Speaking of whom... You'd better pull the easel to the side of the bed so Jeff and Aunt Mandy... Oh, God... Here comes another contraction!"

"Junior's eager to be born," Laura observed as she dragged the easel with the frame propped on it closer to the bed.

Through the frame, one could see the dim outline of a bachelor apartment. On the sofa bed that dominated the room a man groaned and buried his head deeper into his pillow. "Damn it, Laura, go away. I'm trying to sleep!" His words were muffled by the pillow.

"If that's what you want, Jeff... But Mandy will be pissed when she misses the birth of her great nephew, or niece."

Jeff jerked upright.

"What?" He scrambled from beneath the covers, clad only in boxers. He had taken to wearing them after he'd begun sleeping on the main floor of Laura's old apartment, situated in the house that Mandy owned, so they could catch news from Anandria. The problem was, he never knew *when* Laura would come near the painting of her old apartment and open the portal. There had been one or two occasions when Laura had inadvertently neared the picture, and her proximity to it had opened the portal leaving them both staring in stunned surprise at each other – hence his boxers.

It was also the reason why Laura kept the frame well across the room from her own bed since she didn't relish the possibility of a peeping Tom – err, Jeff – when she shared intimate moments with Vaaron.

Diana huffed out a groan, and Jeff's eyes widened. "Don't let anything happen until I get Mandy. She'll kill me if she misses this." He pounded down the stairs.

"As if... I can... control... this..." Diana panted.

"Laura!"

Diana and Laura shifted their eyes to Laura's bedchamber door. Morrigan leaned against the doorframe. Sweat beaded on her brow, and her arms were clasped around her protruding belly. "'Tis time!" she gasped.

"To quote my husband," Laura muttered, "bloody hell, Morrigan!" She hustled across the room and wrapped her arm about her friend's waist. "Two in one bed... Hard to imagine this scenario. If this was in a book, or played out in a movie, I'd scoff at the idiot who wrote the storyline."

Diana's contraction eased, and she sank gratefully into the mattress. Still breathing heavily, she grinned at her mom. "It makes perfect sense here in Anandria, Mom. David and Morrigan were married the same night Manus and I were." She shrugged. "Same wedding night and look what's happening nine months later!" She reached out to Morrigan as her sister-in-law collapsed onto the mattress next to her. A twinkle danced in Diana's eye. "And considering how the magic of Anandria runs through both of us, perhaps there's a little push from that direction, as well."

Laura critically eyed the two women. *Can I do this? Can I see to the welfare of these two powerful women – my best friend, the Goddess of War, and my child, the Moon Goddess?* Both lay panting and grinning at each other, their hands clasped in mutual support. Laura struggled for breath. It was incredible how her world had changed since that day long ago when she had tumbled through her painting into the magical dimension of Anandria, where names and their meanings stirred power.

Laura glanced down at herself. An over-sized T-shirt came to her knees. Thank heavens Vaaron had collapsed after a long day of training the troops or she may have been caught less covered... She shook her head. *Focus! Quit stalling.* She needed to assess the two mothers-to-be.

"Goddamn it!" Morrigan roared with augmented volume.

The walls of the castle shook.

Books tumbled off shelves, and Laura dove to steady the easel that supported the portal. *Crap! Morrigan's goddess voice means Morrigan's in distress.* Talk about a rare event. Morrigan's augmented voice was meant to be used on the battlefield over the deafening clash of warriors hacking it out with their swords.

Laura let the frame go when Morrigan's voice petered out leaving the War Goddess gasping for breath. Her eyes cut to her daughter. Di had to be feeling pretty good, since she hadn't pulled magic from the moon – yet.

Morrigan groaned and set off another mini quake.

"Morrigan!" Laura snapped – the last thing they needed were major repairs to the castle... Laura hurried to Morrigan's side of the bed, took her face between her hands, and demanded, "Where's my son? Where's your husband, David?"

The contraction eased and Morrigan panted, "Sent him... to get... Audrey..."

"The chatelaine of the castle? Why?" Laura asked, puzzled.

"Water broke...Babe coming fast...Audrey knows...midwifery..."

"She does?" Laura was surprised, yet she shouldn't be, she thought with a rueful grin. Audrey had to be the most efficient, hardworking, reliable, bossy chatelaine in the history of Veresah! The woman was remarkable, handling any situation within the castle's walls. *So why not the birth of a baby?*

"I do!" came Audrey's familiar voice from the doorway.

Geez, Laura had been worried about taking on the two births for months. She'd even thought about suggesting the girls spend some time on Earth where modern hospitals handled pregnancies every day. However, the doctors and nurses didn't have the capability to heal instantly if things went wrong – so Laura had sucked it up and steeled herself for this day figuring she'd handle it all on her own.

A tight ball of worry unfurled when her son, and Audrey, strode into the room. Audrey pushed up her sleeves, while David, looking pale and worried, rushed to Morrigan's side. *I'm not doing this on my own.* Laura smiled fondly when David's face went even whiter at the sight of his sister lying next to his wife.

David stuttered, "Di! You, too?"

"Yup!"

From the doorway, another male voice gasped a strangled, "Di!"

Diana's eyes swung to the door. Manus, High Priest of the Lunar Temple of the City of Moyen, rushed across the room to her side and clasped her hand in his. Behind Manus, Vaaron edged slowly into the room. This was not the place for him, Laura noted with amusement. Give him blood, guts, a battlefield, but...

Suddenly another amplified groan reverberated throughout the room as Morrigan's belly rose again. Frantic, Morrigan clutched at her abdomen with two hands. Her eyes widened exposing the whites clearly. Immediately, Audrey dove between Morrigan's legs as she said to Laura, "Have a look see how far along yer daughter be."

Laura stooped to examine Diana.

Di's belly began to tighten with a contraction stronger than anything she had experienced to this point. "Oh God! Oh God! Oh God!" With each expletive, Diana's grip on her husband's hand tightened.

"Di!" Manus yelled in panic. His knees buckled from the pain Diana's moon-enhanced grip caused. "Di!"

Everyone, with the exception of the two labouring women, winced when bones snapped in his hand. It reminded Laura of cereal that went snap, crackle, pop! It looked like Di was oblivious to the damage she had caused Manus.

Manus roared under the excruciating pain. Instinctively, he drew upon the power of the moon. A yellow aura of calming moonglow seeped out of his hands surrounding both himself and Diana. A tad of magic leaked over to Morrigan where Diana's foot touched her, and instantly Morrigan's amplified voice lowered into normal groans of misery, Diana's grip eased, and Manus was able to retrieve his mangled hand.

Laura's head popped up from between Diana's thighs. "I can see..."

Manus peered at his hand when Laura stopped speaking to stare at him in horror. *Christ! None of my fingers are pointing in the right direction.* Spots began to float across his eyes and his knees felt rubbery...

"Crap!" Laura breathed as she hurried to her son-in-law. His face was positively green. Quickly, she cupped his mangled hand between hers and whispered, "Heal thyself!" Power flowed, encasing their hands in a white glow. Magically, his fingers straightened into a functioning hand.

Manus tentatively flexed his digits. "My profound thanks," he murmured and kissed Laura's cheek.

Laura smiled at him. He still looked green!

"Morrigan's babe be almost here," Audrey said as she looked up at David, who was standing still looking somewhat shell-shocked.

Audrey snorted when she noticed Vaaron propped against the wall just inside the door. His face was full of worry and horror. A birthing chamber was no place for men. "Vaaron!" The old warrior jerked when he heard her call his name. "Take the lads to fetch the cradles ye've prepared. Stay outside until we call for them." Vaaron nodded, grateful for the assignment. She snorted. 'Twas not the task perking him up, but the escape without losing face. "Now, Vaaron!" Audrey stressed. The men were barely standing. Sweat dripped off Manus's forehead, and David was swaying.

"Aye," Vaaron replied. He motioned for the men to follow him. Almost reluctantly, both walked away from the bed, but Vaaron noticed the tension in their bodies lessen the further they got from the birthing bed.

David and Manus locked gazes when they stood outside in the hall. "Geez, the pain," David murmured. "I never knew it would be this bad."

"Aye!" Manus agreed. He glanced down at his newly mended hand. "Tis unsettling."

Vaaron threw his arms across their shoulders and steered them down the hall. "Tis why we have been banished."

"We're not banished," David muttered. "We've been sent to get the cradles."

Vaaron shook his head. "'Twas an excuse to get us out of the way. We may be the fiercest warriors able to defend and protect our families, but when our women give birth, we cannot watch them endure the pain. It goes completely against our nature to let them suffer."

A lone man hidden by shadows near the top of the stairs that led down to the main hall, pushed away from the wall. "Tis remarkable how long ye lasted," he said in greeting.

Vaaron snorted at the sight of his nephew, Elfare, smugly smiling at them. "Tis true, we tarried too long for my ease," Vaaron acknowledged. "But 'twas the High Priest who caused our delay.

His wee wife – my daughter – mashed his hand, and Laura had to heal him before we could make our exit."

"Bloody hell!" Manus exclaimed. "My wee wife happens to be the bloody Moon Goddess! And guess what? The moon is high tonight. She is at *full* power. Anandria is lucky she is well inland, miles from the coast. Even so, the tides will fluctuate wildly causing many to evacuate coastal areas when her pain hits its peak and she unleashes her magic." Manus stabbed a finger into Elfare's chest. "In fact, before we came here, we made sure the lower levels of the City of Moyen were abandoned until after the birth."

Elfare brushed Manus's finger aside and clapped him on the shoulder. "'Twas smart to move her well away from the sea, priest. But now, let us move down to the main hall, join the festivities, and quaff down ale until you officially enter fatherhood."

"Hey!" David protested. "I'm married to the Goddess of War. What about my impending fatherhood?"

Elfare slowly eyed him up and down. "'Tis because of *your* wife that I and most of Veresah have awakened at this ungodly hour." He held his hand up when he saw David was about to protest. "'Twas the bellowing of your blushing bride that alerted us to the blessed event." Outright sarcasm was laced through his voice. "But I have to admit, 'twas a pleasant surprise to run into Vaaron when he fetched Manus, and I learned that Diana was abed, too."

Murmuring voices floated up the stairs as they descended to the main hall.

"God almighty!" David breathed when they navigated the curve in the stairs and he saw the hall below them. The massive space was full of people. Men and women chatted and drank tankards of ale while focusing on the stairs. A hush fell over the crowd, but Elfare shook his head and conversations picked up again.

Elfare smirked. "See? Morrigan has awakened the whole town. Now, they await news. There are more outside in the streets – they could not all fit in here." He grabbed a couple of tankards off a passing tray and shoved them at David and Manus.

"But we're supposed to get the cribs..." David protested, eyeing the ale.

"Already done," Elfare quipped as he snagged two more drinks. He kept one and passed the other to Vaaron. "I dispatched some men to see to the task before you three emerged from the bedchamber."

An angry wail from the top of the staircase interrupted the merriment in the great hall. 'Twas the sound of new life thrust from its dark, warm home into the cold, cruel world. David and Manus looked at each other and thunked their tankards down on a table.

"Not yet!" Vaaron bellowed. He and Elfare grabbed their tunics and hauled them back from the bottom step of the staircase. "We wait for the other one..."

Almost as if on cue, a much quieter cry joined the furious wailing of the first babe. Vaaron nodded to Elfare, and they let the two new fathers go. Vaaron followed in their footsteps. He was a grandfather. *Imagine that.* Ahead, he heard their pounding footsteps come to an abrupt halt. He picked up his pace. Audrey, at the top of the stairs, cradled a babe in each arm. One still howled furiously.

"Ah, here comes Grandpa, now," she crooned as she looked at Vaaron with a pleased grin.

The two fathers stood on either side of her gawking at the bundles she carried. "Tis one of each ye have." She turned to David and slid a baby neatly into his uncertain hands. "Tis a boy for you." Then she swung to Manus. "And for you, High Priest, a wee girl."

Manus accepted the bundle. "And my wife?"

Audrey nodded. "Aye, both women be fine. After ye used moonglow to retrieve your hand, Diana got the notion to use it, too, on both herself and Morrigan. Which I might say, made the birthing process much more pleasant. Never before have I seen such serene women in the throes of labour." She patted Manus on the shoulder. "Well done, lad."

"Where's Laura?"Vaaron demanded. He took a peek at the new little faces. The boy was flushed scarlet as he wailed his head off. The girl was snuggled in her blanket, quietly taking in the world with big brown eyes. *Beautiful! Exceptional!*

"She's healing the girls. They'll not have to worry about tenderness after the births. Tis a right handy gift your wife has." Audrey walked down the hall and peeked into the bedchamber. "Bring the babes to their mothers. Laura is finished. All is well."

The men, with their precious burdens, hurried to their wives who held out their arms to receive their new little ones.

"My, this does make a pretty picture," Mandy cooed through the portal. They all looked her way. She and Jeff sat side by side on the end of his sofa bed. Both leaned forward. That was all they could do, because they were Earth bound – not of Anandria – but it was enough. Mandy beamed. "Guess I'm a great aunt, now!"

Jeff reached out and squeezed her hand. "You're always great," he proclaimed with a happy grin.

Mandy sighed. If only Jeff really thought so. She retrieved her hand and playfully slapped him on his bare shoulder. He was still in his boxers, and Mandy was okay with that! Thankfully, he hadn't rushed to dress when he had come to get her. They had reached the portal seconds before Morrigan had given birth to her son, and then within seconds of that event, Diana had given birth to her daughter.

Mandy turned her attention back to Diana and David, whom she called niece and nephew; Laura was like a sister, and her children she considered a part of her adoptive family. "Seriously, though," Mandy said narrowing her eyes at the two siblings. "Have you thought about names? They need strong names – names that will protect them." Her brown eyes bore first into David, then Diana.

David nodded solemnly. "We borrowed your, *Name the Baby*, book and Morrigan and I have chosen a Gaelic name for our son."

Morrigan smiled down at the whimpering bundle in her arms. *Thank heavens the screaming had ceased! Christ, can I feel any more self-conscious in the midst of all these people? I am supposed to be tough...* The War Goddess, right at this moment, knew she was radiating both warmth and softness as she peered down at her son. Her son's eyes opened and connected with hers. Morrigan sighed with delight. His whimpering stopped completely. *Yeah, I can do this... Just let any threat near my son, and the world will see the true measure of my fury.* "Aye, we have chosen a very strong name. He will be known as Raonull, the Mighty One!"

"Good, good," Mandy murmured as her gaze snapped to Diana. "And what are you going to name this precious little girl, Di?"

Diana dipped her head and brushed her lips across her daughter's forehead. Softly, she ran a finger down the little upturned nose. Fierce determination shone in Diana's teary eyes. "I never want her to experience the evil I was subjected to, so I've chosen the name Kathryn in the hopes that it will prevent Lucifer from ever possessing her."

Manus nodded. "At least, that is our hope. Kathryn means, Pure, but it is hard to know what the magic of Anandria will do with that name!"

1

❦

Twelve years after the births

Through the skylights, Mandy Dixon watched the night sky shift and shimmer in a showy display of northern lights. For a month they had been increasing in frequency and colour. Tonight, eerie green curtains undulated with fascinating beauty, and Mandy enjoyed them while she talked to her best friend, Laura.

Their conversation was not unusual for friends of long standing, but the line of communication was. No technology involved – only an inter-dimensional portal.

"So Lucifer is still asleep, huh?" Mandy wanted to know.

"Yeah! Everyone's dubbed it the Unremitting Sleep. He floats horizontally in mid-air. Vaaron keeps a guard watching Lucifer twenty-four seven, but so far, other than breathing, the Dark Lord hasn't moved a muscle."

"That's creepy," Mandy muttered.

"You can say that again," Laura replied. "But as far as I'm concerned, I hope he never wakes up. I'm really enjoying life, and I want it to be a long, happy one." She shuddered. "Just thinking about Lucifer's pursuit of me, makes my stomach clench. The guy is obsessed with the destruction of my soul to prevent my reincarnation. It's hard to believe I'm all that stands in the way of his total domination over the universe." Laura swept one hand down the length of her body. "I still pinch myself whenever anyone mentions I'm the essence of all that is good in the universe, and it's my presence in Anandria that gives them hope for the future."

"You've got to admit," Mandy said, "since you're the only being in Anandria that can heal someone in an instant, and change Lucifer's gargoyles back to their human selves, you are pretty impressive in any dimension."

"Yeah, but it puts a lot of pressure on me. I'm the *only one* stopping Lucifer from dominating the universe."

Mandy shrugged. "True, but you've got a lot of people backing you up. You're not alone."

Jeff appeared at the top of the stairs, his notebook tucked firmly under his arm. He was working from home tonight despite his long day at the lab. "Hey I thought I heard voices up here. How are my two favourite girls?" Without waiting for an answer, he crossed to the couch flopped down next to Mandy with his legs sprawled out in front. "What a day!"

His eyes connected with Laura's. "I wish you could bring that magic touch of yours to Earth. We had another young man – early twenties – get admitted into the program today."

Jeff, a kinesiology major, had pursued research in spinal cord injuries. Currently, he was working on a combination of wireless computer commands that linked to receptors implanted in leg muscles – and he was having some success. "I've never seen a more cynical, bitter person. I think his parents pushed him into the program." Jeff sighed. "It's like he's given up on life, and he's subjecting himself to our study to get his mom and dad off his back."

Laura blinked away a tear. "I wish I could help, too," she murmured. "That's so tragic..."

In an overly bright voice, Mandy cut in with, "Raonull hasn't been to see me in over a month, Laura. Why hasn't he come through to Earth?"

Laura smiled and gave a final swipe to her eye. Leave it to Mandy to steer her away from bleeding heart situations she could do nothing about. "Because he's been too busy getting into trouble. That's why."

"What do you mean?" Jeff asked. "I thought he'd be back soon, so I could show him some more moves."

"I think that was his plan, too, but he's discovered a few new moves here in Anandria."

"Go on," Jeff urged, intrigued by the thought that his fledgling martial arts student had picked up some Anandrian moves.

Laura shrugged. "In Anandria, as children approach puberty, they quite often begin to come into their magical gifts – although the majority don't experience this until closer to sixteen. A few begin earlier, like I did when I lived as Lauren and began healing around the age of five." She shrugged again. "Apparently, Raonull has been flexing his new gift without telling any of the adults about it."

"Mighty One," Mandy murmured. Her eyes narrowed as she contemplated the meaning of his name. "By flexing his new gift, I take it you mean, literally?"

Laura nodded. "My wee grandson, as Vaaron would say, has been drawing upon Anandria's magic to increase his strength. None of us knew he was doing this. He's been tossing boys of all sizes about with little or no effort." Laura honed in on Jeff. "He's using moves *you* showed him."

Jeff grinned. "That's my boy!"

Laura snorted. "Not so fast, Jeff. When he threw the boys, he threw them further than a normal person should be able to throw." She paused. "Mind you, he made sure to toss them into hay bales."

"Well, well," Jeff murmured, his eyes twinkling with amusement.

Laura's eyes twinkled right back at him. "Then the boys dared him to try his moves on General Trymian, who of course, had no idea Raonull was coming into power."

"I think I see where this is going." Jeff ran a hand over his mouth covering his grin.

"The general naturally agreed to spar with Raonull while all the boys watched, and two seconds later, the General had landed in the middle of a river over *fifty* yards away – and he was dressed in *full armour*." Laura nearly choked as she tried to hold in her own laughter. "General Trymian sank like a rock, and David, who fortunately was passing by, had to help pull the General out before he drowned."

"Oh my," Mandy gasped as she stifled giggles. "I bet that didn't go over well."

"Wait! It gets better," Laura wheezed. "As punishment, David grounded Raonull – no dragon riding for a week – and Raonull, in a fit of anger, punched the stone wall surrounding our town of Veresah. The wall was demolished. You could step right through the hole he created."

Jeff whistled. "Impressive! He's a little Hercules, huh? So what did David do next?"

Laura eased the easel holding the portal around so that it faced a window. "Raonull is doing community service for a week."

They all peered out the window. Torches lit up the area where Raonull bent over, shoved his fingers under a massive boulder, picked it up with ease, and set it in fresh mortar a mason was quickly slapping down in the gaping hole in the wall.

"Jesus!" Jeff whispered wide-eyed. "That rock's bigger than he is."

"After he's finished repairing the wall, there's a lot more construction everyone wants done around town, so they're going to take advantage of Raonull's punishment."

"Poor boy," Mandy murmured.

"Not so poor. I think he's really enjoying flexing his muscles." Laura turned the portal back to its usual resting place. "He'll be finished soon for the night, and when he comes into the hall all the ladies will coddle him with delicacies from the kitchen." Laura's voice lowered to a conspirator's whisper, and Jeff and Mandy leaned forward. "But I do feel sorry for the boy, too, because Kathryn's been taking advantage of him."

Mandy sat up straight. "Di, Manus, and Kathryn are in town?"

Laura nodded. "Just got in last night."

"And they haven't been to see me?"

"Easy Mandy. They arrived close to dawn. Diana was beat, and I wasn't available to open the portal."

"So where are they now? "Why aren't they here?"

Laura's smile deepened and her eyes twinkled with mirth. "They're dealing with Kathryn."

"What? Our Kathryn? Our pure, sweet, little Kathryn? What did she do?"

Laura spread her hands. "It seems our little Kathryn is discovering powers of her own, and she's been trying them out on her cousin, Raonull."

"Hey, you guys, are you discussing my daughter?"

Diana, Divine One, Moon Goddess, and Deity of the Hunt, strode into the bedchamber. She thrust her upper body through the portal, planted a smacking kiss on Mandy's cheek, wrapped her arms about Jeff in a shared a hug, and pulled back into Anandria to buss her mom. Greetings done, she collapsed next to Laura on the bed.

Laura smiled at her amazing daughter. Every night one of five moons was present in the sky providing Diana with enhanced strength, incredible hunting skills, and a command over the tides in this world. But during the day, Diana was toast. It was impossible for her to keep her eyes open.

Laura's thoughts strayed to Diana's twin brother David. He was impressive, too, she thought as she idly brushed hair out of Diana's eyes. David meant, Beloved One, and here in Anandria, he was truly that. He had become their premier military leader. His troops adored him, following without question anywhere he wanted to take them. Idly, Laura wondered if the names she had chosen at their birth had created their power, or if fate had dictated her choices allowing them to fulfill their destinies. After all, she had been reincarnated as Laura, another form of the name, Lauren, which she had been known by in her past life. Coincidence? Hmm...

"What's Kathryn done?" Mandy demanded.

Diana's blue eyes fastened on the matronly woman on the far side of the portal. For the first nineteen years of her life, Diana and her brother, David, had lived in Mandy's home – Diana still counted the woman as a second mom. One brow rose in an expression of bemusement as Diana explained, "It seems my little angel manipulated her cousin, Raonull."

The crease between Mandy's brows deepened. "How on earth could a little thing like Kathryn manipulate a big, stocky boy like Raonull?"

Diana sighed dramatically. "Remember those soft, brown eyes she inherited from her father?"

Mandy nodded.

"Well it turns out she's discovered how to get her own way – *every time.*"

"How?" Jeff asked. "Does she bat her eyelashes at Raonull, and he bends to her wishes despite the fact that he's only twelve and a woman that young shouldn't be able to sway him...?" Jeff's skin reddened as he realized what he was implying. He shut up.

Diana chuckled. "Nah... Close, but not quite. She has been blessed with an old Anandrian power that the scholars call, Suggestion."

"Which means?" Mandy asked, obviously intrigued by Diana's answer.

"If she can maintain eye contact with you long enough to utter her wish, she can make you submit to her will."

"No!" Mandy and Jeff breathed together.

Laura grinned. "Diana caught Kathryn compelling Raonull to complete her chores. She was supposed to muck out the dragon stalls just before dawn, but Diana found Kathryn lying on a hay bale with a smug smile on her face while Raonull cleaned the stalls – and that was after the poor boy had been hauling rocks for the last two days."

"And before that, shortly after we arrived," Diana interjected, "I was chatting with one of the servants, who had happened to mention that she had seen Kathryn directing Raonull to unpack and put away her clothing." Diana shook her head. "It was that chat that had me storming down to the stables where Kathryn was caught red-handed lording her power over Raonull. Needless to say, Raonull is furious that she can manage him so easily. But at least he's on guard around her now."

"I can't see that boy handling Kathryn's clothing," Mandy murmured.

They all fell silent picturing the stocky, golden haired boy, blessed with enormous strength, handling the delicate feminine garments that Kathryn favoured. The boy had to be embarrassed. The thought left amused smiles on all their faces. They knew Raonull would do just about anything for his little cousin – *within reason*. They all knew putting her clothes away was *not* within reason!

With a shake of her head, Diana came back to the present. "Guys, there's a reason we've come to Veresah." Jeff, Mandy, and Laura gave their undivided attention to Diana. "Manus and I are worried about Kathryn."

"What's wrong?" Mandy demanded.

Diana shrugged, sat up, and swung her legs over the side of the bed. "It's hard to describe. It's very nondescript, although it's a bit spooky."

"What?" everyone chimed in unison.

"Lately, Kathryn's been falling into trance-like states. Her eyes remain wide open, but no matter what's going on around her, she seems oblivious."

"Night terrors?" Laura asked thinking back to when Diana was little, and would come out of a deep sleep screaming with her eyes wide open.

"You'd think it was that, except it happens at the strangest times, and she doesn't seem terrified. She can be in the middle of a conversation when she suddenly blanks out. When she comes around, Kathryn doesn't seem to be aware that anything unusual has happened, and she carries on as if there hasn't been an interruption."

"Could be something your mom could fix," Mandy suggested, referring to Laura's healing powers.

"Could be," Laura agreed. She shot a sharp look at her daughter. "Anything else unusual in her behaviour?"

"Is that my daughter you are discussing?"

Everyone looked at the handsome, brown-eyed, sandy haired man accompanying Vaaron, Laura's husband, into the bedchamber. It was easy to see where Kathryn's red hair and brown eyes came from when you saw Manus.

Mandy's homely face broke into a grin of welcome. "Manus! You've kept my girls too long in the City of Moyen. I expect you to bring them through to visit me more often."

"Yes, ma'am," he replied, stepping in front of the frame with a curt bow.

Vaaron sat down next to Diana on the side of the bed and took her hand between his. "Manus told me about your concerns for Kathryn." He looked over at Laura. "Do you think you can help?"

Laura shrugged. "I can try, but I was just asking if there was anything else out of the ordinary happening with Kathryn."

Diana sighed, "No..."

"Wait!" Manus faced Diana. "Remember how shortly after Kathryn's *spells* she would talk about something that *might* happen?"

"And each time it did!" Diana exclaimed.

The stunned silence that followed was broken by Vaaron. "Could it be? Could she *also* have the Sight?""

Laura shook her head. "It's very rare that anyone is blessed with two powers from Anandria. Suggestion and Sight. Wow!"

"The Sight?" Mandy queried.

Manus turned towards the frame. "Tis a rare gift. We have recorded only four others in Anandrian history who have masterfully wielded it. Others may experience an incident or two over the course of their lives, but tis very rare to deal with this power consistently. Wait, make that five. Aisling has been recognized as a true wielder of the Sight."

Diana chuckled. "Yeah, it's about time they acknowledged her power. I still remember being freaked out by her prophecies about *us* when I first met you, Manus. At the time, she was only, what, six years old?"

Diana and Manus shared a smile before Manus added, "The one who wields this power catches glimpses of what *may* come."

"Like a prophet?" Jeff queried.

"Aye!"

"Do these visions always come true?"

Manus gave a negative nod. "I said they see what *may* occur. Their visions are often warnings. Sometimes they can see the same thing twice, only with different outcomes." He shook his head in bemusement. "I do not think I have ever heard of anyone wielding more than one magic. Imagine, our little Kathryn with two − Suggestion and Sight!"

"And why not?" Mandy roared. "Look at her lineage. Her grandmother is the essence of all that is good in the universe, and her mother is the Moon Goddess. They're the two most powerful women in Anandria. So why shouldn't she be special, too?"

Laura swung her legs over the side of the bed and stood. "Now hold on. Kathryn hasn't displayed anything concrete. Perhaps this is something completely different, and her words may have been merely coincidence."

Vaaron smirked at Laura. "Kathryn hasn't displayed anything concrete − *yet*."

From his tone, they all took his statement to mean that Kathryn was the real deal, and it was only a matter of time before *he* would be proven correct.

Laura closed her mouth and shook her head. What was the point in arguing over something no one was sure about? Only time would tell, unless a touch of her healing hands rectified the situation. She would examine Kathryn and make sure there was nothing physically wrong. After that, they would have to wait and see.

2

Demon Dience glanced at the sky. He detected faint crackling sounds from above. Multi-coloured lights were weaving across the night sky undulating in a fascinating display. *That* was where the noise was coming from... Magic was stirring! He could feel it. It electrified the air. 'Twas the perfect night to check on his Master, the Dark Lord.

For twelve years, Dience had been peering over the rim of the crater surrounding Lucifer's Lair. He had been observing the vigilant guards the people of Anandria had left to watch over his Master. And now, for the first time, Dience saw exhaustion line the face of the man left to carry out this duty.

Dience stared at the solitary guard and blinked when the man stumbled over to Lucifer's throne where he collapsed and put his head in his hands. Within minutes, soft snores escaped through the man's lax lips. 'Twas the first time Dience could creep close enough to his Master, hovering horizontally in mid-air, to view him.

Lucifer had not aged a bit.

For twelve years, Lucifer had lain unconscious, oblivious to the world around him. He had been put in stasis by the combined magics of Laura and her children. Dience had heard it said that Anandrians were calling Lucifer's floating coma the Unremitting Sleep.

Dience wrinkled his nose with distaste. Thinking about Laura and her daughter, Diana, had his stomach churning. Laura Evans, that paragon of goodness, had outwitted him in many past encounters, which meant his ass had been handed to Lucifer on more than one occasion. And when Morrigan, Laura's friend, had freed Laura from Lucifer's burning stake and had broken every finger on his hands for his part in Laura's capture, Laura had not had the decency to heal his broken digits. *The bitch!* He had been forced to whine and pester nearby gargoyles for help.

Finally, an older gargoyle, fed up with his incessant pleading, had complied. Cruelly, the creature had yanked on his fingers breaking the bones again in order to line up his fingers. Dience could still picture the cruel smile the gargoyle had had on its face when he had screamed in agony. Hopefully, that gargoyle was one of the hundreds Laura had transformed while Lucifer had been knocked out. Dience knew her healing hands had freed many people from the encapsulating black skins that had made them gargoyles.

But even worse than Laura, was her daughter, Diana, also known as the Moon Goddess and Deity of the Hunt! Captured by Lucifer when she had first arrived in Anandria, she had become Lucifer's chief gargoyle, and had looted cities for more slaves to build his forces. Unfortunately for Dience, she had become *his* worst nightmare – the most malicious gargoyle created in centuries. She had hurt him – both physically and mentally. Just thinking about her sent chills racing down his spine. It had irked him when he had heard about valiant deeds she had accomplished since her mother had transformed her back into her human form. Apparently, Diana helped seafaring merchants by regulating and manipulating the tides of the seas. Why, the bitch had even kept Anandrian larders full in the harsh winter months by using her enhanced hunting skills – while he had *starved.*

Life was not fair!

Dience gave himself a mental shake. With the guard nodding off on Lucifer's throne, it was *his* time. He wanted *his* face to be the one his Master saw when Lucifer awoke. He needed to be proactive and gain favour with his Master any way he could.

Dience left the crevice he had wedged himself into. His tread was soundless until a pebble skittered out from beneath his foot. He froze and held his breath. The guard only mumbled a bit before continuing to snore. Dience breathed a sigh of relief, steeled his nerves, and carried on. A few more steps and he stood before the guard. This would be easy. His dagger left its sheath with a soft hiss.

The guard's eyes flew open, and Dience cursed as he lunged wildly. With deceptive ease, the seasoned warrior rose to his feet, sidestepped the descending blade, and drew his sword. Muscles rippling, the guard made a practised thrust into the soft belly of his adversary and ripped up through tender flesh. A grim smile of satisfaction lifted the corners of the guard's mouth.

Dience screamed and dropped his dagger. Slowly he sank to his knees as he clutched his gut and hissed, "Fool! I am Dience."

Horror dawned in the eyes of the guard. His sword clattered to the stone floor of the Liar.

Dience's eyes rolled back into his head as a dark shadow ripped free from his collapsing body. It arrowed towards the guard, who backpedaled until he collided with Lucifer's throne. The guard's mouth gaped open, and the black essence that was Dience slithered into his mouth seeking a new host. A strangled gurgle of protest left his lips before his facial features and body melted into a new shape. The guard became smaller – more compact. His clothing hung off his body until it finally puddled at his feet as he morphed into the little demon!

"Blast it!" the new Dience cursed as he kicked his way out of the smothering garments. "I hate it when I am killed." Gingerly, he massaged a new scar. It puckered along the length of his abdomen, and he knew it would be days before the pain from the sword thrust eased. Mentally, he tallied the number of times he had been through this. This had to be the sixth time he had died – and it *sucked*.

A cool breeze wafted into the crater. It kissed his naked flesh and he shivered. A quick scan of the area had a sigh of regret leaving his lips. The last time he had died, when he had been pushed off a high cliff, he had taken over the body of the nearest mammal – which had happened to be a cat. Now the wee beast lay dead next to Lucifer's floating body, its belly slit, and Dience's old clothes, shredded and bloodied beyond repair, draped over its pitiful form.

Perhaps he could salvage his shoes, he thought as he stepped out of the guard's massive boots and squatted next to the cat's body. Aye, they would do – and his old dagger, too. He needed a new outfit. He attacked the guard's clothing shortening it with vicious strokes of the dagger. The excess material he used to fashion a belt which cinched the material in at his waist. He would manage until he could filch some kiddie clothes off a clothesline in Veresah.

"Dience!"

Dience flinched. Twelve years had passed since he had heard that voice – and it sent chills down his spine. He whirled about and stared at Lucifer hovering a good foot off the ground. Lucifer's head had twisted to the side, and his dark eyes were open and pinned on Dience. "Master! Ye be awake." Dience was not sure if he should be elated or shaking with fear. "How?" Dience edged a little closer.

Lucifer clenched his fingers. They trembled from the effort it took to move them, and sweat popped out along his upper lip. A few sparks snapped off his arms when his elbows began to bend. He relaxed for a moment. His chest heaved and he gasped for breath. Bright colours shimmered above, and he managed a nod towards the heavens. "That's how!" He sucked in a lungful of air and jerked his torso upright. Crackling sparks accompanied his movement. "The lights are caused by a disturbance in the magic separating the dimensions."

Dience backed up a pace, leery of the wild magic that rippled through the air. His master was sitting upright, but his legs remained stretched out in front as he hovered above the ground. *Spooky!* "I do not understand, Master."

Lucifer rested again. "The fabric between the dimensions is deteriorating. It has been ever since Laura destroyed her first portal with fire. As to why I am able to break free, I'll give an educated guess." Lucifer looked about the Lair. "It seems you have died – again. So, with the disintegration of the barriers between dimensions, the release of magic at your death, and the reabsorption of your essence in the vicinity of this powerful magic which holds me, I do believe that you have helped to fragment the magic surrounding me." Lucifer eyed Dience. "I never thought I'd say this, but I thank you, demon."

Happiness welled inside Dience. It was something he had *never* felt since his day of transformation so many centuries ago.

Carefully, Lucifer tried to bend one leg. The magic resisted, and he grunted with effort.

"Let me help, Master," Dience enthused as he rushed over and began to push down on Lucifer's limb. A mini bolt of lightning flashed between them, throwing Dience off. He slammed into the crater wall.

Lucifer let out a roar of pain. "Hands off, you little idiot! Tis a delicate matter to shed this magic."

Dience shook his head, stunned by his impact against the rock, *and* the contempt he heard in Lucifer's voice. Moments ago, the Master had thanked him... He had only tried to help... Dience was at a loss.

Lucifer still panted for breath when he demanded, "How long?"

"Almost thirteen years, Master," Dience snivelled. He dared not gaze at his Master now that he was back in disgrace.

"I've been asleep *twelve* years?" Lucifer sputtered.

"Aye, my Lord."

"My kingdom?"

Dience winced. "Gone, Master." Dead silence greeted this. Dience dared to raise his eyes. Lucifer had forced one leg down and was carefully lowering the second. It looked like Lucifer was sitting in a chair! Magic sparked all around him. This time, Dience noticed that not all the sparks were white. There were black explosions, too, barely discernible except for the glint they picked up from moonbeams shining into the Lair. 'Twas dark magic Lucifer unleashed to counteract the white magic holding him prisoner.

"The Anandrians have been rounding up gargoyles, and Laura has been transforming them." Dience gulped down a fortifying breath. 'Twould be best to get it all out now before Lucifer was totally free. "She has also placed her healing hands on the eggs in your dragon rookery, so now the Anandrians have their own fleet of dragons. Diana has been in charge of their care and breeding."

The Master ground his teeth together and growled. Dience flinched. Diana had been Lucifer's chief gargoyle, twelve years ago, riding his oldest dragon, and leading his troops against her parent's forces. Dience hunched over and clutched at his newly healed stomach before he spit out the last of his news. "All yer old dragons have fled to places far and wide."

Thunder boomed. Lightning streaked into the Lair, surrounding and illuminating Lucifer as he rose to stand tall. His long dark hair floated away from his head. His eyes gleamed with success. He was free! But it had cost him – he was drenched in sweat.

Dience decided it was prudent to pass on one last bit of information before Lucifer's glow of success wore off. "Laura's children have progeny of their own. She is a grandmother."

Lucifer's gaze snapped to Dience. "What are their names and ages? Who are their parents?"

"Both grandchildren be twelve and were born the same night. Raonull, the Mighty One, and Kathryn, the Pure, be their names."

"Any powers, yet?"

Dience shrugged. "I am not certain, Master, except that Raonull is reported to be extraordinarily strong."

"Who sired him?"

"David and Morrigan sired Raonull. Diana and Manus had Kathryn."

Lucifer's eyes narrowed thoughtfully. "Then it's the girl we must watch closely. With her powerful mother and grandmother, she may have astonishing powers."

Lucifer stepped towards Dience and grabbed him by the scruff of his neck. "We will leave the Lair and gather what remains of my forces. Then we will begin recruiting – again."

3

ᏣᏬᏬᎧᎧ

Twenty-two years after the births

Kathryn sat on the back of her favourite dragon, Daisy. Her cousin, Raonull, and his dragon, Rusty, kept her company while they rested on a high bluff. Kathryn had come to live in Veresah as a teen, and she and Raonull were almost inseparable. Her parents, Diana and Manus, had insisted she live with her grandparents since her presence in Veresah had made it possible for her, and Raonull, to cross frequently over to Earth – much to Mandy's delight. And Mandy had become their personal Earth tutor.

At first they had balked at the idea of spending time on Earth where their magic ceased to work. However, the draw of Earth's technologies had made it bearable to be like everyone else on the planet – no magic, but *fun* toys. Indeed, the addictive pull of computers had them spending a great deal of time on Earth, to the point where they had become familiar with all the latest gadgets Mandy and Jeff had provided for them.

Diana and David were extremely pleased both their children enjoyed visiting Earth. They were more than happy to let Mandy and Jeff guide them in their education. Currently, Kathryn and

Raonull were both enrolled at the University of Toronto in online courses and were slated to graduate at the end of the year.

Raonull had followed in his dad's footsteps studying history and in particular, battle strategies, whereas Kathryn had set her sights on a communication degree – Raonull could only shake his head at her choice. Communication? Really? Seemed kind of useless to him...

Right now, however, they were enjoying an early Anandrian night flight on their dragons, and they had set down to give their beasts a moment to catch their breath after the playful session of tag the two cousins had indulged in. Besides, eerie waves of the aurora borealis had begun to crackle above, and they felt it prudent to cease fooling around until the night sky settled. The colours cascading across the heavens seemed to amplify the sense of magic that was always present in Anandria, and it made them uneasy.

Raonull glanced at Kathryn. She was prattling on about something that he had no interest in, and therefore he felt no need to follow. *Blah, blah, blah.* God, she could talk! It was no wonder, he thought with amusement, that she had elected to take communication.

He tuned in for a moment, just in case she asked him a question – she'd be teed off if she discovered he was inattentive! She was going on about some guy who'd made a pass at her when she'd dropped by the university earlier today to straighten out an error she had regarding the number of credits she had earned last semester. *Wait! Whoa! A guy made a move?* Raonull was suddenly all ears. His focus on her prattle became laser sharp.

"His name is Brandon, and he was kind of cute. He wants me to go to the Thursday night pub..."

Raonull interrupted with a loud clearing of his throat.

Kathryn sighed. "What?" Raonull was always hovering. It was hard for her to get to know anyone! She was twenty-two, and she could count on one hand the number of guys she had gone out with – *there had only been two* – not even half the fingers on one hand. And her relationship with them had lasted a few weeks – if you could call *that* having a relationship. And why? In a word, Raonull! *He hovered.*

"If you go, I go!" Raonull declared. Her glare could have knocked him off his dragon, but he'd be damned if he'd leave her alone with some guy who'd just picked her up on a chance meeting. *She's so gullible.*

"Rao..." Her whine of protest stopped in the middle of his name. Colour drained from her face, and her brown eyes widened and deepened to a bottomless black.

"Oh shit!" Raonull flung a leg over the neck of his dragon and slid down its wing. Kathryn's dragon obligingly lowered its wing and within seconds he had slipped behind his cousin to wrap a brawny arm around her tiny waist.

A shiver of unease crept up his back. Her body was rigid. She would have tipped over and crashed to the ground without his support. Thankfully, sessions like these were rare. Sometimes the Sight only lasted a second or two and Kathryn carried on with barely a hiccup, or she'd say, "A feeling is coming on..." Often people didn't even know she'd had an episode. But Raonull always knew, and he would skillfully remove her to a more private place to catch her breath before they discovered what her *gift* had delivered. However, like tonight, there was sometimes no warning, and if he didn't catch her, she might come out with an egg on her head, along with bruises from falling into furniture, or hitting the floor.

He was so glad he didn't have her *gift.*

He liked his Herculean strength. He could smash a boulder into dust with his bare hands when he felt frustrated – although he didn't like the skinned knuckles he suffered afterwards. Luckily, Grandma had always been there to heal him.

Patiently, Raonull continued to hold Kathryn. While he waited, his thoughts turned back to the first time he had held his cousin. They had been twelve, and he had been relegated to community service for tossing General Trymian into the river – a feat that had even surprised him. He had panicked when the General had sunk like a rock. Thank goodness, his dad had been nearby and had pulled the old warrior out before he had drowned! Raonull smiled at the memory of the sputtering, angry, and obviously humiliated man. He had tried to apologize, but his dad had grounded him – no flying his dragon for a week!

He had thought it totally unfair, and had smashed a hole in the town's wall – again, startling himself. That was when his dad, David, had finally condemned him to community service, which he really didn't mind as he got to use his newfound strength. And as a bonus, it had impressed the hell out of his friends. Mind you, he had been tired at the end of every day, but it had been satisfying.

His lips tipped up in a smile. It was during this period of punishment, that Kathryn, Aunt Diana and Uncle Manus had arrived just before dawn on their dragons. The rumble of their landing had had him rolling eagerly out of bed, his muscles protesting, and his eyes blurry from too few hours in bed. He had hurried down to the stables where he knew Kathryn would be tending to the dragon mounts. She had enveloped him in a welcoming hug before telling him to look into her eyes – and the next thing he knew, he had put all her clothes away, *and* had mucked out the dragon shelter. Since then, direct eye contact, while in Anandria, had been avoided so she couldn't compel him to do things he didn't really want to do.

Raonull glanced down. Kathryn was still deep in her trance. Gooseflesh lifted the small hairs along his arms. This always freaked him out. He was dreading her return to consciousness.

The first time she had gone deep, was on that visit when they were twelve. The northern lights had been dancing in the night sky then, too. It was the second night of their visit, and they had been hanging out together when she had collapsed. Her eyes had remained wide open – but no one had been home! Desperately he had gathered her into his arms and had dashed into the castle where he knew all the grownups had gathered to talk to Great

Aunt Mandy and Jeff at the portal in his grandparent's bedchamber. He had rushed directly to Grandma, and she had placed her hands on Kathryn while uttering, "Heal thyself." But unlike the hundreds of times her touch had fixed all that was wrong, this time nothing had happened! He remembered his grandma whispering, "She's not sick."

Then his Aunt Diana had said, "See? I told you. It has to be the Sight."

That had been when Kathryn had stirred in his arms, blinked groggily, smiled, and murmured, "The fabric between the dimensions is tearing apart. Be on guard!"

And it had been that morning, just before dawn, that the relief guard had ridden in on his dragon to report that his fellow warrior, who should have been guarding Lucifer, was not at his post and that Lucifer was *gone*. Where the Dark Lord had vanished to remained a mystery to this day.

Raonull glanced up at the heavens. What would she see this time? He remembered his grandma telling everyone on that night long ago, that the northern lights had something to do with the deterioration of the fabric between the dimensions. *Wow! Where had he dredged that up?* Maybe the memory rose because he vividly recalled the beautiful display he and Kathryn had watched just before she had gone under that first time – and the warning she had issued upon her awakening. He lowered his gaze to check on her. Nope, she wasn't moving. She had been out for more than a couple of minutes. Dread made him shiver. Whatever she was going to say, he was sure it would be momentous.

With a sudden gasp, Kathryn went limp in his arms. "Kath?"

"Mmm?"

"Kath, are you okay?"

She tipped her head back to look at his face. "Ray, where are we? Why am I so sleepy?"

He ran a finger down her nose. He knew it would irritate her. *Yup!* Her head jerked sideways, and she wrinkled her nose while delivering a scowl that would stop a lesser man than he. Pleased by her reaction, he grinned and replied, "We're north of Veresah. Past the Lair. And you, coz, have had one of the longest sessions of Sight I have ever seen."

Her eyes widened as her brain kicked into gear. "Oh my God, Ray!" She twisted in his arms trying to face him. "We have to go home. I have to talk to Grandma and Aunt Mandy."

He held her steady, concerned by the panic threading through her voice. This had to be bad if she felt the need to see Grandma and his aunt. "Christ, Kath, what the hell did you see?"

Kathryn gestured towards the northern lights. "Something's terribly wrong with Anandria. Anandria's magic is bleeding out!" She gripped Raonull's forearms. Her nails dug into his flesh. "And because of this, Lucifer's magic will touch Aunt Mandy." She tried to push his arms away. "Now get off my dragon and mount yours. We have to warn Aunt Mandy!"

Raonull refused to budge. "Not happening, Kath."

"What?"

"I'm staying right here..."

"Fine!" she snapped and patted her dragon, "Get off! Daisy will obey me and take me back to..."

Raonull clamped a hand over her mouth. "You didn't let me finish. I'm staying right here on Daisy's back because I think you need me to hold you upright during the flight home." He released her mouth.

"Oh..." She sighed. "Do you think Daisy can carry us both?"

The runt of the rookery, Daisy was small for a dragon – well under twenty feet in length – but Kathryn had fallen in love with the little reptile, and at the age of five had taken the wee beast under her care naming her Daisy for her sunny disposition. To this day, people snickered when they heard the dragon's name, but the beast returned Kathryn's love with steadfast loyalty and had the heart and determination of a much larger dragon.

"Tis a short trip to Veresah. She'll manage."

Kathryn tipped her head back against Raonull's shoulder. "I'm tired..."

"I know," he whispered in her ear. "Sleep. I'll make sure we get home as quickly as possible." He gave her an affectionate squeeze. "Besides, Aunt Di would kill me if you accidently slipped off Daisy after one of your spells. Why, she'd probably present me as a gift to Lucifer."

Kathryn shook her head at Raonull's silliness and quipped, "She'd have done *that* long ago – if anyone in Anandria knew where Lucifer's been hiding out..."

"Yeah." Raonull nudged Daisy into flight. "It's hard to believe ten years have passed, and no one has figured out where he's holed up. You've got to wonder where he's keeping all the people he's kidnapped."

"You mean enslaved," Kathryn yelled as the wind picked up.

Within minutes, Raonull felt Kathryn's body relax and her breathing even out. Good, she was asleep – something she often had difficulty achieving because, damn it, she carried a secret guilt around that only he was privy to. She thought people expected her to know all the answers, but she had little control over the Sight. When and where it hit was always a surprise – and so was what she saw. She couldn't use the Sight to foretell a specific event.

For that miracle, she often directed people to Aisling, who lived in the City of Moyen. Aisling was older and had developed more control over the Sight as she had aged. She could often force a session of the Sight and direct her vision if an object related to a person, or location, was placed in her hands – but then again, the Sight too often did its own thing, presenting Aisling with obscure information unrelated to what was sought. The Sight was a fickle gift!

Raonull nudged Kathryn. "Coming in for a landing, Kath."

Kathryn blinked. It seemed like she had just dosed off.

Thud!

Touchdown!

Raonull helped Kathryn to her feet. Daisy extended her wing, and within seconds they were down the leathery ramp.

Thud!

Raonull's dragon, Rusty, landed next to Daisy. Black and red scales gave Raonull's beast a burnt orange look under moonlight. It had been a natural leap to come up with Rusty for his name.

Both dragon heads swung towards them.

"Thanks, guys," Raonull said. "Go! Enjoy the rest of the night. Kathryn and I have family business to attend to."

Their dragons gave grunts of pleasure, but waited patiently for the cousins to exit the dragon shelter before they scurried about to the shelter's opening that yawned at the top of the escarpment where the town of Veresah was situated. One by one, they leapt off the edge and soared into the night sky.

Minutes later, Raonull and Kathryn burst into Laura's bed-chamber. The room was dark except for moonlight streaming in through the windows. But it was light enough for the cousins to see Vaaron reach beneath the bed for his sword and begin to roll out of bed.

Laura's arm shot out. She hooked it about his waist. "Vaaron, it's the grandkids. *Relax.*"

Vaaron rolled back onto his pillow. His fierce glare was lit by moonlight. "Did your parents not teach you to knock?"

Kathryn stopped. Heat climbed into her cheeks. *Oh my God. What had they been thinking?* Her grandparents were *old*, but considering the flash of naked flesh she'd just seen they weren't dead, yet. "Sorry," she mumbled.

Laura clutched a blanket firmly under her chin, even as she swatted Vaaron on his chest. Her eyes warned Vaaron to shut up. "What's wrong?" she asked the kids.

Raonull grabbed Kathryn's hand and pulled her up beside the bed – on Laura's side. "Kath had a nasty spell with the Sight while we were on our dragons."

"Oh!" Laura stretched out her free hand to Kathryn. "Are you hurt? You look okay. Did Ray catch you?"

Raonull rolled his eyes. Kathryn was fine – anyone could see that. "We'd set down to let our dragons rest when it hit. I got to her before she toppled off, but it was the longest I've ever seen her go under... And now she's upset."

Laura smiled at Raonull. He was clearly distressed by Kathryn's episode. It was sweet... Her smile turned to a frown when she looked at her granddaughter. Was that a tear on Kathryn's cheek?

"Get out!" The terse order came from Vaaron. "Wait in the hall until your grandmother and I are decent. *Then* we will hear your tale..."

Laura turned her frown on Vaaron.

He glared right back at her "Nothing can be done until we have donned sufficient garments." His eyes swung back to the grandkids. "So get out, until we call for you."

Raonull saw Laura open her mouth to protest, but before she could utter anything else, he grabbed Kathryn's hand and pulled her back to the door. Grandpa could be a real bear when disturbed. Before the door could click shut, Raonull hesitated and stared intently at his grandparents. "Hurry... Please..."

4

Lucifer surveyed his home. A warm glow suffused him. With a start of surprise, he realized he felt satisfied. Ten years of creation had that old spark firing again.

Time to conquer the universe!

After he and Dience had abandoned the Lair, they had travelled to the one place in Anandria so desolate no one would think to look for them there. He had needed time to regroup after the humiliating defeat that had left him asleep for almost thirteen years.

He stretched out a hand and caressed a wall. It felt like sandpaper – and so it should. He had returned to the Badlands Desert – the environment that had almost brought him to his knees after his twenty year exile on Earth. The bleak terrain had suited his mood and had challenged him creatively. Knowing how to fabricate a sun shelter out of the desert sands had given him the idea to construct a new kingdom.

And I've done it!

Melting miniscule molecules of metals found in the sand, he had hollowed out an underground city. Large and small caverns were linked by tunnels. Dience had helped with the construction, since the little demon was a master metal worker. *Probably the only positive thing I can associate with Dience.* The city he had dubbed, Inferno. The never ending heat of the desert, and the method he had used to create the city, justified the name. He sighed. The damned gargoyles, and Dience, kept calling it, the Lair. He was forced to admit that Inferno, hadn't stuck. This was his new Lair.

Now, ten years later, he was delighted that the general population of Anandria still had no clue where he was, nor where he housed his growing gargoyle horde. The Lair covered a lot of underground territory. Two entrances to this Godforsaken place were large enough for landing dragons and were cunningly concealed with a touch of dark magic the dragons could detect. Four smaller entrances for gargoyles on foot were camouflaged by sand dunes and overhangs that cast clever shadows. *'Twas better than the old Lair.*

And the best part? If a gargoyle fell into Laura's hands, her healing touch would restore the gargoyle back to its human form, but its human eyes would never find the secret entrances to his Lair.

Life was good, and it was going to get better...

Lucifer walked out one of the concealed entrances and glanced up at the night sky. A hot wind blew his dark hair away from his face. Above him, the aurora borealis danced in vivid colours. He heard crackling noises. The fabric between dimensions was tearing further apart, and from the sounds of it, he calculated that it was time for action. Laura had best be on guard. He was coming for her – at full strength. Only this time, with her powerful family about her, he needed to find a subtle way to get to her. Through the back door, so to speak...

5

“Calm down,” Mandy ordered.

Kathryn caught a sob at the back of her throat. Laura, whose arm was wrapped around her granddaughter’s shoulder, gave a reassuring squeeze. Vaaron and Raonull simply looked at each other, rolled their eyes, and stifled grins that threatened despite the gravity of the situation.

“We knew the fabric between our two dimensions has been damaged,” Mandy said. “It would make sense that some of Anandria’s magic might leak through to Earth.”

Jeff whistled. “I never thought about *that*.” He frowned. “Maybe I shouldn’t go to that conference in the States.” He looked at Mandy. “Maybe I should stay here with you.”

“Nah,” Mandy said as she shook her head. “I have an idea.” She looked at Laura. “I’ve been trying to finish my latest novel, and so far it hasn’t been happening. I’ve been thinking about heading up to your cottage.”

“It’s May,” Laura said.

“So?” Mandy replied. “No one should be on the lake this time of year. There’ll be no interruptions, *and* my phone won’t work up there – never has no matter what service provider I try.”

“There’ll be black flies!” Laura exclaimed.

"Yeah, perfect," Mandy declared. "I just have to make it from the car, down the hill, then dig in, and start writing – with no interruptions." She shrugged. "Who'd be stupid enough to come visit the Haliburton Highlands at the height of black fly season? Even Lucifer would find those biting bastards a challenge."

Laura opened her mouth, but Mandy jumped back in with, "Besides, I'll be far away from the portal. How the heck could Lucifer's magic touch me up there?" She glanced at Kathryn. "Your visions see what *might* happen, right, Kath?"

Kathryn nodded. "Yeah, but the strength of this vision..."

"Don't worry," Mandy said. "We're changing the outcome of your vision by planning this trip. I'll do laundry today, pack, and leave first thing tomorrow morning. I'll stay up there for at least a month until Jeff gets back, and I'll go to the General Store once a week to use their phone since the summer landline won't be working this early in the season. I'll call at pre-arranged times to check in with all of you."

Laura sighed in defeat. She'd seen that look of determination on Mandy's face a thousand times before. At least Mandy *should* be safe up there. The cottage was well off the beaten path. The nearest town was Kinmount. It barely had enough residents to make it a town. She smiled. If one looked at a map, Salerno Lake, where her family's cottage was located, was next to Irondale, an old mining town. But other than a quaint white church, and a few scattered locals, Irondale could be considered a ghost town. She remembered her grandparents pointing out the foundations of the old town buildings in one of the fields next to a defunct train track. Today, that field was overgrown – at least that's what her kids and grandkids had told her. *Why, I haven't been up there in over twenty years!*

Five generations had visited Irondale to enjoy the spectacular little lake carved out of a massive rock formation called the Canadian Shield, which covered much of the province of Ontario. Laura felt a shiver crawl up her spine. When her mom and dad

had been little, the lake had actually been called Devil's Lake –
and there was still a sign left over from the old days pointing the
way to Devil's Lake if you knew where to look for it. *Nah, that
shiver hadn't meant anything.* "Okay Mandy, check back at the portal
tonight, and we'll set up contact times. I'll make sure someone
goes through the portal to answer your phone calls."

Jeff glared at Mandy. "That better be two calls you make. I won't
be able to concentrate if I'm worrying about you."

Kathryn rubbed her hands up and down her arms. "I don't
know, Aunt Mandy. The vision seemed like a sure thing."

Raonull bumped into her shoulder with his. "Give it a rest,
Kath. She'll be fine."

Vaaron nodded. "We should probably station someone at the
house in case Lucifer puts in an appearance – if that's remotely
possible – because he knows where Mandy lives." He slid his cal-
loused hand down Kathryn's auburn hair. "Does that make you
feel better, love?"

"Yes," Kathryn said and turned into his arms for a hug.

Vaaron kissed the top of her head. "Tomorrow night, I'll fly to
Moyen and let your parents know about your vision. The High
Lunar Priest and Priestess may want to add their ideas to the pot.
And besides, your mother, Diana – Lucifer's former gargoyle leader
– would kill me if I did not inform her about the threat to Aunt
Mandy." He grinned down at Kathryn. "You know how she feels
about Lucifer... However, I don't think they will come back with
me as they have to prepare for the Five Moons Ceremony."

6

Dragons and gargoyles? He had plenty. His magic? He flexed his fingers and felt his power stir. Aye, he could be no stronger. There was no need to expand resources anymore. Now, it was time use his acquired power. If he had read the heavens correctly, a trip to Earth might not be out of the question. There was only one way to find out...

Where on Earth did he want to go?

The Great Wall of China had been built deliberately over the Asian access. Diamond mines intruded into the African access — the miners were clueless, but a nuisance he didn't want to have to deal with. Ice, a mile deep, covered the Antarctica access, and Stonehenge was too damaged to repair with all the tourists around. Australia seemed too removed from the rest of the populated world. That left South America and North America.

Really, there was no question about his destination. The access point in Peru was so isolated it would take days for people to even realize he had come to Earth. So, that left North America, which was conveniently close to the city of Toronto, his old stomping grounds when he had been exiled from Anandria. Plus, it was close to Laura's old home.

He closed his eyes opening himself up to the flow of Anandrian magic. He had always had a talent for reading her invisible power.

KATHRYN HEANEY

That tiny tear that Laura had created in the fabric between the dimensions, when she had destroyed her first portal, had finally ripped wide open. Magic was expanding beyond the boundaries of Anandria. It had been centuries since the last episode, and he relished the excitement thrumming through his body.

Holding his breath, Lucifer climbed the stairs he had fashioned out of the wall until he was able to place his hands on the ceiling. He twisted his wrists apart and splayed his fingers wide. Slowly he sucked in a deep breath pulling magic into his body. It swirled about in his lungs until it seeped into his blood. The purity of Anandria's magic seared at first until the darkness he had nurtured within his soul sought out, latched on, and warped the brightness of Anandria's magic into an ugly force he could manipulate. Concentrating, he gave a gentle nudge. Darkness oozed down his arms to settle in the palms of his hands. The tips of his fingers were spread wide. *Perfect!* His skin rippled as if bugs burrowed beneath his flesh.

Wait for it…

Suddenly, the skin on his hands stretched tight. He was at full strength! Quickly he cleared his mind, except for his ultimate destination, and shoved dark magic into his fingertips. Black streaks shot out – almost like sunbeams, he thought as he eyed the expansive area they covered. The ceiling's sandy surface wavered, like a mirage on a hot desert day, until it finally dissolved leaving an opening large enough for a dragon to fly through – at least on his side, the Anandrian side…

Above him on the Earth side, lay a slab of rock with a long crack running through its centre. Carefully he slid his fingers into the crack and began manipulating the metals in the rock until he had a hole large enough to climb through. Unable to resist, he poked his head up and took his first breath of Earth air. Jumbled rocks above his head formed a small cavern. He wouldn't be able to stand completely upright, but he knew someone who would fit neatly into the small space.

36

Impatience goaded him to crawl completely to the Earth side – but he had to be cautious – he had to make sure he would retain his powers and keep the portal open. Reluctantly he withdrew his head from the other dimension and bellowed, "Dience! Get over here."

Dience skittered around a corner, came to an abrupt halt, and gaped up at Lucifer sitting on the steps beneath an enormous portal, blocked, for the most part, by solid rock. "Master! What have ye done?"

"Get up here. You're going to crawl into the little cave above and see if you can alter the rocks to make it bigger."

Dience eyed the hole in the ceiling. "Where be the cave, Master?"

"Earth!"

Dience shook his head. "Ye know I cannot work metal there, Master. I have no magic on Earth."

"Humour me," Lucifer snapped as he descended, grabbed Dience by the scruff of his neck, hauled him up the stairs, and shoved him through the portal.

Dience stumbled into the cave and averted his eyes to hide his resentment. The Master had lost it. Fine, he would placate the Master and go through the motions of manipulating metals in the rocks. Murmurs too low to be heard fell off Dience's lips. He eyes widened. "Master, look! I have pulled metals out of this rock." He held up his hand where a dull lump gleamed. "How?"

"Magic's not locked away in Anandria anymore," Lucifer replied. "And we're going to get to Laura by a more circuitous route. But first, we need to repair this access point. All the rock above your head has to go, as well as the rock blocking the portal. My dragons need to fly in and out with ease."

Dience gasped when Lucifer started through the hole. Lucifer, from the waist up, was *on* Earth. Dience made a dash to re-enter Anandria, but there was no getting past Lucifer. "Master, ye cannot..." Lucifer grinned at Dience, pushed him away, and began to take the final step into the little cavern. "Nay, Master," Dience protested. "I do not wish to be stranded in this vile dimension. The portal will close when ye come through. There be no return." He whimpered and clamped a hand over his mouth. "Please Master, I want to go home to Anandria," he whined through his fingers.

Thunder rolled outside the cave. Lucifer's grin widened despite Dience's annoying behaviour. His magic was loose on Earth! The thunder rumbling outside was in direct response to *his* feelings that the little demon evoked every time he opened his whiny mouth. Lucifer stepped completely through the portal, watched Dience turn pasty white, and muttered, "Shut your mouth, you little idiot. *Feel* the magic flowing past us."

Dience gaped up at him. "Our magic has come here with us?"

Lucifer nodded. He was hunched over in the tiny cave – but he would fix that before the night was done. Off to one side there was an opening leading to the outside world. If he started there and worked his way back, the jumbled pile of rocks that formed this little cavern would soon be moved and reshaped into the monoliths he required. Lucifer glanced back at the open portal into Anandria. Hell, it was great to be back on Earth. With all his powers intact! No one in this dimension could even remotely suspect what was about to hit them!

Lucifer saw Dience's ears twitch. "What do you hear, demon?"

Dience took a moment, his pointed ears shifting minutely. "Someone approaches, Master." His ears moved again. "I think there be a boat, too. I hear the slap of waves against it."

Lucifer's eyes narrowed. Perhaps he'd add a new recruit to his cause tonight.

7

Damn writer's block! It was the reason she was here easing down humongous, jumbled rocks. Not only that, but night was about to fall, thunder threatened overhead, and she still had to paddle back to the cottage. If she made it home dry, she vowed to remain firmly on her seat at the table writing diligently.

When she had stopped writing sometime around noon, she had stuck her head out the cottage door and had been pleasantly surprised by the lack of black flies. A light breeze had rippled the lake water, and a couple of dragonflies had darted about. Once dragonflies emerged, black flies were doomed. She had decided to take a break. She figured she'd contemplate the next twist in her storyline while she paddled up the lake in the canoe.

However, when she had paddled around the bend in the lake, and her eye had fallen on a huge rock pile dragged there eons ago by glaciers, she had decided to re-enact a childhood adventure. Around the age of twelve, she and Laura had gone exploring up those rocks. They had managed to find a number of small caverns, and had come home tired and dirty.

Mandy had bet she could find some of those caves today, but now she was regretting her decision. She wasn't young anymore, the rocks were difficult to navigate, and she had several scrapes and cuts on her arms and legs. *I'm out of shape.* It was amazing she had actually made it to the top where the view of the lake far below had taken her breath away.

But had it been worth it?

She had an abused body that was sure to hurt like hell the next day, she might get drenched on the paddle home, and she wasn't sure if she could make it back to the cottage in daylight. She'd have to hug the shoreline as she lost the light, which meant emerging mosquitoes would have a feast...

Oh God, what have I done? She sighed. She was only halfway down the hill. *Drat!*

She came to the lip of a rock and peered down. If she sat on the edge and slid, the drop might not be too jarring. With an ungracious huff, she sat and slowly inched her seat forward while stretching her toes down. A few pebbles jostled loose.

Almost there...

8

The house was deathly quiet. Raonull could not recall it ever being so. Jeff had taken off for the States shortly after Mandy had left for cottage country, north of Toronto. Meanwhile he, Raonull the Mighty, was stuck doing overnight guard duty. A week had gone by and nothing had happened on anyone's shift.

He was bored.

He eyed the TV, but didn't want the noise from it to cover up any covert manoeuvres Lucifer might make. He had to keep his ears peeled. Besides, the few times he had tried to watch it on previous nights, the reception had come and gone – very irritating.

Looking for something to read, he searched for Jeff's laptop. It wasn't anywhere on his desk. There went that idea... *Hey, Aunt Mandy has shelves of books – archaic as that seems in this day and age of Earth technology.*

He trotted downstairs to her office. His eye stopped on her desk where a book, sporting the distinctive artwork of his grand-mother on the front cover, rested. He picked it up. *Destiny Calls,* by Kathryn Heaney. *Who the heck is Kathryn Heaney?*

He flipped to the back cover and saw a picture of Aunt Mandy smiling at him. *Hmm... Must be a penname.* Intrigued, he opened it to the prologue and read, "Morrigan peered out of the dense shrubs surrounding the clearing..." *Holy cow! That's my mom in the opening.* He knew Aunt Mandy had written Grandma's story and then a second book about his, and Kathryn's parents, but he'd never read them.

He snapped the book shut and climbed back up to Jeff's apartment. His anticipation was high. The novel would help pass time. He opened it as he collapsed on the couch, but a shadowy movement pulled his eyes away from his find. A large, black spider scurried towards the couch he was sitting on. His stomach jumped, and his nose wrinkled with distaste. He *hated* spiders. The way they moved was creepy.

Little hairs on his arms lifted – the ones on the back of his neck joined in, too.

Yeah, creepy!

He slammed the book down and looked for something heavy to crush the arachnid. If he avoided killing it with his shoe, all the better. The thought of it crunching under his foot sent shivers racing up his spine. *Yuck!*

The spider escaped under the couch. There was no way Raonull was sitting down with that *thing* beneath him. Without thinking, he wrapped his hand around the leg of the couch and lifted. The whole couch rose above his head. "Ah, there you are." He steeled himself for the kill. "All right you eight-legged freak, *die!*" His foot slammed down. He felt the sickening crunch of the creepy crawler.

"Well, isn't this interesting?"

Raonull whirled about, the couch held aloft by one hand above his head. "Kath!"

Kathryn nodded. "That's right, strong boy. Thought I'd visit while you stand watch." She stared at him – then the couch. "So, put the couch down..." She saw the moment Raonull realized what he was doing. "Any idea how you're holding that above your head?"

Raonull shrugged. "Don't know." He slowly lowered it to the floor. "I saw the spider and knew I had to get it before it got me."

"Geez, Ray, you and spiders... I'll never forget trying to watch *Arachnophobia* with you. If it weren't for the rewind feature, you'd have missed the whole movie."

"Shut up, Kath. I just don't like spiders, okay?"

"I still don't understand why you're able to lift the couch over your head."

Raonull balanced on one foot while he scraped the bottom of his shoe on the edge of a step dislodging the mashed spider. "Guess I shouldn't be able to do that, eh?"

"Nope!" Kathryn slipped behind him and tapped him on the shoulder. Raonull jerked around, startled. His eyes met hers which glinted with mischief. "Raonull, the spider you just killed would make a tasty treat, and you're so hungry..." Kathryn clapped a hand over her mouth, unnerved by the sight of her powerful cousin calmly picking up the squashed spider, tipping his head back, and lifting it to his lips.

"Stop! *Don't eat it.*"

The dead spider hovered for a moment over Raonull's mouth. He blinked and really looked at the repulsive mass pinched between his fingers. In a kneejerk reaction, he flung it across the room. *"Eew!"* A shudder of disgust shimmied up his spine, and he turned an angry glare on his cousin. With deadly intent, he began to stalk her as she backed away.

"Ray! No!" she squealed with rising panic. "I didn't think it'd work. It shouldn't have worked... Somehow our magic has followed us to Earth."

That stopped him. He straightened up. His brows drew together thoughtfully.

Kathryn's lips twitched. She couldn't help throwing out one last dig. "But really, Ray, you're such a *wuss.*" With a roar, Raonull lunged for his cousin. Kathryn gasped, spun about, and made for the portal across the room. Her heart sank when Raonull's hand latched onto her shirt and jerked her back.

"And now you *die*." Raonull hoisted her over his head and dug his fingers into her ribs.

A shrill scream split the air, and ended in a strangled gurgle of laughter as Kathryn tried to catch her breath. Raonull was merciless when he tickled.

Beyond the portal in Anandria, a ball of light formed on Laura's fingertips. She transferred it to a rock set in a wooden bracket next to the bed.

Vaaron cracked an eye open. "What the hell, Laura?"

She glared at the frame pulled close to her side of the bed. It had been situated there so guards assigned to Mandy's house had easy access to both dimensions through her portal.

"Grandma, help!"

Vaaron jerked up on his elbow to see what in bloody hell was happening. A few seconds ago, he had thought the voices were all in his dreams. Apparently not. "Raonull, put her down!"

Kathryn hit the floor, climbed through the portal, and plopped down on Laura's side of the bed. "Thank heavens you two woke up. You guys were dead to the world when I crept past to visit Ray."

Raonull shoved his upper body through the portal. "Some visit. She almost made me eat a spider."

"*Made* you?" Vaaron asked with a raised brow.

"Well, he was holding the couch over his head with one hand, so I had to see if my magic worked, too..." Her words petered out. Her body went rigid, and her eyes widened.

Laura wrapped an arm about Kathryn's shoulders drawing her granddaughter close. Vaaron helped lower her onto the bed's pillows when she went limp in her grandmother's arms. Kathryn moaned and her eyes began to blink rapidly until they snapped open and glared at everyone hovering over her. She propped herself up on her elbows and focused on Raonull who had crossed into Anandria to stand beside the bed. "You don't need to guard Aunt Mandy's house anymore. Lucifer won't go to the house."

"Are you sure?" Vaaron asked.

Kathryn huffed an annoying bit of hair off her face. "Positive, Grandpa. He will *not* touch Aunt Mandy at her house."

Laura blew out a relieved breath. It seemed like all their precautions had worked. Mandy was out of danger. "Thank heavens! Vaaron, move the portal back to the wall away from our bed. I want our privacy back." She squeezed Kathryn's hand. "I've been so worried about Mandy. I can relax now that I know Lucifer won't come to the house."

"Is that all you got?" Raonull prodded. "You were out for a solid five seconds."

Kathryn rolled her eyes at him. "Look, muscle man, with the spider phobia, I've told you everything I can remember."

Raonull opened his mouth to protest, but Vaaron took Kathryn's hand and pulled her off the bed as he said, "You two can snipe at each other later. I want everyone out. Your grandmother *needs* her sleep." Vaaron smiled smugly. He had picked up the word snipe off his favorite police TV show that he watched weekly through Laura's portal, and he liked the way it rolled off his tongue.

Laura's eyes cut to Vaaron. Anticipation and amusement twinkled in his eyes. She knew he had *really* missed their privacy, and there wouldn't be much sleeping tonight. Delight skittered up her spine. "Yes, I *need* my sleep."

When their two grandchildren closed the door behind them, Vaaron walked to the wardrobe, pulled out a little yellow dress, tossed it to his wife, and said, "I must check on the night watch. 'Twill take but a moment." He winked at Laura as he slipped through the bedchamber door.

He wants the yellow dress on! How long had it been since he had last peeled it off her body? Too long, she decided as she added stockings and her favourite pair of heels. Thank God, she still had a decent figure so that when the mood to peel things off her sixtyish body hit him, she was happy to oblige! *Oh boy...*

9

❧◦◦◦◦✦

A foot dangled over the entrance to the cave. Whoever it was, they were not making an effort to come quietly down the jumbled rocks. Dience glanced at Lucifer, a silent question in his eyes. Lucifer shook his head. *He* would capture this person, personally.

A husky voice swore. Was their soon-to-be new recruit male, or female? It was hard to tell. Amidst a mini landslide of dirt and gravel, the person dropped. Lucifer lunged, grabbed onto a flailing limb, and then *he* cursed when a large rock fell and knocked his hand away from his intended victim. Protectively, he cradled his injured hand. Blood welled from a nasty gash. *Goddamn it!*

Dience dove past Lucifer, desperate to secure their unexpected visitor. His fingers closed about the person's wrist as the individual landed in an unmoving heap just outside the cavern. Dience glanced up. He could see the path the person had taken down the rock's face. Chunks of rock had broken free, and moss and lichen had been stripped away. Unmindful of his captive's comfort, Dience dragged the body inside the tiny cavern.

"What the hell are you doing?" The victim's question was demanding, yet panicked. "Let go!"

Definitely female. Although the baggy pants that stopped short at her knees, and the voluminous sack that she wore for her shirt, gave no clues to her gender, Dience noted. She struggled to her feet.

Dience yanked hard and toppled her back to the rocky ground. Her head smacked into a boulder. *Damn this is fun.* He rarely got to dish out torment. Usually, he was the one receiving it – *while the Master approved,* he thought with a touch of resentment.

"Well done," Lucifer crooned. "Give her to me."

Dience's mouth gaped open. This was his shining moment. *The Master had praised him.* Obligingly, Dience offered Lucifer her limp arm. She wasn't moving. Wait, she stirred – and groaned. *Guess the knock on her head had only stunned her.*

Unable to stand erect in the cave, Lucifer was on one knee when he seized her arm. His free hand stretched out to push the woman's hair from her face. She was older. Strands of grey threaded through her dark locks. *Pity.* He would have preferred a younger gargoyle.

Her eyes rose, and she blinked him into focus. There was a nasty cut on her forehead, but Lucifer saw determination and defiance in her glare. He sucked in a delighted breath.

Simultaneously, she breathed, "No!"

"Well, well, Mandy. This is a serendipitous meeting."

"Lucifer! How...?"

He smiled and stared deeply into her dark brown eyes. "Be calm, my dear."

All the tension in Mandy's body drained away.

Good. His magic appeared to be at full strength. His compulsion to obey held Mandy in its grip. "Be still and let me minister to you." He dropped her arm and she remained complacent, her eyes wide and focused on his face. Lucifer shifted his hand to her chest, while he kept the other one resting upon her forehead. His lips parted, and he began the chant of transformation.

Dience sidled up. Excitement lit his eyes. Rarely did he get to see the moment of transformation when Lucifer made a new gargoyle. Usually, he was sent away on an errand, or he was pulled away by other gargoyles to be tormented for their pleasure while the Master was occupied. But today, he would hear every reverent word uttered by his Master, and be a witness to the miracle of his dark magic.

As the chant neared completion, Lucifer drew the hand on Mandy's forehead back and forth in a gentle massage. It was the final act that pushed his dark magic into her.

He almost paused, but caught himself before he ruined the transformation chant. Nevertheless, his stomach clenched. Blood was smeared all over Mandy's forehead. Belatedly, he realized a good deal of it was *his*. Despite the fact that his immortality had healed his wound, he had neglected to wipe away the remaining blood before touching Mandy and the open wound on her head. *What will be the repercussions for mixing my blood with hers?*

Blood magic tended to be powerful – and extremely unpredictable...

10

Magic swirled about the tiny cave. Lucifer waited impatiently for it to settle. Unlike the usual transformation from human to gargoyle, no black leathery skin began to encase Mandy's body. *What the hell was the magic doing?* He knew it was working. He could *feel* it.

He glanced down at his hand. Drying blood from his former wound, and blood from the cut on Mandy's forehead, glistened. He had *never* mingled his blood with another soul. His eyes returned to Mandy and he gasped. She lay serenely on the rocky floor with her eyes closed. But she had begun a transformation so radically different from any other, that he sat down hard, stunned by what he saw.

Subtle changes were taking place. Grey hair turned ebony, skin smoothed out into the freshness of youth, cuts and bruises vanished, while her bone structure shifted – *all over*. Her once sturdy body developed curves – *in all the right places*. Her cheek bones became more prominent. *She looks striking!* Even her lips plumped and darkened in colour.

Lucifer took a deep breath and froze.

Hell, her scent was the most intoxicating he had ever encountered, and by his body's reaction, she had to be emitting pheromones by the barrel. When was the last time he had truly desired a woman? Oh, he had had fun with thousands, perhaps even millions. Who knew? But he had *never* had this gut reaction to a woman before.

Her eyes opened and regarded him.

I am lost. Desire hammered through him. Her eyes were so dark they were almost black. He watched the corners of her lips tip up as if she was delighted by his presence. *Shit! What's happening to me?*

"Lucifer." Her voice was pure sin – husky, yet sultry. His name on her lips had the small hairs on the back of his neck prickling with delight.

Dience leaned over Mandy from the other side.

"Get away from her!" Lucifer's hand shot out, latched onto Dience's tunic and, with deceptive ease, he tossed the demon forcefully through the portal into Anandria.

Mandy rolled up onto one elbow. Her smile widened into a grin. She stretched out a hand and ran a single finger down Lucifer's chest, stopping just shy of his obvious hard-on. She chuckled, the sound a throaty enticement. "My my, you are indeed the very devil himself."

She licked her lips, and he *had* to watch. He needed a taste. He began to lean over, but she stopped him with a finger to his lips. He arched an imperious brow.

She chuckled again, *not* intimidated by him. "I am yours, Lucifer. But not on a cold, rocky floor."

Delighted, Lucifer pulled back. He waved a hand towards the portal indicating she should precede him.

Mandy shook her head. "I cannot. I am not from Anandria."

His mouth tipped into a wicked lopsided grin. "You are now... Amanda."

Several exhausting hours later, Lucifer rubbed his cheek against Amanda's silky black hair. This new incarnation of Mandy was incredibly intoxicating, and he couldn't equate this woman he held in his arms with the homely, middle-aged Earth woman, whose best friend was Laura. For the first time in his long existence,

Lucifer felt an emotional connection to another being. *Blood magic... Who knew?*

Mandy stirred, and he heard a soft sigh of contentment. His gut clutched. *What the hell was that about?* He felt loath to disturb her after their amorous bed play, but he had a portal to construct – one large enough for his dragons. It would take hours to reshape the metals in the rock. But once the portal opening on Earth matched the size of the opening in Anandria, and a ring of standing stones was constructed, he could imbue the stone circle with a mixture of his dark magic, and the magic of Anandria, so that it remained continually open – whether he was present or not. And that, right there, was the beauty of Anandria's escaping magic – magic bathed the portal on both sides. He was no longer tethered to one dimension. He sighed. It was time to get up and begin wielding magic. Dience was present, so he could exploit the demon's abilities to work his dwarf magic on the metals in the rocks, too. Slowly, he began to pull his arm out from beneath Mandy's head.

"Lucifer?"

Her sultry voice made his stomach tighten with hot desire. "Go back to sleep, my dear. I have work to do." The next time he crawled into bed with her, he wanted it to be a comfortable Earth bed and not the hard rock platform, topped with a thin mattress of straw, they currently lay upon.

"Okay," she murmured sleepily and snuggled under the blanket.

Eagerly, Lucifer donned his distinctive white robes. The sooner he got to work, the sooner he would be revelling in Earth luxuries. Oh, how he had missed Earth technologies and the comforts they provided. *Hopefully, Anandria's magic won't screw that up too much...*

11

ↄ๏ⵌↄ

Mandy stretched on the bed and gazed up at the ceiling with delight. It was polished to a fine gleam and reflected back her new body with brilliant clarity. For the first time in her life, she was stunning, a real knockout, a vision...

She could go on. *Oh why not?* She was a veritable goddess, a curvy nymph, a voluptuous vision. And even though she was rumpled from vigorous bed play, she had never looked sexier *in her life*. Why, she looked thirty years younger – like a woman in her prime, and not some worn out hag in her sixties.

A throat cleared and she glanced at the entrance to Lucifer's bedchamber, unconcerned by her nudity. A repugnant creature leered at her. Its skin was leathery and black, its eyes, bright yellow with black slits down the middle. But over its arm was draped a soft, green garment.

"The Master selected this for you to wear," the creature rasped.

"You're a gargoyle." Mandy heard the sultry, dulcet tones of her own voice and smiled. *Add siren to the list.* It was strange how she didn't fear the creature. She'd written enough about them, while telling Laura's story, that she knew she ought to be afraid. *Interesting.*

"Aye, my lady."

"Ooh, *my lady*... I like that!"

Another gargoyle stepped up to the doorway. "I have your breakfast, my lady."

"Lovely!" She waved them in, took the garment, and slid it over her head. The gargoyle offered a metal belt made of fine silver links to wrap about her waist. She looked up and the sight of herself reflected back from the polished wall took her breath away. The medieval, floor-length robe nipped in at her waist. It complemented her creamy pale skin and shiny black locks – which seemed to have grown overnight. She tossed her head. *Gorgeous!* Her usual bob had disappeared. Her hair was almost down to her bum. *Spectacular!* Lucifer would definitely prefer this new look to her old baggy shorts, shirt, and short hair she had sported last night.

Absently, she took a proffered piece of toast from the second gargoyle and, keeping her gaze on her reflection, bit into it. She gagged and spit. "What the hell are you feeding me?"

The gargoyle bowed. "Tis toast, my lady."

"No butter? No jam? Nothing else?"

"Tis all we have here in the Lair."

"Unacceptable. Take me to Lucifer."

Both gargoyles spun about without question.

Excellent! She followed them a short distance through extremely wide tunnels. Off to one side, she caught sight of a gargoyle leading a dragon down another corridor. *Oh. My. God.* Both creatures were magnificent.

"Up there, my lady," one of her escorts said, pointing up to the portal in the ceiling.

Mandy, without hesitation, ascended the steps carved into the wall and stepped through the hole. She felt a mild resistance as she passed from one dimension to the other. *Hmm, has to be Lucifer's blood that lets me move between dimensions.* Curiously, she glanced around. The cave on Earth was larger. She could stand upright now. Off to her left she heard soft chanting, and she watched in fascination as Lucifer and Dience laid their hands on rocks and molded them into new shapes. "Lucifer!" she called loudly. "My breakfast was totally unacceptable."

Annoyed by the interruption, Lucifer glanced over – *and froze, stunned by the sight of her – and his violent gut reaction.* She was an Amazon! Tall and curvy, with gleaming black hair that swirled about her luscious ass, she projected an assurance only a truly beautiful woman possessed. *If I have a fantasy, Amanda is it!* "'Tis all the fare we have in the Lair, my dear." *Great, my voice sounds strangled.* He cleared his throat.

"Well it's not good enough."

"What do you suggest?" Lucifer asked, amused and fascinated by her aggressive and, he had to admit, rather sexy manner and look. He walked to her and found he eagerly anticipated her reply.

"I can cook," she said with a gleam in her eye. "I've always been able to cook, and there's a cottage down the lake filled with supplies." Her chin rose, and she stared down her nose at him. "I'm leaving."

Lucifer's stomach clenched. *"No you're not!"* God, he'd said that from between clenched teeth. What the hell was the matter with him? Why did her threat irritate him? He could kill her – eliminate her hold over him. One hand about her throat – her creamy, long throat... No, he couldn't do that. *What the hell?*

"Of course I'm leaving. We'll not be fed the same swill your demon and gargoyles consume."

"We won't?"

"Definitely not! I'm starving, and I'll eat a whole lot faster if you help me paddle my canoe back to the cottage."

She wasn't leaving him. She wanted to cook for him.

Mandy placed her hands in the small of her back, arched so her breasts thrust forward, and said, "And I'll not be sleeping on that rock you call a bed again. There's a perfectly good bed back at the cottage. Understand?"

Lucifer nodded dumbly as he muttered over his shoulder to Dience, "Carry on." He had a sneaking suspicion he knew what people meant when they said a man was 'whipped'. He just had to make sure his tongue wasn't hanging out and drool wasn't dripping off his chin. *Christ, this is the last blood magic I'll ever do.*

12

The moon was high in the night sky, and stars covered the heavens in a dazzling display one never saw in the city. It was a lovely night, with a slight breeze that kept the bugs at bay. Mandy should have been content, but she felt restless as she stood on the end of the dock waiting.

Apparently she was too much... A distraction...

A sly smile lifted her lips. *She was a distraction!* That left a glow of satisfaction. All her life, men had looked past her at other women – *make that, they looked at Laura.*

She sighed. Her smile turned into a frown. She *needed* to be with Lucifer. How many nights had he left her alone at the cottage telling her to work on her book?

Why is he leaving me so much?

Mandy knew she had pleased Lucifer when he had enthusiastically dragged her into Anandria to that hard platform he had called his bed, torn off her clothes, and had brought her to one orgasmic peak after another. His cries had been loud, too, she mused. Since then, he had refused to take her with him, and he barely had time for a quickie when he returned before he collapsed on the cottage bed utterly fatigued. Six nights had gone by without him. *Unacceptable!* However, Lucifer had assured her that the enlargement of the portal was almost complete, and the ability to bring his dragons and gargoyles through was near.

She sighed and eyed the paddle boat. It would take *forever* to reach the bay where the portal was situated in that. Lucifer had the canoe – paddle boats were useless except to bask in the sun while you bobbed on the lake. Besides, although Lucifer would be delighted by her appearance – their chemistry was undeniable – he would be incensed by the delay her arrival would cause. *And she would make sure she caused a delay.* He wanted to take over the world – blah, blah, blah... She was sick and tired of hearing about his glorified plans. Why couldn't *she* come first in his plans?

Mandy gracefully sank down on the dock curling her legs beneath her. Idly, she trailed a finger through the inky black water. The stars, reflected in the lake, shimmered and dissolved as the ripples she created spread over the water's surface. With a start, she realized she had missed yesterday's check-in time. Laura would have been expecting her call. *Now, that would have been an interesting conversation.* "I'm fine, and by the way, I have a new boyfriend. His name is Lucifer..."

Her lips tipped up.

Too late. The call was missed. The boyfriend news would have to wait. How to tell her? She loved Laura – and she loved Lucifer. *Now there's a conundrum.*

The moon's light flickered for a moment. Mandy glanced up and sucked in her breath. Three dragons cavorted across the heavens doing dives, spins, and turns at dizzying speeds. Her heartbeat tripled. They were magnificent – and frightening. But it wasn't the dragons that had her heart racing. Her man, dressed in white, sitting astride the largest dragon, his head thrown back, his joy undeniable, filled her with fierce desire and pride.

Suddenly, he dove straight for her. She scrambled to her feet instinctively trying to dodge the deadly talons of his dragon. But the beast was too fast, as was the man on its back. She found herself snatched up by a powerful arm that wrapped possessively about her waist. Lucifer's lips touched her ear as he seated her in front of him and he said, "Tis done, with the exception of some standing stones Dience will work on. This world is mine. Come share it with me."

Her heart rate quadrupled. Her hands actually rested on the scales of a dragon. Wind buffeted her face as they raced across the sky. Best of all, the man behind her *wanted* her. Ho hum Mandy was finally getting a taste of adventure and romance! His hard body cushioned hers as the wind pushed her back. "Yes," she yelled through the whipping wind.

Momentarily, her conscience pricked when she thought about Laura. She was aiding and abetting Lucifer, Laura's mortal enemy...

To hell with Laura! Laura had always been beautiful and loved. Laura had abandoned homely Mandy for a new life in a new world. *Well now I, Amanda, am beautiful, and have a man panting after me...*

She frowned.

What about Jeff? She had been waiting years for Jeff to make a romantic gesture. Her eyes watered, and it wasn't from the wind hitting her face. *Damn!* Jeff had never wanted her the way Lucifer craved her – yes, *craved!* Somehow, the thought of Jeff left a pang in her belly. *To hell with him, too.* She didn't owe him anything. He had nothing to offer her. Why should good old Mandy be relegated to the background, waiting pathetically for life to begin?

As far as she was concerned, Mandy was gone. Amanda was starting a new life – *right now.* "Yes," she whispered defiantly once more. She would go with Lucifer and support his dreams. Besides, her conscience whispered, Laura was far from harm. If Lucifer wanted to take over Earth, what difference would it make?

She finally had a man!

"Excellent," Lucifer crooned into her ear. His lips closed over the sensitive flesh on her neck and suckled. Goosebumps prickled her flesh, and he heard her gasp with pleasure. "Let us get settled in our new home." He reached past Mandy and patted the dragon's neck. "Hades, we're heading south and slightly west."

"Southwest?"

"Aye, Amanda, my dear. We're settling in Toronto."

Mandy glanced right and left taking in the two dragons flanking them. Gargoyles rode on both. She yelled over her shoulder. "There's no place for dragons to land at my house."

Again, Lucifer lifted his lips to her ear. His hot breath elicited more enticing chills, which she savoured – no, *craved*.

"Tis not your home we go to, Amanda. I have a place downtown..."

13

Laura fussed with Kathryn's hair smoothing it off her face. She was worried and knew she wasn't the only one. Vaaron was checking Raonull's backpack, and was appalled that his grandson was not going to be carrying weapons. Neither of the grandkids would be armed. Laura knew this was inconceivable to Vaaron, a man who slept with his sword beneath the bed, and a dagger under his pillow.

"Explain to me again, why you cannot take, at the very least, your dagger. Does a man not have the right to defend himself?" Vaaron demanded.

Raonull grinned at his grandfather. "If we go on a plane, we have to go through security. They have sophisticated technology that'll pick up a weapon. No weapons are allowed on board a plane in case someone might hijack the plane, or worse, kill everyone like on 9/11 in New York City."

"You've both got your passports?" Laura fussed. "And you're sure England's where you have to go to?"

"Yes, Grandma," Kathryn replied. "The Sight showed me Stonehenge. Ray and I need to go there. And no, I don't know why. All I know is if we don't go, some great tragedy will befall all of us. I don't want to chance that happening. This vision felt very urgent to me."

Raonull watched his grandmother reach out to fuss some more over Kathryn, so he quickly grabbed Kathryn's hand. "Come on Kath. We've done our research. The Stonehenge you saw on the Internet was the one in your vision." He held up a folder. "I've got our reservations – except for accommodations. Every place I contacted was full. There's some damn festival going on in the area, but I'm sure we'll find something once we get there." He pulled Kathryn towards the portal.

"I don't like this," Laura muttered. "I don't like the two of you going so far away. Being out of touch. Your Aunt Mandy has missed checking in with us. I can't imagine what's wrong with her."

Vaaron wrapped an arm about Laura's waist. "She probably got caught up in her manuscript and lost track of time."

"Yeah, but five days late?" Laura stomped her foot. "All I can do is worry. I feel useless stuck here in my bedchamber hoping she'll call."

Raonull pulled Kathryn through the portal. "Once we're settled in I'll call. Keep Elfare, Audrey, or even General Trymian handy to answer the phone."

Everyone laughed. No one could picture the general stepping through to Earth to answer a phone. If it wasn't magic, he was highly suspicious of anything technological. There was no way he would pick up a receiver and speak into it.

Laura waved at the grandkids. "Go on. I'll make sure someone is here to take your call."

"Okay, bye," Kathryn called over her shoulder as Raonull yanked her down the stairs. "Stop pulling, Ray."

"Well then, hurry up. Airways Transit is probably waiting at the curb to take us to the airport."

Their voices faded, and Laura turned in Vaaron's arms. "I'm glad Raonull is always with her." She shivered. "I can't imagine what would have happened if he hadn't jumped on Daisy's back when Kathryn zoned out in mid-flight. But why would her vision send them off to England? You'd think her visions would be limited to Anandria, where magic exists."

"You forget, love, magic has been escaping to Earth. Look what the children were able to do in your old apartment – Raonull lifted both the couch, and Kathryn, over his head. And Kathryn compelled Raonull to eat a spider." He shook his head. "I think they are following the magic."

14

"Oh! Welcome to Avebury Inn." The petite woman with the ebony hair grinned sheepishly. "I do apologize. I thought I was alone."

She stepped away from the wall she had been rubbing her back against, to greet Raonull and Kathryn at the registration counter. "Lately, I've had this awful itch between my shoulder blades, and two strange bumps have come up." She paused. "But then, you don't want to hear about that, do you? Too much information." She grinned. "Here I am blathering on..."

Raonull bit his lip. He would *not* laugh. She was enchanting, with slightly slanted green eyes that sparkled with good humour – and a curvy little figure, too. *A sight for sore eyes.* And they were sore after that overnight flight they had endured, plus the car rental from hell. He had never had to drive manually on the wrong side of the road before, which he had had to do since their automatic pilot was on the fritz. And Kathryn had tried to navigate using her phone's GPS, but the damn device had malfunctioned and they had had to use an old-fashioned paper map – very archaic, if you were on Earth – not so much in Anandria.

And talk about a disappointing destination. Stonehenge was an ancient ruin – period. Tourists flocked around it snapping pictures. The cousins had not found an active magical site like they had hoped for. So, why had Kathryn's vision brought them there?

Next, they had driven around aimlessly after leaving Stonehenge, because Kathryn had had no idea what to do next, and every inn, hotel, and motel they had stopped at had been full – except for the dirty little dump they had booked into last night. Raonull swore his eyes hadn't closed. He had heard skittering roaches every time the lights went off. It didn't take long before he had dragged Kathryn back to the car to sleep – if one could sleep in a car. Neither one had felt refreshed when the sun had come up.

Determined to find a better place, Raonull had driven aimlessly until Kathryn suddenly snapped to attention and insisted he take a side road to the little town of Avebury, and stop in front of the Avebury Inn. It looked quaint, and very old, and the inn's sign hadn't been lit up, but they had called the number on it anyway – they were too tired to get out if there was no room available. The connection was a bit garbled, but much to their delight, they had determined that there was a vacancy.

Right now, all Raonull wanted was somewhere to rest his head and shut his eyes. Tomorrow, they would figure out what the hell Kathryn's vision had been about – if anything. However, the petite brunette who stood blushing behind the counter had definitely grabbed his attention.

A tall dark-haired man strode out of a back room to join the five-foot nothing woman behind the counter. "I say, are you the people who just called?"

Raonull heard Kathryn suck in a sharp breath. He glanced out of the corner of his eye. Kathryn's eyes were wide, and her mouth gaped open for a second before her lips curved up with pleasure at the sight of the handsome man.

Raonull scrutinized the man. *Handsome, and about the same height as me, and it looks like he works out. Probably the woman's husband.* He turned his gaze back to the petite innkeeper, surprised by the jolt of disappointment he felt at that thought. "Yes. We're not sure how long we want to stay. My cousin," Raonull indicated Kathryn with a flick of his wrist, "has always wanted to explore Stonehenge. We drove past and were disappointed by all the tourists, though."

The man nodded. His dark eyes twinkled as they settled on Kathryn. "Stonehenge has all the press, but our town of Avebury is much more interesting. Despite our close location to Stonehenge, you'll find our community is fairly quiet, and..." he paused dramatically, "if you haven't noticed, our whole town is situated within a stone circle older than Stonehenge."

"Really?"

Raonull noticed the breathy quality of Kathryn's voice. *Oh yeah, she was interested in the information – and the man.*

A pregnant pause hung in the air. Kathryn and the man stared at each other. Finally, the petite woman cleared her throat, nudged the man, and said, "Douglas only reserved one room for you, but I suppose you'd prefer two, as you're cousins. Maybe adjoining rooms?"

"Yeah, that'd be great," Raonull said as he passed her his credit card.

She glanced at the name and said, "Thank you, Mr. Evans."

"Please, I'm Raonull, and this is Kathryn."

She flicked a look up at him through her eyelashes. "I'm Ella Donella, the owner of this fine establishment. I, *and my cousin,* Douglas Adair, will be your hosts." She efficiently handed back his card along with an old skeleton key. "The loo is shared between your rooms. Doors open to either side separating your rooms."

"The loo?" Raonull asked.

"The bathroom, coz," Kathryn supplied on a yawn. She slapped a hand over her mouth.

"That's right, she's brilliant," Ella confirmed. "And there'll be muffins in the morning. Tea and scones every afternoon at four."

"Thanks. Come on, Kath..." Raonull was about to grab her hand, but wrapped an arm about Kathryn's waist instead, pulling her back against his chest. She had gone ramrod straight. *Damn.* Her eyes were open, but unseeing.

Douglas walked around the end of the counter. "What's wrong? Is she okay?"

Raonull hesitated to answer, but Ella rounded the end of the counter, too, watching Kathryn with considering eyes. "She's all right." He shrugged. "It's just that she has these..."

"Visions?" Ella breathed. "Is she having a vision?"

Raonull nodded.

"Brilliant!"

"How'd you know?" Raonull asked, dazed by Ella's easy acceptance.

Ella stared at Kathryn in fascination. "Anyone born within Avebury Circle sees things a little differently than most folks. My granny used to predict events on a regular basis, and even I have seen things. But I've never gone under as deeply as Granny was wont to do."

Kathryn went limp, blinked her eyes, sucked in a deep breath of air, drilled a look at Ella, and declared, "You're a fairy!"

Ella tilted her head quizzically. "What are you on about?"

Kathryn shrugged and pulled out of Raonull's arms. "I see magic in your blood. *Fairy magic.*"

Ella smiled. "Now that would be interesting, if it were true." She held her hands out. "But I see no wand, or fairy dust, and I've never flitted about like Tinker Bell." She spun about. "See? No wings."

Kathryn's brow puckered. "But that's what I saw." Her lips pushed into a pout as she rubbed her eyes. "Truly you *are* a fairy."

"Look, we've just endured a trans-Atlantic flight, customs, a British car, a night sleeping in said car... You're almost asleep on your feet, Kath. The quest can wait until tomorrow." Raonull's head ached, and he was sure Kathryn had to be suffering, too. He reached over and drew Kathryn back into his arms.

"But," Kathryn protested, "we need to figure this out. It's important."

"No buts, Kath." He stooped and hoisted Kathryn over his shoulder. He didn't want to argue. He was too tired. This was the easiest way to get his cousin to comply. "Which way to our rooms?"

Ella stepped up to Raonull, tapped his bulging biceps, and poked him in the chest with a sharp fingernail. "You're a strong one, aren't you?"

Kathryn's muffled voice floated up over his shoulder. "You have no idea."

Raonull stared down into Ella's green eyes and got lost for a moment. Mentally, he shook himself. He and Kathryn were exhausted and needed sleep. "Our rooms?"

Ella smiled. She liked the hulking man. "Follow me." Two doors down, she stopped. "There you are. If you need anything let me know."

Raonull thrust his key in the slot, shoved the door open, stepped in, and closed it in Ella's face.

Ella whirled around and grinned at her cousin. "Things have just become interesting in the town of Avebury. Did you hear? They're on a quest!"

Douglas nodded thoughtfully. "I did." He slipped behind the counter to grab a sweater. "I'll be heading home now. I'll see you close to lunchtime. Perhaps, we can learn more about our guests and their quest then."

15

Lying on her stomach across Raonull's bed, Kathryn flipped through a ratty old book while she waited for him to come out of the bathroom. The sun wasn't up, but they were both wide awake. Obviously, they weren't on British time yet.

Raonull appeared in the bathroom door, his toothbrush hung out the side of his mouth, while he buttoned up his shirt. Around the brush he said, "I can't believe Aunt Mandy still uses books. When Christmas rolls around, we should convert her books to eBooks."

"She'd hate that." Kathryn's finger stilled on a page. She had spotted Aunt Mandy's baby name book when they had come through the portal to Earth and, *following a feeling*, had grabbed it to take on their trip across the ocean. "Ah ha! Here it is. Ella." She tapped the page. "Ray, her name means, Beautiful Fairy!"

Raonull began to brush his teeth while he watched his cousin. He knew better than to interrupt when she was on the hunt. She was already scanning another page.

"Yes!" Kathryn crowed. "Donella, her surname, stands for dark-haired elfin girl."

Raonull held his toothbrush up in a salute. He didn't dare speak or toothpaste would spill out of his mouth. He did tip his head and raise an eyebrow in question, though.

Kathryn immediately dove back into the book. "Douglas... Douglas... Douglas..." she muttered, running her finger down another page.

Raonull saw her frown.

"Douglas means dark stranger, or dweller by the dark stream." She looked up at Raonull. "Guess he's not a part of whatever we've got ourselves into."

Raonull held up his hand and ducked into the bathroom before he reappeared wiping his mouth. There'd been disappointment in her voice. "Check out his last name... Ella said it was Adair."

Kathryn flipped to the appropriate page. "From the dark oak tree ford..." she muttered.

Raonull shrugged. "Maybe it'll come together later." He grinned. "At least both his first and last names have something to do with a stream or river. That might be coincidence, or it might be something significant. Keep an open mind, Kath. Oh wait, you're the one who can't stop the freakin' universe from putting *visions* into your head."

Kathryn chucked a pillow at him. He ducked and dove onto the bed. His fingers dug into her ribs and she let out a shrill scream. "Stop!" she gasped. "No!" She had difficulty catching her breath as she continued to shriek.

Someone pounded on the door, and the cousins froze on the bed. Kathryn met Raonull's gaze, and they burst out laughing just as the door to Raonull's room clicked open.

Raonull sucked in his breath. His little fairy – *yeah, she looked like a fairy* – stood in the doorway, her ebony hair a tangled mess, her green eyes narrowed with fury, and a key clutched tightly in her hand. A short bathrobe that barely covered her assets seemed to be all she wore. *Hot damn.*

"Bloody hell," she hissed. "I thought someone was being murdered."

Raonull rolled to his feet. "You heard us?"

"How could I not? My room is right next door."

Kathryn pushed hair off her face. She felt the heat of embarrassment colour her cheeks. She levered up onto her elbows to look at Ella. "Sorry," she muttered. Her eye fell on the name book, and she grabbed it up holding it high. "I was right, though. Ella means beautiful fairy."

Ella shook her head. "Total rubbish." She glared at them both. "Do you two realize what time it is?" She didn't wait for a reply. "And why are the two of you up and dressed?"

Raonull crossed the room and leaned against the doorframe to tower over Ella. "Can't sleep." He glanced over her head to peer down the hall. "Where's Douglas?"

"He went home."

"Home? You mean he left you here all by yourself? At night? With strangers? All alone?"

Ella poked him in the chest with that sharp fingernail she had used on him earlier. "Butt out, strong man. It's my inn. Douglas helps me, but he has responsibilities, too."

"But you're alone with strangers," Raonull sputtered going nose-to-nose with her.

Her eyes lowered to his lips and she felt the heat of his breath on her cheek.

"He shouldn't have left you," Raonull declared hotly.

Ella realized the hand she had used to poke him with was now lying flat against his broad chest. Startled by her attraction to the big guy, and the way he made her lose focus, she gave a disgruntled shove. Raonull didn't budge. He still peered intently into her eyes.

"Back off, Ray," Kathryn said. "Give the girl breathing room. She's not related to you, so quit trying to intimidate her."

Raonull straightened up and glared at his cousin. "I don't try to intimidate..."

"Ha! That's total rubbish," Ella said as she breezed past him to sit on the bed next to Kathryn. "Did you hear about the cruise ship that capsized in the Mediterranean a month ago?"

Kathryn nodded, bemused by the abrupt change in topics.

"My mum and dad, along with Douglas's parents were on board. They didn't make it..." She choked on the last couple of words.

"Christ!" Raonull sat down on the bed next to her. "They're still diving at that site. It's supposed to take months to raise the ship."

Ella nodded and dabbed at her eyes. "Now the inn is mine, and Douglas has his parent's estate, along with its accompanying responsibilities, that he's still trying to sort out."

She pasted on a watery smile. "You're my first guests. When Douglas got your call inquiring about rooms, I decided it was time to give it a go. I felt like I might be able to handle two guests..." She hiccupped and drew the sleeve of her robe across her nose. "I guess I was wrong. I'm sorry..."

"Nonsense, lass," Raonull chided. "My cousin and I can't help but admire how well you're holding up considering the circumstances."

Ella sniffed. "Having Douglas nearby helps. It's less than a five minute walk to his place. I don't know what I would have done if he hadn't been here." She turned a tremulous smile towards Kathryn. "The sun's about to rise, and Douglas should be up soon. Once he's completed the ritual his parents used to do every morning at dawn, he'll come back to the inn."

"A ritual?" Kathryn asked as she looked over Ella's head at Raonull with a raised brow.

Ella sniffed again, and Raonull handed her a tissue. "Yeah, at dawn his parents always sat at the base of the old oak tree on the banks of the river, Winterbourne."

"Ray..." Kathryn said.

"Yeah, yeah, I'm with you, Kath." Raonull crooked a finger under Ella's chin turning her to face him. "Do you think you could take us there? Are you up for that?"

"Or, are we pushing too hard?" Kathryn interjected.

Ella stared into Raonull's eyes. Something about him helped to settle her. She sniffled again and accepted another tissue from him. As she blew her nose, she caught her reflection in the mirror over the dresser. Could she look any worse? Her hair was a mess, her face was splotchy – and she was sitting next to Raonull with only a skimpy bathrobe on. Horrified barely covered what she felt.

Suddenly, she realized both cousins were sitting quietly waiting for an answer. What did they want with Douglas and his weird ritual? "I suppose I could take you, but give me a sec to throw on some clothes."

She rose from the bed and dashed out the door.

16

"Lovely," Ella breathed. "Just lovely." She gestured towards the stone cottage with its thatched roof situated on the banks of the Winterbourne River. The horizon was turning pink as the sun began to rise, birds twittered overhead, and she was pleased to see Kathryn and Raonull gazing with pleasure at the idyllic scene.

"There he is," Ella whispered with a flick of her wrist.

Backlit by the predawn light, Douglas approached a huge tree. He sat down cross-legged at its base facing its massive trunk. The first rays of the sun speared up from the horizon, allowing them to see the distinctive leaves of an oak tree.

"Douglas," Ella called, visibly startling him.

Douglas rose, and dusted off the seat of his jeans.

Kathryn gaped. Had Douglas looked that hot last night? Or, had she been so fatigued the full beauty of the man hadn't registered? She remembered thinking he was handsome, but this morning he looked like a god!

"Ella?" He looked perplexed by their presence.

"They needed to see you," Ella replied. "So I brought them."

Raonull nudged Kathryn's shoulder with his. She was staring at Douglas with a stupid look on her face. When she failed to respond to his nudge, Raonull fisted a hand, rapped her on the forehead, and shoved his face in front of hers. "Hello? Anyone in there?"

Her gaze snapped to his. Total annoyance showed on her face. "Ray, go jump in the river."

Raonull's eyes went wide. He lurched upright and faced the river. Breaking into a run, he flung himself out over the water and landed hard on his belly. They all heard a loud, *thwack!*

Kathryn flinched. "Crap, I keep forgetting I can do that on Earth."

Raonull broke the surface with a roar of fury. Ella and Douglas watched sheer terror settle over Kathryn as Raonull thrashed to shore. "Kath!" he roared.

"No, Ray," Kathryn squealed. She whirled about – and ran smack into a hard chest. Muscular arms wrapped about her. "Let go!" she screamed as she struggled to escape.

Douglas tightened his hold. Raonull was mad as hell, and Kathryn was panicking. *Why? What madness infects these two Canadians?* "Not a chance," he whispered into her hair. "I've got you."

"No! I can outrun him until he cools off."

"I think he's cool enough," Douglas chuckled, eyeing the water streaming off Raonull.

"No! You have to let me go."

"Too late." Douglas was fascinated. Something had happened, and one glance at Ella proved that she was clueless, too.

Raonull stormed up. "You've gone too far, Kathryn."

"Oh God, I'm in trouble," she whispered. Raonull never called her Kathryn unless he was furious with her. She buried her face against Douglas's chest. His large hand shifted up to cup the back of her head.

Raonull reached for Kathryn.

Douglas shifted, sliding his body between the cousins. "What's your problem? Give her a moment."

"No way." Raonull grabbed Douglas's arms and pried them apart. Kathryn screamed and tired to duck under the two men, but Raonull's hand clamped down on her arm stopping her escape.

When Douglas tried to help Kathryn, Raonull knocked his feet out from under him, and pinned him to the ground, holding him there with his foot on his chest.

Shock had Douglas gaping up at Raonull. He couldn't budge. The bloke was a bloody Hercules! How could Raonull hold him down so easily? *Christ, I work out daily, and my build and size are comparable to his — but I can't move!*

"Ray, don't," Kathryn pleaded.

With his hands free, Raonull scooped Kathryn up, and swung her back and forth gauging her weight. "As the British say, not bloody likely." He let go, and Kathryn flew through the air. Raonull lifted his foot and freed Douglas just as Kathryn hit the water. A grim smile curved his lips when she bobbed to the surface sputtering.

"Well," Ella huffed, nonplussed by the whole situation. "Look at the two of you. This is just brilliant. You're both soaked to the skin, and the temperature is just a tad above freezing." Ella paused to take a deep breath. "Douglas, go help Kathryn out of the water, while I take strong man into the cottage to warm up by the fire."

Raonull glanced down when her hands wrapped around his biceps and pulled. He snorted. *As if she can move me! I'll move when I damn well want to move. Right now, I'm relishing my revenge.* But then his eyes met Ella's...

They snapped at him with irritation. "Move it," Ella muttered as she tugged again. "You'll catch your death if you stay out here, you stupid blockhead."

Whoa! His little fairy was bossy, and had a temper. He paused. *His?* He was thinking of her as his? *Damn.* He'd known her for less than twenty-four hours. He was contemplating giving in to Ella's tugging when Douglas sloshed up with Kathryn wrapped in his arms. She was a shivering, teeth-chattering mess.

Douglas sneered at Raonull as he passed by and muttered, "I want an explanation."

17

The stone cottage was tiny. Kitchen and living room formed one room, which was dominated by a large brick fireplace. A fire crackled and popped on the hearth, perfect for the chilled people in the room, and their wet clothes strung high above on a line between the rafters.

Raonull emerged from the bathroom. His broad shoulders tested the seams on his borrowed T-shirt. Luckily, he and Douglas were close in stature so the sweat pants were a comfortable fit.

"Sorry," Kathryn muttered when she saw him. She was huddled in a forlorn heap at the end of the couch, her eyes averted and downcast.

At least she has the decency to let me decide for myself if I'll accept her apology. She has to be feeling really bad. "I forgive you, Kath." Raonull strode over and tucked a lock of hair behind her ear. "Don't do it again."

"I won't. It was uncalled for, and I keep forgetting I can do this on Earth." With her nerves still on edge, Kathryn adjusted the massive terry robe, Douglas had provided, about her legs. She also made sure it didn't gape open at the neck. It was weird to sit there knowing she was totally naked underneath. Surreptitiously, she buried her nose in the fabric and sniffed. *It smells like Douglas.*

Out of the corner of her eye, she saw him sit next to her. He kept looking quizzically between her and Raonull.

"Just what in blazes is she apologizing for?" Ella asked, clearly mystified by Kathryn's apology. "If anyone should be begging forgiveness, it should be you, Raonull. You should be grovelling at her feet." Ella latched on to the bottom of Raonull's T-shirt and pulled. He toppled onto the loveseat next to her. She glared at him. "You *let* me do that, didn't you?"

"What do you think?" Raonull smiled at his little fairy. *There I go again.* Kath had him believing she was a fairy!

Douglas threw a protective arm around Kathryn and drew her close. "Yes, why should she apologize? *You* tossed her into the water. I didn't see anyone throw you in."

Raonull noticed Kathryn was looking everywhere but at him. Her colour had deepened, too. He was enjoying her discomfort, so he decided to turn the screw a bit more. "Perhaps, my cousin should tell you what she did to me."

Kathryn threw him a panicked look. "No, Ray."

"Yeah, Kath, tell them why I'm so ticked off with you."

Douglas and Ella watched her fidget with the tie on her robe.

"Umm..." she began. "You guys accepted, pretty easily, the fact that I experience visions." She watched them nod before she flicked her fingers at Raonull. "You might have noticed Raonull's extraordinary strength."

"I bloody well did," Douglas groused. He was damned if he could explain how Raonull had pinned him so easily.

Kathryn smirked. Douglas had no idea magic was at work. She cupped Douglas's chin and turned his face to gaze into his eyes. "Douglas, listen and truly hear me." Instantly, Douglas closed his mouth. His focus shifted exclusively to Kathryn.

"Kath," Raonull growled in warning.

"Shut up, Ray. They have to understand, because we *need* them."

Ella cocked her head. "And why would we be wanting to help you?"

Kathryn sighed. Could she explain it? "Because if you don't, and we fail, a powerful evil will be unleashed on Earth, which is capable of enslaving humanity for all time."

"Go on," Ella scoffed. "You're pulling my leg."

Kathryn shook her head. "I, and my family, have extraordinary powers which should never work on Earth, but they're doing exactly that."

"Are you hearing this, Douglas?" Ella sputtered. "Total rubbish."

Douglas stared silently at Kathryn.

"Douglas?" Ella prodded again. "Hey, Douglas!"

"He can't say anything, Ella," Raonull said. "Kath has put a compulsion on him to listen."

Ella leaned forward and snapped her fingers. "Cut it out, Douglas. Say something."

"I have to release him before he can speak," Kathryn explained.

"Kath, let him go," Raonull ordered.

She nodded once, and leaned towards Douglas. "I think you've heard enough. Now let us hear from you freely."

Douglas blinked, his hand rose and massaged his temple before his face contorted with a snarl and he grabbed Kathryn's arms. "What the bloody hell did you do to me?"

"I did the same thing to you that I did to Ray. I *told* you what to do."

"Huh?" Douglas shot a glance at Raonull. He saw a smug smile curl up Raonull's lips.

"Douglas," Kathryn gasped. "Please let go. Your fingers are digging in, and you're hurting me."

Shocked, Douglas thrust her away. Confusion clouded his eyes when he turned to Ella. "She *made* me listen. I had no choice. I couldn't talk. All I could do was listen."

"And she *made* me jump in the river," Raonull added.

Douglas eyed Raonull intently. "She did, didn't she?"

Raonull nodded. "Finally, you believe. Now you understand why I was angry and threw her into the water."

The men exchanged looks of total understanding.

Ella leaped off the loveseat and planted herself between the two men. "It's time for tea and a fascinating tale." Her eyes locked with Kathryn's. "I'm sure there's a lot more to the telling."

"I'll help," Raonull declared.

"Oh no, strong man," Ella said emphasizing each word with a poke to his chest. "There's only room for one at the sink."

Raonull winced and danced away. She had damn sharp nails. His foot caught on a rug and he stumbled. He grabbed a shelf – one of many lining the whole northern wall of the cottage filled with books. "Hey!" Raonull pulled a familiar book off the shelf. "Will you look at that? Not many own this in an actual book format, anymore – my Aunt Mandy being one of them. Everyone else has it in digital."

"What've you got, Ray?" Kathryn asked.

"*Destiny Calls.*" His eyes passed over the English cousins. "Have you both read this?"

"Of course. Kathryn Heaney's one of our favourite authors," Douglas replied.

Raonull grinned and gestured at the book. "Then you know our grandmother's story."

"Sorry?" Ella muttered as she plugged in the kettle.

Raonull held the book higher. "Our Aunt Mandy wrote this. Kathryn Heaney's her pen name. She uses her mom's maiden name for this series since she's one of the actual characters in the book." He reached for another book. "I see you've got *Destiny Reclaimed*, too! That's our parent's story."

"What?" Douglas grumbled.

Ella marched back with a plate of biscuits. She nodded at the books clutched in Raonull's hands. "We've read both of them."

Kathryn grinned. "Well that's a relief. We won't have to explain too much."

"Whoa!" Douglas huffed. "They're fiction."

"Nope," Kathryn quipped. "And I have a feeling book number three will be our story. If we survive..."

Douglas stared at her for a moment. "It's not fiction?"

"Nope! 'Fraid not."

Ella put the biscuits down. "We're talking magic, Lucifer, dragons, and gargoyles?"

"Yeah," Raonull confirmed.

"That's brilliant!" Ella exclaimed as she sat down next to him. "But why are you two able to use magic here on Earth? And how did Lucifer come out of his coma? That was how the second book ended, right?"

Raonull stared at her, amazed by her easy acceptance. "You're not joking are you? You're taking our word at face value without question."

Ella grinned up at him. "When you've lived your whole life within Avebury Circle, you grow up believing in magic." Ella nodded towards Douglas. "After all, I'm related to a Druid."

Kathryn started to glance sharply at the man sitting beside her, but a movement at the window distracted her. "Ah, Douglas?"

"Yes?"

"Do you always have squirrels knocking on your window?"

"What? Jesus Christ! The tree..." Douglas exploded out of his seat and raced to the door.

Kathryn raced after him. She watched the squirrels keep pace. Behind her, Ella said to Raonull, "It's like an animated Disney movie. Look, the squirrels are patting the trunk of the tree with their little paws – so cute."

Douglas flung himself down at the base of the tree, closed his eyes, and began chanting something in an ancient language. Reverently, he slid his hands up the tree's massive roots. A long crack at least three feet in length split the bark vertically on the tree's trunk.

"It's not working you know." Douglas glared up at Kathryn as she approached. She was staring intently at the tree. "The sun has cleared the horizon." She placed a hand on his shoulder.

He shrugged her off and kept chanting with desperation in his voice. Kathryn was right, it wasn't working. His hum of power was gone, and he felt no connection to the tree. *What have I done?*

Kathryn squatted next to him. "It's all right, you know. This is supposed to happen." He kept chanting. "I know you and your kin have kept the tree well and alive for many centuries. Now, it can give up its secret to us. This was meant to be."

His voice deepened. He began to rock his body and rub the exposed roots harder, ignoring her...

Raonull was seeing small 'tells' that let him know Kathryn was experiencing a number of rapid short sessions of Sight. But whatever she relayed to Douglas was being ignored. Raonull grinned. If looks could kill, the glare Douglas directed at his cousin would have keeled Kathryn over on the spot.

Ella tugged his hand. "Ray, listen to the tree."

Raonull's attention snapped to the towering oak. A hissing, sizzling sound had him inspecting the long split in the tree's bark. The gap was widening. The bark was curling back. Even the wood beneath was cracking open. The squirrels leapt to the ground. He didn't have a good feeling about this...

He shifted his gaze back to Kathryn and Douglas. They were glowering at each other oblivious to the changes in the tree.

Crack!

With a grunt, Raonull tossed Ella into a bush well behind him. Then he sprinted like hell to the tree.

I can make it.

His arms wrapped about both their chests, and with a mighty heave, Raonull sent Douglas and Kathryn flying through the air to land in the river at the exact moment the tree exploded.

Splintered wood became deadly shrapnel. Whole branches careened through the air. The ground heaved as the roots tried to pull free.

Ella extracted herself from the bush. Wood blew by, and instinctively she ducked. She thought for sure she was a goner, but the spear-like branch, heading for her face, veered off at the last second as if it had hit an invisible wall – *like a force field*, she thought numbly. But the most horrific sight she saw was Raonull, tossed high in the sky by the explosion, his body limp and unresponsive. Like a rag doll. There was blood, too. She began to run. If Raonull wasn't already dead, he would be if he hit the ground from that height. She wasn't sure what she was going to do, but she had to do something...

Pain exploded between her shoulder blades, and her feet left the ground. *God, what's hit me?* She closed her eyes waiting for her own crash landing, but they quickly sprang open when she realized she was still heading towards the heavens. *How?*

Thwack! Thwack!

She looked over her shoulder and her eyes just about fell out of her head. *I've got wings! They're beautiful, large, iridescent, fairy princess wings. And they're driving me up to meet Raonull.*

18

Kathryn hit the water hard. Her oversized terry robe immediately tangled with her legs and dragged her down. She wanted to untie and shove the garment off, but her fingers were covered by long sleeves, and the belt was secured tightly at her waist. Her lungs ached, and panic threatened to overtake reason.

Something brushed through her hair. She couldn't tell what it was because of the murky water, but it came back and latched on to her hair with a yank that made her wince. An arm wrapped about her chest. *I'm not going to die.*

She reached the surface and dragged in blessed air.

"That was too close," Douglas murmured in her ear. "I couldn't find you at first." Floating wood rammed into him. "Ow! Mother of God, my tree..."

Kathryn looked towards shore where the tree should have stood. "Ray!" she cried in horror.

Simultaneously Douglas gasped, "Ella!"

Douglas stroked furiously towards shore, pulling Kathryn in his wake, while he kept an eye on the drama unfolding overhead. Ella flew – *yes, flew* – up to Raonull, whose limp body was falling through the air.

Ella intercepted and wrapped her arms about Raonull. She flapped her beautiful wings *hard*. It didn't stop his fall, but it slowed their descent enough that their touchdown would only result in a few minor scrapes and bruises. Ella landed on top of Raonull with her new wings draped over his still form.

Douglas reached the shore and raced over. Kathryn had to struggle with her soggy robe.

A few feet away from the downed pair, Douglas bounced off an invisible barrier. Stunned by the impact, he staggered. Kathryn sloshed up beside him. "Ella," Kathryn called softly. "It's all right. Douglas and I are here to help. Let us in."

Ella lifted her head. Tears streamed down her face. "He's breathing," she choked out. "He's *alive*."

"Let us in," Kathryn repeated as she placed her hand on the invisible barrier separating them.

"I'm doing that?" Ella asked, confused by the power swirling about her.

"Yeah. It must be an instinctive act of protection. Calm yourself. Let us help. Take a few deep breaths." Kathryn smiled. Beneath her hand the barrier dissolved. She grabbed Douglas's hand and pulled him forward. Together they knelt beside Ella.

Relief washed across Ella's face. Silently, her wings curled up and slipped through her skin. "Oh!" she cried, startled. She was left with two small bumps situated between her shoulder blades and her spine and a ruined T-shirt – her wings had bashed through it ripping it apart.

A pregnant pause held them all – until Raonull moaned.

Kathryn leaned over and examined the nasty gash on his temple. There were other cuts, mainly down the right side of his body, which had taken the full brunt of the explosion. "He probably saved our lives," Kathryn murmured. "His magic gives him a strong constitution. Perhaps that's why he survived."

Douglas pushed to his feet. "I'll be right back."

"Where's he going at a time like this?" Kathryn hissed at Ella.

"It's all right. He's a Druid and knows a great deal about healing. He's probably fetching one of his powders, or ointments. The townspeople clamor for them when they're hurt or sick."

"Ow, my head," Raonull groaned.

Ella grabbed his hand as it headed for the injury. "Lay still, strong man. You're hurt and bleeding."

"What happened?"

"The tree blew up," Kathryn muttered as she tried to hold back tears of relief. "Thank heavens you've got a hard head. But just to set my mind at ease, I want you to wiggle your toes and squeeze my hand." Raonull obliged and Kathryn gasped, "Don't squeeze so hard! Geez, any harder and you'll break my fingers."

Raonull dropped her hand and propped himself up on his elbow. He sucked in a sharp breath and quickly eased back down to the ground. "Damn, my head hurts like the very devil – and the world's spinning."

"Duh, cousin, you've got a concussion. We'd better get you checked out at a local hospital, since Grandma's not around."

"Move aside ladies. I'll take care of him." Douglas fell to his knees. In his hand he held a jar. The stuff inside looked like peanut butter.

"Wait till you see this," Ella hissed to Kathryn. "Douglas rarely uses this cream as it's hard to make. It's a product made from the tree." She glanced back to where the tree once stood and sputtered, "Oh. My. God."

"Oh my God is right!" Kathryn breathed. From the ragged remains of the stump, something golden gleamed. It was lodged in the vertical crack in the stump.

Without taking her eyes away from the unusual sight, Ella said, "Hurry up, Douglas. There's something else you need to see."

"Hmm?" Douglas murmured as he applied brown cream to the gash on Raonull's head. Raonull's hand came up to grip his wrist painfully. Douglas eyed his patient. There was dire threat in Raonull's gaze. Douglas chuckled. "Let go, Ray. I know what

I'm doing, and I promise you'll feel better before five minutes have passed."

Raonull held Douglas's wrist a tad longer before he released his hold. "Are you sure I don't need stitches? There's a lot of blood."

Douglas clucked his tongue. "The bigger they are, the harder they fall. And, no, you won't need stitches. Hold still. I'm almost done."

"Douglas, hurry up," Ella urged. She was peering into the split trunk.

Kathryn moved up to join her. Tentatively, she poked her hand through the crack, and hissed in surprise when a surge of power swept through her body. She jerked back, checked out her hand, and breathed a sigh of relief. Nothing was damaged. It looked normal.

Meanwhile, Raonull was experiencing Douglas's magical healing touch. His head no longer hurt, his cut had ceased to bleed, and, as Douglas applied cream to his other lacerations, Raonull was pleased to see them heal within seconds.

"That's the last of it," Douglas said as he spread cream onto a gash just under Raonull's ribs.

"That stuff is miraculous," Raonull said. "You'll have to make more."

"I can't. It came from the tree's acorns."

Their eyes travelled across the yard. It looked like a bomb had exploded.

"Guys?" Kathryn called. "I need help."

Douglas held out a hand, and pulled Raonull to his feet.

Raonull smiled when the world stayed steady. "I'm surprised I only had a few cuts and bruises. The last thing I remember, I was being thrown high in the air."

"Could've been a *lot* worse if it weren't for Ella."

"Ella? Ha! I tossed her into a bush."

"Yeah, and she came screaming out when she saw you up in the air."

"What'd she do, catch me?" There was derision in his voice.

"You could say so."

"Ha! I'd flatten her. She's tiny."

"She didn't catch you on the ground."

"Well, where the hell else would she be catching me?"

"In mid-air. It seems Kathryn's right about Ella being a fairy."

"What?"

"You heard me. Beautiful wings, too."

Raonull stared at Ella, whose head was close to Kathryn's as they looked inside the stump. He didn't see any wings, but her T-shirt had two massive rips near her shoulder blades – *right where one would expect wings...*

Kathryn stepped aside. "Look."

Both men peered through the crack in the trunk. Something golden was lodged in the stump.

"Whoa!" Raonull breathed.

"Yeah, you can feel the magic, too," Kathryn remarked, and patted him on the shoulder.

"I'll get my axe," Douglas said as he wheeled about.

"No!" everyone yelled together. They didn't want Douglas damaging what was stuck in the stump with an axe.

"Stand aside," Raonull ordered. "I'll get it out." His hands gripped the two sides of the crack, and the muscles in his upper body bunched when he strained.

The wood gave way with a loud crack. Douglas reached past Raonull and tried to dislodge the object. "Looks like a box," Douglas grunted. It didn't move. His face started to turn red. "It's stuck. I can't budge it."

Raonull nudged him aside. Douglas went flying. "Oops, sorry," Raonull murmured. "Keep forgetting about my strength on Earth." Still staring at Douglas, Raonull reached in with one hand and lifted the object out of the stump – *with no visible effort.* "It's a bit weighty," Raonull drawled. "I think it's made of gold."

Ella stepped between the two men. "We don't need a pissing match between the two of you. What we need is to bring it inside where we can examine it. I'll make another pot of tea, and we can all catch our breath."

Both men nodded. The way Ella was glaring at them they knew the wisest course of action was to follow the little fairy into the cottage. But just to make sure the men complied, Kathryn grabbed Douglas's arm, and Ella snagged Raonull's free hand.

Raonull's brow rose. She was a fierce little thing. He glanced down at the golden object in his hand. His hand ached a tad. *It's bloody heavy.* "Just a minute, Ella." He slid his hand out of hers and shifted the object into the crook of his arm. Then he reached for her and tangled their fingers together. *Nice!*

19

Carlos Ricardo stepped out onto one of the four terraces gracing his two story penthouse. With drink in one hand, and cigarette in the other, he was content to wait for word about his latest transaction. His men knew where to find him.

The only thing missing on this moonlit night was a beautiful woman. Perhaps he should call Lilly. She could warm his bed and share a celebratory glass of the bubbly when the cash was secured in his impressive bank account. Using forefinger and thumb, he rubbed tired eyes. No, his little *chica* would have to wait. Exhaustion was catching up with him – although it never reached the same level as it used to when Lucifer had run the show.

He took another sip of whiskey, his drink of choice, and ran through the last twenty plus years since Lucifer's demise.

On paper, he, Carlos Ricardo, had always been the front man for Lucifer. Cars, condos, and the yacht had been purchased in his name, even though it was Lucifer who had financed and enjoyed the frivolous luxuries– until Lucifer had died. What a liberating day that had been! Experts were still trying to explain the absence of Lucifer's body after his car had crashed. Caught on camera, driving the car that had torpedoed through a railing on an overpass ramp to crash a hundred feet below on a major highway, authorities had expected to find Lucifer in the mangled wreckage. But no remains could be found inside the car. No body parts had been splattered in the vicinity, either.

It had taken Carlos years to stop looking over his shoulder and to begin enjoying the luxuries already listed in his name. At first, he had thought Lucifer had somehow walked away — the man had always seemed invincible, often surviving things that would kill an ordinary man. Carlos remembered fingering a hole in one of Lucifer's discarded shirts. It had been dead centre — a shot to the heart — yet the man had lived. How? He remembered laughing when the forensic teams had found nothing of Lucifer at the crash site. Obviously, his boss had outwitted them again, he had thought. So, he had waited for Lucifer to return. And waited...

Gradually, the men had come to him for direction, and reluctantly he had given orders, hoping Lucifer would approve. Eventually, after several years had gone by, he had accepted that Lucifer had indeed perished. He had begun to do as he pleased.

He'd come a long way from the small time operator he had been when he had first met Lucifer in prison. Becoming Lucifer's new drug consortium CEO, he no longer did dirty work. He had flunkies for that.

Carlos puffed on his cigarette and placed his drink on the coffee table. Maybe he'd stretch out on the couch for a while and close his eyes while he waited for word about the deal that was going down tonight. Life was pretty sweet. He put his feet up on the table. At first he tuned out the city sounds. Being right next to the Royal Ontario Museum — or ROM, as people called it — on a major downtown Toronto artery, there was always street drama. But tonight, the noise had escalated to unusual proportions. Multiple sirens screamed down below. People shouted. And there was more than one person screaming.

What the...?

Annoyed, he rose and crossed to the plexiglass panel on the edge of the terrace. Cars stood at a standstill, emergency vehicles converged, and lots of people stood gawking. They looked up and pointed. He looked up, too — and froze.

Swooping between the high rises of downtown Toronto were three dragons – yeah, *dragons*. They were massive. How did they stay up? Was it a movie stunt using remote controlled robots? If it was, they had his attention. What a fabulous bit of advertising!

Sweet Jesus, they were headed his way! They would pass right by his condo. Would they fit between the buildings? Hopefully, whoever controlled the dragons would make sure there was no contact with any buildings – the damage would be substantial. Just in case, Carlos stepped away from the edge of his terrace. He didn't want to get clipped by the enormous wings he heard beating the air.

The largest dragon dipped low and swept past. Carlos sucked in a horrified breath. *It couldn't be.* A man and woman straddled the base of the dragon's neck. The man was dressed in white from head to toe, his long black hair caught at the nape of his neck. "Couldn't be," Carlos muttered. "Lucifer is long dead and gone." *Had to be an actor operating the controls flying the dragon – same with the costumed guys on the other two dragons. Great costumes, too. Black and ugly as sin. Very convincing.*

He chuckled, surprised by the unexpected rush of nerves that had made his belly clench. Maybe he should call Lilly after all. She could give him a massage before they crawled into his bed for the night. He turned to head back inside the condo. A powerful gust knocked him forward, and he barely got his hands out to brace his fall. A blood chilling screech, and sudden darkness, was all the warning he had before something massive hit his terrace.

The building shuddered.

Carlos rolled to his back and ran into a wicked looking talon attached to a dragon's foot. The beast's large wings retracted neatly against its body. *Sweet Jesus, this is no mechanical robot. This is real!* Carlos crab walked backwards. He needed to get inside – *now*. He had one hand over the threshold when he heard a voice he would never forget – a voice he had hoped never to hear again...

"Hello, Carlos."

20

It was a book! At least a thousand pages, filled with indecipherable script, and it was latched on the side so that it looked like a large box. It had them all stumped.

The cottage had been abandoned in favour of the inn. Computers had never worked within a hundred yards of the cottage – magic and technology *never* meshed well. So, here they were at the inn, in fresh clothing, checking images on an old fashioned, wired desktop computer to find writing of a similar nature as that in the book. Ella said that wireless service never worked inside the Avebury Circle, either.

Ella pulled Kathryn to one side. "Let's flip through the book from the beginning. See if something jumps out at us while the guys stick with the computer." She tugged on Raonull's shirt. "Close the book and open the front cover, strong man, so we can explore."

Raonull and Douglas were the only ones who could lift the cover of the book since it was incredibly heavy.

Ella turned back to Kathryn. "And while we're going through the book, explain to me again why I've got wings."

Kathryn had to use both hands to lift and turn over the first massive, gilt-edged page. "The fabric between our two dimensions is torn. That happened when Grandma burned up her portal. The tear has been getting larger, and Anandria's magic is seeping out. That's why I can compel people to do things, and Raonull is inhumanly strong."

Douglas grinned. "That's a relief. I was beginning to wonder if everyone doubted my manliness when I couldn't lift the damn book out of the stump."

Ella grinned right back at Douglas. "I don't think you have to worry, coz. I think Kathryn fancies you despite your lack of muscle."

Kathryn pretended to not hear Ella. She cleared her throat and tried to carry on nonchalantly. "And the Anandrian magic makes it possible for me to see visions, too." She tipped her head to the side and said, "You and Douglas must have Anandrian blood."

Ella reached behind and felt the bumps on her shoulders. "And that's why I've got these? Because my ancestors were left behind the last time a portal was sealed between Earth and Anandria?"

"That's that theory," Kathryn confirmed. "Grandpa is always telling stories about how Anandrians have come to Earth in the past, and when portals were sealed, some were left behind – which is where myths about dragons, gargoyles, and fairies came from – because they really were real. It wouldn't surprise me if you probably have Anandrian blood, and now that there's more magic filtering through to Earth, your latent ancestral powers are becoming evident."

"And Douglas is a sorcerer?" Ella continued.

"Well, yeah. He's a Druid. Wielder of ancient spells..." Kathryn paused. "That morning ritual he kept repeating by the oak tree had to be a powerful protection spell for this book." She squinted down at said book. "Ray, when you opened the book for me, I think you accidentally picked up the first page with it. Will you flip the pages back for me, so we can check to make sure nothing was missed? My arms are getting tired."

Raonull moved next to the girls, and with one hand, lifted the couple of pages Kathryn had already turned. Sure enough, there was the first page. Ella slapped her hand down. Her finger slid over a diagram filling the page. Her eyes widened with excitement. "Bloody hell," she breathed. "Douglas come look at this. Tell me what you see."

Raonull shifted behind Ella to peer over her head.

Douglas moved behind Kathryn to rest his hands on her shoulders. He felt her start at his touch, and then to his delight, she relaxed and leaned back. *Nice.* His eyes drifted down to the book. His fingers clenched. Kathryn flinched. Never taking his eyes off the incredible drawing in the book, he simply lowered his hands to her waist and pulled her back against his chest with a muttered, "Sorry."

Ella, watching him, gave a nod of satisfaction. Douglas recognized the diagram. "It's Silbury Hill, right?"

"Just what I thought."

"What's Silbury Hill?" Raonull demanded. Ella waved a hand at the full-page sketch. Raonull snorted. "That tells me a lot." Ella spun about and poked him in the chest. "Ow! Would you cut that out? Your nails are sharp."

"Is he always this whiny?" Ella asked Kathryn with a mischievous grin.

Kathryn rolled her eyes. "You have no idea."

"Good, makes me feel much better," Douglas added.

"Hey!" Raonull roared.

Ella sighed and looked up at him. "Get back on the computer and pull up aerial shots of Avebury."

"Yes *ma'am*," Raonull muttered. He moved away and brought up the requested image.

"Ma'am? What's this *ma'am* thing you're calling me?" Ella demanded.

Raonull's brow rose when he looked at her. "I once knew an *ancient* woman. She was a bossy old librarian– very similar to this fairy I know..."

"Fine!" Ella harrumped as she gave one last poke to his chest. She spun about and moved her finger to the computer screen. Her shoulders suddenly hunched and her hands began to shake as if with palsy. Raonull rolled his eyes. She had morphed into a curmudgeonly, old librarian. Her voice trembled as she said, "This is Avebury, inside the standing stone circle. Notice some parts lie outside the circle."

Raonull nonchalantly lifted his hands and dug his fingers into her ribs. The librarian role dissolved, and he had his fairy back gasping with laughter in his arms. "Better," he murmured. "I like fairies better than librarians."

"Noted," she wheezed, and leaned back against him. Her finger pointed towards the screen again. "There are other structures beyond Avebury, like Windmill Hill, and Silbury Hill..."

Raonull whistled. "Silbury Hill is *massive*. What is it?"

"Silbury Hill is the biggest manmade mound in Europe, and no one has a clue as to its purpose." Douglas reached past Kathryn and pulled up an image of the hill itself taken from the ground. Everyone took one look at it and compared it to the sketch in the book.

"Same shape," Raonull muttered.

"Ray?"

"Yeah, Kath?"

"I'm going under..."

"Move aside," Raonull bellowed. Kathryn's eyes rolled back into her head. Her body stiffened.

"I've got her." Douglas shot a peeved look at Raonull since he already had his hands on her.

They all jumped when her mouth opened and her naturally light voice came out almost an octave lower than normal. "Listen and heed."

"Christ!" Raonull swore. "She *never* talks when she's immersed in Sight. What the hell...?"

"Shut up!" Ella ordered. "I've got paper here. I'll try to write down what she says."

Kathryn's eerie voice continued. Ella wrote furiously. The men hovered, and fear shone in their eyes. This wasn't normal. Finally, Kathryn went limp in Douglas's arms. She groaned and brought a hand up to her throat. Her fingers massaged her vocal chords. Her eyes flickered open. When she spied Douglas peering into her face, and she realized she was lying across his lap on the sofa, her brows drew together. She reached up and patted his broad chest. She opened her mouth, but a raspy whisper was all she could manage. Confusion marred her brow.

"Don't talk, hon," Douglas whispered. "You've already told us a great deal." She shook her head. "You don't remember anything?" She shook her head again.

"Then look at this." Ella shoved a pad of paper under Kathryn's nose. "I wrote the whole thing down, just the way you said it."

Through a broken veil of magic,

Evil has come to stay

Bloodlines lost, forgotten,

Knowledge locked away

Look back in time, remember well,

Your heritage, your past,

Angel, fairy, sorcerer,

To help complete the task

Into the light the key has come

To help unlock the door

For mystery, myths, and legends,

Are the norm on Earth once more

Douglas shifted Kathryn in his arms and peered into her eyes. "It's about the tear in the fabric between our two dimensions."

Kathryn nodded dumbly. For the first time, she had no memory of her session of the Sight. She *always* remembered her visions.

"That's us!" Ella exclaimed pointing to the line about bloodlines being lost and forgotten. "We knew nothing about our ancestry, and Douglas your parents didn't have time to completely instruct you about Druid practices before they passed." Her finger moved down to the bit about knowledge being locked away.

"Look back in time, remember well, Your heritage, your past, Angel, fairy, sorcerer, To help complete the task," Raonull murmured, looking over Ella's shoulder.

"Well, I'm the fairy. Douglas has to be the sorcerer. Where do we get an angel?" Ella asked. Raonull cleared his throat. Ella shot an incredulous look at him. "You?" She poked a finger at his chest again.

Raonull looked at Kathryn. "Our Aunt Mandy always had a theory that since Lucifer is a fallen angel, Anandrians are most likely angels put in Anandria to keep Lucifer in check with our magical capabilities. We don't know for sure if she's right, but if so, Kath and I are angels. Grandpa kind of agrees with Aunt Mandy."

Douglas glanced sharply down at Kathryn. His brow rose.

She shrugged.

"Where are *your* wings?" Ella demanded as she spun Raonull around to feel his massive shoulders for bumps like hers.

Raonull nestled into her touch as he said, "I think that's where the folks on Earth got us confused with fairies from Anandria. We all have magic, but only fairies and dragons have wings." Ella swatted him between his shoulder blades and spun him back. He wrapped his arms about her waist. "Now the bit that says, An ancient tree of wisdom, Cousins all well met..."

"Jesus!" Douglas breathed. "The old oak, the book... *And,* we're all cousins."

"Into the light the key has come, to help unlock the door, For mystery, myths, and legends, Are the norm on Earth once more." Kathryn glanced around at everyone. Her voice was gaining strength, and she was sure the insight flooding into her mind was her gift from the Sight. "I think the myth and legend part refers to Earth's past. Anandrians have been here before. When they left, the history of their coming eventually became myths and legends over time. I mean, how did we get dragons and gargoyles playing such prominent roles in several cultures around the world?"

Raonull jumped in. "But what is the damn key, and where is the blasted door? I'm clueless."

"Angels shouldn't be able to curse," Ella admonished with another poke to his chest.

He grabbed her hand and raised it to his lips. His eyes twinkled as he retorted, "When the world's at stake, and fairies keep attacking, an angel can have the occasional slip of the tongue."

Douglas whispered to Kathryn. "I think she fancies him."

Kathryn nodded. "Same for Ray. I've never seen him pay attention to a woman like this before. Usually, he's hovering over me, destroying any chance I might have for a love life."

Douglas gave her a squeeze, mashing her up against his chest. "Good! With Ella around, I might have a chance with you."

Kathryn glanced up sharply at Douglas. "I'd like that."

The inn's phone startled them all. Ella was the first to spring into action. "Avebury Inn, how may I help you?" She listened politely. "No, I'm sorry, sir, but we're full up at the present time." She hung up and turned in time to see Raonull's eyebrow shoot up. "What?" She nodded at the golden book. "We're going to be busy, so I can't accept more guests." She shrugged. "I've already turned on the *No Vacancy* sign and forwarded calls to voicemail. The locals won't think it's strange. You're the first guests I've had since my parents passed. They'll just think I did too much, too soon. So, no worries."

"So, any suggestions as to our next move?" Raonull asked.

Ella pointed at the golden book. "I say we take a look at Silbury Hill. We'll go after dinner." She slapped her hand on Raonull's chest. "And you'll carry the book."

"Why should I carry the book?"

"Because you can lift it easily."

"No, I mean, why bring the book to Silbury Hill?"

"Why not? If we get there and find we need the book, we'll have wasted time. If we don't need the book, then you, strong man, have had a lovely stroll with the benefit of some much needed exercise."

"I need exercise?"

"Uh huh," Ella quipped. "If you're with me, you have to keep up."

"I'm *definitely* with you, and I assure you I can keep up – *after* I get some sleep." Raonull grinned down at her. "Jet lag's taking its toll, so I'm going to drop my cousin off at her room, and then head for mine. Silbury Hill will still be here a day later." He yawned and held his hand out to Kathryn.

Douglas and Ella watched the two cousins disappear into their respective rooms.

"Well?" Ella asked.

Douglas shook his head. "I'm feeling a bit stunned right now."

"Because of the girl, or the magic?"

"Both," he replied. "I just wish Mum and Dad were here. They told me that on my twenty-fifth birthday, there'd be a wealth of information to be passed on to me. I wonder if they knew about the book. I wonder if they knew about our ancestors." His fist clenched. "Life's not fair..."

She glanced at him, her green eyes brimming with tears. "No it isn't." She wrapped her arms about his waist. "But I think an adventure is about to start that no one could have prepared us for." Her lips lifted in a tremulous smile. "I'm a fairy. You're a sorcerer. And we know two angels. Imagine that!"

21

❦❧❧

The check-in person had grumbled, "Have you seen the news? No one is flying in or out of Toronto. Radar and computer functions have gone haywire for both the control tower and planes attempting to land."

Of course Jeff had seen the news. Who in the world hadn't? His chest had tightened with anxiety. Mandy hadn't. She'd have no clue that Lucifer had come to town – *with dragons and gargoyles.* The cottage had no internet. And Laura needed to find out about this, too. How the hell had Lucifer pulled this off?

The closest flight he'd managed was to Buffalo. When he'd landed, ground transportation wasn't going to Toronto. Period! However, a bus was scheduled to leave for Hamilton the next day, so he'd stayed overnight in a cheap hotel – all decent accommodations had been full – people were waiting for airlines to determine when it was safe to fly. He'd bussed to Hamilton in the morning – a mere fifty minute drive from Toronto. But finding someone to take him from Hamilton to Toronto was proving to be a problem.

He glanced up at the TV and bit into his airport lounge sandwich. They were saying three dragons had swooped down to various underground parking lots – the largest settling under the condo building called Museum Place. It had calmly carried out a

Rolls Royce, a Jaguar, and a BMW into the middle of Bloor Street and had left them in a pile that blocked traffic.

It was nesting! There was a chilling thought. And the other two dragons were doing the same at other underground parking lots.

Guns fired at the beasts were useless. Bullets stopped when they met the beasts' scales and fell to the ground. Even a dragon's vulnerable belly seemed invincible.

Some fool paparazzi had been stupid enough to walk right up to Lucifer's dragon while shooting pictures. Then his camera had malfunctioned when he had been standing beneath the dragon's nose. The dragon had simply opened its mouth and chomped down. Another news camera, much farther away – probably on a neighbouring rooftop – had zoomed in catching it all, even the aftermath with the beast licking its chops.

That had people backing off!

Jeff flipped open his wallet and eyed his credit card. He'd tried renting a car, but others had beaten him to all the available vehicles. He scanned the lounge. An Airways Transit driver sat at the next table staring intently at a TV. The man's face looked bleak. He had an air of desperation about him. Pulling his card out, Jeff smoothly left his booth and slid onto a chair at the driver's table. He nodded at the TV screen and said, "Bad for business."

The driver blew out a frustrated breath and shook his head. "You have no idea. My run is between Hamilton and Toronto, and the company has cancelled all my trips. I just got married, and the bills are due." He wiped a hand across his glistening forehead. "I told my wife not to go overboard with the wedding, but would she listen? Fifty thousand dollars she spent. I told her I didn't have fifty thousand dollars, but she wouldn't listen. And to make matters worse, she's pregnant! So I took out a loan, see? And now they want their money..."

Jeff waved his credit card under the guy's nose. My limit is ten thousand. Do you think that will buy me a ticket to downtown Toronto?"

The driver straightened up. His brows crashed together. "Ten thousand... That would keep them off my back."

His eyes flickered up, and Jeff saw fear. "You wouldn't have to drive past Museum Place. Where I want to go is close, but not directly in line with all the action," Jeff reassured.

The driver swiped an arm across his sweaty forehead, and came to a decision he wasn't totally okay with. "When do you want to leave?"

Jeff grinned and clapped him on the shoulder. "How about right now?"

22

c̃ↄⓒↄↄↄ

Resentment boiled beneath his skin as he stared up at Museum Place from the sidewalk below. He'd been put out on the street like the trash. "How humiliating," Carlos seethed under his breath. "No thanks for minding the shop all these years. No opportunity to be host for my old boss. It's *my* penthouse, not Lucifer's. *I've* lived there for over twenty years."

He had nada – nothing. Just a terse, "Get out," from Lucifer after the man had somehow compelled him to write out codes to accounts, and surrender keys to both the condo and his luxury car. Carlos snorted. He had been dismissed. Discarded.

Turning his back on his home, Carlos stalked away checking his cell phone every few feet to see if he had reception. Four blocks away, two bars came up on his cell. "Gary?" he said into the phone. "You got my annual retainer for your services a couple of days ago, right?" He smiled when he heard Gary Russell's reply. "Well, my friend, you're about to earn your money."

Carlos paused to listen to the private investigator. He remembered when Lucifer had hired Gary and had said his name meant, spear bearer, so he should be good at pointing and shooting at anything, even with a camera. Why that had stuck with him over the years, Carlos had no idea. "Yeah," Carlos muttered into the phone. "What I want has something to do with Lucifer. He's back.

But first, I want you to put me up for a while. I don't care if I have to sleep on your damn couch. Just give me your goddamn address. I'll be there shortly."

Carlos ended the call and turned to make his way to the PI's home when he saw the chief of police conversing with an Emergency Task Force team, or ETF, as the locals called them. Without hesitation, Carlos marched up to the chief and stuck out his hand. "Chief, Carlos Ricardo, here to make your day a little sweeter."

The chief regarded Carlos with a 'Yah sure,' look on his face. He knew who Carlos was – had tried to bring him down, and his drug operation, but had been unable to find anything that would stick. "How do you propose to make that happen, Mr. Ricardo?"

"My former boss just kicked me out of my condo. No gratitude. Nothing." He couldn't help scowling. "But there's a hidden staircase Lucifer had built into the penthouse when the building was originally constructed. He was behind the corporation that had Museum Place built. Lucifer's name was never recorded on any documents. He was really careful about that kind of thing." Carlos shrugged. "Lucifer wanted an escape route – just in case." And Carlos remembered using it before Lucifer had disappeared.

Carlos pulled out his wallet and slid a credit card out. "This is the key that'll take you and your team in through the back door. Even present day management has no clue this exists. Lucifer made sure anyone connected with the original planning and construction had some kind of unfortunate accident."

"I remember people being reluctant to move in," the chief murmured. "Rumours of it being cursed had floated about." He looked sharply at Carlos. "Are you sure you can get us in? That looks like an ordinary bank card."

"Oh yeah. But I don't know how well your guns will work on Lucifer. They were pretty lame with the dragons – God, I can't believe I'm actually talking about freaking dragons."

The chief nodded. "I know. Everyone's still scratching their heads over the actual existence of dragons, and how ineffective our guns are." He gestured to the ETF team. "So we've got canisters of tear gas and stun guns with us instead."

"Then follow me," Carlos said. He had to restrain himself from rubbing his hands together with glee – too cliché. He was too cool for that.

Retracing his steps, Carlos boldly passed by Museum Place. He waved at the cringing concierge, who had worked there forever and was peeking over the top of his desk. However, at the sight of the ETF team following Carlos, the old concierge smiled and gave him two thumbs up.

Carlos took them around the side of the building. Tiny grooves in its concrete wall ran vertically down the side of the structure. Carlos didn't do anything until he hit the rear corner. He placed his hand on the wall and began walking backwards counting the grooves silently to himself. When he hit number thirteen, he stretched his arm up high and began pulling the card down the tiny groove. When he reached the ground, a section of wall retracted with a quiet *whoosh*. Carlos pushed, and it silently swung in revealing a narrow staircase wide enough to accommodate one person.

"Tight," muttered the chief.

"It is, but it opens into the rear of a walk-in closet that can hold about five men."

"Should be enough," the chief grunted. "There's Lucifer, the woman, and those two creatures that arrived with him on the dragons. Five to four – good odds. Let's do this."

"I want to be one of the five men," Carlos said softly. "I know the layout inside." He held up his credit card. "And how to use this when you reach the top."

The chief eyed him speculatively, motioned for one of his men to pass over a stun gun, and said, "Done." He knew Carlos was well versed in weaponry, and despite the fact that he'd like nothing more than to lock the drug lord up, he'd rather take down Lucifer even more. He'd been on duty the night Lucifer had supposedly died. He'd had to leap out of the way when Lucifer's car had come directly at him. Until now, he had thought justice had been served when Lucifer's car had careened off the highway ramp to be crushed upon impact. Now, he was feeling rage – he had a score to settle with Lucifer. "Lead the way, Mr. Ricardo. Stan, Clyde, and Charlie, you're with me. The rest of you wait here."

Carlos promptly took the team up to the nineteenth floor. He was glad he had always made his daily workout a priority when he heard the heavy breathing of the men behind him. *Considering these guys are supposed to be an elite team, you'd think they'd be in better shape.*

The top of the stairs appeared to be a dead end, until Carlos bent over and slid the card across the bottom of the wall. Again there was a soft whoosh, and the wall popped back towards them. This time, Carlos pushed the wall to one side, like a pocket door, and stepped into a walk-in closet. The lights, working on motion sensors, popped on. Behind him, the other four men piled into the cramped space.

Carlos held up a hand, and waited for everyone to catch their breath. He ran a critical eye over them and revised his opinion of the team. They were in great shape. Their heavy breathing was due to the gear they carried – Kevlar vest, guns, heavy boots, helmets... *How many pounds did all that paraphernalia add up to?*

Cautiously, he cracked the closet door. The bedroom was empty. He waved them out, and they spread out on either side to flank the door. Seconds later, they had left the bedroom and were standing on an exposed balcony that stretched the length of the condo. It overlooked the living area below. A sweeping staircase went right down the middle. Below them, was the woman who had accompanied Lucifer on the dragon, sitting on a white couch.

Lucifer stood before her. He tipped his head back, made direct eye contact with Carlos, and simply said, "Hello, Carlos."

Carlos shivered. *Same greeting as before...* Lucifer was too damned cool. And why couldn't he take his eyes off his former boss? *Just like the last time… Shit.* Beside him, Carlos was aware of the ETF team lining up along the railing, their guns pointing down at Lucifer. *Why isn't Lucifer trying something?* This wasn't good.

"I'd wondered if you'd remembered the back stairs. One of my gargoyles told me you had ventured around the side of the building." Lucifer shook his head as if disappointed. "At least you brought me more recruits."

Why can't I stop staring at Lucifer? Recruits? What the hell does Lucifer mean by that?

"Carlos, come down and join me."

Damn, I'm walking down the stairs. Behind him, the chief was yelling at him – but it was gibberish in his ears. He *had* to join Lucifer.

A gun fired, and Carlos flinched as he continued to walk down the stairs. Nothing hit him, and he felt a rush of relief – until a bullet bounced down the stairs past him. *They tried to shoot me! Thankfully, that damn bullet didn't function any better than the ones used against the dragons in the streets.*

Two canisters bounced past him. Gas billowed in their wake. Carlos kept walking towards Lucifer who casually twirled his hand. A wind came out of nowhere and pushed the gas out the open terrace doors. With the threat gone, Lucifer held out his hand to Carlos. Carlos couldn't help himself. He reached out and put his hand in Lucifer's. *What the fuck is wrong with me?*

Lucifer pulled him into a hug before he placed one hand on Carlos's forehead, and one on his chest. He whispered, "Carlos, I never want to have to worry about betrayal again." He broke into a low chant.

"Hey," Mandy said. "That's what you did to me."

Lucifer ignored her.

Carlos stiffened. His eyes rolled up into his head. Patches of black rose up through his skin and began to meld together. The last bits to be encased in the leathery substance were his hands and feet. Fingers and toes grew nasty talons on their ends. His toes pushed against the ends of his dress shoes until they split wide open, leaving his talon-tipped toes sticking out in all their mishapened glory. Carlos blinked and let his new, eerie, goat-like, yellow eyes with vertical black pupils bisecting them, survey the living area. They stopped on a mirror, and Carlos began to shuffle awkwardly over to it in his ruined shoes. Half way across the room, he stopped and impatiently ripped them off his feet. Everyone heard the leather tear easily with his new enhanced strength. Carlos threw the remnants of his shoes across the room and continued traversing the room.

His ugly hands clutched the sides of the mirror as he stared at his reflection. His breathing escalated. He began to whimper. In a last fit of human rage, Carlos smashed the mirror. Glass flew everywhere – and he turned an accusing glare on Lucifer.

Lucifer waited, enjoying the angst of his old friend. *Ah, there goes the last of his humanity.*

Carlos bent his head in a curt nod and rasped in a new voice, "What would you have of me, Master?"

Lucifer smiled, looked up at the gaping ETF team, and said, "Our numbers are more even now. Four of them, to four of us." He held up a hand when Mandy opened her mouth to protest that she made five for their side. "Amanda, my dear, there is no need for you to dirty your hands when I, and my gargoyles, are here. Sit back and watch your servants in action."

"My servants?" she whispered with delight.

"Always," he murmured as he walked over, picked up her hand, and placed an open mouthed kiss on the back of it.

"Chief," one of the ETF team members muttered. "We need to go."

Murmurs of agreement met this suggestion. The chief gathered his stunned wits, and barked, "Fall back, and make it fast." Three gargoyles were already mounting the stairs. *Shit, gargoyle Carlos still wore his suit and tie.* Automatically, the chief drew his gun. He fired, but the bullets fell to the ground the minute they came close to the gargoyles.

The chief ran for the bedroom closet, where his men shoved at each other as they tried to get into the narrow staircase. They were panicking. "One at a time," he bellowed, and nodded when they settled down and filed into the narrow aperture.

Gargoyles, followed by Lucifer, crowded into the closet before the chief could escape. The chief of police fired three more times before he threw his useless gun down and pulled out his stun gun. It crackled to life – then promptly died. He whirled to dash down the stairs, but a hand, tipped in talons, clamped down hard on his shoulder and squeezed with inhuman strength. He collapsed to his knees and two of the gargoyles pinned him to the floor.

Lucifer hovered over his head. Gently he placed a hand on the chief's forehead and one on his chest. His lips moved in a soft chant. He was amused when the chief tried to fight his gargoyles – there was no breaking their hold.

Suddenly, Lucifer lifted his hands and wiggled his fingers as he stared at them. "My magic is blocked." He eyed the chief with a speculative eye. "Rip off the Kevlar vest."

"No!" the chief screamed.

Carlos, with ridiculous taloned feet sticking out of the bottom of dress pants, attacked the vest with his talons. At first his talons were ineffective, but then one caught in a fastener and tore it open. Within seconds, the chief's chest was exposed. Carlos took great delight in running a single talon down the front of the chief's shirt. The material tore easily, and a shallow cut, beaded with blood, was left behind.

Lucifer brushed Carlos away, and once again placed his hands on the chief's forehead and chest to resume the chant.

The chief's throat closed up on a scream. Fine hairs on his body came to attention, and his skin began to tingle. His eyes darted erratically from side-to-side at the horrific creatures holding him down. A patch of black rose up on his forearm...

23

⨒

Kathryn lifted one eyelid. Crap, the clock said three o'clock. She still felt groggy, but she knew there'd be no more sleep for her. She was restless now that she was awake. She rolled out of bed and stumbled into the bathroom to turn on the shower. A quick rinse would wake her up so she could be civil at the dinner table. She stepped into the stream of water and relished its heat. After a few minutes, she reluctantly turned off the water and wrapped herself in a plush towel provided by the inn.

"Kath?"

She pulled the door open a crack on the opposite side to her room, and peered out into Raonull's room. He sat on the edge of his bed looking rumpled and sluggish. "Ray? You okay?"

"Yeah. I'm hungry. I woke up when I heard the shower turn on."

"Sorry."

"Nah, it's okay. I'm just feeling restless. How about you get dressed and we'll go find Ella and Douglas? Maybe they've got something we can snack on before dinner... I think Ella said they serve tea at four."

"Yum, count me in." She closed the door. As her shirt went over her head, she heard Raonull swear. "What's wrong?"

"I opened the curtains and it's pitch black outside."

"What?"

"You heard me. It must be three in the morning, not three in the afternoon."

Kathryn left the steamy bathroom. "They let us sleep right through dinner." She yawned. "What time is it back home?"

"Ten at night. We're five hours ahead." He grabbed her hand and pulled her into the hall.

"Where're we going?"

"To find food." They went behind the registration counter to a door marked, PRIVATE. Without hesitation he turned the knob. "I noticed a pass through to the dining room earlier. This has to be the kitchen."

Kathryn tried to plant her feet. She felt funny entering an employee only room, but of course, her efforts were useless against Raonull's strength. It was dark beyond the door, except for a dim glow coming from the far corner of the room.

"Oh!" A small figure straightened up and spun about. Wings simultaneously erupted with a loud *thwack!*

Raonull grinned. *Ella!* She stood backlit by an open fridge door. She looked adorably rumpled. His eyes widened appreciably. The nightie was indecently short and kind of transparent – like her enormous wings. You could see the light from the fridge right through them. His mouth went dry.

"Ella!" Kathryn cried with delight.

Ella nodded on a sigh of relief. Her wings curled up and slid silently back into her shoulder blades, but her arms tightened – one across her chest, the other much lower down.

Kathryn shrugged out of her hip length sweater, and ran to Ella. The little fairy gratefully slipped an arm into it. Kathryn let out a low whistle. The wings had done major damage to her baby-doll nightie. The back was in shreds.

"Thanks," Ella breathed.

Footsteps pounded down the hall, drawing rapidly nearer.

Ella's wings unfurled again, almost knocking Kathryn over. Thankfully, only one arm was in the sweater, so no more clothing was lost.

Raonull grabbed a wicked looking butcher knife off the counter and went into a defensive crouch, but he relaxed when Douglas burst through the door.

Kathryn sucked in an appreciative breath at the sight of Douglas clad only in boxers. The guy was in shape! Talk about washboard abs. *Impressive.*

"What's going on?" Douglas demanded. "Ella, your wings are out!"

Ella grabbed on to the refrigerator door to steady herself. "Douglas!" Her wings curled up and slid beneath her skin. "I was getting a snack. These two startled me, and my wings popped out. But they disappeared when I realized who they were." Kathryn grabbed Ella's other arm and shoved it into the sweater. "When we heard you running down the hall," Ella continued, "they burst out again."

"Okay," Raonull said. "Your wings react to fight or flight situations. You feel threatened, they pop out." He carefully laid the knife down. Everyone was staring at him. "What? It was handy, and we weren't sure who was out there. I was taking precautions."

"I'm glad you waited before throwing. It would have sucked to have to make a trip to the hospital to have a knife removed from my chest."

"I had my suspicions it might be you, Douglas, so I held off throwing until I was sure." Raonull's stomach let loose with a long, low growl. He grinned. "As long as we're all up, why don't we have a snack? Then we can head to Silbury Hill. There'll be no one around at this time of night – and I don't think any of us will be able to fall back to sleep."

Douglas rubbed his eyes and sighed. *The bloody Canadian – no wait, Anandrian – was right. There'd be no going back to bed.* He gestured towards his cousin. "Ella made sandwiches before going to bed. She figured they'd be ready whenever the two of you woke up. I'll fill a knapsack and you can eat as we go." He shooed Ella away from the fridge. "Go put something on, love. Leave this to me."

Ella frowned at him. "*You* need more than your boxers, you know."

"True, but men are quicker when it comes to getting ready."

Ella ran a hand over her shoulder and felt the bumps on her back. "Maybe in this case that's true. I've got a halter top buried in one of my drawers somewhere, and I think I've got a shawl. If my wings unfurl again, they shouldn't do too much damage in those clothes."

Douglas frowned. "Are you talking about that little black halter?"

She sent him a cheeky grin as she sailed out the door. "What other halter do I own, Douglas?"

Douglas opened his mouth, but she was gone.

Raonull clapped a commiserating hand on his shoulder. "That bad, huh?"

Douglas rolled his eyes.

Raonull smirked. "Then I'm sure I'll *love* it."

"Sod off," Douglas snapped as he brushed Raonull's hand off his shoulder. "Go fetch the book and your car keys while I pack the food."

24

&

They tromped through the grass at the base of Silbury Hill. The horizon was growing lighter, and they no longer needed the 'torch', as Douglas called the flashlight – which really hadn't been much good since it kept flickering on and off. However, there was really nothing to see, Raonull thought. The hill was enormous and covered in vegetation. If he had to compare its size to something, it could have housed a Canadian football field within it and the accompanying stadium seats.

The book was growing heavy – even for him. He'd been lugging it around the hill, and he was annoyed that the girls had insisted he bring it along, *just in case,* whatever *just in case* meant. He grunted and shifted it to his other arm. They had to be halfway around the hill and there was nothing to see. What a waste of time and energy...

"Ray!" Ella's touch was soft but insistent on his arm. "Ray, *look.*"

Kathryn and Douglas were up ahead. The Druid had Kathryn's hand in his, their fingers entwined. Raonull narrowed his eyes.

Ella stomped her foot and tugged him to a halt. "I'm *not* talking about Kathryn and Douglas. Look at the hill."

Impatient with the whole situation, Raonull dragged his eyes from the couple and dutifully looked at the hill. "Jesus!" he whispered. Something glowed beneath the hill's vegetation. He stepped closer and watched it intensify.

"Hey, you two," Ella called to Kathryn and Douglas. "We've found something."

Raonull took another step closer to the hill. The soft glow morphed into a piercing light. Startled, he stepped back. It dimmed to a soft glow. He inched forward – brighter, again! Experimentally, he retreated, placed the book on the ground, and stepped forward. The glow didn't change.

He retrieved the book, stepped forward, and... It brightened with every step he took towards the hill. "Bloody hell," he groaned. The girls had been right. It was all about the book!

Kathryn darted forward, her hand outstretched.

Douglas snagged her about the waist and pulled her back. "Hold on, hon, we need to go slowly. It could be dangerous."

Kathryn snorted. "Seriously? Think about this. Ella's a fairy, you're a sorcerer, and your family has been guarding this book for generations. Just which side of good, or evil, do you think you're on?" She struggled out of his grip. "My visions brought us to England, and right now, I can see the outline of a door, along with something glinting beside it." She flicked her fingers at him dismissively. "Stand back and let me go to work." She took one step away from Douglas.

Douglas wrapped an arm about her waist once more. "Here," he said to Raonull. "Watch your cousin for me."

Raonull shifted the book to the other side and wrapped a meaty hand about Kathryn's upper arm. "Got her."

"No you don't," Ella cried. She stomped down hard on Raonull's instep.

"Bloody hell," Raonull yelled as he dropped Kathryn and the book – which landed on his *other* foot. He sat down hard and pushed the weighty book off his foot. Blast it, his foot was puffing up. His hand whipped out and he grabbed Ella's ankle.

Thwap!

Ella's wings rammed into the side of his head and knocked him over.

Raonull gaped stupidly up at Ella. Kathryn moved next to Ella, and they linked arms. Ella immediately enveloped them both within her iridescent fairy wings covering them from neck to toe.

"Ella, what are you doing?" Douglas demanded.

Ella's chin came up. "This is an equal partnership. You two won't be pushing us to the sidelines. I won't have it. The risk is ours to take as much as it's yours. If one of us is truly in danger, the rest will come to their aid." She drilled both men with her green eyes. "Do I make myself clear?"

"Perfectly," Raonull muttered as he massaged both feet. He lifted one hand and flipped it towards the hill. "Please, after you. Go right ahead." *Goddammit my feet hurt – my head, too. Fairy wings aren't as fragile as they look.*

Kathryn pinned Douglas with a look. "We haven't heard anything from you, Druid."

Douglas stepped back, bowed from the waist, and swept an arm out as he said dryly, "Your wish is my command. Go uncover our discovery."

Ella's wings opened, and retracted, releasing Kathryn. "Nice," Ella whispered. "I think I'm getting the hang of these wings."

Kathryn, aware of the two men watching her, stepped boldly up to the glowing door-shaped outline. She'd be damned if she backed down now. *Courage.* Besides, she had a good feeling about this, and she rarely ignored her feelings. She was pleased that her hand barely trembled when she reached out to push vegetation aside.

As ivy fell away, a large metal plate, with a raised design swirling across its surface, was exposed next to the door. Her hand brushed across the plate. She felt nothing, except disappointment. She had expected something magical...

Large hands fell on her shoulders and she heard Douglas say, "I've seen that design before." His head cocked to the side. "It's very familiar." He glanced back at Raonull, who grunted softly as he hefted the book. "Well, I'll be... It's the book," Douglas sputtered. "Look at the design on the book."

Raonull ran a hand over the book's cover. "Yeah, it's real pretty…"

Douglas snorted. "Ray, it matches the metal plate like two pieces of a puzzle that fit together."

"That's brilliant!" Ella enthused. "Put the book on the plate, and let's see what happens."

Raonull limped over, and flipped the book to match its design with the one on the metal plate. They all flinched at the harsh screech of the two metal surfaces rubbing together before the book dropped into place.

The air stirred, and a door swung inward leaving enough room for a single person to enter. Beyond the door lay darkness. Douglas shook his 'torch' and flicked the switch on and off. Nothing…

Kathryn placed her hand over his. "Don't bother. Magic interferes." She passed by him and felt a slight pull when she crossed over the threshold. *Welcome.* Behind her she heard both men call out. Ella stepped through, too, followed closely by the men. "Did you feel it? Did you feel the barrier give way in welcome?" Kathryn demanded.

"Jesus, Joseph and Mary," Ella gasped. "Was that what that was? A barrier?"

"Yeah." Kathryn sighed happily. "Keeps out the unworthy. This place is a sanctuary." Raonull stomped over and went nose to nose with her. Kathryn calmly raised her hand and said, "We're partners. Remember our talk a few minutes ago?" She glanced at Ella who nodded in agreement, then returned her attention to Raonull. "Ray, I knew everything would be all right."

His eyes narrowed thoughtfully. "The Sight? You had a mini session of the Sight?"

"Yeah."

"You could have said something before you stepped into the hill."

"I know. I'm sorry, but I felt compelled to move forward after my vision." She patted Raonull's arm. "This is a sanctuary, and we are welcome. Retrieve the key, Ray. We don't want anyone else trying to enter."

"The key?"

"Aye, Ray," she said, mimicking the vernacular of her grandfather. "The book *is* the key."

"Bloody hell!"

Douglas moved up beside her, snagged her hand and said, "I've been guarding the key to Silbury Hill? I wonder if Mum and Dad knew?"

Raonull turned to retrieve the book. It was visible from inside the wall, as it had sunk halfway through the structure, allowing one to grab it inside the hill. He curled his fingers over the edge of the book's cover and pulled. It slid into his hands, and the door immediately swung shut – *with force.* Raonull jumped back with a curse on his lips, startled by the inky blackness that suddenly cloaked them.

"Douglas!" There was a hint of panic in Ella's call.

"Yeah, I know, Ella. I'm trying, but the damn light won't turn on."

"Ella?" Raonull called, concerned by the fear he heard in her voice.

"She's claustrophobic," Douglas murmured. "She can't stand dark, enclosed spaces."

Kathryn raised her hand, and a ball of light gathered on her fingertips. She glanced around. A single tear rolled down Ella's face, her wings were out, fluttering with apprehension, and sweat beaded on her forehead. Beyond Ella, Kathryn spotted a rock set within a bracket on the wall. Calmly, she walked past Ella and transferred the light to the rock.

"That's bloody brilliant!" Ella gushed. She rushed to Kathryn, threw her arms around her in a hug, and sealed them in with her wraparound wings.

Kathryn laughed with delight. The sensation of softness, strength, and protection was surprising whenever Ella's wings held her.

The men stared at the fairy whose head rested on Kathryn's shoulder. Her eyes were closed, and her lips were tipped up with happiness. Slowly her wings curled up and slipped into her shoulder blades. It was the first time Raonull had had an unobstructed view of the infamous black halter top – Ella's shawl lay in a heap on the floor. *Holy cow!* The top was short, revealing a good portion of mid-riff, and when she straightened up – he gulped at the sight of the plunging neckline. *Damn!* No wonder Douglas had been worried.

Douglas sidled up to him and hissed, "Shut your mouth, and stop gawking at my cousin."

Oblivious to the men, Ella planted a noisy kiss on Kathryn's cheek. "How'd you do that?"

Kathryn stooped to retrieve the shawl and draped it about Ella's shoulders. "It's basic magic. Anyone over the age of five in Anandria can do it."

"I remember," Ella squealed with excitement. "I remember Vaaron telling Laura how to create light in *Destiny Calls*, the first book of the *Anandrian Series*."

"Try it," Kathryn urged. "Make a fist. Gather energy in your core. Think cool light. Send it up to your arm and down to your fingertips. When the magic gathers there, open your fingers and transfer it to one of those rocks on the wall." She nodded and everyone followed her gesture. Brackets, with rocks nestled in them, lined the walls that disappeared into the darkness in either direction. For the next five minutes, Kathryn instructed both Ella and Douglas in the creation of light.

Bored, Raonull went back to the door. By the time they had mastered the simple magic, Raonull approached everyone and cleared his throat. "There's something you need to know. I went back to the door..." He looked at Ella. "There's no plate to set the book on *inside* the door. We can't open it. We're stuck."

Ella's wings exploded out.

25

Jeff turned the key and opened the door. It creaked and he winced mentally chiding himself for not getting the WD 40 out. He'd meant to do that months ago. Stale air hit him in the face. *So, Mandy must still be at the cottage...*

He shoved the door closed, disarmed the alarm, and headed for the stairs. He needed to talk to Laura and Vaaron. Hopefully, he wouldn't have to wait too long before Laura opened up the portal.

The portal was nowhere to be seen when he reached the second story, and he was shocked by feelings of desolation. The trip through the city hadn't helped either. Cars had streamed away from the downtown core, which had looked like a movie set – eerily deserted, with bits of paper blowing down the streets. His driver, from Airways Transit, had only been too glad to leave him when they had reached Mandy's house.

Jeff collapsed on the couch, weary beyond belief. His head tipped back. He closed his eyes. A picture of the dragon he'd seen flying between buildings popped into his head, and he hoped his driver would make it back to his new, expectant bride. Perhaps he shouldn't have engaged the young man, but he had been desperate...

"Jeff?"

His head snapped up, and he rubbed furiously at his burning eyes. Drool ran down his chin. *Geez, I must have dozed off.* He swiped his arm across his face.

"Jeff! Thank heavens, you're here."

Jeff blinked his eyes into focus. The oval portal hung in the air, and Laura sat beyond it in her medieval bedchamber. "Laura! You have no..."

"Mandy hasn't contacted me in over a week! I've been here every day waiting for her."

Jeff slashed a hand through the air. "Laura, listen. Better yet, get Vaaron and anyone else who's available. And hurry!"

Laura narrowed her eyes. "Why?"

"Lucifer's *here*. Get everyone, and I'll explain."

"Lucifer!" Her eyes widened with horror. "Is Mandy okay?"

Jeff shrugged. "I think so. She should be at the cottage." He shooed her away with a flick of his wrist. "Hurry!"

The portal disappeared on Jeff's side when Laura walked away. Unable to settle, Jeff strode to the fridge and yanked it open. Curdled milk soured the inside of the fridge, so he yanked out the carton, dumped it down the drain, ran water to flush it away, then grabbed a glass from the cupboard and filled it with water. His stomach growled. He yanked open the freezer. Every store, restaurant, and venue he had passed on the drive into the city had been closed. He reached for a freezer bag containing a single portion of lasagna – Mandy was always stashing home cooked meals in his freezer.

The air in his living room wavered, solidified into Laura's portal, and revealed a number of familiar faces. Laura, Vaaron, General Trymian, Elfare, and even Audrey, looked expectantly at him. Jeff felt the hard knot in his stomach loosen. He wasn't alone anymore. These people dealt with the threat of Lucifer every day of their lives.

Vaaron nodded to Jeff. "What did you mean when you told Laura, Lucifer is there?"

Jeff grinned. Vaaron always got right to the point. "Lucifer is here on Earth. In Toronto. He's been here several days." He shrugged. "I just got here. It took me days to get home after the news spread globally. Everyone's avoiding Toronto."

"It's been on the news?" Laura's voice sounded tight.

"Yeah, at least whatever footage they can get out. None of the reporters' cameras, or weapons the police and army have, seem to be working properly. TV newscasts have been kind of sketchy. Sometimes, the broadcast is perfectly clear, then the next minute, all there is, is static. But what I've gleaned is that weapons are malfunctioning, and flights in the Toronto area are impossible – there's no reliable radar, communication systems keep going down, and some aircraft have crashed."

Vaaron held up a hand. "'Tis magic interfering with Earth technology. How did Lucifer arrive in Toronto?"

Jeff blew out a breath. "He came on a dragon with a woman sitting in front of him. Two more dragons flanked him carrying gargoyles on their backs. He's taken over the penthouse condo at Museum Place across from the Royal Ontario Museum, and his dragon has cleaned out the condo's underground parking so it has shelter during the day."

"What is a penthouse condo?" General Trymian growled.

Laura turned her head and replied, "Private lodgings on top of a tall building that houses other private lodgings."

Vaaron broke in with, "Police have tried to subdue him?"

"Police, the armed forces..." Jeff looked at the general. "Those guys are Earth's warriors. They tried to bring him down. The ETF team attempted to breech his condo, and the chief of police was captured and turned into a gargoyle – at least that's what I *think* happened. I caught a small blurb on the radio as I rode into town. The men on the ETF team were pretty freaked out by whatever has happened."

The microwave dinged, and Jeff pulled lasagna out. He blew on the steaming meal and dug in as he said, "I'm not staying long. I want to find Mandy. I don't want her coming back to Toronto. If she does, Kathryn's prediction might come true – Lucifer would have a chance to work his magic on her."

"But Mandy's got the car. How are you going to get there?"

Jeff grinned. "Before I went to the States, I finally got that old clunker of a motorcycle I've been tinkering on to work." He sighed. "I just wish I didn't feel so tired and beat up."

Laura waved him over to the portal. A calculating gleam shone in her eye as she reached through the portal. "If Lucifer is there with his dragons and gargoyles, and Raonull and Kathryn were able to use their powers before they went to England..."

"The kids went to England?"

Laura smiled. "Yeah, Kathryn had another bout of Sight, and Stonehenge was the focal point of her vision, so they took off to see what that was all about. I'm just glad they got out before Lucifer came to Toronto."

Jeff cleared his throat. "I hope they got out. I hope magic didn't interfere with their flight. No one knows for sure what the exact status is of anything in the Toronto area..."

Laura's hands cupped Jeff's face. Her brows drew down with worry. "I have to believe they made it out. Kathryn was sure they were *destined* to be in England. But," she rubbed Jeff's stubble covered cheeks with her hands, "I think I can help with the fatigue. Heal thyself."

Everyone in Anandria gasped as her magic flowed beyond the portal into Jeff. "Bloody hell," Vaaron breathed.

Jeff watched a large purple bruise on his arm disappear and felt his energy ramp up. "Oh, my God, Laura! I've heard about what you can do, but to actually experience it..."

Laura stared into his eyes with a full grin on her lips. "I know. It kind of blew me away the first time I used it." Her grin disappeared. "Now, finish up that lasagna, and get on that bike. We have to keep Mandy safe."

Vaaron nodded. "We will confer while you look after Mandy." He shook his head at the others. "How the bloody hell did Lucifer get the dragons to Earth? And *where* did they come through to Earth? How can we combat him?" He looked up as Jeff shoved the last of the food in his mouth. "Are you still there, Jeff? Hurry! Warn Mandy not to budge from that cottage."

"On my way," Jeff replied. He tossed his plate on the counter and pelted down the stairs.

26

Ella's wings had finally retracted. Raonull's suggestion that she light the rocks on the wall, so they could find an exit, had worked well as a distraction. During moments of fatigue, Ella had *allowed* Douglas to try his hand at lighting the rocks until she felt strong enough to carry on. Invariably, Douglas was done in by the time Ella wanted to take over.

Kathryn's stomach growled. They had been inside Silbury Hill for a long time. She felt impatient. Ella wasn't proficient at wielding magic. Kathryn glanced down at the old fashioned mechanical watch she wore – the only kind that worked around magic. It was close to six in the morning, and her stomach knew it. Thank goodness Ella had made enough sandwiches for a small army. "Anyone want a snack?" Kathryn asked.

"Me!" Raonull dropped the book and slid his back down the inner wall of Silbury Hill.

"Ray!" Ella cried, and fell to her knees to fuss over the dropped book.

Raonull prodded the book with his toe. "The book's encased in metal, the floor is dirt, let it be, Ella. It's fine." His arm snaked out and wrapped about her waist. With an efficient tug he toppled her into his lap.

"Oh!"

A wing thwacked him in the face, and his nose began to bleed. "Jesus Christ, woman." He cupped his nose. "I can't get within a foot of you without getting hurt."

Ella giggled, and her wings retracted. "It's your fault. Stop startling me."

Douglas caught Kathryn staring at them with a goofy grin on her face. "I *love* that girl! She's not fawning over Ray. Back home in Anandria – here on Earth, too – women trail after him cooing over his physique. He can do no wrong. Ella, on the other hand, calls him out the minute he steps out of line. But the most fascinating thing about the whole situation is that he *lets* her."

Douglas dropped the knapsack, snagged her hand and slid down the wall pulling Kathryn with him. "Chemistry," he muttered.

"Yeah, looks like," Kathryn agreed. "I've never seen Ray like this with any other woman." Kathryn felt Douglas's arm settle across her shoulders. Tired, she gave in to temptation, closed her eyes, and let her head fall back on his shoulder with a sigh of contentment.

"I'm hoping there's some kind of reaction between us, too," Douglas whispered.

She jerked upright. Heat flamed instantly in her fair cheeks. At that precise moment, her stomach let rip with a long, low growl – even Raonull and Ella turned to stare at her.

With an unconcerned chuckle, Douglas reached for the sandwich filled knapsack.

In an attempt to regain some composure, Kathryn let her eyes wander. The lit rocks, Ella and Douglas had left behind, had significantly cut through the gloom. A lot was still cloaked in darkness, but there was something in the centre of the hill. "Ray!" Kathryn breathed. "Look in the middle." She rolled to her feet and broke into a slow jog. "Ray! You *have* to see this," she yelled over her shoulder when she hit the halfway point.

Behind her, the others began to stir.

Raonull and Douglas started to run.

"Hey!" Ella yelled from behind.

Thwack!

Ella's wing beats reverberated throughout the hill, and the other three stumbled to a stop as they watched Ella rise then glide effortlessly to the centre where she touched down on a raised, round, stone platform. "This is amazing," Ella yelled.

Douglas and Raonull started running again. Within seconds, they caught up to Kathryn and matched their pace to hers until they reached the centre of the hill and Ella. Ella was squatting on the carved surface of the round platform. Her hands whisked over it feeling its deep grooves. "What can it be for?" Her wings slipped silently into her back.

Kathryn leaned over and put her hands on her knees as she tried to catch her breath.

Raonull nudged her almost knocking her over. "I told you, Kath, you need to work out more."

Her foot shot out. It hooked around Raonull's ankle. Her hands grabbed his arm, and she gracefully levered her cousin over her head. He landed on his backside.

"Personally," Douglas murmured patting her shoulder, "I think you're in great shape."

His hot breath brushed her neck, and Kathryn felt annoyed by the chills *that* elicited.

Ella stepped off the platform and planted herself in front of Kathryn. "How'd you do that? You're only an inch or two taller than me. Can you teach me? Can you do that to Douglas? I mean, you're so short. These guys are huge."

Kathryn lifted her hand to her shoulder and let it rest on Douglas's hand, but in the next instant she yelled at Ella, "Move!" as Douglas went over her head.

Ella's wings snapped out.

"Oomph!" Douglas landed hard next to Raonull.

"It can be taught," Kathryn said looking up at Ella who hovered overhead. Ella descended to the floor and retracted her wings. *Ella's getting good at that.* Feeling better, Kathryn linked her arm through

Ella's and pulled her back to the stone platform. "Let's have a look at this..." Kathryn caught her breath. "Ray! Get over here."

Raonull rolled to his feet. Douglas hissed at him, "Next time warn me." Raonull grinned and sauntered over to his cousin.

"Ray, it looks exactly like the Moon Table inside the Lunar Temple in the City of Moyen. How can that be?"

"Are you sure?"

"Duh, Mom and Dad let me play on it for most of my childhood. Of course I'm sure." Abruptly, Kathryn fell silent. She crawled onto the platform and ran her hands over its carved surface. "Could it really be this simple?" she muttered. "Ray where's the book?"

"Back there," he said jerking his thumb over his shoulder. "Why?"

"I think we've got the key to more than just the door to Silbury Hill. Go get the book."

By the time Ray got back, they were all standing on the stone slab, except Kathryn who remained on her knees. She pointed at the stone surface. "The book goes there."

Raonull moved around her. A pattern, etched into the stone, mirrored the one on the book – they would mesh together. *Bloody hell!* He leaned over and slid the book about trying to match the patterns. The metal cover on the book screeched, but it finally engaged. Magic lifted their hair, and the world dropped away...

27

Vaaron ran a finger through the condensation on his tankard of ale. Everyone in Veresah knew what he, the Anandrian military leaders, and the Town Council, had been discussing for the last twenty-four hours. *Lucifer. On Earth. With dragons and gargoyles.* By now, everyone also knew that he felt it was *their* responsibility to help the people of Earth. His problem? The only practical way to do that was if their dragons were part of their offense.

It would take Laura forever to paint a portal large enough to accommodate them. Her paintings were detail oriented. Vaaron sighed, raised his tankard to his lips, and swallowed. It was Laura who had pointed out their need for dragons. She had drawn a quick sketch of downtown Toronto effectively illustrating what skyscrapers looked like for the Anandrians. They were nothing like trees in a forest. The bloody big structures blocked sightlines – trees, at least, let you see through their branches, which meant that Anandrian troops had some idea that dragons, with gargoyles aboard, were almost upon them. Hell, it would be impossible to fight Lucifer on Earth unless they were airborne, too.

Vaaron glanced about the tavern. Every man present was discussing the possibility of going to Earth. Vaaron sighed again. They could send troops through Laura's portal until there were hundreds of Anandrians present. But then what? How to strike? How to contain the Dark Lord and bring him back to Anandria? They had to get Lucifer home and repair the tear in the fabric between their two dimensions.

"Vaaron."

A soft feminine voice had him turning about on his seat with a smile on his face. Kimberly, Guardian of the Royal Forest, had slipped through the rowdy crowd unnoticed and was staring at him pensively. She was a shy little thing, and he was surprised by her presence. Vaaron inclined his head in greeting, and murmured, "Kimberly," as he scooted over so she might join him on his bench. "What brings you out of your quiet forest into this boisterous mass of male camaraderie?"

"Vaaron, I have an idea." She blew out a nervous breath and shook her head. "Forget I said that. Coming here was a mistake."

Vaaron placed a large hand over her forearm stalling her as she rose to leave. "Nonsense. There must be some merit to your idea, since you have ventured far from home. I would hear it. Perhaps 'twill be the very thing to sort out my whirling thoughts."

Kimberly plopped down with her head bowed. Her face was hidden behind a fall of golden hair. "Audrey told me Lucifer has his dragons, and you do not, because the beasts cannot go through Laura's portal. At first, I thought I should provide Laura with a bigger canvas, but then I realized 'twould take too long to paint a dragon-sized portal."

Vaaron nodded and smiled encouragingly. "Go on, mistress."

"I began reading the books of lore my parents left in my care after their passing. I wanted a solution – and I might have found it." She peeked up at Vaaron and was encouraged by his unwavering look of interest. At his nod, she continued. "There are many plants that use the magic of Anandria. They just need a little boost from me to make their magic work. There's Crimson Pygmy Barberry, Dwarf Boxwood, Blue Mouse Ears Hosta, Munchkin Hosta, Slim and Trim Hosta, Thumbelina Hosta, Dragon Wort, and finally, Forget-me-not..."

The tavern's door banged open. All conversation ceased as patrons checked out the new arrivals. Two large men, wearing distinctive clothing from the far south, barged in. "Is Vaaron here? Tis where we were told he would be," the dark haired warrior of the two bellowed.

"And ye be?" the bartender demanded as everyone fingered their weapons. Strangers were scarce in Veresah. "And why would ye be looking for Vaaron?"

With a flourish, the dark haired, dark-eyed warrior bowed low as he said, "I be Paul, yer humble servant." He straightened and just as dramatically swept an arm out towards his companion. "And this be Michael." He waggled his eyebrows. "We be two of the fiercest warriors Anandria has ever seen. Ye may have heard of our exploits."

Both men were very young.

"I cannot say that I have," Vaaron murmured sarcastically under his breath to Kimberly before he stood. All eyes shifted his way. "Tis fine names you bear," Vaaron noted. "Michael, a gift from God. Paul, humble – to a fault, I gather."

Paul inclined his head. "Most certainly. I have yet to meet with a deed that intimidates me."

Vaaron stalked up to them. They were brash indeed. Both were solidly built, carried swords and daggers of the finest materials, and stood eye to eye with him. As dark as Paul was, Michael had icy blue eyes and hair that was almost white. "Why were you looking for me?"

Michael smiled with lips that were almost white, too. "Ye be Vaaron. Good. Tis action we seek."

"Aye," Paul agreed. "The Southern Hemisphere is secure from all threats, and we had heard Lucifer stirs again."

"That he has. The Dark Lord has ventured onto Earth taking his magic with him."

"Tis all we have heard since passing through the gates of Veresah. Tis more than we had hoped for." Paul caressed the pommel of his sword.

"Aye," Michael added.

Vaaron eyed them, assessing them. Paul was the braggart – *humble my ass.* If there was a humble bone in his body, Anandrian magic would have to dig for it. Michael, on the other hand, was a man of few words – a man to watch – very intense and serious. They were young and eager to test their mettle in a real battle, Vaaron concluded. *Probably more of a hindrance than a help.* "If you wish to join our ranks, meet me on the practice pitch tomorrow morning. I have unfinished business to attend to before I determine if you can handle yourselves with my men."

Vaaron turned to the bartender. "Set these men up with a tankard each. They have come a long way..." Vaaron's eyes narrowed. The bench he had been sitting on was empty. Kimberly had slipped away – and not out the front door, since he was currently standing in line with it. The only other exit was through the back. "Excuse me. My unfinished business just slipped away."

Agilely, Vaaron cut through the crowd, vaulted over the bar's countertop, and passed through a curtain into a back storage room. He arrived in time to see Kimberly's dark green cloak slip through the closing back door of the tavern. The shy, middle-aged woman had been about to make a point back there, before the brash young warriors had interrupted them, and he wanted to find out what her litany of plant names had to do with their fight against Lucifer.

28

❧◎◎❧

Kathryn squealed when the stone platform liquefied into a swirling silver mass and she, and the book, sank through it. The book
landed with a thud far below. She remained on hands and knees
– her knees one step above her hands. Holy crap! She was at the
top of a long flight of stairs carved out of a stone wall. She winced
when a softer thud announced Douglas's impact – on top of the
golden book. *That can't be good. He's not moving.* "Douglas!"

Frantic, she scanned below for Ella and Raonull. A gust of wind
made her look up. Ella, using heavy beats of her wings, lowered
herself, and Raonull, safely to the floor below muttering, "See?
When it's important, I'm always saving your arse."

Touchdown, Kathryn thought with relief as the pair tumbled to
the floor. But Douglas still wasn't moving. Collecting herself, she
sprinted down the stairs keeping one hand firmly on the wall from
which they had been carved. "Douglas," she cried, falling to her
knees next to him.

He groaned. His breath puffed out in agonized pants. "Move...
the... book..."

Ella and Raonull joined her.

"Ribs... hurt..."

Raonull reached out to lift Douglas off the book, but changed
directions at the last second when Kathryn stiffened. He had to

steady Kathryn before she toppled on top of Douglas. The Sight had the worst timing...

"Ray! Don't touch him," Kathryn gasped as she came out of the Sight.

"Why not?" Ella asked.

Kathryn frowned. "There's more to his injury than we can see." Douglas bit off a groan. His face looked unnaturally pale, and sweat beaded on his upper lip. "Get... off... book... Hurts..."

Raonull bent over Douglas's face. "You heard Kath. She said if I move you, we could do real damage to you. But I could try to pull the book out from under you. It'd be risky, but if the girls steady you, we might make you more comfortable."

"Yes," Douglas hissed between clenched teeth.

"Okay, buddy. I'll do it smooth and quick. Kath, stabilize his shoulders. Ella, you hold his hips. When I pull on the book try to minimize his movement. Ready girls?" Raonull knelt, gripped the book, and carefully pulled it from beneath Douglas. Douglas groaned with relief, but continued panting with pain. "You okay?" Raonull asked running a critical eye over the Druid.

"Better..."

Ella brushed a lock of hair off Douglas's forehead. "What are we going to do? Douglas needs more help than we can give him. Blast it, he's going into shock. He's shaking." Her wings snapped out, and she blanketed one wing over his quaking body.

"Warm... Nice..." he murmured.

"She's right," Kathryn conceded. "He needs medical attention." She looked up the stairs to the swirling silver ceiling. "It could take hours for us to find an exit from Silbury Hill." She leaned close to Raonull and whispered, "Time, I don't think he has, if my vision is correct."

Raonull knew Kathryn was serious. Her gift of Sight was pretty accurate. Seeking inspiration, he checked out their surroundings and whistled. They were inside an enormous, round, underground cavern, and that disturbing, liquid-like ceiling swirled overhead.

There were no corners, or sharp angles, other than several sets of stairs carved out of the walls in various locations. The swirling ceiling extended over those stairs, too. And dead centre, a tiered conical structure also touched the churning ceiling. Its base was spread over a large portion of the floor, and the tiers leading to its apex allowed anyone to march up the cone from any point at its base. *Wait.* Stylized drawings on the bottommost tier took his breath away. "Kath, check out the drawings."

Kathryn gasped in surprise. Etched into the stairs was a distinctive outline of the Lunar Temple, a dragon, and a gargoyle. "Ray," she breathed. "Do you think it'll take me home?"

"I don't know, but I'd say we have a better chance going up there than back to Silbury Hill."

"Ella, are you okay if Ray and I check out the centre staircase? I think I might find help there, but just in case it takes me somewhere else, I want Ray as backup." Kathryn saw fear and indecision flicker across Ella's face. "Remember when we entered the hill, my vision told us it was a sanctuary? I'm pretty confident we should be safe wherever we end up."

Ella's wing curled a bit tighter around Douglas.

"Too... tight!" Douglas bit out.

Ella jerked with fear as she loosened the wing covering her cousin. The little fairy was losing it. Whatever they did they had to do it *fast.*

"Just hurry." Ella swiped her thumb across Douglas's cheek wiping away a tear.

Raonull reached across Douglas to cup Ella's chin. He raised her eyes to his. "I promise we will not desert you. Whatever we find up there, we will return ASAP. Understand?"

"Okay. Just go!"

"Come on, Kath."

29

Kimberly hurried through dark streets nervously peering right and left. It had been a mistake to leave her forest. She started panting. What had she been thinking? She had been thinking it would be easier to catch Vaaron after the sun had gone down, and most folks had settled in their homes for the night. But she had not counted on so many warriors gathering in the tavern. She remembered how her stomach had clenched when she had realized she had to cross through the brawny men to reach Vaaron at his corner table. She had almost left. But she had a tantalizing idea, and she had had to voice it.

And look at me, she thought with disgust – *running away, back to my forest, without explaining myself to the Protector. Perhaps my idea is not viable...*

"Gah!" Her hand flew to her throat where her cape cut into it. Her feet nearly slipped out from beneath her. Fear threatened to send her into a debilitating panic. *No!* She whipped about to see who held her cape. Her action nearly strangled her a second time when the cloth tightened uncomfortably about her neck.

"Easy," Vaaron said as he released his hold. "You are a fast one, mistress." He gestured towards a side door in the castle. "'Twill be much quieter in my home, Kimberly. Surprised I was to see you venturing into the tavern tonight. I am sorry I left you before you finished telling me your idea."

Kimberly, flushed from exertion and embarrassment, murmured, "Tis nothing, Vaaron. Really..."

"Nonsense. You made the trip in from your forest because you have something to offer. Come into the castle, and Laura will brew some tea. You will be able to voice your thoughts much more comfortably there than in the tavern."

Kimberly's brows rose before she sighed and turned towards the door.

Laura, Kimberly is here. Put the kettle on, love. She has piqued my curiosity with an unusual conversation we began in the tavern, Vaaron broadcast to his wife.

Kimberly? In the tavern?

Aye! She listed plants that might somehow help with our lack of dragons in Toronto.

How would they help?

I do not know. She ran away before I could find out. There was a disturbance that interrupted our conversation. She slipped out the back door.

Ah, now that sounds more like Kimberly, our forest recluse. The only time she was in the castle was when you surprised me with that beautiful frame and canvas she carved out of a single piece of wood she had nurtured. She was so excited, that I think she was unaware of the people watching us.

Aye! Vaaron reached past Kimberly and pushed the door open. Beyond, Laura stood removing a steaming kettle off a wood stove.

"Oh, tis the castle's kitchen!" Kimberly exclaimed.

"Hello, Kimberly. It's lovely to see you again." Laura watched Kimberly glance around. "Everyone has settled in for the night, so it's just us. Why don't you have a seat at the table while I pour the tea?"

"All right," Kimberly murmured. "I can do that."

Vaaron and Laura sat down across from her. Laura passed her a cup of tea, and they waited patiently. Kimberly had a sip of her tea before she began to speak. "You need to get the dragons to Earth.

The portal is too small to accommodate them. With the plants I listed, when I spoke with Vaaron earlier, I believe I can create a potion that will shrink our dragons down to tiny reptiles that could easily go through your portal. My father was a sorcerer. He passed on a great deal of knowledge to me, as well as his legacy of an extensive library that I can use. It is what I do when I am not tending my plants; I am constantly reading my father's journals. He was a great sorcerer in his time."

Vaaron cleared his throat. "Tis a wonderful idea, Kimberly, but we need our mounts to be dragon-sized."

Kimberly beamed. "Tis why I included forget-me-not. Once through the portal, the dragons will pee out the potion, and the forget-me-not will return them to their former size and shape."

"It is worth a try," Vaaron acknowledged intrigued by her idea.

"What happened to your father?" Laura asked, fascinated by the thought of Kimberly possibly wielding spells.

Kimberly frowned. "When Lauren was a babe, and Anandria was close to being overcome by Lucifer, my father used every drop of his life force to create an invisible barrier around Veresah, thus giving Vaaron and Lauren a chance to grow into their powers." She sighed regretfully. "The barrier held for years – until Lauren was ten and transformed her first gargoyle. But I lost my father – he was so worn down from maintaining the magic. I never really knew him."

The outer door, that Vaaron and Kimberly had used to enter the kitchen, banged open. Elfare barged in dripping rainwater off his tunic. "Christ, it has turned into a nasty night out there." Dismay marred his features when he looked down and saw the puddles he was leaving behind on the pristine floor.

"What are you doing here?" Vaaron demanded eyeing his wet cousin.

"Tis the tavern, Vaaron. The barkeep sent me to collect you. The two new lads are up to their necks in a fight."

"They started a fight?"

"Nay! The warriors in the bar decided to test their mettle. They did not like their snobby air."

Vaaron sighed and rose to his feet. He was getting too old for this kind of thing. "We had best hurry before the lads can no longer walk."

Within minutes, Vaaron, with Elfare hot on his heels, burst into the tavern.

"Appreciate the ale," Paul said with a nod to Vaaron as he casually sipped his foamy beverage. Michael held his tankard up in silent thanks, too. Both young men leaned against the bar with one foot propped on the rail at the bottom. Bodies lay everywhere. Some were moving. Some were not. An occasional groan wafted through the air. Blood trickled off several warriors.

Vaaron did a quick survey. The furniture was either smashed or toppled over. The two young men appeared without bruise, or cut, to mar their handsome faces – although their clothes looked at bit mussed up. Twelve seasoned warriors against two young pups. *Impressive.* Perhaps Paul had not bragged when he had stated that he had not met with a deed that had intimidated him. Vaaron narrowed his eyes. "Fetch Laura, Elfare. I need my men back on their feet so I can chew them out for their foolhardy actions that have cost our good friend, Randolph. They owe him restitution for the damage they have caused in his fine tavern."

"No need, Vaaron." Laura pushed into the tavern. "I figured there'd be casualties." She looked about wide-eyed. "But I never imagined the casualties would be these men!"

Randolph kicked a broken chair. "Restitution, Vaaron, will be high. Tis the second time in three months your men have destroyed my place."

Vaaron let loose a mental sigh. *I would love to retire. Spend quality time with my wife.*

Laura picking up on his thoughts, grinned at him – sounded good to her. Unfortunately, with the possibility of Lucifer in two dimensions, every able bodied man was on call.

"Heal them, Laura, quickly, so we can retire to our chambers," Vaaron murmured with disgust.

Laura passed through the room. One by one, men regained their feet and almost universally glared at Paul and Michael before sheepishly meeting Vaaron's gaze. When they all stood before him, Vaaron held up a hand for silence and stated, "Each of you is in debt to Randolph. I want him to list the coin, barter, or labour he will garner from each warrior. I personally guarantee Randolph will be compensated for this foolish act this eve." His cool gaze swept over his men. "Tis unbecoming that my men initiated an unprovoked attack on two strangers."

"They provoked us," someone muttered.

Vaaron's brow crashed down. He tried to locate the impudent man, but failed to identify him. "How did they provoke you?" He directed the question to the room at large.

Patrick stepped forward and met Vaaron's eyes squarely. "Tis a peg or two they needed to be brought down with all their bragging."

Vaaron calmly reached out and ripped a patch off Patrick's shoulder effectively demoting him to the general ranks of his troops. Patrick paled, but held silent when Vaaron continued to speak. "Tis not bragging if you can back it up." He took the time to make direct eye contact with each man. "They backed it up." He took a deep breath. "They were forced to. Not one of my warriors should have instigated a fight in Randolph's Tavern. Tomorrow, Paul and Michael would have had their mettle tested on the practice pitch – and you *all* knew that."

Vaaron turned to face the newcomers. "Where do you lay your heads this eve?"

Michael gave a negligent shrug of his shoulders. Paul said, "We have just arrived in Veresah."

"Then come," Laura interjected. "We'll find you a room in the castle. Won't we, Vaaron?"

"Aye, but after I confer with these two young warriors."

Laura smacked Vaaron on the shoulder. "Let them settle in and rest." She headed out the tavern door with Elfare and the two young men in tow.

Vaaron shook his head and caught up to Laura in the street. "Lucifer has been terrorizing Toronto..."

"Duh, you don't have to tell me, but tomorrow is soon enough to talk shop."

Vaaron's hand slid about Laura's waist. She was sassing him again. He gave her a squeeze and guided her through the castle's kitchen door. He knew what battles to pick.

Kimberly still sat at the kitchen table clutching her cooled cup of tea in white knuckled hands. "I was not sure if I was to stay."

Laura rushed to her side and removed the cold cup from her hands. "Of course you were supposed to stay. Vaaron is truly interested in your idea, and I insist that you stay the night with us."

"But I *need* to have my father's books and gather the plants."

Elfare blurted out, "I will go with you and help." The tips of his ears turned red when everyone in the room stared at him. "She will need someone to carry and fetch," he said in defence when no one said anything but continued staring. "She will need me to protect her should anyone, or anything, try to stop her."

"Oh!" Kimberly's cheeks burned a bright pink. "But I have no room in my hut for you to rest."

Elfare went down on one knee and clasped her hands between his. "I'll take my rest across the threshold of your abode. Please accept my protection, Kimberly. Long have I admired you, and it would please me to get to know you better."

"Oh!" Kimberly's cheeks flamed a deep red.

"Do you remember when we were young, and you came to the town's celebration? We danced around the bonfire." He watched Kimberly nod. "Do you remember the kiss I stole?"

Kimberly's hands flew to her cheeks, but she nodded.

"I have tried to get to know you, on several occasions, but you always disappear into the forest. No matter how proficient my tracking skills, you melt into the woods, and I can never find you." He pulled one of her hands away from her face and twined his fingers through hers. "Give us a chance to get to know each other."

Kimberly peered down at him and their entwined fingers. Elfare raised her hand to his lips and brushed her knuckles with a soft kiss. Kimberly gasped, but did not pull away. Slowly she nodded. "I would be pleased to have you accompany me. I would be pleased to have you protect me. I would be pleased to get to know you better." She smiled tentatively at him and felt her tummy tremble when his eyes sparkled with happiness.

Elfare rose to his feet while maintaining his hold on Kimberly. His gaze swept the room. "We will see you tomorrow at sunset, if not sooner. Come Kimberly, we have work to do."

"Well," Laura said after the couple left. "I always wondered who Elfare was saving himself for. I guess we now know."

30

Kathryn's head cleared the cool silver substance. She couldn't help but cry out, "Yes!"

Raonull's head popped up next to her. He glared at her. He was pissed that she had shot up the stairs ahead of him.

"We're home," she sighed. "Where is everyone?"

"It's midnight Anandrian time. Your mom and dad should be here with their priests discussing what their collective powers should be used for tonight."

"Midnight?"

"Yeah, remember the time difference? Anandria is aligned with Grandma's port in Toronto, not some obscure town in England."

"Don't let the cousins hear you say that about their town." She stepped up and her body cleared the silver mass. "Of course!"

"What?"

"Once a year, all five Anandrian moons are full at the same time. Naturally, this enhances anyone's gift of moon power. Mom and Dad take the priests and priestesses to the rooftop so the domed roof inside the Lunar Temple won't amplify everyone's power to unimaginable levels. Whole towns could be wiped out due to someone's careless manipulation of the tides."

"So they're up on which roof?" Raonull asked as he lifted Kathryn so her feet cleared the swirling mass of the Moon Table and placed her on the floor before joining her.

"Where the dragons land. It's the only roof large enough to hold them all."

"Let's go. There's no time to waste."

They careened across the room. Raonull bashed through one of the large wooden entrance doors to the temple – he barely caught the door before it smashed against the wall – jogged down its sweeping staircase, and ran up the stairs leading to the dragon landing area.

"There they are," Kathryn crowed.

Her voice cut through a moment of silence in a communal chant. Priests in their robes, their cowls raised over their heads, their arms extended towards the heavens, all turned and stared reproachfully at her. Having grown up in the City of Moyen, and being the only child of the two most powerful moon people, the priests knew she knew better than to interrupt.

"Kathryn? Ray?" Diana, Divine One, Moon Goddess, and Deity of the Hunt, cried out in total shock.

Taking that as their cue, Kathryn and Raonull dashed forward. Kathryn grabbed her mom's hand and tugged forcefully. "You've got to come with us."

Raonull stepped in front of the High Priest. "Uncle Manus, we need your help, too. Kath says you've got a spinal board somewhere."

Diana pulled Kathryn to a stop. "I thought you were in Veresah."

"Nope, England." She pulled harder until her mom moved.

"I don't understand. England?"

"You will, Mom. Just hurry."

Raonull and Manus veered off to the first aid station, located nearby for incoming wounded – both people and dragons. Grabbing the spinal board they followed Kathryn and her mother.

"So how did you get here?" Diana prodded as she was dragged off the roof by her daughter. "And why were you in England?"

"You'll see, Mom." Kathryn struggled to fling open one of the massive doors to the temple. Diana, with her enhanced moon strength, nudged her aside and did it for her. "Thanks Mom."

Diana didn't reply. Her mouth hung open when she saw the swirling top of the Moon Table. "Manus! Oh my God! Check out the Moon Table."

Kathryn grabbed her hand again and tugged. "Gawk later, Mom. Douglas needs help – and fast."

Diana allowed her daughter to pull her across the floor. "Who's Douglas? Where is he?"

"He's a Druid, and he's beneath the Moon Table." Kathryn bent over the Moon Table and stuck her hand into the swirling mass. "Ah, there's the top step. Be careful where you step. You don't want to miss the top of the stairs and end up like Douglas." Kathryn lifted one foot and let it sink through the top of the table.

Diana flung off her ceremonial robes and boldly stepped after her disappearing daughter.

Manus mumbled under his breath, "Bloody hell," when Diana's head sank beneath the table top.

"Feel for the steps," Raonull cautioned again. "It's a long way down."

Manus nodded and prodded with his boot. He had also rid himself of his ceremonial robes, but Raonull couldn't help smirk when he saw his usually fearless uncle grip the pommel of his dagger so hard his knuckles whitened when his foot entered the Moon Table.

Raonull followed hard on Manus's heels. Oohs and ahs came from the watching priests who had followed them, but their chatter was cut off when Raonull's head passed through the liquid Moon Table top.

Below, Kathryn and Diana were racing to Douglas. Raonull smiled when Aunt Diana realized it was a fairy wing that Ella was using to cover Douglas. "A fairy! I've always wanted to meet one," Diana cried. Ella retracted her wings and made room for Diana next to Douglas. As Diana reached for the injured man, she met Ella's eyes and said, "We'll talk later."

Without hesitation, Diana placed her hands on Douglas's torso. A pale yellow glow surrounded the Druid and Raonull saw Douglas's tension and pain fade away as his eyes slowly closed. Moonglow from the high priestess was powerful stuff. Although unable to heal instantaneously like Grandma Laura could do, Diana was able to speed healing and sedate people with her moonglow.

Working quickly and efficiently, they stabilized Douglas and got him on the spinal board. The stairs were tricky. Eventually, they decided Diana, with her enhanced strength, would carry the front of the stretcher, and Manus, who also enjoyed the moon's influence, took the rear. With the tiered steps, they were able to carry the stretcher sideways for most of the trip up the conical structure, but towards the top, Diana had to go first with Manus hoisting the stretcher above his head to keep Douglas level.

Kathryn simply hovered. She followed them up the stairs, monitoring Douglas's breathing. That left Raonull and Ella staring at each other. "You did really well, Ella. You kept him warm and calm." Raonull held out his hand. "Let's go join my aunt and uncle in Anandria."

Colour rushed into Ella's cheeks. She tucked her hands behind her back. "I think you should bring the book with us. You're tired. You'll need two hands to carry it." There was no way she was going to let Raonull feel her tremors of relief. She had feared that Raonull and Kathryn would fail to return for them, and she and Douglas would perish – first Douglas from his injuries – then her from a lack of food and water – *all alone*. If it hadn't been for Douglas peering up at her, relying on her, she wasn't sure if she could have kept it together as well as she had. The place was spooky with its echoing emptiness.

Raonull sighed, picked up the book, and began walking with an exaggerated limp towards the stairs. "Duty first," he mumbled loud enough for Ella to hear his words. "But wait until I'm home, fully rejuvenated. Fairies can't resist a strong man."

She had to agree with him. She smiled and followed him up the stairs. *Imagine that, we're going into Anandria!* Her belly unclenched a little. Douglas was safe. She giggled nervously. Raonull was half in and half out of the swirling mass. She was the only one completely on this side of the silver swirl. A few more steps and she would join the rest of them. Raonull's last foot pulled through, and Ella pushed off hard, anxious to get out of the cavern.

"Ow!"

Her head cracked against solid rock, and inky darkness descended. Her wings shot out. Thwack! The noise echoed endlessly around her. Her hands clutched her aching head, and she could feel a warm trickle of blood. *Oh God, oh God, oh God...* At least her wings gave off an iridescent glow. *Oh God, oh God, oh God...* It was solid above her head. *Solid! Where's the silver swirl?*

"Ray!"

She screeched his name over and over. Sobs tore from her throat. She would die here. *Alone.* Her hands pushed at the ceiling. Her nails scraped the rock leaving streaks of blood in their wake. There was no give.

Buried alive! No, please no...

31

Where the hell is she?

Jeff had arrived at the cottage somewhere around noon, weary and worried, but somewhat relieved that Mandy's car was parked at the top of the hill. He had called her name as he had run down the path, but everything had been eerily silent. He had felt even more spooked when the cottage door had been left wide open with just the screen door keeping the bugs out. Several lights had burned inside. A quick tour – even up to the old outhouse and to both boathouses – hadn't turned up any sign of Mandy.

The canoe and paddleboat were tied to the dock, and the small motorboat and the ski boat, were resting inside their respective boathouses. Perhaps someone on the lake had picked her up to go into Kinmount, the nearest town. Or, they had taken her for a boat ride. But why leave the cottage wide open? Something wasn't right.

Now, well past midnight, Jeff felt his stomach clench. He was beyond worry. He was frantic. *What the hell should I do? Dammit. Where else can she be?*

One thing was certain, he needed sleep. Unable to fight the weariness dragging him down, he rubbed his aching eyes. Tomorrow, his brain would function better and he'd be able to make a plan. Tonight... He yawned and fell onto the bed.

Where is she?

32

⚜

"You won't take me shopping. The TV doesn't work. So what am I supposed to do?" Mandy was on a tirade. With her brand new body, and living high in Toronto, she wanted to go out on the town – New York, perhaps, since Toronto was a ghost town – and be seen on the arm of the most gorgeous man in the universe. She wanted the lifestyle, clothes, and accessories that went with the penthouse. Instead, Lucifer was obsessing about where to stash his dragons and how to feed them.

Damn his 'plan' to take over Toronto.

Thankfully, the police chief had rectified the dragon problem a few seconds ago when he had suggested using the Roger's Centre. With its retracting roof and spacious ball field, it would make an excellent dragon nest. He had even suggested herding Torontonians into the stadium – most were out of shape and would make tender snacks for the dragons.

She tapped her foot impatiently and glared at Lucifer – the one responsible for her gorgeous transformation, and therefore the one who should deck her out in style and show her off to the world. Really, she was beginning to doubt his devotion, and was fed up with his silly plan to rule the universe. Her bottom lip stuck out in what she thought was an adorable pout, and her brows were lowered with displeasure. "The least you can do before you go out and conquer the city is fly me back to the cottage so I can retrieve my manuscript. It'll give me something to do until you have time for me!"

Lucifer rolled his eyes. The incessant whining was getting to him. It had not ceased since he had commandeered the penthouse. If it weren't for the drugging pleasure he received when he used her body...

He *needed* her. It was irrational and bugged the hell out of him. "Fine, I'll take you back. Hades has enough time to make it there before the sun comes up. Besides, it will give me a chance to check on Dience. He won't be expecting me so soon. If he hasn't got those standing stones erected by now, there'll be hell to pay."

Mandy turned a blinding smile upon him. It took his breath away. He was relieved his concession had mollified her. He watched her hips sway as she walked towards him, and he felt his body tense with desire. He drew in a determined breath. If they didn't leave now, the rising sun would prevent his dragon from taking them north. Then he would be stuck for another twelve hours listening to her bellyaching. *Sex can wait.*

"Why are you constructing a ring of standing stones on top of the portal?" Mandy asked. "All your creatures are passing from one dimension to the other quite easily." She slid her hand into his and drew him into the private elevator that would take them to the parking garage where their dragon, Hades, waited.

"The stones will magnify my dark magic here on Earth once I infuse them with it. The portal will be continuously open whether I'm there or not, and they'll act as a homing signal to my dragons and gargoyles so they are never lost in this world."

"You're brilliant, dear," Mandy said as she drew his head down and brushed her lips across his in a teasing game of nip, suck and retreat.

Hell, just one small concession, and she's all over me, and she's interested in my plans. But he knew retrieving her manuscript wasn't going to placate her for long. *Perhaps, a little shopping foray.* What would she do for him then? He lowered one hand to her ass and squeezed just as the elevator door slid open.

"Master?"

A mini storm, complete with flickering lightning in the elevator, indicated his irritation at being interrupted. He broke their kiss and sliced a look at his newest gargoyle. The creature still wore the chief of police's hat on its head. "Master, only four residents are left to evict, and then the building will be secured. The most difficult one, I gave to Hades to devour. The man got on my nerves."

Lucifer's mood lightened. "Good." He glanced down at Mandy. "What about the concierge? Is he gone yet?"

"No, he keeps mumbling something about being at Museum Place from the beginning. And not abandoning his post. And help should come soon. So far I haven't tossed him out, or fed him to the dragon – yet. The old geezer looks like he'd be stringy to eat – not much meat."

"Excellent! Keep him here. He may be of some service. He'll know where to look for exclusive clothing stores. I want to keep my Amanda happy." Despite the fact that he could alter the structure of Amanda's clothes to conform to any style she desired, the thought of having her out of the way while he waged war was vastly appealing.

Mandy let out a delighted squeal.

"Where are the other three gargoyles?"

"They're breaking down doors. The building should be ours within the hour."

"Excellent." Lucifer tugged on Mandy's hand to pull her out of the elevator and up Hades wing. Once they were seated, the giant beast ambled up the ramp to street level. Lucifer glanced down the deserted street. When all his dragons and troops were installed in Toronto, he would perform a door to door extraction of people, transforming the fittest, and giving the rest to the dragons to appease their appetites. Despite the eerie hush hanging over Toronto, he knew there were still hundreds of people within

KATHRYN HEANEY

the city limits. But right now, it was time to see to Amanda's needs, and rattle Dience's confidence.

Hades took off without incident. Below, Lucifer could see an occasional car. A shiver of delight raced up his spine. One of North America's largest cities was his. Too bad reception on his TV was so sporadic. He would have loved to have seen, and heard, all the reporters covering his story. Reporters were great at inciting terror. It was almost like they worked for him.

He sighed. Television reception was poor because of his presence and the Anandrian magic that flowed about him – it was *the* top whining point for Amanda. He tightened his arm about Mandy's waist and lowered his lips to nibble on her neck. Her head dropped back and he was pleased by her dreamy smile. *Lord, she is gorgeous – and tempting.* Dience could wait. They'd stop at the cottage first, and... *Well, look at that!* They were over the cottage already.

Hades flipped his tail up and soared down. With barely a thud, Hades touched down on the dock running along the shoreline. Lucifer smirked. Hades only shook the ground when he sought to make a dramatic entrance. Otherwise, the old dragon used centuries of finesse to land soundlessly – only the thwack of his braking wings gave warning to those below.

"I'll just be a minute, Lucifer. I'll get my manuscript."

He stopped her from rising by tightening his hold. "I'll come with you, Amanda."

"No need. It'll only take a sec... Oh," she cried when his hand cupped her breast and gave a gentle squeeze. "Oh... I see..."

"Wait for us, Hades. We won't be long." A giggle bubbled up from Amanda's throat. It sent pleasurable anticipation skittering down his spine, particularly when she dragged him down Hades wing to the porch and through the door. She made a sharp right into the bedroom and stopped dead in her tracks. Sprawled across the mattress was an old friend.

"Jeff," Mandy breathed.

Lucifer peered over her head. Jeff Davies lay on the bed. A small lamp burned on the night table. Lucifer's eyes narrowed. Jeff had imprisoned him on Earth, in an Earth jail, without the use of his magic, long ago. An unpleasant chill made him shiver as he remembered Amanda destroying Laura's first portal back to Anandria, while Jeff had held him captive. Amanda, now that she shared his blood, he had forgiven. Jeff, he would never forgive. *But, what's with her breathy voice? Does she desire him?*

Mandy dropped Lucifer's hand and rushed to the bed. "Jeff what are you doing here?"

Jeff blinked bleary eyes. "Mandy?" He blinked again. He was mistaken. A strange woman leaned over the bed. "Who are you? You're not Mandy. Where is she?"

Lucifer stepped back into the darkness of the cottage and narrowed his eyes. Jealousy speared his heart. He wanted – *no, needed* – to see what his mistress would do.

"Yes! It's me, Mandy." She wrapped him in an exuberant hug.

Jeff tried to disengage. "Mandy?" Her long, black hair hung about her face obscuring her features. Maybe his eyes had played tricks when she had awakened him, but he could have sworn she was a young, hot babe with a full curvy figure.

"Why are you here?" she asked while still squeezing him close.

"You didn't check in with anyone, and when I saw Lucifer had arrived in Toronto with dragons and gargoyles, I was worried. I couldn't help but think about Kathryn's prediction that Lucifer's magic would touch you." He wrapped his arms about her. She sounded like Mandy – although her voice was a bit deeper, like she had a cold. Very sultry... "When I got here and you weren't here, I panicked – but I was so tired, I had to get some sleep."

"Nice to know you care," Mandy whispered in his ear.

"Of course I care. You're my best friend."

Mandy stiffened and pulled away. "Yeah. *Best friend.* That's all I've ever been to you, isn't it, Jeff?"

Jeff's eyes widened. "What have you done to yourself? You look different... You're gorgeous."

Mandy gave him a smug smile. "I *am* gorgeous. And I'll *never* be more than a friend to you." She flipped her hand towards the dark doorway. "I've finally found a man who adores me – loves me – and I'm sure, *hates* you – almost as much as I do."

"What?"

"Think of all the years you passed me by for other women."

Lucifer stepped through the doorway into the light. A delighted smile graced his angelic face. *Amanda had been scorned by Jeff. Retribution and revenge were in order for them both, it seemed.*

"You!" Jeff hissed as he rolled to his feet. Lucifer didn't look any older than he had forty years ago. A wisp of envy cut through Jeff – there was silver in his hair, fine lines creased his brow and the area around his eyes, and grooves ran from the corners of his mouth to his chin. He had aged considerably compared to Lucifer.

Jeff's eyes cut back to Mandy. She looked thirty years younger, and had somehow reshaped her body and facial features. For the first time, he *looked* at her the way a man can't help looking when a beautiful woman walks by. *She's dynamite! Any man would drool over her.*

"Hello, Jeff," Lucifer drawled.

Their eyes met and held. Jeff stiffened. He couldn't look away. *What the hell...?*

"Not only have you wronged me, but you have scorned Amanda since the day you met her." Lucifer tut-tutted. "Payment is due... I believe there's an Earth saying, 'Karma's a bitch'. Well Jeff, Karma has just caught up with you. Come here."

It was a demand Jeff couldn't refuse. With steps that were stilted and wooden, he tried resisting. Sweat broke out on his brow. *Hopeless.* His limbs weren't his to control.

Lucifer stepped forward and placed one hand on his forehead, the other on his chest.

"Hey, he's already good looking..." Mandy stopped speaking. Horror washed over her. Jeff was undergoing transformation – he wouldn't be gorgeous anymore. Her eyes hardened. Jeff had been gorgeous *all* his life. Women had flocked to him. *Let Jeff see what it feels like to be rejected – to repulse others.* Lucifer would get no opposition from her.

Lucifer chanted and dark magic stirred inside the cottage.

Black patches erupted over Jeff's skin, and his eyes rolled up into his head. Mandy watched with fascination as her old crush transformed into a hideous beast. But, when he opened his gargoyle eyes, she did feel a twinge of regret for the loss of his dark, bedroom eyes. However, when Jeff caught his hideous reflection in the dresser mirror, and his cry of anguish cut through the night, her pang of conscience subsided. Finally, Jeff had a taste of what it had been like for her *all her life.* She had never liked her reflection in the mirror – never was truly accepted by beautiful people. She had been tolerated because she was Laura's friend.

Lucifer slid an arm about Mandy's waist. "Amanda, my dear, I couldn't help but overhear the grief this man has put you through. So to even the scales, I wish to gift him to you. He will be your devoted servant, dogging your every step, awaiting your commands."

Lucifer turned his head towards Jeff. "Do you hear that Jeff? You belong to Amanda. You will be at her beck and call. Every whim she has will be yours to fulfill."

Jeff tipped his head in acknowledgement. "Yes Master." His yellow eyes shifted to Mandy. "What do you wish, Mistress?"

"Wait by the dragon, Jeff." Mandy smiled, sat on the edge of the bed, and patted a spot next to her in invitation. "Lucifer and I have business to attend to. We won't be long."

Jeff gave a curt bow and tried to shuffle past them, but talon tipped toes stuck out the ends of his ruined sneakers, and he had to pause to tear them off his feet.

Mandy laid her head upon Lucifer's chest once Jeff was gone and whispered, "Thank you. He's finally *mine.*"

33

"You're going to be fine," Kathryn said as she sat down on the edge of the bed. "Mom's touch of moonglow stopped the internal bleeding." She brushed Douglas's hair back, more for her comfort than for anything else. "You'll live."

"Good to know," Douglas replied dryly.

Kathryn chuckled. "Give Mom's touch time. It's not instantaneous healing like Grandma Laura's. But eventually, within a few days, you should be right as rain."

Diana pushed off the doorframe. "That's right. As long as you remain still, and let my moonglow repair the damage the book caused when you landed on it, it should take a couple of days, give or take, to heal."

"Impressive," Douglas breathed. "And unbelievable. But I think I'd like a pain killer while your mojo works on my body."

Diana rushed to the bed. "No problem." Her hands cupped his face, and a soft yellow glow enveloped his head. His eyes drooped, his breathing became less laboured, and his body visibly relaxed. "There, he should sleep peacefully."

Kathryn looked around. "Hey, where's Ray and Ella? Why isn't Ella here worrying about her cousin?"

Diana put her hand on Kathryn's shoulder and a faint yellow glow seeped off her fingertips as she said, "Stay calm."

"I hate when you say that, Mom. And stop trying to zone me out with your magic."

Diana grinned at Kathryn, shrugged, and dropped her hand. "Ray is searching for the spot on the Moon Table that fits the design on the book."

"Why?"

"He came through ahead of Ella, and the Moon Table solidified before she could follow."

"What? She's stuck down there? Isn't there a pattern on the Moon Table like the one on the book?"

"Apparently not, but we have every available priest scanning the table top."

"This'll kill her!"

"There seems to be a lot of similar patterns, but nothing that fits..."

"Oh my God! I just got an idea. Mom, stay with Douglas while I run to the temple."

"Of course."

It wasn't far to the Lunar Temple, since their living quarters were attached. Kathryn barreled up to Raonull and gasped, "Turn the book over."

"Huh?"

"Turn it over, Ray. Maybe the pattern on the other side unlocks the Anandrian portal."

Raonull flipped the book exposing the beautiful pattern on the back cover. "Christ! Kath, you're right." He put the book down, slid it around, and cursed when it didn't mesh under his frantic touch. All he could think about was Ella stuck in limbo, all alone, and sealed in. He had to calm down.

"Let go!" Kathryn hip checked him and calmly took over sliding the book about. Mom had done a fine job with the moon-glow – her hands were steady, and she felt no panic. "There!"

The book sank through the stone, and the table top swiftly melted into a swirling silver mass. Raonull bent over and shoved his head through. There she was, her head cradled on her arms, her wings lying limply over her and spilling down the stairs — they looked lifeless — dull — their iridescence noticeably faded. Her sobs were heartrending. And through her sobs, she was calling his name — over and over...

"Ella!"

She jerked up. Light sprang into her wings, and wild cries of relief shook her body. He held his arms out, and she rushed into his embrace. Her body trembled violently. Gently, he tucked a finger under her chin to raise her face. His lips brushed across hers and tasted tears. Silently, he vowed she would never be left alone again. Their kiss deepened and her arms rose up to tighten about his neck. Ella sighed into his mouth as she calmed. Raonull knew he was lost.

He nipped her lower lip and straightened up, drawing them both through the Moon Table until they stood next to it. In return, she melded her petite body to his and plunged back into their kiss, encouraging him with soft licks. Raonull tangled his tongue with hers. It wasn't until he heard the deep clearing of a throat that he cracked an eye open to see Uncle Manus staring at him, while priests gaped at... *Oh hell, Ella's wings are wrapped around me.* Reluctantly he tried to pull away. "Ella, love, I'm trapped."

She peeked up at him through wet lashes. A hint of mischief twinkled in her eyes as she replied, "Yes, you are."

"We've company."

"Oh!" She whirled about. Her wings knocked Raonull off his feet.

Stifled guffaws erupted around the temple, and even Manus had to control his laughter before he could sputter out, "Welcome, Ella." Then he lost the battle, and let out a deep chuckle.

"Oh!" Ella whirled back. "Who are these people?"

Raonull, in the act of standing up, ducked back down to the floor narrowly missing another wing whack. *Hmm... Wing whack — perfect terminology.*

Ella's wings began to droop and grow dim. Raonull knew panic was setting in.

"Where are Kathryn and Douglas? Why aren't they here?" Ella whispered.

"Uncle Manus," Raonull implored as he swept Ella into his arms. "Can you help?"

"Aye," Manus said. He reached out, touched Ella, and released a bit more than a touch of moonglow, being careful to limit its reach – he didn't want Raonull to collapse, too.

Ella went limp in Raonull's arms, and her wings silently slid into her back. Raonull grinned when he heard a collective, "Oh," of wonder come from the priests. A fairy was a first for them, he thought as he gazed down at her exquisite features.

"Take her into Kathryn's room, Ray. Then we'll talk. I want to know how my daughter, and nephew, who were supposedly in *England*, ended up here with a fairy and a..." He raised an eyebrow in inquiry.

"A Druid, Uncle Manus," Raonull supplied. "Douglas is a Druid, and I think you had better prepare yourself, because Kath has fallen hard for the sorcerer."

Manus snorted and nodded at Ella cuddled protectively against Raonull's chest. "As hard as you have fallen for that little sprite in your arms?"

Raonull sighed and looked down at the dark-haired beauty. "Aye, Uncle Manus – as hard as that."

Manus patted him on the shoulder, looked past him at the swirling top of the Moon Table and said, "Do not be long, Ray. Tis a tale we all need to hear."

Raonull was placing Ella on Kathryn's large bed when Kathryn popped her head into the room. "How is she?"

Raonull smoothed a cover over Ella. "Your dad calmed her down. She should sleep. I'm heading back out to the temple to tell everyone what happened to us. Are you staying with Douglas?"

"Yeah. Mom dosed him really well with moonglow, but I want to be there in case he wakes up in pain. If he does, I can go get Mom."

"Okay," Raonull straightened up. "Wish me luck. I'm sure they'll grill me for the next hour or so."

Kathryn grinned. "Glad it's you and not me."

Raonull pushed Kathryn out of her room and into the guest bedroom where Douglas slept. "Keep an ear open in case Ella wakes – but I doubt she will."

With that, Raonull walked down the hall, and opened the door to enter the temple.

Manus eyed his nephew. "England to Anandria, huh?"

Raonull nodded at his uncle. Priests and citizens were crowded into the spacious Lunar Temple to gawk at the swirling surface of the Moon Table. Raonull took a deep breath and began talking. No one uttered a sound while he spoke. They left that up to their leader, Raonull's uncle, the High Priest, Manus, who finished up with, "So Ella had no idea she was a fairy, and Douglas, although he knew of his Druid heritage, did not know he had been protecting the key to the portal? And no one in England had any inkling about the purpose of Silbury Hill? Unbelievable," Manus muttered on a tired yawn.

Others also tried to hide their fatigue, but the rising sun was beginning to take its toll on the priests. Soon they would all be asleep on their feet, Raonull thought. He, on the other hand, felt jacked. And who wouldn't, after finding this incredible link between dimensions? Thank heavens Kathryn hadn't inherited an affinity for the moon either. As children, they had managed to get into a lot of mischief, when her parents were out for the count, after the sun had come up. "There are several more staircases down there. I'm assuming they're portals to other locations."

"Fascinating," Manus said through another yawn. "We will explore later."

Murmurs of agreement met this statement, and Raonull watched as they filed out to fall into their beds. It was time to venture back through the Moon Table and find the elusive exit from Silbury Hill. *That should help settle Ella's fears if she knows there's a way back to her home.*

He had one foot through the Moon Table when he heard, "Going somewhere?"

Drat! Caught in the act. He smiled, amused by his melodramatic thought. "Kath, I thought you were with Douglas."

"Nice try, cousin. You're trying to sneak away without me." Kathryn smiled. "Mom checked on Douglas a few minutes ago, doused him again, so he's out for the day. She checked Ella, too." She looked at her watch. "It's a new day. The sun is up. By tonight, Douglas should start feeling more like his old self."

Raonull lifted his foot out of the table. "Why are you still awake? I thought you'd crash by now."

"Are you kidding? My body has no idea what time zone, or dimension, it's in."

"Yeah, mine, too."

"I can't believe you were going to enter the table without checking to see if I was around. You were, weren't you?"

Accusation rang in her voice – something she was very good at whenever he tried to ditch her. "Yeah." A warm grin spread across his face. *She's gonna come with me.* He knew there was no way around it. She could compel him if he tried to leave without her. Better to give in, he had learned over the years, than become her puppet. Besides, he liked sharing adventures with her.

He held out his hand.

Smugly, she slipped her hand into his, and together they descended into the in between place where the book lay at the base of the conical staircase. Kathryn watched while Raonull scooped it off the floor. "What's the plan?"

"I want to find the exit to Silbury Hill. We should be able to find it a lot faster without the English cousins along."

"Fine, but I'm going up the stairs ahead of you. I don't want to be stuck in limbo like Ella was. That'd be creepy."

"Agreed," Raonull said as he looked around the cavern. "Only one problem, Kath."

"What?"

"Which stairs lead to Avebury? They all look alike."

"Hmm... They do look the same. I think it's this way. But for now, put the book down, and let's take a look around. We never had a chance when Douglas was hurt."

"Okay." He dropped the book.

"Hey, careful with that."

"Why? It falls every time we open the portal."

"I guess..." Kathryn conceded.

It didn't take long to complete a circuit around the cavern. All the staircases carved out of the circular wall seemed identical, and with the conical staircase in the centre, there was no reference point to determine which set of stairs they needed.

"Where do they all go?" Kathryn wondered as they stood next to the book again.

"There has to be a way to differentiate between them." Raonull glanced down at the book and scooped it up. "I've got an idea."

"What?"

"Remember how the door appeared leading into Silbury Hill when I walked past it with the book?"

Kathryn nodded. "You mean, maybe the book will expose something? Give it a try, Ray."

Slowly, they approached a staircase. A small circle appeared at its base. It glowed brighter the closer Raonull and the book got. Within the circle was an irregular shape. "What the hell is that? It looks like a blob with points on it," Raonull complained.

"Don't know," Kathryn admitted. "Let's move on to the next one and see if it helps us figure it out."

"Okay." He moved to the next set of steps. "What the...? Same circle, but the blob in this one looks more elongated and vertical...

Fatter at the bottom... Kinda looks like a pig's head if you squint at the bottom left side."

Kathryn gasped, and whacked Raonull on the shoulder. "That's *England*. And that dot, right there, *has* to be Avebury, or Silbury Hill." She grabbed his elbow and pulled him back to the previous set of stairs. "Oh my God, Ray. That's Australia." She kept walking and dragging him behind her. She stopped and stared at the circle at the base of the third set of steps at a loss for worlds.

"Holy mackerel, Kath. That's home!" Raonull cried.

"Yeah, those are definitely the Great Lakes, and that dot looks like it's slightly north of Toronto. Should we go there first?"

"Nah, let's go back to England and find the hill's exit. I want Ella feeling more comfortable with the whole situation. We'll come back to this later. See where it takes us."

"Okay, but first, let's walk around the cavern and see where the other stairs go." She dragged him onward and he smiled. She was always dragging him places. Good thing he *let* her.

"Ray, this one's in South America – Peru, I think."

"Maybe the Incas knew about the portals," he said nodding at the dot marking the location of a portal. "If I recall, their writings talked about people from another world. Interesting, huh?" Kathryn didn't answer, but kept tugging him along until he whistled. "That's definitely Africa, Kath. I think this one's in jungle territory."

She whirled about to look at him. "I think there's a staircase for every continent on Earth. What have we got left? Asia and...?"

"Antarctica."

Sure enough, the next circle contained an outline of the icy continent, and finally, they came to the last staircase. Raonull squinted at its base and whistled again. "Looks like the Chinese built one hell of a wall right over it."

"The Great Wall of China?"

"Uh huh. See?" He pointed at a double line that fell on either side of the dot. "Astronauts can see the wall from space, and that double line sure looks like it's in the right spot. Maybe the wall was built to be more than just a border. Maybe it's supposed to prevent visitors from another dimension from visiting." He winked at Kathryn. "There are a lot of dragons in Chinese culture. How did that happen, I wonder?"

"Guess we'll never know for sure," she said.

But he could tell she was intrigued by the idea. "Guess not, but let's head up to Silbury Hill and find that exit. I know we've only been gone from Earth a few hours, but I think Ella is suffering from a severe case of homesickness. Her arrival in Anandria was traumatic, and I want her to be comfortable in either dimension..."

"You like her, don't you?"

"Yeah."

"Oh my God, you're serious about her!"

"Yeah."

Kathryn loved the soft look on Raonull's face. *Love at first sight?* The thought made her smile. "Ray, she's wonderful."

"Yeah." Raonull felt his face heat up. *Damn.* Kathryn was bound to tease him later.

"Come on, tough guy. Let's find Ella's way home."

"After you, Kath."

"Naturally, 'cause the book has to go last." Kathryn hurried up the stairs and pushed through the swirling ceiling. Yup, she was inside Silbury Hill. The swirling table top reflected light off the hill's domed ceiling.

Raonull bumped her from behind. She got the hint, and stepped off the table allowing him to come through. She walked forward, and as the table solidified behind Raonull taking the light with it, she broke the inky darkness by releasing little light balls off the ends of her fingers. Finally, she reached the outer wall and lit a rock nestled in a wall bracket. "Your turn," she quipped when Raonull came up behind her. "I'm starting to get tired."

"Gotcha covered, coz."

They walked, and Raonull lit the way for them. He was lifting his hand to light yet another rock when the wall directly to his right slid soundlessly open. He looked down at the book in his other hand. *Nope, nothing unusual happening with the book.* He stepped back several paces and the wall slid back into place leaving no evidence of a door behind. He put the book down and stepped forward. Again the wall slid open. He stepped back and it closed. He turned to his left. Kathryn had lagged behind. She had her back to him and was examining something on the wall. "Hey Kath, hurry up and come over here."

"Yeah, yeah."

She was oblivious to his find. "What the heck were you doing back there, Kath?"

"I found some marks on the wall. Sort of looks like a game someone was playing to pass the time. I was trying to figure it out." She moved up to him. "What's up?"

"Go stand over there by the wall next to the last light I lit."

She gave him a funny look, but said, "Okay." She walked over, and the same section of wall slid open. "Oh my God!"

"Yeah, you can say that again − and no book needed. It's like a supermarket door. It lets people out, but not in. Step back and close it up, Kath. We don't want any passersby to see this."

"Yeah."

"Ella will be relieved when we show her this. Now, let's head back to Anandria and grab some shuteye. You're starting to sway on your feet."

Kathryn yawned. "All those time zones and dimension changes are catching up with me."

"We'll explore the Ontario stairs after we wake up." He winked at her. "Besides, I think Uncle Manus and Aunt Diana will want to join us."

Kathryn shook her head. "Uh uh. Mom and Dad have one more ceremony to complete. It'll help boost the power of the other priests for the coming year. We interrupted them, so they didn't complete the ceremony last night. All five moons will still be visible tonight, so they'll be busy. And with Mom occupied, I want to stay close to Douglas. Make sure he's steady on his feet."

"Okay Kath, I guess this'll have to wait." Disappointment washed over him.

They returned to the centre of Silbury Hill and lined up the book. Silently it slid through the platform. Raonull placed his hands on Kathryn's waist and boosted her up over the edge. He didn't release her until she had found the stairs beneath. He followed her down, retrieved the book, and climbed up behind her into Anandria where the Moon Table solidified into solid stone. *Amazing!*

He looked back over his shoulder before entering his Uncle Manus and Aunt Diana's apartment. He'd be on his own tomorrow night – wasting a good opportunity. Douglas would need another night of recovery, and Ella and Kathryn would most likely want to spend time with him. Women always fussed.

Raonull clenched the book. Any other item would have been squashed by his superior strength – but not the book – how infuriating. He needed an outlet. No, he needed to see where that portal came out in Ontario. Kathryn would kill him if he went without her. *I should wait... Nah, I can't wait. I'll try the stairs.*

34

Raonull was wide awake. He had been in bed for over two hours. Aunt Diana and Uncle Manus had to be out of the apartment and well into their intricate ceremony. Kathryn was spending the night on a cot in Douglas's room, just in case he needed aid. He had heard her shuffling about getting food and drink a little while ago, which she had taken back into the Druid's room. Nor had Ella stirred. Uncle Manus and Aunt Diana must have really zapped her with moonglow. He'd have a word with Debra before he left to make sure she'd greet Ella when she awoke. Debra could give Ella a bite to eat and then a quick tour of the city. Debra would *love* taking care of a fairy.

He rolled out of bed, slipped into jeans and t-shirt, and added a spare dagger he kept in Moyen to a sheath on his belt. He eyed his sword. *Nah, too unwieldy if I end up in a tight spot. Plus, I have to lug the book about.* He bent over and picked up the book. *Now to sneak out…*

He cracked the door. No one was there. A soft glow from the rocks on the hearth illuminated his way as he crept across the living room. He didn't want to alert the girls. The last thing he wanted was to piss off his cousin who would insist he wait another night. Nor did he want a hysterical fairy tagging along. He'd explore first, beg forgiveness, then after telling everyone what he had found, let them join him. No surprises. No hysterics. Simple. Kathryn and Ella could deal with that.

A bowl of fruit and a couple of sandwiches sat on a large platter on the table behind the couch. He smiled. Aunt Diana, or Debra, had been thinking about him. He bit into one of the sandwiches and swiped an apple out of the bowl. He chewed with relish and started for the door.

"Going somewhere?"

Jesus. He nearly jumped out of his skin. He whirled about. A dark head popped up on the far side of the couch. "Umm..." Where the hell was his usual smooth drivel that he could dish out to women?

Ella rolled off the couch, swiped a sandwich off the plate, and stalked over to him.

Oh hell! The little fairy was seething. Anger and irritation were written all over her face. Her finger poked his chest. Her nail dug painfully into his skin. He refused to show any reaction. He knew the force behind the poke was deliberate.

"You were going to leave me here in a *strange* place, with *strange* people, in a totally *strange* dimension."

"Kathryn's down the hall with Douglas, and I was going to tell Debra to look out for you." He stared at the floor.

She poked him hard, again. "Who the hell is Debra?"

"She looks after Kathryn's family. You know, cleans, cooks..." Ella's frown deepened. *Bloody hell. Time to change tactics.* "Kathryn and I went back through the Moon Table after everyone went to bed, and we found the way back to Avebury."

Ella froze in the middle of a poke. "You found..."

Raonull grabbed her finger and gently redirected it. "A way back to Avebury. Kathryn and I went back to Silbury Hill, and we found the exit. You can go home."

Her face broke into a grin. "That's brilliant." Then her brows crashed back down. "I can't believe you were going back to Avebury without me tonight. How could you?"

Raonull held up both hands, and shook his head. "Nah, I wasn't going back to Avebury, Ella."

She pouted. "Then where were you going?" she asked, pointing at the book in his arms.

"I *think* I was going home."

"What?"

"Remember the other stairs?" Ella nodded. "Kathryn and I discovered tiny maps at the base of each staircase. We think there's a portal for every continent. So, I was going to see if the North American stairs took me to Ontario. The dot on the map looked like it was just north of Toronto." He was gratified to see Ella was somewhat mollified by his answer – until she frowned again. *What now?*

"You were *still* abandoning me."

"I thought you were *still* sleeping." He flinched. Even he could hear the exasperation in his voice.

"So?" she insisted.

"So, I figured you needed rest after the trauma you went through last night."

Her back stiffened and her wings *thwacked* out.

Oh, this is not good.

Her nose lifted, and she huffed as she poked him again. "Listen strong man, I'm not some fragile, shrinking rose. Granted, I was petrified when the ceiling solidified, but now that we know *why* it solidified, and we can prevent that from happening again, I'm *not* going to break into hysterics on you." He opened his mouth, but she carried on. "And don't think I haven't figured out that you thought exactly that. *Oh, the hysterical little fairy,*" she minced.

Raonull winced. She had him. Ella took a huge bite out of her sandwich and calmly chewed while she stared at him. Raonull blew out his breath. Reluctantly, he made direct eye contact and felt irritated when he saw her smug little face. "I wanted to have fun exploring, and I didn't want you freaking out on me ruining everything... And I'm sorry."

She swallowed the bite of sandwich, rose up on her toes as she pulled his head down, and placed a soft kiss on his cheek. "This time, I'll forgive you. But if you *ever* exclude me again..."

"Duly noted." Raonull crushed her in a big hug. Her wings curled about them both. *Nice.*

"Well, there be a sight for this old girl to see."

Ella lifted her head off Raonull's chest. An older woman stood grinning from ear to ear watching them.

"Ella, that is Debra," Raonull groaned into her hair.

"My wee bees told me the fairy was up, and her wings were out. They like yer wings, by the way. I like them, too. They be beautiful!"

"Bees?"

Raonull mumbled, "Debra's name means, bee. She can talk to them – and just about any other insect, too. But bees really like her and keep her informed about lots of things."

Debra harrumped and added, "Aye, they tell me, lad, that ye have hurt the wee fairy."

Ella giggled. "I *like* you."

Raonull met Debra's gaze. "I apologized."

"Good," Debra grunted. "Now where be ye taking the book?"

"Uncle Manus and Aunt Diana will be busy tonight, and I think it's important to expand our knowledge about the book. I'm going for a look see so that when they're available everyone can make informed decisions."

"And I'm going with him," Ella chimed in.

Debra's gaze softened when Ella stepped away from Raonull and her wings slid into her back. *She's charmed by my little fairy*, Raonull thought eyeing Debra.

"Well then," Debra said, "if Raonull has a wee fairy with him, he will be fine. Will ye be gone long?"

"Not if we can help it. No more than a couple of hours," Raonull guessed.

"Fine, I will have a hot lunch waiting when ye get back."

Ella skipped across the floor, let her wings snap out, and proceeded to wrap both her arms and wings about the woman. She peered over Debra's shoulder at Raonull. Her message was clear. *See, I have control.* "Thank you, Debra."

Debra hugged her back, speechless with delight and wonder. Raonull passed by them to hold the door to the apartment open. "Come on, Ella. Let's see what trouble we can get into tonight."

Ten minutes later, Raonull eyed Ella. She looked pale after passing through the Moon Table – he couldn't blame her. He slipped his hand into hers. Colour began to bloom in her cheeks when a map started glowing at the base of the nearest staircase.

"Ray! I see it. And I, a Brit, who's never been out of the country, recognize the Great Lakes." She pulled eagerly at his hand, to hurry him up the stairs.

But when she went to thrust her head through the ceiling, Raonull had second thoughts and stopped her. "I need to go first. Just in case..." Deliberately, he placed the book on the top step. "Without the book, the portal *will not close* behind me. Stay put. I need to make sure it's safe."

Ella clutched his arm. "Ray, don't leave me alone."

Raonull caught an annoyed sigh just in time. Hysterics were close – he really didn't want to deal with that – which was the reason he had tried to sneak out in the first place. He patted her hand. "A couple of seconds, Ella. I'll poke my head out. You can still hang on to my hand." She bit her bottom lip, drawing his eyes there. She tempted him... They were alone... He gave himself a mental shake and told himself not to go down that road.

"What if something grabs you?"

His free hand slid his dagger out of its sheath. "I'll have a surprise waiting, love."

She still looked unsure, so he gave in to temptation and drew her in for a kiss. *A distraction might take her mind off the situation.* She stiffened, but then her body became pliant. She grabbed his head to participate more fully – *and it was fully* – in their kiss. *Bloody hell!* Now *he* was distracted.

Slowly, he pulled away from their kiss. He was here to gain information and, he admitted to himself, he wanted to be the first to know what lay at the top of those stairs. "I'll only take a peek. Hold onto my hand, Ella."

He pushed through the swirling ceiling. His head met with resistance, startling him. However, the resistance proved no problem for his extreme strength. The barrier gave way. Dirt tumbled into his face, and he had to spit it out of his mouth and wipe his arm across gritty eyes. *What the hell?* He blinked furiously. Dirt lingered on his long eyelashes. Overhead, he waved his dagger about blindly until his vision cleared.

Moonlight spilled over a serene forest scene. There was no danger. A jolt of recognition washed through him, and he gasped with delight at his emerging childhood memories. He ducked back into the portal and grinned. Ella was covered in dirt! It coated her face, her hair, even her wings. *Hmm… Her wings are out. Not terrified, huh?* Raonull eyed the lovely appendages. Moss clung to them. He tried to stifle his amusement, and he must have succeeded, because in the middle of swiping her hand through her hair, Ella's eyes swept up, and her face beamed at the sight of him. Her wings slid quietly into her back.

"Where'd the dirt come from?" she asked as she flung herself at Raonull and hugged him tightly.

Raonull plucked a twig out of her hair. "This," he said inspecting the stick between his fingers, "is a little piece of home."

"Yes," she replied. "We're back on Earth."

Raonull shook his head. "No, Ella – I mean, yes, the minute we step through the portal we're back on Earth, but I'm also home. This portal is located at the top of a hill that you have to descend if you want to reach my family cottage. Kathryn and I used to climb up here and play directly on top of this portal…"

"I don't understand."

He tugged her hand. "Come on." He pulled her through the portal as he sheathed his dagger. They stepped out onto flat stones at the edge of a circular clearing. Large shrubs arched over creating a tunnel effect. "See? This 'tunnel' is the only way in or out of the clearing. Raspberry canes and some other kind of thorny bushes enclose the clearing. Kathryn and I pretended this was our fort."

Ella checked out the clearing, enchanted by its beauty. The only blemish was the ragged hole in the moss they had climbed through that now revealed the swirling silver beneath it.

"Stay here. I'll be just a sec. I want to retrieve the book." Raonull stepped back into the portal, gripped his nose as if he were diving in for a swim, and sank out of sight.

Ella giggled at his antics and squatted down. She fingered the dirt next to the portal. Moss covered the whole clearing! Soft and velvety to the touch, it was what had crumbled and dropped all over them when Raonull had burst through. Carefully, she raked away more moss beside the open hole, and sure enough, she exposed a larger expanse of the swirling silver surface. *The whole clearing would look like this if the moss was removed. A person would fall right through if they stepped anywhere on the mossy expanse.*

Raonull rose out of the hole, the book clutched in his hand. He stepped next to her onto the flat stones of the natural tunnel leading away from the clearing. Behind him, the portal hardened into stone. He watched Ella pull up more moss. He bent over and helped her, using his dagger to scrape the moss aside. Soon, they saw engravings etched on its surface matching the engravings on book.

Ella slid her hand back into his. "All the times you and Kathryn played here, you had no idea that there was anything special beneath the moss?"

"Heck no." He grinned down at her. "We were too busy defending our fort from imaginary invaders."

"You're sure this is the same clearing?"

Raonull squeezed past her pulling her through the break in the vegetation. "Wait till you see Checkley's Lake. There're lots of beavers in it. No cottages. It's too small. I'm surprised they even call it a lake and not a pond. There it is! You can see moonlight reflecting off its surface."

"How pretty!"

"Yeah, it is. But if we head down the hill, we'll cross over a dirt road that cottagers use to access Salerno Lake before we pick up the path that takes us down to the cottage. My Aunt Mandy is here. She likes solitude when she writes."

"I get to *meet* her? She's Laura's best friend, right? She's the author, Kathryn Heaney, right?"

Raonull chuckled. "Yes you get to meet her. She might even have old copies of her Anandrian books handy that she can sign for you."

"Really? Oh Ray, this is so exciting!"

"Yeah, yeah. Ella, pick up the pace. It's a long way down the hill to the lake, both my hands are occupied, and the bugs are starting to bite..."

Secretly, he was just as excited as Ella. Aunt Mandy was going to meet Ella, a real live fairy – the first girl he had ever brought home for her to meet. *Damn!* Only days since he had met Ella. Love at first sight? Nah, lust was first, he thought with amusement, which he had to admit had quickly changed and grown into something deeper. *Most disturbing!*

35

"Shh!" Raonull pulled Ella down behind a small cedar tree. "Don't let your wings pop out," he whispered.

Her brows rose.

He wrapped an arm around her and drew her back against his chest. Slowly he rose until their heads poked above the greenery. They were high enough up the hill behind the cottage that they had a clear view of its roof and the dock along the shore. Moonlight glistened off the lake making it easy to see.

Ella sucked in a horrified breath. A real dragon had touched down on the dock – and two people were descending off its back – a man and a woman. She felt Raonull's breathing increase as they watched.

"Lucifer," he hissed. His eyes narrowed. The woman looked a lot like Aunt Mandy. Maybe a close relative? Like a sister? Except, Aunt Mandy didn't have any sisters – or cousins. *Who the hell is that?*

Ella peeked up at him, and Raonull held a finger to his lips. The couple were heading to the cottage. Quietly, Raonull stepped out onto the dirt path they had been following down the hill and pulled Ella with him. Raonull hoped that the night air didn't send their scent to the dragon idly trailing a talon through the dark water while it waited.

The path ended at the rear of the cottage where the bedroom jutted out from the bulk of the main building. They huddled next to the bedroom wall. Thankfully, there were no windows on this side. The uninsulated, thin summer walls made it easy to hear conversations. Ella felt Raonull squeeze her hand almost painfully when they heard *three* voices - one woman and two men. Spit in her mouth dried up as dark magic stirred. Her skin crawled. It felt unclean... An agonized cry from a man at the magic's apex had her clutching at her throat and swallowing a scream.

"Come on," Raonull whispered in her ear.

His hot breath, and the feel of his hand tugging on hers, sent a rush of relief through her. Gratefully, she stumbled back up the hill behind him.

By the time they reached the dirt road, they were panting heavily. Raonull drew her further down the road to a parking lot hidden by trees. "*That* was Aunt Mandy – although she didn't look like herself," he mumbled. "And, Lucifer has just turned Jeff into a gargoyle!"

Their eyes jerked up. Huge wings beat the air as the dragon took off. Ella swallowed a cry when the beast's silhouette crossed the moon. Three beings added to that silhouette – one definitely a gargoyle. Ella's wings *thwacked* out. Raonull glanced down, startled by their appearance. She pulled her hand out of his, as her wings fluttered experimentally. Delight made her grin when her feet left the ground.

"Ella?"

"Don't try to stop me," she cried as she zipped higher out of his reach.

"Ella, what are you doing?"

She hovered over his head. "Reconnaissance!"

"Ella, get back down here!"

She shook her head. Moonlight lit his face. He wasn't happy. "I promise I won't be long."

"What are you going to do?"

Her eyebrows rose at his angry tone. "I'll stay well back and close to the trees. If they only go a short distance, we might be able to find out how Lucifer brought his dragons to Earth. Bye..."

"Ella!" Raonull roared. She disappeared into the woods. Furious, he dropped the heavy book and sat down hard on top of it. *Bloody stupid woman.* Nervous, he drew out his dagger and threw it over and over into the ground. *Wait till she gets back...* His stomach clenched. *What if she doesn't come back?* HIs hands fumbled his dagger. It clattered to the ground, and he stared unseeing into the dark forest.

A gust of wind hit him from behind. The air glowed softly from a source that wasn't the moon. Raonull whirled about on his seat. "Ella!" He surged to his feet and crushed her against his chest before she could completely touch down. He went nose-to-nose with her. "Don't you *ever* do such a foolish thing again!"

Annoyed, Ella swung her wings forward and clapped him on either side of his head.

"Ow!" Raonull dropped her to clutch his ringing ears.

With an easy flutter, Ella shot back into the sky to glare at him. "We're equal partners, remember? I will *not* be ordered about by you, or anyone else. If I see an opportunity, I will take it. I hope I've made myself perfectly clear." She flew up the remaining portion of hill to the portal. The soft glow of her wings disappeared as she crested the top of the hill.

Well, damn! I've made a mess of this again.

Wearily, Raonull picked up the book and made the long trudge up to the clearing. Ella was sitting on a rock at the edge of the portal. "Ella?" She ignored him except for a quick, reproachful glance his way. He thought he heard a little snort. *Well, if that's the way she wants it...*

He slid the book onto the portal and watched it fall through. Before he could step into the portal, Ella zipped by, her wings fluttering madly as she plunged ahead of him through the swirling silver surface. Quickly, he followed. He was in time to see her fly up the conical staircase into Anandria. She wasn't waiting for him. He retrieved the book and climbed into Anandria in time to hear Ella say, "Debra, get Diana and Manus. I've got news about Lucifer."

Debra slid her hand into Ella's and pulled her over to her apartment door. "I will be getting them soon, lass. The moon ceremony be almost done. Meantime, ye need a bite to eat." Debra looked over her shoulder. "Oh, there ye be, Raonull. Come along. Tis some soup, cold meats, and biscuits awaiting ye."

Ella stiffened and pulled her hand out of Debra's grasp. "I'm not hungry. I'll go wait in Diana and Manus's apartment."

One could hear a pin drop as Ella crossed the hall to the other apartment. Debra narrowed her eyes and focused on Raonull. "What did ye do?"

"Something stupid," Raonull replied, as he turned towards his aunt and uncle's apartment.

"Well tis obvious 'twas something stupid," Debra muttered, as she watched him barge through the door and close it with a resounding *thud*. She wanted details...

Raonull leaned back against the door taking in the full measure of Ella's glare. "I'm sorry. I was worried about you." The room remained silent. "You're such a wee thing..."

Ella snorted.

"And I don't know what I would do if something happened to you. I care for you... Deeply." A startled look passed over her face, so he decided to press on. "I know we've only known each other for a couple of days, but when you flew off, my gut was screaming at me. I didn't want to lose you."

"You're gut was screaming at you?" Raonull's gaze shifted to the hallway. Kathryn stood there with a smirk on her face. "You really need to work on your romantic repartee, cousin."

Ella swung around and stomped across the room. "Butt out, Kathryn! He was doing just fine."

"Whoa! Okay," Kathryn put her hands out to ward off the little fairy and backed down the hall. "I'll leave you two alone."

Ella felt Raonull's arms slip about her waist. Giving in, she let her head fall back to rest on his chest.

"Perhaps we will have a future together," he murmured.

"Do you really mean it?"

"Yeah."

Ella twisted about in his arms. Both black brows rose as she took a moment to contemplate the look of him.

Raonull held his breath.

She lifted a hand to his cheek and stroked the scratchy bristles growing there. "Every time you leave without me to face the unknown, my gut screams, too." Her brows crashed down. "Remember that when you dash off to save the world."

"Understood, love. If at all possible, we'll *try* to stay together. Partners."

She nodded. "Yeah, partners."

The door to the apartment burst open. "Easy, Di, or I'll have to replace another door," Manus said with a shake of his head.

Diana ignored him and sailed into the room. Her nose was quivering. "I smell the cottage!"

Raonull chuckled and brushed a piece of moss out of Ella's hair. "You've got that right, Aunt Diana."

"You two went up the stairs without me?"

Everyone whirled about to face the hallway. Kathryn had reappeared with Douglas leaning on her for support.

Raonull sighed again. How did he manage to keep pissing off the women in his life? He shrugged. "I couldn't sleep, and I knew you were staying by Douglas as he recuperated. I figured it was the perfect time to see where the stairs came out. And, Kath, you'll never guess where the portal is." He didn't wait for her guess, but blurted out, "The clearing where our fort was up the hill. It's under all the moss!"

"No!" Kathryn breathed. "All those years we played there, and we never knew."

Raonull frowned. "But the most disturbing thing we saw was a dragon landing on the dock." Everyone gasped. He nodded and continued. "Lucifer, and a lady who looked a lot like Aunt Mandy, were on its back. At first, I didn't think it was Aunt Mandy. She looked so different – beautiful and curvy – but then when they entered the cottage, and Ella and I snuck up to the outside wall, we heard their conversation. It was Aunt Mandy all right, and Jeff was inside. It was a surprise to them that he was there." Raonull reached out, grabbed Diana's hand, and took a deep breath before dropping his bombshell. "Aunt Di, Lucifer turned Jeff into a gargoyle – and he made him Aunt Mandy's servant."

"What?" Diana gasped. Flashes of her own time as a gargoyle ripped through her head. "Why would Lucifer give Aunt Mandy a gargoyle? Why would she be with him? And why was Lucifer at the cottage?"

"I can answer that last question," Ella said drawing everyone's eyes to her. "I flew off after the dragon when it left with everyone on its back, and..."

"You did what?" Douglas roared.

"See? I'm not the only one who worries about you," Raonull muttered as he rolled his eyes towards the ceiling.

Ella glared at them both. "Would you two shut up and let me finish?" Her fisted hands rested on her hips. "The dragon flew around the bend in the lake into the next bay, where there's a huge jumble of rocks. They landed there."

"Why?" Douglas demanded.

"Quit interrupting and I'll tell you," Ella fumed. "Near the top, Lucifer has constructed a rocky platform, with a ring of standing stones large enough for a dragon to pass through."

Diana's brows crashed together. "Did you see the three of them go through the portal on the dragon?"

Ella nodded. "They flew right in."

Kathryn groaned. "The Sight was right. Lucifer's magic *did* touch Aunt Mandy. She's never been able to enter a portal, but somehow, Lucifer has given her the ability to cross over. And it was also right when it told me there was no need to guard Aunt Mandy's house in Toronto." Kathryn stomped her foot. "The blasted Sight just omitted the part about the cottage."

Diana caught Manus's eye as she huffed out a worried, "Suggestions?"

Manus wrapped an arm about her shoulders. "We dispatch a dragon with a messenger to Veresah. Laura and Vaaron need to know Lucifer is on Earth. Then tomorrow night, we'll send men to do some reconnaissance. We'll find out just where Lucifer's portal comes out in Anandria."

"I think I might be of some use," Debra said from the entrance to the apartment. "And we would not risk any men."

"Explain, please," Manus said, his eyebrows rising in surprise at this unexpected offer.

"Take a few of me bees through the portal to Earth. They can fly right through Lucifer's portal to his new hidey hole and report back to me. We will finally know where he hides in Anandria!"

36

Lucifer stepped back, satisfied with the night's work. Amanda had kept herself amused by ordering Jeff to do nonsensical tasks — like moving a stone from one location to another. She obviously garnered great pleasure from Jeff's state of slavery. Without her pestering him, he had been free to inspect the ring of standing stones Dience had constructed around the portal. The portal measured about thirty feet across — perfect for a dragon to pass through while in full flight.

He walked around the ring of stones, pausing at each monolith to draw intricate patterns over its surface with his fingers and softly chant until dark magic seeped into it. As the sun came up, he rested his forehead on the last stone and watched the gigantic portal emit a resonating wave of dark magic. The standing stones worked. The portal would be open 24/7, whether he was present or not, giving access to Earth for his gargoyle horde and dragons. It would also be a homing beacon guiding his slaves back to Anandria.

"Amanda, my dear, I'm tired. Let's retire back to the cottage."

Mandy climbed up a small rock to stand next to him. She gaped at the massive opening. It was mind blowing. She turned adoring eyes on him. "You must be exhausted."

"Aye, love. But a good day's rest will do much to restore me. The sun's up, so we'll have to take the canoe back. Let's get going before I collapse."

Mandy noted that there were fine lines at the corners of Lucifer's eyes. It was the first time she had seen him look other than flawless. The powerful magic he had just dispensed had drained him. It was something a day's sleep, topped with home cooking, could look after, she decided as she slipped her hand in his, kissed him softly on the cheek, and tugged him to the edge of the platform. "No need for you to exert yourself any further." She turned to look at *her* gargoyle, still dressed in shorts and a muscle shirt. "Jeff! Get your butt down to the canoe and get us back to the cottage, pronto," she shrieked.

She smiled up at Lucifer. Her voice lowered into that of sultry lover. "You can sit at ease in the middle of the canoe. I'm sure I can fashion a comfortable backrest with the life jackets. Then I'll take the front seat and help Jeff paddle."

She released his hand and slid over the edge of the platform heading for the shore down below. Lucifer's face split with a delighted grin. She could morph from lover, to shrew, and back to lover within seconds. She was so entertaining!

Had he ever been this happy? *Ever?*

Not even thoughts of world domination made him smile foolishly the way he did when Amanda was around. Would conquering the universe top the feelings of contentment and happiness she made him feel?

There was only one way to find out...

Tomorrow night, the majority of his dragons and gargoyles would settle in Toronto. The dragons could make several trips to get the horde there, but he would leave a skeleton crew in the Lair to guard his Anandrian home – really, it was a senseless precaution, as the Anandrians would never locate his home beneath the desert sands. No one went near the Badlands.

An unpleasant memory of his time in the Badlands, when Anandria had called him home from his imprisonment on Earth, solidified his opinion that no sane person would *ever* venture across the extensive desert. If he were not immortal, he doubted he would have survived his grueling trip to the City of Horval.

Lucifer settled into the canoe. By the time they returned to Toronto, the chief of police – one of his newest gargoyles – should have rounded up a goodly number of plump humans and jammed them into the Rogers Centre. His dragon fleet would feast well before retiring at dawn the following day.

The shapely bottom of his concubine captured his attention. Amanda was stretching forward to dip her paddle into the water. Her curves were emphasized by her tightening clothes. Lucifer grinned in appreciation. He would take her, and Jeff, on the first run to Toronto. He glanced back at Jeff. Jeff would remember from his human life, all the ins and outs of Toronto. If he teamed Jeff up with the concierge at his condo, they could probably keep Amanda happy shopping while he dealt with his troops.

37

Dience gaped at the luxurious lodgings. It was hard to believe the Master had brought him to his personal abode in Toronto. Although, when he had heard Lucifer say through clenched teeth that, "Dience should come on the first dragon ride. I don't want the blithering idiot out of my sight for too long. With my luck, he might damage one of the standing stones." Dience had to admit he had felt infuriated, especially when one of Lucifer's gargoyles had latched onto his tunic and had dragged him up the wing of the nearest dragon.

But now, here he was in the most palatial building he had ever seen. Already, Jeff and Mandy had headed out to shop, and Lucifer had left to direct gargoyles about the city as they arrived from cottage country.

Dience peered out of the corner of his eye. On the couch sat a man Lucifer had briefly introduced as Gary Russell. Gary had been there to greet them when they had landed. It turned out that Gary wanted to offer his services to his old boss, Lucifer. Dience had wanted to wipe the satisfied smile off the private investigator's face when Lucifer had welcomed him back into his employ. Instead, Dience had ground his teeth as he had held back his anger.

Years ago, after Lucifer had returned from Earth to Anandria, Dience had heard about Gary. According to Lucifer, Gary had kept a low profile as he had spied on Laura and her family. Gary had been clever using his photography to enter Laura's artistic world. Gary had befriended Laura and had been drawn into her confidences. Gary had never bungled a single fucking assignment. Gary, Gary, Gary...

Gary was eyeing him speculatively. "Hello demon. I've heard about you, but I never thought I'd meet you. Lucifer often compared me to you."

"Really?" Dience replied cautiously.

Gary's eyes sparkled. "Yeah, I heard you're quite daring."

"Aye, I be that," Dience admitted warming up to the man.

"Then perhaps you might like to join me."

"What for?"

"Who is the one person Lucifer wants to destroy?"

Dience sucked in his breath. Maybe... Just maybe, Gary would make the perfect partner. "Laura!"

Gary nodded and waved his hand towards a gargoyle wearing a suit that was pilfering the contents of the fridge. "I've been having a very informative chat with Carlos while I was waiting for Lucifer to return. It seems like Amanda – or good old Mandy – has chats with Laura through a portal in Mandy's house. My guess is that Laura will be sending the troops through – so to speak – since Mandy has failed to check in."

Dience nodded with growing excitement.

"Right now, Lucifer's attention is focused on the city of Toronto as he secures a place for his horde. What do you think he would do if we delivered Laura to him?"

Dience crossed to the couch. He had to hop up to sit on it – 'twas the most comfort he had ever felt in his extensive life. "I be interested. The Master would finally appreciate my devotion to him. With your brains and my daring nature, we would be a most interesting team."

"Good, good," Gary murmured. He looked at Carlos and shuddered. The last thing he wanted was to end up as a gargoyle.

Becoming indispensable to Lucifer, should guarantee my cushy human life.

"I know Mandy's residence well. I believe a stakeout might be in order while we concoct our plan."

"Stakeout?"

"Yeah, we watch the house for a bit..."

Dience groaned.

"Problem, demon?"

"I hate sitting in bushes," Dience replied vehemently.

Gary chuckled. "Here, in Toronto, I much prefer the comfort of my car. But if you want to sit in a bush..."

Dience had no idea what a car was, but anything was preferable to a bush. "Nay! I will go with the customs ye practice on Earth."

Gary held out his hand. "Fine, we'll start tomorrow night."

Dience slowly extended his hand – no one had *ever* taken it in a pact before.

38

Vaaron watched a dragon lift off the ground bearing Paul and Michael on its back. The pair of southern warriors had wanted to venture through Laura's portal to Earth, but Vaaron felt it prudent to send them off on another quest – his men were still smarting from their defeat in the tavern. Once Paul and Michael had discovered they were to bring Diana, the Moon Goddess, and her husband, Manus, the High Priest of the Lunar Temple, up to speed with the Toronto situation and bring them back to Veresah, they had been eager to fly to Moyen.

Vaaron smiled. He had heard Paul say to Michael that they had held their own with David and Morrigan on the practice pitch, so the Moon Goddess should be a piece of cake to defeat. Secretly, Vaaron hoped his powerful daughter 'wiped the floor' with those two. His grin increased. Earth idioms were clever indeed. He could easily see Diana demolishing the pair.

He turned away from the window and crossed to Laura who fussed with David and Morrigan. "Leave them be, Laura. The troops await word. David knows this is a scouting exercise only, and he will take extra precautions. Besides," he nodded at Morrigan, "his wife will not let him do anything rash."

Laura gave a last pat to David's shoulder, kissed Morrigan on the cheek, and waved them towards the open portal before collapsing on the loveseat situated a few feet away so that the portal would remain open with her proximity.

David went first, and Morrigan followed, saying, "We will not be long. It should take minutes to ascertain that the house is empty." Silently, David motioned for them to go downstairs.

They arrived on the ground level and, as planned, separated to cover the main floor. It rapidly became evident that no one was home. David ran back upstairs, stuck his head through the portal and yelled, "All clear."

Immediately, Anandrian warriors filed past Laura. They stepped through to Earth, and Laura heard their boots clatter downstairs to the main floor.

Vaaron's hand landed on her shoulder and squeezed. "Kimberly is ready, Laura. The dragons all know they have to pee once they are outside the house."

"And she's made enough potion to bring them back home?"

"Aye, Laura. David carries a vial with him..."

"But what if something should happen to David? Our poor dragons will be stuck on Earth. They could perish if they have no shelter when the sun comes up."

"Morrigan and Elfare also have vials of potion, and they have been through the portal enough in the past to understand the structure of Toronto. I only wish Diana and Manus were here. There's no one better on a dragon's back than our Diana."

"Don't worry, Mom," David said from the Earth side of the portal, "Di will be here soon. She won't want to miss out on this. And everyone is carrying a map of Toronto. We're taking squadrons of dragons into different districts to see what Lucifer's response to our presence will be. Ah, here comes Kimberly now." David smiled. Behind Kimberly were twenty of the cutest little reptiles ever seen in Anandria. Some walked, while others fluttered little wings and flew in her wake. About six inches long, they were a ferocious bunch ready to fight.

Laura couldn't help giggling at the sight of the tiny dragons. "Are you sure the forget-me-not will return them to their full size, Kimberly?"

"Absolutely," Kimberly answered. "With Elfare's help, I collected more plants than we needed. We can send dragons back and forth constantly as long as magic exists on Earth. Kathryn's dragon, Daisy, kindly offered to volunteer to be the first dragon to test the potion. One drop was all it took on her tongue to have her shrinking. I had advised her to drink before the experiment so she could pee and immediately regain her stature. It all worked beautifully! I had dragons lining up after that, ready for an adventure in another dimension. They are bloodthirsty creatures, and all are eager to pit their fighting skills against their distant cousins."

Laura nodded and turned her attention to David and Morrigan. "Be safe. Remember we are just testing the waters tonight. Do not do anything foolish."

"Gee, Mom, you sure know how to take all the fun out," David groused good-naturedly.

Morrigan elbowed him in the ribs. "Do not worry, Laura. I will be in this dimension making sure my husband – your son – complies."

"There you go sounding like a Borg again, Morrigan," David teased as he walked away. He knew Morrigan got his reference. She was an avid *Star Trek* fan.

Vaaron leaned down to whisper in Laura's ear. "They will be fine, love. Now, make room on that tiny couch for me. I will prop my sword on the arm in case we get any unexpected visitors from either dimension!"

39

"Strike while the iron is hot," Gary murmured.

"Iron? What iron be ye talking about?" Dience demanded. Dience snuggled back in the plush leather seats. Earthlings knew a thing or two about comfort, and he was loath to leave this newest haven called a car.

Gary's eyes sliced sideways. "It's an old Earth saying." He gestured towards the silent house. "We saw the troops come out, we witnessed the unbelievable growth of those lizards into dragons, and for five hours we've seen nothing else. I say we try a strike now."

"I did not see Vaaron come through the doors. He will be with Laura."

"Maybe, maybe not. If you stay out of sight, I can think fast on my feet if need be."

"So I can stay here?" Dience enthused patting the car's seat.

Gary's lip curled with distaste. No wonder Lucifer had praised his performance if this is what he had had to deal with over the centuries — and it had been centuries. Dience had provided background info over the last couple of hours to help curb boredom. It was interesting to discover that the famous book, and movie, *Destiny Calls*, wasn't fiction at all. "Yes, stay here. If I'm successful, think about what we'll do with Laura. Where to take her? How to secure her for Lucifer? Obviously, we can't count on a gargoyle to help. The dumb beasts are terrified of her. I'm counting on you to come up with a holding cell if I'm successful." God, he could see Dience's chest swell with pride. The pitiful demon was starving for approval – it was obvious even for someone who had only taken Psych 101.

Dience smiled, revealing pointy teeth. "I know exactly where to hold her." He patted the seat again. "And this beauty can take us there – no dragons or gargoyles needed."

"Fine, fine," Gary murmured. He opened the door and stepped out. Whether Dience had a place to put Laura, or not, he'd make sure she faced Lucifer. It was unfrigginbelievable how the world had suddenly altered, and he would be a survivor no matter who he had to sacrifice.

The door to the house proved to be no problem; it was unlocked and unguarded. He walked right in. A swift search of the main floor revealed nothing unusual. Gary couldn't believe the disappointment he felt at the mundane look of the place – *I mean, dragons and warriors had come out of here!*

Next he eyed the stairs. There had to be something supernatural up there...

He tiptoed up the stairs and tried peeking into the area at the top before he was fully revealed to whomever, or whatever, might be up there.

He heard voices.

He froze.

"Laura, stop worrying so."

Holy crap! Laura was alive! He hadn't seen her in forty years – and he had looked for her. Every time he had approached Mandy, as Laura's friend and fellow artist, Mandy had insisted they meet outside the house to talk, and then she had evaded talking about Laura by saying Laura was in a witness protection program. It had never made sense, and had bugged him – until Lucifer had shown up in Toronto – on dragons! There was more to this story, so here he was discovering the *more to this story.*

"I can't help worrying, Vaaron. People I love are out there dealing with Lucifer while I sit here hiding. Think about what he might do to them to get to me. And they've been gone five hours! They should be back by now."

Gary heard a door crash open. He jumped and felt a moment of panic until he realized it had come from beyond the top of the stairs. A new voice boomed, "Vaaron, come quickly. A dragon from Moyen has landed, and 'twill not surrender its note addressed to you. Even Audrey was ignored!"

Vaaron sighed. "The beast must have passed by our dragon carrying Paul and Michael. I had best see what the beast has brought from Moyen. It must be important if it will not deliver its missive to anyone but me. Stay here by the portal, love, in case our warriors return. I will be but a moment." Gary heard the smack of a quick kiss. "I think you are safe for the few minutes 'twill take to retrieve the note."

"Hurry back, Vaaron."

Gary's mind whirled. It was happening. Opportunity was knocking! He had to seize the moment. He heard the men leave and Laura sigh. *Okay, I have to be smooth. I have to be her old friend.*

Depending upon years of undercover work, Gary pasted a delighted smile on his face and took the final steps up into the second floor apartment. His smile almost faltered when he saw the oval opening suspended in mid-air, but it widened when he saw Laura sitting on a loveseat in a medieval bedchamber looking down at her lap where her fingers idly played with the stretchy hem of her yoga top. His step wavered for a moment when he noticed a wicked broadsword propped on the loveseat's arm. Well, Laura had no reason to reach for it – after all, he was an old friend – at least, she thought so.

``Laura! Oh My God! How many years has it been?"

Laura glanced up. Her eyes widened and she came to her feet. "Gary!"

He extended his arms, but came up hard against an invisible barrier. "Ouch! Damn! That hurt," he cried shaking a sore wrist.

Automatically Laura stretched her hand through the portal. "Heal thyself."

Gary gasped when a white glow engulfed the hand that rested on his forearm and spread over his body eliminating the minor pain he felt from the collision with the invisible wall. Not only did the pain disappear, but he felt energized and extremely alert. For one stunned moment he gaped at her before giving himself a mental shake. He had to make a move.

He grabbed her hand as she began to pull away and yanked hard enough that she lost her balance and tipped forward through the portal.

"Gary! No! I have to go back," Laura cried.

"Not tonight, Laura. Sorry." He scooped her up in his arms and began descending the stairs to the main floor. It was tough going, because she wasn't passive; she struggled, hit, bit, and screeched like a woman possessed. But his hold was solid. The front door to the house banged open. Gary steeled himself for more trouble, but it was only Dience.

The demon's eyes lit up. "I heard her coming." He nodded his head. "She be a hellcat to control."

"Then help me, you idiot. Can't you see I have my hands full?"

Dience chuckled and slid a set of handcuffs from the pouch hanging at his waist. "I snatched these from the chief of police. They be not conjured, so Laura will not escape me this time."

"You mean escape us..." Gary emphasized as Dience grabbed one of her flailing arms and snapped a cuff on her wrist.

"Of course," Dience groused as he made a small leap into the air to nab her other arm. He chuckled with delight as the other cuff clicked shut. Laura shrieked even louder and thrashed harder in Gary's arms.

Gary dropped her.

Laura hit the carpeted floor and struggled to roll onto her knees as she gasped for breath. She tipped her head up, her eyes snapped with fury as they stopped on Gary. "You have no idea what you have done."

The vehemence behind her words, and the betrayal Gary saw in her eyes, made him want to step back from the promise of retribution he sensed. Flustered, Gary snapped at Dience, "We have to get moving. Vaaron will be back anytime now."

Dience only smiled wider. "Relax. The portal be closed. Vaaron cannot reach us. Laura does not possess dark magic that will keep her portal open indefinitely like our Master. We be at risk only from warriors and dragons already through the portal."

Gary glanced out a window. "Then let's get as far away from this house as we can. They won't stay away forever!"

"Aye!" Dience agreed as he calmly reached into his waist pouch and drew out a handful of sand.

"What the hell...?" Gary watched, speechless, as Dience let the sand fall in a line on the carpet, while he chanted a few words as his fingers moved over the sand. Magically, the sand morphed into a delicate chain.

"She be a runner and a fighter. Hold her still." Dience picked up the chain and looped one end around an ankle he had grabbed. As the end of the chain completed the loop, it magically melted together sealing the loop about Laura's ankle. There wasn't much length left, but Dience managed to secure her other leg in his hand and wrap it in the chain, too.

Laura was hobbled – unable to move her feet. She couldn't step, or shuffle – and probably not even hop. Nevertheless, she struggled mightily when Gary took her shoulders and Dience her feet. They heaved her off the ground and out to the waiting car parked down the street. She screamed until her throat became hoarse, but the street was deserted, and a lack of lights in all the homes gave her little hope. She was back on Earth, and Vaaron was in Anandria. *Separated again!*

40

Audrey peered over Vaaron's arm, trying to read the missive from Moyen. They were walking quickly back to Laura. "Read it out loud," Audrey insisted.

"Raonull and Kathryn are in Moyen. They found a portal in England that took them up through the Moon Table. And there are other portals connected to the Moon Table – one of which opens onto the property my wife's family has owned for generations, where they go to relax away from the city." Vaaron gasped. "Mandy is with Lucifer, and Lucifer has changed Jeff into a gargoyle. The portal Lucifer is using is just down the lake from Laura's family cottage."

Vaaron crumpled the note in his fist and broke into a run taking the stairs to their bedchamber two at a time. He shouldered the door open. "Laura, the grandkids are..." Vaaron stopped dead in his tracks. His heart thumped as he surveyed the empty room. "Laura!" he bellowed.

Audrey, puffing behind him said, "Why be ye bellowing for Laura?"

"She is not here."

"What be ye talking about? She has to be here. Where else would the lass be? Ye were not gone that long for her to disappear."

"She is not here!" Vaaron emphasized as panic seized his chest making it difficult to breathe. "Audrey, assemble the staff. Search the castle from attic to dungeons. I want everyone to report back to me within the next five minutes."

Audrey swung about and hustled down the stairs to the bell at the base of the rail. Three sharp rings had servants running into the hall. 'Twas a signal they all knew. Usually 'twas used when the castle was in danger of attack. "Laura be missing – within the last few minutes. Vaaron says, search the castle and report back here as quickly as possible."

Vaaron waited at the top of the stairs as the staff scattered. Laura had to be somewhere in the castle. She could not have gone far in the time he had retrieved the note from the dragon. He glanced back into their bedchamber. The portal was closed. It was simply a painting of her old apartment on Earth. Vaaron's stomach roiled. *If she has gone through and left me again, can I survive?*

At the base of the stairs, servants were returning. Each person gave a negative shake of their head. Vaaron began to descend the stairs. His step became more determined. *Aye, he would survive.* He glanced at the note clutched in his fist. *This time there was another portal.*

"Audrey, I will need food for a trip to Moyen tomorrow night. Tis too late to start tonight. Notify me if Laura should somehow have escaped our notice and shows herself before I leave."

"And where be ye going, Vaaron?" Audrey asked.

"I have to talk to General Trymian."

Audrey nodded. "May I make a suggestion?" She did not wait for his reply. "Take Daisy and Rusty with you, along with some of Kimberly's vials. I imagine Kathryn and Raonull will be insisting upon participating – as will Diana and Manus. Tis my guess that the portals in Moyen cannot accommodate dragons any more than the portal here can."

Vaaron paused and swung back going nose-to-nose with Audrey. "Thank you, Audrey. You have a clear head in a crisis, and I value your counsel."

"Harrumph! I just want your wee wife home again," Audrey sniffed.

"Me too!" Vaaron gave Audrey a smacking kiss on her cheek and left her gawking at his backside.

41

It hadn't taken long for Anandrian warriors to arrive! Lucifer
ground his teeth in frustration. They were on dragons, too! How
the hell had they accomplished that feat? Laura couldn't create a
portal that large, unless she had been painting it for a very long
time. She needed intricate detail to open one of her portals —
she didn't have his advantage of centuries of experience with
dark magic.

It was strange, though. Every time his horde encountered
Anandrian warriors, the warriors veered away from his dragons —
they did not engage in battle. That, at least, allowed his dragons to
complete their trips north to collect the rest of his gargoyle horde.
He had left behind only a few gargoyles in the Lair to watch the
'home fires' while he was here on Earth.

As for the strange behaviour of his enemies, he took an educated guess that they were scouting out the situation. He would do
the same in their shoes.

One more trip north would complete his complement of gargoyles, but first he wanted to check in with Gary Russell and put
his private investigating skills to use. He might as well use the man
to find out how the Anandrians were coming through to Earth
with dragons in tow.

Lucifer brought Hades down on one of the terraces of his penthouse. "Wait here. I won't be long." He slipped off the dragon and went through the sliding doors. Amanda was back and she had bags and packages spread all over the living room.

"Ooh, Lucifer! Sit down. Let me show you what I got tonight." Mandy pulled a red sequined dress out of a box. "I thought the red was a bit devilish – perfect for a night out with you, my love. Of course you can only truly appreciate it on my body. So sit down, and I'll just be a minute putting it on."

"Very nice," Lucifer muttered brushing her aside. "I will see it later. There is still a lot for me to accomplish this evening. Where is Gary?"

Mandy stuck her bottom lip out in a practiced pout – she'd been working on it in every dressing room she had stepped into tonight – that was a lot of practice. The old concierge had directed them to many exclusive clothing shops, and Jeff had either ripped their doors off, or smashed in their display windows. "Who cares where Gary is. You've got me. And you've ignored me all night long. Don't you think it's Amanda time, Lucifer? Huh?" Her lip went out a little further. Her fingers toyed with the buttons on her blouse. She swayed across the floor to the open doors leading to the terrace. "Hades, go get the rest of the gargoyles from up north. Lucifer is busy with me right now. He'll be free when you get back."

The old dragon snorted and lifted off before Lucifer could countermand her order. He stalked over to her and grabbed the hair at the back of her head. "Just what the hell do you think you're doing? I don't have time for..."

Mandy threaded her fingers through his hair and yanked him down. Her lips left a bright red smear across his. He opened his mouth to protest, and she thrust her tongue down his throat, her body grinding hard against his length. She untangled one hand from his hair and let it slide down his body – lower than was decent, but sure to 'grab' his attention. She heard Lucifer groan, and she smiled against his mouth. "You're ride's gone, hon – now I'm volunteering..."

Hell, he was beguiled. *Outwitted by a woman determined to have her way.* As he kissed her, he glanced over her shoulder. Jeff stood nearby watching, and if Lucifer wasn't mistaken, the gargoyle looked like he wanted to kill him. *Hmm... Interesting...* Perhaps, by making Jeff Amanda's possession, Jeff felt misplaced affection for *his* concubine. Lucifer stooped and lifted Mandy over his shoulder. She squealed with excitement. "Jeff, is Gary here?"

"No, Master."

"Where is he?"

"I don't know."

"Dience!"

"Master, Dience went with Gary."

"Why?"

"I don't know."

Lucifer began carrying Mandy up the stairs to the bedroom, and Jeff fell in behind. "Stay down here, Jeff!"

"But Amanda is going up there."

Lucifer reached the top step and turned around – Mandy giggled as she hung upside down over his shoulder. "When Amanda is with me, you will find other ways to employ yourself." He gestured at the bags littering the living room floor. "Put all of that away."

Jeff grinned, and his long, mucous coated tongue swiped over his lips. "Then I'll see you in a moment."

"Why?" Lucifer demanded.

"The closet where I'll hang these is in your room."

Lucifer stopped dead in his tracks. "Forget the bags. I want you to find Gary and Dience. Understood?"

Jeff cocked his head. "Understood... Master."

Lucifer smashed open the bedroom door. There had definitely been insolence in Jeff's reply. After he was done with Amanda, he would deal with Jeff. But now... He flipped Amanda off his shoulder and he heard her giggle as she hit the mattress. His anger deepened. He had wanted to do so many other things tonight – and *she* had stopped him.

"My, how forceful you are tonight, Lucifer," she crooned as she ran her hands down his chest.

Lucifer grabbed her hands. Rage built, and his heart pounded as he looked down at Amanda. *How the hell have I ended up in bed with her?* Nothing had gone right tonight. How had the Anandrians come through with their dragons? Where were his spies when he needed them? Why was there that underlying sense of insolence in Jeff? *And how have I lost control of this evening so fast?* His dragon had left without him. *Unacceptable.*

Lucifer ran a critical eye over Amanda as she lay panting beneath him. There was no denying the effect her allure had upon him – *and right now it pissed him off.* She dictated his actions too much. That had to stop *now.* He transferred both of her hands into one of his and reached for a scarf draped about her neck. It slid off easily and he wound it tightly about her wrists before securing it to the headboard of the bed.

"Ooh, Lucifer! Such a bad boy," Mandy crooned.

Lucifer smirked down at her. "Just figuring that out, my dear?" His hand cracked across her cheek before he jerked up her skirt. Her cry of pain drew an ugly smile from him. He would use her to still the hot blood raging through his body – *but that was all.* There would be no tender loving – no playfulness... He freed himself. His smirk grew.

Mandy's tear filled eyes widened, and she gasped in pain as he thrust into her. "Lucifer!" Her body wasn't ready for this rough treatment. "Lucifer, stop! What are you doing?"

He gave no reply, but Lucifer noted his sense of satisfaction bloomed the more she panicked. He grunted as he pounded into her. It didn't take long before he stiffened and shuddered with release. Then without a word, he rolled off her and straightened his clothes as he left the room.

"Lucifer!" Her breath caught when he didn't stop.

Good, her panic is escalating. He heard her increase her efforts to escape her bonds. For the first time since he had mingled her blood with his, he felt a measure of control. *Now where the hell is Dience and Gary?* He needed information, and he needed it fast.

Jeff looked up at the second floor as he emerged from the bedroom. He was sitting on the couch idly flipping through TV channels that rarely worked. Lucifer felt his irritation grow. *The damn gargoyle is supposed to be locating Dience and Gary.* "What the hell are you doing? I asked you to look for my two spies." He continued down the stairs as he glared at Jeff.

Jeff shrugged. "I looked. They were nowhere in the building."

"Did you send others out to locate them?"

Jeff shook his head and continued to flip through channels. "No, you just told *me* to look for them. I looked. They aren't here." Lucifer ground his teeth. Jeff was extremely intelligent. Jeff knew what he was doing. Jeff's insolence was intolerable. *Jeff has to be acting this way on purpose.*

Above, Lucifer heard Amanda screeching demands for release in between sobs. *Damn, she's hard to ignore.* He still desired her – and that realization made his anger escalate. Especially when he knew that if he released her, she would wind him around her little finger, and stall his plans for the rest of the night. He couldn't afford that right now. His attempt to take Toronto was in jeopardy!

Lucifer turned at the bottom of the stairs. He sent a contemplative look up to the bedroom door. Amanda had to stay put while he went to war. "Jeff!"

Jeff slid his yellow eyes sideways. That was all the acknowledgement he gave to Lucifer.

Lucifer's blood began to boil. "Jeff, listen well. You are Amanda's loyal servant. But I am giving you direct orders you must obey over any that Amanda will issue." Jeff blinked, but didn't say anything. "You will safeguard your mistress. That is your priority. I will bespell the door so that she may not exit the room. Once I have left tonight, you may enter and release her bonds. It will be your responsibility to make sure she is well fed and no one else enters the room. Understood?"

Jeff looked at him fully. "I will see to Mandy's welfare. I will protect her and prevent others from entering her room."

"Good. Finally some co-operation." Lucifer stepped out onto the terrace. A large dragon was soaring down Bloor Street towards him. He stepped onto the rail of the terrace and launched himself onto the passing dragon's back.

The last Jeff saw of Lucifer, he was disappearing around another high-rise. Jeff turned his attention to the screams and sobs coming from the upstairs bedroom. The Master was gone. He would tend to Mandy. When he reached her door, he saw Mandy's body thrashing and heaving on the bed. Tears streamed down her bruised face, and her wrists looked like they had been rubbed raw.

"Jeff!" Mandy sobbed. "Help me!"

Jeff walked across the open expanse of the massive room and silently began to work on the knots.

"I don't know why he did this. It wasn't like other times when we played and teased. He was cold, angry, and brutal. He raped me! That was *not* making love." Mandy rubbed her freed wrists then wiped the tears from her cheeks. Her brown eyes looked into Jeff's yellow gaze. "I don't know what I did to deserve such callous treatment. I'm leaving!"

She swung her legs off the bed and was startled by how sore and shaky she felt. Damn! If he thought he could treat her that way... Mandy crashed into an invisible barrier. It felt like the portal that Laura had created – the one that always refused her entrance to Anandria.

Jeff laid a taloned hand on her shoulder. "Lucifer has left me to see to your needs and provide protection."

"Protect me? From what? Him?"

Jeff smirked. "I think it's Lucifer who needs protection from you, Mandy." He ran a talon down her arm. "Lucifer has little control around you, and it infuriates him." Jeff walked past Mandy and out the door. "I will bring you food."

Mandy stepped forward in his wake intending to follow, but there it was again, there was that damn invisible wall she couldn't go through. Her eyes narrowed. "If he thinks I'll take him back into my bed, Lucifer has another think coming."

Feeling impotent in the luxurious bedroom, Mandy strode to the bathroom. She needed a shower. She needed to scrub all traces of Lucifer from her body. She'd be damned if she'd reek of that jerk anymore. She fingered her cheek. She needed an icepack...

42

Dience clenched his teeth. Laura was tied down in the back with seatbelts. Between the belts and the chains he had wrapped around her, there was no way she was escaping. However, her screams, sobs, curses, and now her hiccups, were giving him a headache. No matter what dimension he captured her in, the bitch always grated on his nerves. The only time she had shut up was when she had asked Gary about his duplicity. Gary had smirked as he had told her how he had befriended her to keep tabs on her for Lucifer. *That* had shut her up for at least five minutes.

"Are you sure you know where we're going?" Gary asked for the tenth time.

"Absolutely." Dience did not hesitate. He could feel the pull of the standing stones – just as Lucifer had promised. Currently, they followed a dirt road. Moonlight glinted on water far below. "Over the next hill, there be a driveway on yer left. Pull in. From there, I will carry Laura down the hill and we can paddle to the portal."

"What? We can't drive there?" Gary slammed on the brakes when the promised driveway suddenly appeared, and he wheeled in.

"No road," Dience confirmed.

Gary hit the brakes again. He'd nearly hit a car and motorcycle parked in the small parking lot hidden by trees. "Who else is here?"

Dience unbuckled his belt and leaned over his seat to look into the back of the car. Laura glared up at him. "They be owned by Mandy and Jeff. No one else be present." Dience pulled a bandana off his neck, grabbed Laura's chin as she tried to avoid his touch, and stuffed it in her mouth – sound carried at night. He got her out of the car and slung her over his shoulder. Ten minutes later, they were down the hill. Dience pointed up the lake. "The portal be beyond that bend in the lake."

Gary eyed the canoe on the end of the dock. He shook his head. "I'm not getting in that. Laura's struggles would have us dumped in the water. There's a rowboat on the neighbour's dock. It won't tip."

Dience sighed. "Perhaps ye be right. Laura would like nothing more than to dip her ankle restraints in the water and dissolve them." So they pushed through dense brush along the shoreline, and Dience heard Laura's muffled squeals every time a tree or sharp branch connected with her body. Sweet music to his ears! When he finally lowered Laura into the rowboat, regret washed over him that her torment was over – for now.

Gary pushed off and settled the oars into the locks.

"I be the rower," Dience declared.

Gary took a few strokes ignoring Dience. The boat glided easily through the still water. "I've got it."

"Nay," Dience said, and pushed him off the seat. The boat rocked ominously. "I will not feel safe until she be locked away." Dience grabbed the bobbing oars and pulled. His enhanced demon strength made the bow of the boat pop out of the water. A sizable wake was left behind. "I only be interested in getting the job done quickly, since Laura has been my downfall more than once."

Gary pulled himself off the bottom of the boat. If looks could kill, the little demon would have expired immediately. "It's no wonder Lucifer barely tolerates you. Subtlety is not your strong point." Gary placed one foot on Laura's stomach to stop her struggles. He looked up and his mouth dropped open. They were already rounding the bend in the lake and impressive standing stones up high on the side of a hill gleamed under the moon's rays. "Holy shit!"

"Aye!" Dience agreed as he directed the boat towards shore. It crunched against rocks, and Gary flinched at the grating sound. However, he quickly jumped out and secured the boat to a nearby tree. Dience deftly slung Laura back over his shoulder, and they began the long climb up to the portal. It really was no accident when Laura's head smashed into a rock and she lost consciousness.

As they crested the top, Gary had to admire the stamina of the demon. Dience wasn't winded at all. Amazing, considering Dience had carried Laura without any help.

"Stay here!" Dience ordered as he stepped to the edge of the standing stones.

"Like hell," Gary declared and stepped up next to Dience. He sucked in a breath when power surged around his body flapping his clothes and lifting his hair. *What the hell?*

Dience stepped forward past the standing stones. Gary watched the demon walk onto the top step of a massive staircase that wound down a wall into a gigantic hole. As soon as Dience cleared a few steps, Gary advanced to follow. His foot hovered over the top step. He transferred his weight forward, but his foot hit an invisible barrier. "Dience!"

Dience glanced up and grinned from ear to ear. "Ye be not of Anandria. Ye cannot enter the portal." Dience ran the rest of the way down the stairs. *What a coup! I have Laura all to meself. I need not share success with Gary.*

Dience hit the bottom of the stairs and bolted down a passageway. He had thought long and hard about this during the car ride up here. He had the perfect cell in mind to hold Laura. There would be no escape. There could be no quick rescue. He chortled with delight. *Perfect! Absolutely!*

He turned left into a small vertical hollow — it was too small to be considered a cave — and pushed Laura unceremoniously into it. She hit the wall hard, and Dience grinned. *She will feel that later.* He kept one hand on her chest holding her senseless body upright against the rock.

Dience immediately hooked a foot around a boulder that lay off to the side and dragged it in front of the opening. Chanting quickly, he began melting the boulder to the edges of the hollow. He hooked another one with his other foot and dragged it over. Good, now he could work without having to hold Laura in place. Quickly he snagged other loose boulders and piled them on top of the ones forming the base in front of Laura. He was just tall enough to see Laura over the top as he worked, and he was grati fied to see horror in her eyes when she finally came to and realized she was being entombed in the small space. Muffled cries accompanied her struggles.

Dience rolled another boulder over so that he could stand on it and gradually lift other smaller rocks into higher places effectively sealing the hollow up. After an hour's labour, he stopped to admire his talents. 'Twas a wall that could not be dissolved with water as he had not changed the structure of the metals in the rocks, but the dark magic, infused in the wall, would make it virtually impossible to destroy. All that remained was a small slot – big enough to insert a dinner plate and keep her breathing. Damn, 'twas great watching Laura panic.

He scrambled off the boulder and hurried to a nearby section of the Lair where a fresh water supply bubbled up from deep beneath the desert. Dishes were stacked next to the spring. He grabbed a plate and dipped it into the water. Carefully, he balanced it as he took it back to Laura's cell. There was a slight lip which kept most of the liquid on it. Dience hesitated before he dipped his hand into his pocket and pulled out the key for Laura's handcuffs. He added it to the water on the plate.

The hole in the wall was a little high for him, so he pushed the plate onto the boulder that he had stood upon to finish sealing up the hollow. Then he climbed onto the rock, picked up the plate, and slid it through the slit he had left in the wall. "Here's a little present from me to you," he crooned as he flipped the plate and sent the water – and the key – flying. He pulled the plate back and watched.

Laura desperately grabbed for the key and managed to snag the cord attached to it. Within seconds, she had the cuffs undone. The conjured metal of the chain about her ankles sizzled and gave way to the water to become sand once again. Her hands lifted to her mouth, and she pulled the disgusting scarf out before she slammed her body against the wall Dience had created. Unfortunately, her effort was useless. It was *rock solid*. Unable to admit defeat, Laura thrust an arm through the slot. Her fingers curled into Dience's tunic. "Let me out, demon."

Dience only smiled. She could do him no harm "Nay, my lady. Ye be truly caught. When Lucifer arrives in his domain, he can take his time to plan a fitting demise for you. Perhaps, he will simply shove lit kindling through this hole I have conveniently left." Dience pried her fingers off his tunic. "Think about that while ye stew in there..."

43

Douglas couldn't sleep. Raonull, Kathryn, Ella, Diana, Manus, and the two new warriors, Paul and Michael, had gone through the Moon Table with a small swarm of bees. It had been an eerie sight to see everyone slip through the swirling silver mass. He wished he was with them, but he was still sore and a bit shaky. Thank God for Diana's moonglow. She had let a bit flow through his healing body tonight, but despite its relaxing effects, he still couldn't sleep.

Douglas propped himself on a chair outside the Lunar Temple next to Debra. According to her, her bees would fly back home from Lucifer's new Lair. Douglas eyed the older woman. She had the patience of a saint as she awaited word from her bees.

Inside the temple, a troupe of priests hovered over the Moon Table. Swords were hidden within the folds of their robes. They were the backup team. Should any of the *away team* get into trouble – it helped to think in *Star Trek* terms, since this was so freaking insane – they would help, Douglas thought.

In fact, priests were stationed throughout the in between space between portals forming a long line. Kathryn would stand guard on the Earth side of the portal, Ella would fly the bees down the lake and show them where Lucifer had his portal, and Diana, Manus, and Raonull would scout the immediate area surrounding the cottage. Douglas wasn't sure what Paul and Michael were doing, but if trouble raised its head, the impressive duo would be on hand. They had almost beaten Diana on the practice pitch after they had arrived in Moyen, until Manus had stepped in to join her. Then it was no contest... For the first time, Paul and Michael had conceded defeat, bowing down in deference to the powerful moon beings.

Douglas sighed. He wished he was part of the away team. Their plan seemed solid. If trouble arose, Raonull would let out a whistle. Kathryn, in turn, would relay the message that they needed help, to the priests in the in between place, who would then notify those still in Anandria. It seemed like a slick plan.

Douglas frowned and stared at his fidgeting fingers. They were tapping an erratic rhythm on the arm of his chair. His nerves were on edge. Ella was flying to Lucifer's portal. He wasn't happy about that, but he'd had to concede that Ella was an essential player. Even Ella's assurances that she would fly through the woods, and not down the centre of the lake, had failed to ease his dread. He sighed, and fidgeted even more. At least Kathryn was stationed in a relatively safe location.

"Druid, tis the role you are fated to play," said an unexpected voice. Douglas looked up. An exotic woman cradled a massive book in her arms.

"Aisling! Tis glad I am to see ye," Debra gushed. "Be ye bringing the lad a wee look into the future?" Debra leaned over and murmured to Douglas, "Aisling, here, be a powerful prophet. She helps Kathryn with her gift of Sight."

"A prophet?" Douglas muttered.

"Aye! I see things," the woman agreed. "Now, whether one believes what I say, is up to the individual." Aisling stood in front of his chair. "Are you willing to listen to me?"

Douglas blew out a breath. "Why not? Anything's possible, it seems." Aisling bent forward and placed the oversized book on Douglas's lap. His first thought was, *Are all books in Anandria huge and cumbersome?* His hands closed over the edges of the book, and he felt a surge of energy run up his arms. His clothes puffed out, lifting off his skin as energy swept by, his face prickled, and all his hair stood on end.

Aisling nodded. "Aye, you are a true sorcerer. The book only releases its energy to one who can wield it. 'Twas my father's, and no one, since his passing, has met the book's requirements." She waggled her fingers at Douglas. "Open it."

Douglas lifted the cover and scanned the first page. His brow rose in inquiry as he perused the ancient language inside. "The book might like me, but I can't do anything with it. Not a clue what it says." He continued to flip pages.

"Patience," Aisling cautioned. "Keep speaking."

"This is useless. You may as well take it back..." Words froze in his throat. Letters floated across the open page. Freaked out, he resisted an urge to push it off his lap. "What's it doing?"

"The book is learning. The more you speak, the more able it becomes at translating your words. My father used only an ancient Druid dialect. So, welcome the book. Thank it for its willingness to pass on centuries of knowledge to you."

A bit dazed, and wondering if Aisling had a screw loose, Douglas bent over the book feeling self-conscious and silly. "Welcome book. Thank you for accepting me and letting me in on your knowledge."

Letters whirled across the page.

"Tell it what problem we are dealing with," Aisling urged. She began to tap her foot when Douglas hesitated.

"Okay... Lucifer is on Earth with dragons and gargoyles. My cousin and my new Anandrian friends are trying to stop him in his tracks. We need to rein in Lucifer and Anandria's escaping magic."

Pages flipped madly. Douglas nearly fell out of his chair – there was no breeze to make the pages move. Three-quarters of the way through, the book lay still in his lap. "Sweet Mother of God," he breathed. "I can read it."

Aisling nodded. "The book wants you to begin reading there. It will help you with the situation." She patted Douglas on the shoulder. "Glad I am to have paid attention to the Sight that sent me to you. I should not have doubted, but there have been no known sorcerers in Anandria since I was a wee child. Now a word of caution... The book can guide, but tis the Druid who interprets and utilizes the knowledge revealed to him." Aisling whirled about and ran down the stairs of the Lunar Temple.

"Wow!" Douglas looked at Debra. "Is this for real?"

Debra bobbed her head. "Aye! We all witnessed the book's energy melding with ye. Tis a powerful tool in yer hand. Read it carefully while we wait for everyone to return."

Douglas lowered his eyes to the open page. No more fidgeting. He *had* to read. As he read, he thought he heard voices matching the words in the book. "Torn is the fabric. Mending must commence..."

He glanced up, and the murmurings in his head stopped. He dropped his gaze back down, and sure enough, the book was talking to him as he scanned its pages. *Amazing.*

Several hours later, he brushed at an irritating buzz near his ear. Something pinged off his face. Annoyed, he looked up and came face-to-face with a bee. The significance of the little guy's presence suddenly hit home. His spine straightened, and he directed his gaze at Debra, whose head drooped to one side, while soft snores whistled through her lips. "Debra," he called quietly – he had no desire to jolt her awake.

Debra remained comatose.

"Debra!" Douglas nearly jumped out of his skin. He looked down. The book glowed in his lap. Damn, he could feel magic. *It must have amplified my voice.* He looked over at Debra again. Hair blew off her face, her jowls jiggled, and her eyes popped open. Douglas immediately lifted the book off his lap and placed it on the ground. The wind died. "Debra, are you okay?" *Good, my voice sounds normal.* But Debra looked like a fish out of water gasping for air. "Just nod if you're all right," he added.

Debra nodded then managed to sputter, "By all the moons in the sky, be that wind and voice yer doing?"

"Yeah," Douglas confirmed. "I think the book helped me when you didn't wake the first time I called your name."

Debra eyed the book suspiciously. "It took ten years off me life," she groused. Then she grinned and said, "Tis truly amazing."

"Yeah, it is. I'm learning so much."

"So Douglas, me boy, why did ye want me?"

Douglas looked around. "He was here a moment ago..."

"Who?"

"A bee. He was hovering in front of my eyes."

Debra came to her feet. "Scared him, ye did, I be thinking. Ah, there he is."

A bee buzzed over and landed on her shoulder. She listened intently, then murmured, "They found Lucifer's portal...They went through and found an underground city... They found an exit... Sand all around... Bees have remained, except this one, who came back through our portal to me...The rest are flying from Lucifer's Lair, to Moyen... No idea the length of time..." Debra paused. The bee hopped on her shoulder emitting erratic buzzing noises. Debra grinned. "Everyone is fine. They be coming home." Debra glanced up at the horizon. "Tis almost daybreak. Good timing. If they be any longer, Diana and Manus would need a place to sleep on Earth."

"You got all that from the bee?" Douglas peered at the bug, but he only saw a regular bee.

"Aye, my beauties tell me many things."

"Wow!" Douglas pushed to his feet. He swayed for a moment, and his face screwed up with disgust. "Useless," he muttered as one hand rose to finger the remains of a lump on his forehead.

"Not according to Aisling," Debra snapped. "Be thankful for yer blessings. If ye be not here, Aisling would not have been able to bequeath her father's sorcerer book to ye." Debra tilted her head. "I be thinking, ye have a significant role to play. Patience, sorcerer. Patience."

Douglas sighed, and carefully bent over to retrieve the book. Slowly he stood up with the book in his hand. The world stayed in place this time. "Come on Debra, let's go greet everyone when they come through the portal."

Thud!

Both Douglas and Debra looked up at the nearby rooftop.

Thud! Thud!

Three dragons had arrived. Two were empty, but the man getting off the third dragon was in a hurry. "Tis Vaaron!" Debra cried recognizing Diana's father. "What be he doing here?"

The door to the temple crashed open behind them, and Kathryn rushed out of the Lunar Temple. "Debra what do the bees say?" She pulled up short when she saw her grandfather pelting down the stairs from the dragon's landing area. "Grandpa?" Her eyes touched on the dragons on the rooftop. "And Daisy and Rusty?"

Diana and Manus appeared behind Kathryn. "So what did Debra say...?" Diana stopped, stunned to see her father. "Dad?"

Vaaron looked like hell. He passed Kathryn and grabbed Diana's forearms. His knuckles whitened as he said, "Your mother is gone."

"Gone?" Diana breathed. "How can she be gone?"

"I left our room to retrieve the missive you sent from Moyen explaining why Raonull and Kathryn were here." His grip tightened, and Diana winced. "When I returned, your mother was missing, and the portal was closed. I am here to use the new portal. I need to go to Earth."

Kathryn placed a hand on one of Vaaron's. "Grandpa, let go, or Mom won't be in any shape to help you."

Vaaron glanced down and pulled his hands off Diana. "Bloody hell! Sorry," he muttered. "Our warriors went through Laura's portal with the dragons, and I thought she would be safe while I retrieved your note."

Diana inclined her head. "Yeah, we know about Lucifer in Toronto and the warriors of Veresah going through Mom's portal, since Paul and Michael arrived just before dawn yesterday."

Raonull, with his arm about Ella, pushed through the door of the Lunar Temple laughing at something Paul and Michael were saying behind him. "Hey, did we find out what the bees are saying?" He stopped dead in his tracks. "Grandpa, what are you doing here? Where's Grandma?" His eyes flickered up. "What's Rusty doing here? And Daisy?"

Manus put an arm around Vaaron's shoulder. "Let us move into the apartment and sit while we exchange information. We will have exactly one hour to figure out what is happening before the rising sun knocks me, and Diana, out for the day."

Vaaron nodded dumbly and let Manus pull him into the apartment. Diana followed them as Kathryn linked arms with Douglas and tugged, dragging him along. Raonull, still clutching Ella to his side, fell in behind. Naturally, Debra — with Paul and Michael — brought up the rear to join the family.

An hour later, Diana and Manus tumbled into bed. They'd go through the portal tonight, taking their dragons with them. That was the only plan they had so far. Perhaps sleep would clarify their strategy by the time the moon rose again. Perhaps the bees, which had gone through Lucifer's portal and were right now making their way back to the City of Moyen, would help crystallize that plan. Perhaps...

The last of the moon disappeared and pink rays of sunlight lit the morning sky. Diana and Manus relaxed as their breathing deepened and sleep stole their last conscious thoughts.

Down the hall, Vaaron was dead to the world. His daughter, Diana, had touched him as he had entered the guest room, infusing him with moonglow so that he might be refreshed for tonight's mission. Ella, Kathryn, and Raonull had gone to their respective beds, and Paul and Michael had put their heads together for a few minutes before they finally left for the barracks.

But Douglas pored over the sorcerer's book. He was wide awake and felt strangely refreshed. Energy hummed off the book and seeped into his body. And whenever he reached the end of a page, it would flip over without a touch from him! Oh, the things he was learning...

44

⚜

Laura tried to tamp down her panic. Barely able to move in the tomb of solid rock Dience had sealed her in she bent her knees and felt her bum scrape down the wall behind her. At least she could look through the slit in the rock. *Still nothing to see.* It was dark, and she shivered in the damp underground air. She slid an arm through the slit and called forth a ball of light on her fingertips. *At least my magic still works.* The light lasted seconds before it extinguished, but it was enough to see that a large boulder rested slightly beneath the slit – the one Dience had stood upon. Again, she made a fist to make light. She tipped her hand over and let the light seep into the boulder.

A spark of delight shivered through her when the light was absorbed by the boulder. In fact, it spread down the tunnel and seeped into the walls of her prison. *Better.*

She pulled her arm in and looked at her hands. In the soft glow she examined the damage she had inflicted upon herself. Her nails were destroyed, and her fingers were raw and bleeding. At first, she had tried using the key from the handcuffs to widen the slot, but it only left a few white marks behind. Now, it lay twisted on the floor of her prison. She had spent hours searching for cracks with her fingers, and then digging them into the slightest fissure.

She sifted from foot to foot. She wanted desperately to sit down, but there wasn't room. She looked down. Was there was a piece of loose stone – a pebble – anything that could be used as a tool on the opening in the rock? If it was hard enough, she might be able to bash away parts of the entombing wall. A hysterical giggle bubbled up. What was she thinking? Even if there was a rock, she couldn't bend over to pick it up.

Damn! No way out – unless Dience came to release her. With a sigh of despair, Laura whispered, "Heal thyself." A brilliant white glow surrounded her abused hands leaving behind unmarred flesh. She tipped her head back against the wall. The headache she had had from the bash on her head was gone, but she felt a tear creep down her cheek. Despair rolled through her. Even her magic failed to energize her. *How could this have happened to me?*

She jerked when her head nodded and bumped against the wall in front of her. God, she needed sleep. Her eyes ached, her throat hurt from screaming, and because of being forced to stand, her leg muscles screamed from being in a perpetual state of tension. She desperately needed to lie down.

Her head tipped forward again to rest against the wall. She closed her eyes. Even if her legs gave out, there was nowhere for her body to fall. She let her leg muscles relax and felt her knees start to bend – they ran into rock and would go no further.

She jerked.

Something was hitting her face! *How annoying.* Her eyelids cracked, and she was startled by the low glow of her magical light. Time had passed. *I must have slept.* "Ow!" *What the...?* Something hit her face, again! Her knees straighten, and she called up more magic to brighten her prison. She tipped her head forward and peered out the slit. She heard a low hum. "Ow!" That hit had stung! *OMG! Bees!*

Laura?

Vaaron? You can talk to me?

Bloody hell, yes, love. I heard your bees comment. Where are you? Why are you so scared?

Gary, my photographer friend, showed up at the house and pulled me through the portal. Turns out he works for Lucifer — always has. He's an informant. And he's working with Dience. They cuffed me. I'm not sure exactly where I am, but I'm close to the cottage. Dience carried me up the old rock pile on the lake, but he knocked me out. I have no clue where I am now. Wherever it is, Dience has entombed me in solid rock. I can't get out. I can't sit or lie down. I can't move. He left a small slot — I guess it's for air. He has to keep me alive. Hey! Why are we talking? Why didn't we talk before this?

I went back to the portal in our room. It was closed. You were gone. I did not think it possible to communicate with you. I did not reach out to you, or listen for your thoughts. All I thought about was how I had lost you again. I forgot about Anandrian magic being on Earth.

Laura nodded and regretted moving when her forehead scraped against rock. She winced. *I guess, when I was pulled through to Earth, and saw my portal close, I didn't think I could talk to you, either. I wasn't listening, or trying to broadcast to you. I'm an idiot.*

That makes two of us, love.

So why did you hear me thinking about bees?

I was drowsy with sleep, and I suppose as I drowsed, my thoughts stopped churning about the new portal I will attempt to come through tonight, thus my mind was open and I could hear you...

A new portal? How? I haven't made any other portals.

Tis an ancient portal. Opening on the hill above your cottage. I planned to come through and head to Toronto to rescue you.

The cottage!

Aye! The grandkids found it when they went to England, entered a portal that brought them to Moyen, then discovered other portals leading to the various continents on Earth lying under the Moon Table.

Really? Hope welled in that one word.

Aye, love. And the wee bee bashing into your face is one of Debra's bees. We are waiting for them to report back to us so we know where Lucifer's latest Lair is. And since there is a bee trying to talk to you, you must be in Lucifer's new Lair, somewhere in Anandria. Hopefully, they will return to Moyen before nightfall. We will be coming through the portal with our dragons tonight.

The portal is that big?

Nay, Kimberly's potion will shrink the beasts down. Tis why I await the night, so 'twill be safe for the beasts.

Tears glazed Laura's eyes. She shoved both arms through the slot and was able rest some of her weight on her arms. A hysterical laugh of relief chortled up her throat. "All right, bees, get out of here. Everyone in Moyen is waiting for you to lead them here. I need help, and I need it before Lucifer arrives..."

45

Dience breathed a sigh of relief. After spending several hours clinging to Gary's stiff back under the hot sun, he was glad to arrive at the condo. He knew Gary was peeved that he couldn't go through the portal to see what had been done with Laura.

Dience swung his leg over the back of the motorcycle and stretched. Instead of returning to Toronto in the comfortable car, Gary had decided to commandeer Jeff's motorcycle that had been left with the key in the ignition. He had argued that they would have an easier time entering the city on it.

Dience eyed the bike. He had to concede it had worked well. They had cut across fields, the closer they got to the city, avoiding human patrols, since more of Earth's military had converged on Toronto in the last few hours.

Dience stiffly hobbled to the elevator ignoring Hades, who had opened one eye when the bike had roared in. However when the beast saw Dience, he had snorted and closed his eye again.

The elevator whisked them up to the penthouse. Its doors opened to reveal Lucifer standing, with a snarl on his face, and his arms crossed over his broad chest. He was not happy. "Master!" Dience stepped out and fell to his knees. "Master, I have great news."

Lucifer glared over Dience's prone body at Gary. "What the hell is he talking about?"

Gary smiled. It was painfully obvious how terrified Dience was of Lucifer. He stepped around the prostrate demon. "Lucifer, I have secured Laura for you."

"Nay, Master! Tis I who secured her. Tis I who took her through your portal and entombed her in stone."

"What?" Lucifer's eyes sliced toward Dience. "You have entombed her? Is she alive?"

"She be breathing when I left her," Dience stated in a bolder voice.

Lucifer pushed Gary aside and stepped up to Dience. "Exactly where have you put Laura?"

"She be in the Lair, Master, walled into a shallow hollow. I left a slit so air might reach her, and gargoyles could feed her."

"Did you instruct the gargoyles to feed her?"

Dience scuffed one foot across the hardwood flooring. "Nay, Master."

"Idiot!" Lucifer ran a hand through his long hair and turned back to Gary. "You did nothing to ensure Laura's safety?"

Gary shrugged. "I couldn't follow Dience – wherever the hell he took her. I had no idea what he had done to her until he told you about her just now. But I was the one who snatched her through *her* portal. I left it up to Dience to secure her until you could deal with her."

Lucifer blew out an agitated breath. Plans had to change – again.

He looked up at the second level of the condo. After he had left Amanda, he had ridden his dragon, driving people into the Rogers Centre stadium, much like a cowboy herding cattle – the dragons would eat well. Then, he had taken one last flight over the city, greeting the last of his arriving gargoyle horde and directing them, and their mounts, to the stadium. *A most satisfying night.*

But, his good mood had flown south when he had returned to his condo at dawn. Gary and Dience had not shown up, and Jeff had smirked when he had climbed the stairs to Amanda's room where she had flatly refused to entertain him in their chambers. She had glared at him while cupping her bruised cheek. *Damn, he'd really smacked her.* A momentary twinge of conscience had pricked him, but he'd shrugged it off, and had tried to compel her to do his bidding. Much to his disgust, she had been immune to his compulsion. *Damn blood magic.* She had even glared at him and said, "It'll be a cold day in hell before I let you back in my bed."

Too tired and annoyed to force her, again, he had reasoned that if he let her have her way, she might think it was an apology. She'd eventually come around. She couldn't keep her hands off him. He was irresistible. *And so is she.*

But, Jeff had smirked at him again as he had come down the stairs. *Damn gargoyle seems to have no fear or respect for me, the Master.*

Lucifer stalked past Gary and fell onto the opposite end of the couch from Jeff. Things had to be done on Earth if he wanted to keep the momentum going. Toronto was his. It had fallen without a whimper – *within forty-eight hours.* Earth technology had left its citizens without protection. Its conquest had been, well, boring. Whereas centuries ago, the inhabitants of a more primitive Earth, had had a strong belief in magic, and had given him a decent fight. Now, with the arrival of Anandrians and their dragons, the fight to expand beyond Toronto had suddenly become interesting.

He sighed. The timing of Laura's capture couldn't be worse. He was torn. Which first? Subjugate Earth? Or take care of Laura? If he neglected Laura, she could die, because his damn gargoyles might not feed her. She'd be reincarnated – again.

Laura first, he decided.

Lucifer ignored Jeff when the gargoyle left the other end of the couch and climbed the stairs to the second level.

"Mandy?" Jeff's rough voice rasped as he entered the bedchamber.

Mandy, face-down on the bed with her face pushed into a pillow muttered, "What?"

Jeff sat on the edge of the bed. He stretched out a taloned hand and gently pulled strands of her hair through his mishapened fingers. "They have Laura."

Mandy lifted her head. "Huh?"

"Lucifer has Laura."

Mandy groaned and pushed her face back into the pillow. She shifted until she could peer at Jeff out of one eye. "Why tell me? I'm stuck here." She groaned. "And I don't feel well. I'm nauseous."

Jeff's talon tapped her shoulder. "You don't have to be stuck here."

Mandy slowly rolled over. "I'm about to puke. Why the cruel tease?"

"I'm not teasing. Lucifer made me yours to command – your servant. By his very decree, I can only do what is best for you. Lucifer's not best for you. He cannot command me."

"Oh God!" Mandy rolled off the bed and dashed for the bathroom to heave up the contents of her stomach. Her eyes were closed as she hovered over the toilet bowl and gasped for breath. She was alone – and so unloved. What had happened to Lucifer? He'd adored her. What had she done to deserve such harsh treatment?

A hand wrapped in a damp cloth, cupped her forehead. She opened her eyes and slowly straightened up as Jeff gently wiped her sweaty brow. She met his yellow eyes in the mirror over the sink. "What I wouldn't have given to have you be so attentive to me when you were human, Jeff."

The cloth slid down the side of her face as Jeff watched their reflections in the mirror. "I've always been your friend, Mandy."

She turned in his arms. "I wanted more than friendship," she stated bluntly.

For a moment they stared at each other, until Mandy broke eye contact and turned away as she asked, "What do you mean I don't have to stay here?"

Jeff held up a credit card. "I can get you out without Lucifer knowing."

Mandy's brow rose. "A credit card? What the hell's that for? It's useless in Toronto. And I don't want to go shopping. I want to leave, but Lucifer has bespelled the door." Jeff grinned, and Mandy shuddered at the sight of his mucous coated tongue. Suddenly, she wished he was his old good looking self. It had been fun ordering his gargoyle self about – a petty kind of revenge for the times he had ignored her – but now, she wanted her old buddy back, despite his lack of romantic interest.

Hell, she wanted Laura, too. She wanted to confide in her best friend – a friend she had callously betrayed. She had to be honest. Yes, she resented Laura, her good looks, her fabulous husband, her magical powers, and her perfect children. But... Laura hadn't lorded it over Mandy when she had landed Vaaron, a hunk of a husband – or for that matter, all the boys she had attracted over the years. And now, Lucifer had Laura captured again!

For a moment, an undeniable pull of lust at the thought of Lucifer overcame Mandy – but it was squashed as another wave of nausea forced her over the toilet. Again, Jeff held her head until she was finished, and could splash cold water over her flushed face. God, she felt awful.

Her nose scrunched up with distaste. One minute she lusted after Lucifer, and the next she was repulsed by his actions. *He is a beast in the shape of an angelic man!* She shook her head. Lucifer's appeal was gone, ripped away when he had raped and battered her. And...

Is Jeff sniffing my neck?

Jeff growled low in his throat. "You're breeding, Mandy."

"I beg your pardon?"

Jeff nodded. "Women smell sweeter to gargoyles when they're pregnant. Don't ask me how I know. It's a built in feature for gargoyles." He smiled. "Gargoyles find pregnant women repugnant." The corner of his mouth tipped up. "But I serve you nonetheless."

He steered her out of the bathroom. "The odour has only developed since you were with Lucifer last night."

Her hands came to rest over her protruding belly – it had always been slightly rounded all her adult life. "I can't be carrying his child. It's only been a few hours since I was with him. It's too soon for anyone to know."

Jeff tapped his nose. "I know. There is no disputing the evidence."

Mandy's brow rose. "I won't believe it until I have irrefutable evidence."

Jeff nodded. He held up the credit card. "We'll get out of here, and on the way to your house, we'll pick up a pregnancy kit at a drug store."

"The credit card's for a pregnancy test?"

Jeff clicked his tongue – a very repulsive looking act. His long tongue left sticky mucous streams hanging off his lips which he promptly licked away. "The card is our key out of here. We don't need it to buy the kit. We'll smash a window and grab a test kit when we pass a drug store."

"Oh... I still don't understand what the card is for."

He grabbed her hand and pulled her into the closet. "The chief of police told me about a passageway Lucifer has in this closet and showed me how to open the doors." Jeff ran the card along the bottom of the wall at the back of the closet until they heard a click. "That does it." He hooked a talon under the door and pulled.

"Wow!" Mandy looked down the narrow staircase. She stepped forward fully expecting to hit Lucifer's force field, but there was nothing there.

Free!

She glanced back. Did she really want to leave Lucifer? She sucked in an angry breath. *Yes! I'm too good for him... But he made me into a gorgeous woman... He desires me... He used me! He brutalized me! And, now he wants me to welcome him into bed with open arms as if nothing has happened. I don't think so.*

She stepped onto the first step.

She had always wondered why women stayed with abusive men who begged forgiveness as they climbed back under the covers. *Well damn, I get it now.* She longed for sweet loving Lucifer. Even now, she was trying to rationalize the rape he had committed on her last night. *Nope! It's time to leave. And yes, he's dangerous – the most dangerous man in the universe.* He would probably kill her if he got his hands on her after she left. *Hell, he is going to kill Laura!*

Her feet picked up speed propelling her down the steps. It was time to admit to herself that *she* had been malicious. When Lucifer had given her a fabulous body, *she* had dumped Laura to fraternize with the enemy.

Mandy watched Jeff slide the credit card down a vertical slit in the wall at the bottom of the steps. A door slid open and sunshine spilled in blinding her. It was hard to admit, that Laura had had her own share of tragedy. The girl had lost her family – first her parents, then her husband, and finally, her children. Mandy had offered Laura sympathy, but really, she had reveled in the fact that Laura's life had sucked, too. *What kind of friend does that?* Mandy stifled a sob as she ran down the street behind Jeff. She had to make things right between them. She frowned at Jeff's backside. He had a blanket thrown over his head. "Jeff?"

Jeff paused, waiting for her to move up beside him. "What?"

"Why the blanket, and where are you taking me?"

Jeff pointed up. "The sun dries my skin." Then he pointed down the street. "We're going home."

"Is that wise? Won't Lucifer look for me there?"

"Maybe," he said grabbing her elbow and urging her on. "But the Anandrians are there taking shelter inside the house. They will help to protect you. But I think, even though Lucifer obsesses over you, he obsesses more over Laura. He will go for Laura before coming to find you."

"Shit!" Mandy muttered.

"Exactly!" Jeff agreed as he stopped while Mandy threw up on the curb.

46

◈

Mandy climbed the steps to her home. Jeff tagged along behind. Without hesitation she opened the door and pushed inside. Immediately she heard little claws scrabble across the floor, and her eyes caught tiny shadows scurrying into other rooms. The man on the couch cracked an eye open and jackknifed up as he reached for his sword leaning against the arm of the couch.

"David!" Mandy snapped. "Put that down, and come give your Aunt Mandy a hug."

David gaped at the woman with the gargoyle in tow. This was Aunt Mandy? This voluptuous woman with the long black hair was Aunt Mandy? *No way!*

The kitchen door banged open, and Morrigan backed into the room saying, "I thought we could use a snack before we turn in when Elfare comes to relieve you. I cannot believe that Laura has left us stranded. Good thing we have plenty of potion so the dragons could take shelter..."

David cleared his throat. "Ah, Morrigan, we have company."

Morrigan whirled about almost losing the contents of her tray. As it was, milk spilled over tall glasses that slid precariously.

"I see you found the chocolate chip cookies I had in the freezer," Mandy quipped, as she folded her arms over her chest and raised her chin in the air.

Morrigan placed the tray on the coffee table. She rested one hand on the hilt of her dagger tucked in at her waistband. Her gaze went past Mandy to the gargoyle. "You are new," she said to him. "I do not know you."

Jeff tipped his head as he rasped, "Oh, but you know me very well, Morrigan. I have had the pleasure of sparring with you on many occasions."

Morrigan narrowed her eyes as the gargoyle whipped past 'Aunt Mandy' and lashed out with his foot effectively disarming her with a move only one man had developed and mastered. "Jeff?" Morrigan gasped. The gargoyle grinned. "Bloody hell, tis you!"

Morrigan peered hard at the woman. "Damn, tis Mandy, too."

"What?" David said stupidly.

"Tis Aunt Mandy. Look into her eyes, David. *See* the woman. She has been *altered*."

Mandy nodded. "Lucifer tried to change me into a gargoyle, but our blood accidently mixed and this happened." She ran her hands down her body, preening for them. "Lucifer can't keep his hands off me." She gestured towards Jeff. "Lucifer also gave me my own personal servant."

David bit his lower lip and glared at the stunning woman. Jesus Christ, it *was* Aunt Mandy! Kathryn's vision had come true. Lucifer's magic had touched her despite their precautions. "Why are you here, Aunt Mandy? Why did Lucifer let you leave?"

Mandy touched fingers to a fading bruise on her cheek. Her brows lowered as she hissed, "I left him! He doesn't deserve me."

Mandy nodded at Jeff. "He got me away from Lucifer." She smiled at David. "I knew Anandrian warriors had come to town. Had to be via Laura's portal – although, I can't figure out how the dragons got through." Mandy frowned. "And Laura's been captured."

"What? Back up, Aunt Mandy. Mom's been captured? How? Where is she?"

Jeff's raspy voice cut in. "Gary and Dience snatched Laura through her own portal. They took her north to Lucifer's portal, and Dience entombed her within some rock." Jeff shrugged at their gasp of horror. "Don't worry, Dience left her an air hole."

"Who got entombed?" Elfare said as he entered the room.

"Mom!" David cried, horrified by Jeff's announcement.

Elfare froze when he glanced at Jeff. "What is a gargoyle doing here? And who is that woman?"

Mandy laughed. Sitting on Elfare's shoulder was a tiny dragon. The shadows scurrying away when she had entered house must have been other little dragons. "I'm really beginning to like magic. Who came up with the idea to shrink the beasts?"

"No one you would know," David murmured. He stepped closer to Mandy. "Why are you here, Aunt Mandy? I can insinuate, from what you said, that you and Lucifer have been intimate. Won't he come looking for you?"

Mandy pulled David into a hug. "Of course he'll come looking for me – but probably after he deals with Laura." She tipped her head to whisper into his ear, "But I've had it with him. He mistreated me. I'll have nothing to do with him. I'll not be a punching bag for an egotistical immortal. So, I've come home. I knew warriors here could protect me, as well as family. Family can forgive me... I hope." She shook her head. "I'm still trying to wrap my head around what I have done. It's like a fog lifted when Lucifer struck me. I can see him for the sadistic bastard he is – and I realize what a vindictive, selfish bitch I've been..." Mandy covered her mouth, pushed David away, and made a mad dash for the washroom.

"Hormones," Jeff rasped into the heavy silence following her exit. "She's breeding."

Morrigan cut a sharp look at Jeff. "Breeding? Then why did Lucifer abuse her?"

Jeff let loose a raspy chuckle. "Amanda, as he calls her, is Lucifer's temptation. Mandy distracts, which ultimately thwarts his plans when he succumbs to her charms. Last night, Mandy ordered his dragon away before he'd finished his mission. Lucifer couldn't resist her charms, and resented her for his weakness. I believe, that's why he snapped and lashed out at her. Her allure is his Achilles' heel – a threat to his goals. The man is pulled in two directions, by two desires."

Morrigan walked around Jeff. "Why did you help Mandy leave? I *know* the compulsion to serve the Master. I was a gargoyle. In other words, why did Lucifer let *you* leave?"

"I'm not Lucifer's gargoyle. Lucifer gave me to Mandy to serve and protect. The moment he abused Mandy, it became imperative for me to protect her." Jeff shrugged. "I brought her here to friends and family."

"Then you fight with us?" Morrigan asked.

"I fight to protect Mandy. She will not fall into Lucifer's hands again while I still live."

"Good! Now about her breeding..." Morrigan began.

"There is no doubt," Jeff said. "She smells!"

"Since when?" Morrigan insisted.

"Since she was with Lucifer last night."

"So Lucifer has no knowledge of this?" Morrigan flipped her hand towards the bathroom where everyone heard Mandy puking.

Jeff grinned, and Morrigan could swear his yellow eyes gleamed with amused pleasure as he said, "Lucifer has no clue."

"Excellent! I want no word of this leaking out. Lucifer must not know." Morrigan patted Jeff's arm. "You can bunk in the basement. All other floors are occupied to the max. Besides, sunlight won't blister your hide down there."

Jeff glared at Morrigan. "I stay with Mandy in her bedroom."

Elfare stepped between Jeff and Morrigan. "I just left Mandy's bed, and had assumed David and Morrigan would occupy it next. Others are sleeping on the floor. We have a full house."

Jeff turned to David. "You and Morrigan, find another place to sleep. I'll stay with Mandy – *in her bed.*"

Mandy staggered out of the bathroom looking pale and shaky. Jeff hustled to her side and drew her down the hall to her bedroom.

Elfare scrambled after them muttering, "I better follow in case someone awakens and sees a gargoyle in the room."

Morrigan turned to face David. "Well, this is unexpected!"

"Yeah," David agreed. Worry creased his brow. "I wish Dad was here to bounce ideas off him. Do we split forces – one to stay in Toronto, and one to fly north? Do we all go for Mom and leave Toronto to deal with whatever Lucifer has planned for tonight?" David expelled a worried breath. "Why the hell was Mom alone at the portal? Where was Dad?"

Morrigan grabbed David's hand and they tumbled onto the couch. "There will be no answers, until we rescue your mother." She leaned her head against her husband's shoulder. "If she is killed, nothing will stop Lucifer." Morrigan smiled. "Therefore, the decision is made. Let us sleep. We fetch Laura."

David arched an eyebrow. "I'm commander-in-chief. I make the final decisions."

Morrigan smiled slyly at him. "But I am the War Goddess. I *let* you think you are in charge. Ultimately, your decision will match mine, so do not fret – listen to your wife." She snuggled into his embrace. Her acute hearing picked up heated words coming from Mandy's bedroom. Elfare was having difficulties. She finally lifted her head when Elfare came back down the hall. "Is everything all right?"

Elfare grunted. "Nearly had a battle break out when I woke the crew in Mandy's room and they saw the gargoyle. But those drills we keep running paid off. They snapped to attention when I bellowed at them." He grinned. "But I nearly lost control when Mandy objected to Jeff climbing into bed with her. Jeff bluntly told her he would let no other sleep in her bed, and since no vacant spots existed in the room, she had better shut up and let him protect her if she didn't want him to hand her back to Lucifer."

Elfare ran a hand down his face. "When I left, I swear Mandy was looking pleased when Jeff pulled the comforter over them."

Morrigan stood up drawing David with her. "Come on, lover. I'm tired and I want some sleep. Time for Elfare to take the watch."

"Where do you suggest we go? Aunt Mandy and Jeff have the bed, now."

"We take the basement. I remember where the camping gear is, and I'm sure we can sleep on an air mattress."

David shuddered.

"Do not worry, hon. If there are spiders, I will kill them for you."

David eyed his petite wife. "You really have no understanding how your son, Raonull, and I, feel about those creepy eight-legged freaks, do you?"

She giggled and pulled him down the basement stairs. "I really think you have nothing to worry about tonight. Most of the dragons are down here and they have been snacking on them..."

Elfare smiled as the pair disappeared. *Spiders.* Who knew two of their fiercest male warriors could be brought to their knees by spiders? Truly, a secret he would not tell their troops!

47

Paul tapped Debra's shoulder halting her before she entered her apartment. "Michael and I would have a word with ye."

"Aye," Michael muttered leading them down the front steps of the temple to a small patio where a circle of four chairs waited. Douglas was already settled there with his new book. "Douglas," Michael said in greeting as he lowered himself into the chair next to him.

"What be ye wanting?" Debra asked curiously.

"Yer bees," Paul said succinctly.

"Me bees? Why me bees?"

Michael held up a small vial of purple liquid.

Paul continued. "Everyone waits for night before venturing through the portal with the dragons. But we have an idea which would give us an advantage."

Michael nodded. Douglas smiled. It was obvious Michael was not one for words and left the talking to Paul.

"And how would me bees give us an advantage?"

Michael raised the vial and Paul said, "We have some of Kimberly's potion. We shrink down and ride yer bees through the portal and into Lucifer's Lair. No dragons needed! Then we can eliminate the gargoyles he has left behind, and the troops arriving at sunset will find no resistance – until Lucifer comes. And, we think Lucifer will come, despite his success in Toronto. Laura be too valuable. He must deal with her."

Debra slowly nodded. "Aye, I see where ye be going. Let me call me bees and see if they be amenable to carting ye great brutes on their backs." Debra tightened her lips, and blew until she emitted a low buzz. Instantly bees appeared. "Hello, me beauties." Her hand flicked towards Paul and Michael. "These two want to shrink down in size. They be looking for a ride through the portal and then through Lucifer's portal. Be ye willing?"

Debra sat quietly. Two bees separated from the rest, one going to Paul, the other to Michael. They landed on the arms of their chairs. "Ye have yer answer gentlemen. They be willing."

Paul grinned. "Excellent! The book is lying on the floor next to the Moon Table. I think the two of us can heft it onto the table and slide it in place before we shrink down."

Douglas remained silent, but he followed them into the temple clutching his sorcerer's book and watched as the golden book sank through the Moon Table. Next, both men took turns touching their pinky fingers to the open vial, and tipping it. Carefully, Paul corked the vial. Douglas felt his stomach clench when they sucked the potion off their fingers. *Damn, it worked.* Paul and Michael shrank until they were mere specks. Unfortunately, that was all that shrank. Clothing and weapons lay on the ground – full size.

Debra laughed. "Me bees want to know how they will fight gargoyles naked."

"Douglas?"

Douglas looked behind him. His mouth gaped open at the sight of a very rumpled and sleepy Kathryn. "Kath? What are you doing up?" She had left an hour ago, as had all the others. Only Paul and Michael had stayed up, their heads close together, hatching their questionable plot.

"Douglas, use the book," Kathryn said through a yawn. She gestured at the sorcerer's book tucked under his arm. "Open it. Tell it what you want." She yawned again, rose on bare toes, and pecked his cheek with a kiss, before turning about to stumble back to her bed.

"Well," Debra breathed. "She be getting as good as Aisling at using the Sight. Now, hurry Douglas. Open yer book."

Aware of Kathryn's receding footsteps, Douglas snapped open the book. "Paul and Michael need clothes and weapons reduced to a more appropriate size."

Debra gasped when little sparks of light rose off the page, swirled through the air, and landed softly on the pile of clothing and weapons. All items began shrinking. When the spell was complete, Douglas had to squat to see two little specks scurrying about on the floor. He blinked when two bees landed and the specs climbed on board. Pride washed through him. The bees took off and began to sink through the swirling silver table top. He'd done it!

"Well, I never!" Debra declared.

Her words brought Douglas out his self-congratulatory stupor. He snapped the book shut and pelted after Kathryn, hoping to catch up with her. "Hey!" he yelled before she could step into the apartment.

Behind him Debra sputtered, "But there be more in the book. Ye must turn the page..."

He ignored Debra.

Kathryn paused and gave him a disgruntled look. Her eyes ached with fatigue, and no matter how attracted she was to Douglas, she needed sleep. "What?"

Whoa, sheer annoyance in her voice. Drat! Not the response he had hoped for. "I just wanted to say thanks. Here..." He reached out and unlatched the apartment door. "Let me walk you to your room." He snagged her hand. She didn't protest, so he stepped forward and closed the door behind them with a whispered chant.

Kathryn's brow rose. "Impressive. How'd you do that?"

Douglas nodded at the book tucked under his other elbow. "It's a primer for sorcerers. It teaches me how to *be* a sorcerer." They arrived at Kathryn's bedroom. "Well, goodnight." Douglas reached for the latch behind him on the opposite wall. "I think I'll try for some shut-eye, too."

"Wait!" Kathryn snapped.

"Huh?"

"Don't go in there."

"Why not? Where else should I sleep? The guest room is housing Vaaron, now. Diana said I could share Raonull's bed."

Kathryn frowned. "Ella thought you'd be up reading like you've been doing the last couple of days."

Douglas shook his head. "I feel a lot stronger, and I want to join you when you go through the portal tonight. So, I should sleep."

"Are you sure you don't want to continue studying? We might need something from the book."

Douglas's eyes narrowed. "Why don't you want me to go into Raonull's room, Kath?" His fingers lifted the latch.

Kathryn dove across the hall and grabbed his hand. "Why don't we go for a stroll? I haven't seen much of the sun, and I think a little vitamin D would help."

Douglas ignored the pressure of her hand as it tried to pull him away from the door. Determined, he opened it to find Ella curled up against Raonull's back, spooning him. One wing drooped over the side of the bed to rest on the floor, while the other was draped over Raonull's body covering him from neck to knees. A blanket ran under her wings covering Ella's body from sight. "What the...?"

Ella turned her head and cracked an eyelid. "Buzz off, Douglas," she mumbled sleepily.

Douglas stepped into the room. "Ow!" He covered his face with both hands. His sorcerer book dropped to the floor, and his nose bled profusely.

Kathryn smiled. Ella was using that force field power she had used to protect Raonull when the oak tree had exploded.

"Get out," Ella hissed as Raonull snored on. "You'll wake him. Debra told me fairy dust from a fairy's wings helps with sleep – and Ray needs his sleep. He hasn't slept well since Silbury Hill. I'm trying to help him. So far it's working. If he's going into battle tonight, I want him alert so he'll be coming home. Don't blow this."

Douglas stooped and scooped up the book with one hand as he eyed his cousin. Kathryn latched on to his arm and pulled him back into the hall. "Great," he grumbled. "What am I supposed to do now?" He flicked his fingers and a hanky appeared in his hand. Carefully he began cleaning his bloody face.

"Come with me," Kathryn cooed as she opened her bedroom door. "I've got a wash basin in here where you can clean up."

Douglas followed her inside. A bowl and jug rested on a dresser. But all Douglas saw was an enormous bed with rumpled sheets.

Kathryn wrung out a washcloth and stepped up to Douglas. Ignoring the butterflies bashing about in her stomach, she went up on tiptoes and gently wiped the cloth over the lower half of his face.

Douglas caught her wrist. His eyes bore into hers. "I'm serious, Kath. Where am I supposed to sleep today?"

Kathryn raised her other hand and transferred the cloth to it and continued wiping away blood. Her gaze remained firmly on her task. "You could sleep here."

"Pardon?" Douglas stiffened. She winced, and Douglas realized his grip on her wrist had tightened. "Sorry," he muttered, releasing her.

"I said you can sleep here, with me." She bit her bottom lip.

His eyes fell to her mouth. "You're serious, aren't you?"

"Uh huh." Kathryn dropped the cloth, walked to the bed, and slid beneath the covers. "If you need help, I could compel you..."

Douglas grinned. "That's one compulsion I don't think I'd mind." He held up his hands when her gaze pinned him. "But, I think I can manage on my own." He whipped his shirt over his head, slid his trousers off, and dove under the covers Kathryn held up wearing nothing but his boxers. His arms slipped about her and pulled her in close. "Good night," he quipped, as he snuggled his nose into her hair and took a deep breath before closing his eyes. His body went lax.

Kathryn gaped at him. Despite drawn curtains, enough sunlight filtered through the edges that she could see him clearly. Had he really just jumped into her bed and fallen asleep within seconds of his head hitting the pillow? Was she really so undesirable? "Douglas?" she whispered.

Douglas slit his eyes and noted the disappointment contorting her face. With a whoop, he pounced, claiming her lips as he rolled on top of her.

She felt a deep chuckle rumble through his chest. She pushed him away and landed a solid punch on his shoulder. "What the hell?"

He pulled her back in. "Had to be sure," he grumbled amiably.

She slid her hand between their lips. "Sure about what?"

He grinned down at her and kissed her fingers. "Were you offering me a place to sleep? Or a place to *sleep*?

"Huh?"

"Shut up, Kath." His hands roved up her back until he cupped her head. "I know a great way to relax." He rubbed his lips over hers.

Kathryn stiffened, and her eyes went wide and unseeing.

"Great! The Sight. Really? Bloody hell!"

Kathryn blinked. She was back. She was smiling.

"What does that smile mean?" he asked warily. "What did you see?"

"Us," she whispered happily. "Now show me how to *relax*, Druid."

48

⌒◯⌒

"We need to explore the Lair entirely before we pee," Michael yelled over the buzz of their bees.

Paul's brow rose. When Michael spoke, he paid attention. "It could take a long time."

Michael shook his head in disgust. "We don't walk. We get the bees to fly us around until we understand the layout."

"Oh," Paul mumbled.

Michael nodded with satisfaction. He would get his way – again.

They popped out of the portal above the cottage, and the bees sped up the lake to Lucifer's portal. Within minutes, they descended into the ring of standing stones. Two gargoyles at the bottom, shooting dice and laughing, merely waved taloned hands about their heads to brush away what they perceived to be buzzing insects. Paul ducked despite his bee's agility, and peered at Michael who grinned as they left the gargoyles far behind.

Within thirty minutes, they had pretty much covered the entire underground lair. Bees were fast! They had found two major openings large enough for dragons to enter and exit, and four smaller openings for gargoyles to sneak in and out. At each access point, two gargoyles were stationed. In mutual agreement, Paul and Michael decided to strike first at the gargoyles guarding the portal.

If the gargoyles there were gone, their troops would face no opposition when they arrived.

"Whoa!" Michael pulled his bee to a hovering stop. Two gigantic female hands were thrust through a slot in the rocks. They hung limp and still.

Paul patted the fuzzy head of his bee. "Would ye please move closer?" His bee landed on one of the hands which jerked with the tickling sensation. "Careful!" Paul yelled to his bee, or the person attached to the hands – he wasn't certain which.

Blue eyes peered out of the slot. A feminine mouth frowned just before it said, "Oh, I thought you'd be long gone. I need Debra to send the troops to rescue me."

Paul realized she was talking to the bee. She hadn't noticed him. But he recognized her! 'Twas Laura! "Laura! Hey, Laura."

Laura's frown deepened as a second bee landed on her hand next to the first. "Seriously, guys," she hissed, "you need to tell Debra I'm here and get help before Lucifer arrives."

Paul glanced over at Michael. "She cannot hear us."

Michael nodded. "We be so tiny, we be specks to her." He twisted about on his bee to look over his shoulder. "I hear the gargoyles at the portal. They be around the next corner. Let us fly there, pee, take care of the creatures, then come back to rescue the lass."

Michael had talked again! Would miracles never cease? Paul usually got one grunted word here, a two-word sentence consisting of subject and verb there, or a rude gesture from his boyhood friend. Michael was using full sentences – and he was linking them together. In fact, Michael had said more since their arrival in Veresah than Paul could ever recall. "Agreed," Paul said as he urged his bee to take flight. Laura would have to wait a few more minutes for her rescue.

Their bees landed behind a small boulder. Paul and Michael hopped off giving each bee an affectionate pat of thanks before the insects took off. In unison, the men faced the wall of the tunnel and started emptying their bladders. As the last ounce dribbled out of their bodies, they stared at each other waiting for their miraculous return to normal stature.

Nothing happened!

Paul flexed the muscles across his shoulders. His tunic ripped down the centre of his back, but he remained tiny. "Hell, I only got a wee bit bigger, and look what happened to my favourite tunic."

Michael nodded as he flexed his biceps and watched the seams in his sleeves tear apart. "Mine, too." They eyed each other with critical eyes until Michael said, "The bloody Druid's spell must have done something to interfere with Kimberly's potion. Tis the only explanation."

"Aye," Paul agreed flabbergasted by Michael's eloquence and their unusual situation. "I say we go for the gargoyles anyways. They will ne'er know what hit them. We just have to take care not to get stomped on, or squashed by a swatting hand. We must bedevil them until the others arrive."

"Aye," Michael agreed reverting back to his usual one word statements. He took off in a determined charge only to pull up swiftly. The speed of his advancement *dazzled* him.

Paul zipped up beside him. "Whoa!" he hissed. "We move like blurs. 'Twas a sight to see ye fly across the ground. 'Twas a heady experience to do the same when I raced to yer side." Michael smiled as he looked up at the seated gargoyle throwing the dice directly in front of him. Paul could practically read his mind. He knew that steely look. Michael was about to attack! Paul followed Michael's lead and pulled both dagger and sword free. He ran a skeptical eye over their weapons. They would be nothing more than pin pricks to the gargoyles – if they even felt them. He nudged Michael with his elbow. "Stab hard, and pull out quickly. Move to another area and repeat. Do not let them squash you."

Michael nodded and blurred off into action.

Paul followed.

Both went for the same gargoyle, and both aimed at its gigantic butt. Together, they plunged their weapons through its leathery hide, yanked them out and sped away. The gargoyle flinched and ran an annoyed hand over its rump. "Damn mites," it muttered.

Paul and Michael grinned with delight. "Take the other one," Paul hissed. "Keep striking with your weapons and changing locations." Michael was gone in a flash. Paul selected an area on his gargoyle's thigh and sped off to do as much damage as he could with his teensy weapons.

Within seconds, both gargoyles were slapping at their butts and legs. They rose to their feet, one grumbling about fierce no-see-ums. Paul crossed paths with Michael. They both still moved with incredible speed. It was obvious Michael was having the time of his life as he jammed both his dagger and sword into the ankle of his gargoyle then sprinted away. The gargoyle reached down to slap his ankle. Paul sighed. It was like watching a beautiful dance. Michael manoeuvred in and out, hitting his target with ease. Now it was time he added his own moves back into the mix. *What fun!* Gargoyles stomped and hopped from foot to foot. He and Michael were forced to weave from beneath massive taloned feet time after time.

A raspy voice up above growled, "I am leaving. The portal be damned. I will face Lucifer's wrath rather than these invisible pests."

"Agreed," the other gargoyle gasped as he grabbed his spear leaning against the wall and took off after his comrade who was already a hundred feet down a tunnel.

With chests heaving, Paul and Michael grinned at each other. There were minor cuts and scrapes on their bodies – some from talons that had nicked them, and some from crashing into rocky walls when they had not stopped fast enough. "Fantastic fun! Do we go after them?" Paul gasped.

"Nay, we wait."

Paul nodded. "If they come back, we will do more of the same. If not, we greet our kinsmen and get Douglas to fix us."

"Aye," Michael agreed. "If they can see us..."

49

Lucifer climbed the stairs inside his condo. He had spent the day with his top gargoyles plotting his next move. Now the creatures were on their way to gather his troops. The majority would engage the Anandrian warriors and their dragons in combat, while he headed north with Dience in tow. *I can be rid of Laura within hours.*

But first, he *needed* to charm his way back into Amanda's bed. He *needed* to get her out of his system so he could fully concentrate, because no matter how engrossed he became in his plans of domination, thoughts of *her* kept intruding, stirring his blood at the most inappropriate times. His lust *needed* immediate release.

"Amanda, my love," he purred as he opened the bedroom door. He paused. *Where is she?* His gaze settled on the partially closed bathroom door. *Ah, in there.* He crossed to the rumpled bed and smoothed out the covers, folding the top sheet back in invitation. "Amanda, my dear, come let me love you."

Silence greeted his invitation.

He sat on the edge of the bed facing the bathroom door. *She's stubborn. Perhaps if I apologize...* "I know I may have been a little rough..."

He waited. *Still nothing.*

Lucifer crossed to the bathroom door and gave it a gentle push. The hinges creaked, but he heard no one moving beyond it. Impatient, he stepped boldly over the threshold. The room was large and luxurious, but it took seconds to see that no one rested in the tub, or lay upon the chaise lounge.

"Not possible," he hissed through clenched teeth. *The bitch has found a way to leave me.* She hadn't left through the bedroom door – his spell was still intact, binding her to the confines of the bedroom. *But how?*

"Jeff!" he whispered. Jeff had been nowhere to be found earlier when he had called all his top gargoyles to his war table. He had simply assumed Jeff had sequestered himself with Amanda in the bedroom. *Oh, and he had.* That bastard had found a way to get her out.

Lucifer charged back into the bedroom. His eyes roamed, searching. He stomped to the window. *Too high.* The only other access to the room was through the main door... "The closet!" He whirled about, and charged into the walk-in closet. The carpet was scuffed and, if he wasn't mistaken, he could make out a small footprint in the pile. "Argh!" He turned and charged out of the bedroom. *Where would she go?* He punched the wall. His fist went through, and his rage grew.

"Lucifer?" Gary stood below in the living room looking up at him. "What troubles you, my friend?"

Lucifer sucked in a calming breath. "Amanda has fled." He locked gazes with the private investigator. "Find her."

Gary nodded. "Was she alone?"

"Nay," Lucifer ground through his teeth. "Jeff is with her. The damned gargoyle took her out through the secret staircase."

Gary picked up a set of keys from the coffee table. "Leave it with me. They have probably fled somewhere familiar. I'll start with her home."

"Gary?"

"Yes?"

"If you bring her to me, you will be richly rewarded."

Gary grinned. "That's all I ever wanted from our association, Lucifer. Now, deal with Laura. Take Dience. He's the only one who knows where she is, since I can't pass through your portal. I'll bring Mandy here when I find her."

"Excellent!"

50

David looked up. He had had very little sleep during the day. Restless, he had given up on sleep and had sat on Mandy's front porch to contemplate their next move. There was still an hour to go until sunset. The sky was shrouded in clouds. Not much chance the sun would slip through. They could get an early start...

"David?"

He looked back at the front door. Aunt Mandy and Jeff – the new version of both – stood in the doorway. He wasn't sure what to think about them. Did he trust them? He wasn't sure. Both were products of Lucifer's magic. Logically, that meant they were Lucifer's minions. But there was something different about them. Jeff sneered whenever Lucifer was mentioned, and Aunt Mandy seemed to despise the Dark Lord. How was either situation possible?

Mandy walked over and sat down next to him on the porch swing. Jeff stood stoically beside her. "David, I want to go with you."

"Huh?"

"If I stay here, this will be the first place Lucifer will come looking for me. I have no car, no way to leave the city, and I know everyone here will head north on a rescue mission for your mother. I would be a sitting duck. If I go with you, and your troops, I'll be heading back into Lucifer's territory – but I would have protection." She glanced sideways at him.

David silently noted the way her hands cupped her belly, which seemed twice as large as it had early this morning. *She looks pregnant!* He stared down at his hands. He was ready. There would be no harm in revealing his plans, now. "Only Morrigan and I will go after Mom. The rest will engage Lucifer and his horde here in Toronto under Elfare's leadership. The carnage has to be stopped. Did you know he's herding people into the Rogers Centre so his dragons can feed?"

Mandy gasped, "I didn't know."

David surged to his feet. He didn't trust Aunt Mandy, he realized. Perhaps keeping her within sight might be prudent. Once they rescued his mom, Laura might be able to use her healing powers to get the old Aunt Mandy back. "There's great cloud coverage. As soon as I wake Morrigan and take our dragons out for a pee, we'll be leaving."

"A pee?"

David grinned at her. "Kimberly made a shrinking potion for the dragons. However, to regain their normal size they have to pee it out."

"Oh... Interesting..."

David turned to go through the front door of the house. He paused, momentarily startled by the sight of the gargoyle standing next to Mandy watching them. It was particularly disturbing that it was clothed in Jeff's shorts and a somewhat tattered T-shirt with *Canada's Wonderland* splashed across the front. Jeff certainly did make an impressive gargoyle, but David hoped his mom could fix *that* situation, too.

51

Douglas stood on the end of the dock. His mouth hung open. Daisy, Rusty, and – he wasn't sure of the names of the other dragons – were, one by one, growing to alarming sizes as they peed.

They were a small party. Vaaron was in charge of the rescue mission, since they were rescuing his wife. Then Diana, and Manus, sort of seemed to be second-in-command, depending upon which one of them you talked to. Raonull was their much needed muscle –according to Kathryn's Sight. And that left Kathryn and Ella. Both women had tagged along – he wasn't sure why, but Aisling had appeared insisting they be part of the rescue party. Vaaron had protested the girls' involvement, but Manus had assured him that Aisling's prophecies were *never* to be ignored. Douglas sighed. Hopefully, they'd be the lucky seven. Hmm... There was a movie called, *The Magnificent Seven...*

Dark water lapped at the edge of the dock as true darkness settled over cottage country. His sorcerer's book glowed under his arm just as it had when he and Kathryn had awakened an hour ago. Douglas felt guilt eat a small hole in his gut. Why hadn't he turned the page when Debra had yelled that there was more to the spell he had placed on Paul and Michael? Christ, he had been too besotted by Kathryn's retreating figure and had ignored the wise old gal. Now he prayed that the two brave warriors were safe and would remain so until he got there. Would he be able to find them? He recalled how tiny they had become – mere specks!

Vaaron waved everyone over. "We'll mount up and head directly to the portal. I want to leave the dragons on this side, with the exception of Daisy. She's small enough that if we need anyone to evacuate suddenly, she can get them to safety without trampling everyone to death. So, Kathryn, you fly right in as soon as the rest of us climb into Lucifer's Lair. We must assume Paul and Michael were ineffective, considering the fix they are in, and there might be gargoyles left on duty."

Douglas felt his face flame red.

Kathryn squeezed his hand and pulled him over to Daisy. "What's done is done. No crying over spilt milk. The die is cast..."

"Yeah, yeah, the devil is in the details. I'll remember that the next time we have to go up against Lucifer. Now, how do I ride this creature?"

Kathryn's eyes sparkled with amusement. "We're going to walk up Daisy's wing, and I'll sit at the base of her neck. You'll sit behind me and hold on to me for dear life!" She giggled as she tugged him up the wing. "Look, Raonull and Ella are already ready for takeoff." Kathryn stopped in her tracks and pointed down the lake. "Grandpa! Two dragons. Incoming!"

Diana and Manus exchanged looks. "How can Lucifer be here already? Darkness only set in a few minutes ago," Diana said.

Manus shoved his fist in the air. "'Tis David and Morrigan's dragons. Make room for their landing."

Dragons shuffled to the edge of the forest to clear a space for the approaching dragons.

Thud!

Thud!

Raonull threw his leg over his dragon's neck and slid down the beast's wing to greet his incoming parents. "Mom, Dad, what are you doing here? And how'd you get here so fast from Toronto? The sun just went down."

Vaaron walked up eyeing the passengers Morrigan and David had brought along with them. Suspicion filled his eyes. He recognized the clothes on the gargoyle, and the woman looked like a relative of Mandy's. "Who are they?"

"Hi Dad!" David glanced at the people and dragons milling about the family cottage and grinned with approval. His sister, Diana, and her husband, Manus, were there – both good to have at his back in a tight situation. "Here's the abbreviated run down, since I think we're all on the same mission and would like to get it over with before Lucifer shows up." David stood and helped Mandy walk down the dragon's wing. "This lovely lady is Aunt Mandy. She's been under Lucifer's thrall – as far as I can tell – and she's expecting his child."

"What?" Vaaron roared.

"Yeah, that was my reaction, too," David quipped as he started telling everyone the situation concerning Mandy and Jeff. David breathed deeply at the end of his twenty-second recital.

Vaaron studied Mandy intently. "Tis truly you, Mandy? How did he alter you so completely?"

Mandy fell against Vaaron and wrapped her arms about his neck. "It's me!" she wailed dramatically. "My blood mixed with Lucifer's." She stepped back and swept her hands down her curvy body. "And this is what happened." She looked up at Vaaron through her eyelashes. "Lucifer found me irresistible."

Jeff joined her. "Not irresistible enough. He harmed you."

Vaaron stared at Mandy for a few seconds before turning his attention to his son. "David, will Elfare be able to hold Lucifer in Toronto?"

Morrigan snorted, and interjected, "The Dark Lord does what he wants. If he knows Laura is here, he will come despite Elfare's best efforts."

"Tis what I thought," Vaaron muttered. "Di, you and Morrigan bring Jeff and Mandy with us. I do not want Lucifer making a stop here while we are elsewhere. Mandy needs to be well rid of him."

Diana smiled. "I'll take Jeff on my dragon. It's been a long time since I've flown with a gargoyle."

Morrigan grabbed Mandy's arm and yanked. "I will deal with her."

Diana planted a hand in the middle of Jeff's chest when he tried to follow Mandy. "You're with me, Jeff."

Five minutes later, they had landed outside the ring of standing stones. The dragons used a nearby stand of dark evergreens to help camouflage their presence. Jeff and Mandy were placed behind a boulder out of sight – no one quite trusted them, since they had been created and influenced by Lucifer. But Jeff seemed fixated on keeping Mandy safe from Lucifer so they left him watching Mandy. Ella fluttered off to keep watch down the lake and the rest, with the exception of Kathryn, made their way into the portal.

There was no sign of Lucifer's gargoyles. The portal seemed deserted. Douglas sent a puff of colourful magic up signalling for Kathryn to enter. She and Daisy dove into the portal. Daisy eloquently braked with her wings as she touched down soundlessly.

Douglas felt useless. He had no fighting experience. It was something he would rectify. Hell, even Kathryn could best him – he knew, because he had seen her in practice. He moved off to one side, while everyone else aligned themselves in a pattern that allowed no one to penetrate their ranks from any direction. "Ow!" he hissed and slapped at his ankle.

The others looked back, clearly annoyed by the noise.

"Jesus!" Douglas yelped and hopped from foot to foot, slapping at both ankles. "Bloody hell!" He froze and peered suspiciously around.

Vaaron strode back and muttered, "What the bloody hell are you doing?"

"Careful! Watch where you're stepping."

"What?" Vaaron let his gaze rove over the floor.

"I think Paul and Michael are here. Anyone see teeny specks moving about?"

"There!" Diana cried, her acute Deity of the Hunt eyesight easily picking up what the others were missing.

Douglas knelt and opened his sorcerer's book. Two specks jumped on the page. "There you are." He twirled his hand in the air over the book. "Small, to accommodate these two men, but now it is time, they've peed, you ken?"

Kathryn was leaning over his shoulder. "That's it? That's a spell?"

Douglas looked up at her, annoyed. "I've told my magic what I want it to do..."

Wind whipped through the tunnels, and the pages of the book snapped shut spitting out the specks that began to grow at an enormous rate until Paul and Michael stood grinning at everyone, their swords and daggers in hand. "About time ye found us," Paul griped. He smiled slyly. "Although, Michael and I had fun bedevilling the gargoyles stationed here at the portal. Drove them mad with our swords and daggers which were big enough to cause a nasty sting. We had exceptional speed, too. They thought we be little mites eating their flesh, and they ran away crying like babes. 'Twas a sight, I tell ye."

Michael grunted and all eyes turned to him. "Laura be that way."

Vaaron grabbed the front of Michael's tunic. "Then take us there, lad. I hear every moment of her despair in my head. Entombed in stone, unable to move, claustrophobic she has become, though she has never been so before."

"Follow me," Paul broke in with a wave and bow to everyone. "We tried talking to her, but we were so small, all she saw and heard were the bees we rode on."

Kathryn moved up next to Raonull as they moved through the tunnels. "Ray, this has to be why the Sight insisted you be here. You're going to bust Grandma out!"

Raonull grinned down at his little cousin and fisted his hands. "She'll be out in no time."

52

Lucifer stood on the terrace of his penthouse and watched the greater downtown area of Toronto fall. Dragons from both sides flew between high rises, their riders armed to the teeth. He looked over his shoulder. Inside his home, his chief gargoyle, and the former chief of police were huddled over a three dimensional map he had conjured. His chief gargoyle made sure plans were being executed correctly, while the chief of police plotted the next sector to strike — and it was working like a well-oiled machine.

He spun about and strode through the French doors into his condo. It was time to deal with Laura. They didn't need him here. Fleetingly thoughts of Amanda tugged at him. He still wanted her. *And he would have her.* Gary would secure her and bring her home. Lucifer ground his teeth. Damn, he wished he'd had a round in bed with her before he left to look after Laura.

His fists clenched. Thankfully, despite his wishes, Amanda *wasn't* here. He *needed* her too much. Which was exactly why he had lost his temper with her the other night. She alone had the power to alter his plans — all because he desired her. He sighed. Toronto would be his by tomorrow morning, and then he didn't care how much time he spent in bed with that beguiling witch.

"I'm leaving the campaign in your capable hands," Lucifer said to the two gargoyles. "I have bigger fish to fry." He chuckled. *Laura will indeed fry!* By tomorrow morning, no one would wield healing powers. His gargoyles would be his forever. Ultimate power over beings in the universe would soon be his. Everyone would bow down to him. *Well, maybe not Amanda. She'll reign at my side.* Only Amanda intrigued and delighted him. Unless he recaptured Diana... Lucifer smiled. Diana had challenged him, yet had given him the respect that was his due. She had been magnificent!

And speaking of Diana... *Where the hell is Dience?* Di had loved tormenting the little demon. It had been a source of unending amusement to see what she would cook up next. Whether it was humiliating, painful, or even tortuous, as she sliced the demon until he almost died, her ingenuity had always amazed him. "Dience!"

"Master," Dience answered as his head popped up on the other side of the sofa.

"Get your butt over here. Tis time you fetched Laura for me. Tis time we rid the universe of her righteousness." Lucifer grabbed a handful of Dience's tunic and lifted the demon over the back of the sofa as he passed by.

Dience scrambled to get his feet beneath himself, but the Master's long stride did not allow for this. He was dragged ignominiously into the elevator where he finally came to rest next to Lucifer.

Lucifer latched onto Dience again when he exited the elevator to find Hades. The beast had made himself at home, Lucifer noted. Mounds of soft grass had been dragged in and bones were all ready spread throughout Hades' newest nest. Hades lifted his head and swung it towards Lucifer. "We head back to the portal, my friend." Hades extended his wing and within minutes Lucifer was seated with Dience behind him.

The ancient dragon headed up the ramp to street level. "The battle is well under way, but it should be clear for us. My gargoyles have been instructed to draw the Anandrians away, but be sharp, Hades. You never know if those damn warriors will pull something unexpected." Hades cleared the parking ramp and beat his wings to take off. The sky above twinkled with stars. No dragons with warriors on their backs swooped past. "Step one completed," Lucifer muttered.

A dragon screech made Lucifer smile. *A death call!* A dragon further down the street was falling to the ground with a spear stuck through its throat. He watched Anandrian warriors leap off its back. One landed on an awning over a store's door, the other managed to land on a balcony and roll to his feet. Immediately some of his horde was there to engage them in hand-to-hand combat. *Nice!*

The city fell away. Roads, deserted and dark, branched away from the city. It would have been a two hour drive if he had taken his car. Flying as the crow goes, it would take about half an hour – if that long. More time than he actually wanted to spend in the presence of Dience – but it was a necessary evil. The demon knew where Laura was entombed.

53

Raonull pounded the rock wall with every ounce of force he could muster. "Don't worry Grandma, I'll get you out." Another fist joined his. Everyone felt the ground tremble with the force of the double hit. Raonull glanced about to see who had given assistance. He grinned at his grandfather.

Vaaron shook out his hand before cradling it against his chest. "Bloody hell, I think I have broken it."

Laura thrust her hands through the slit in the wall. "Give me your hand, dear. Heal thyself." A white glow surrounded their clasped hands. She was feeling hope despite her predicament. Everyone knew where she was, and they were here to help. They would get her out.

"I'm next," Raonull declared holding out bloodied knuckles.

Laura obliged, and healed his lacerated hands. Worry furrowed her brow as she contemplated the wounds her men were acquiring in their effort to free her. Earlier, Raonull had slipped his hands through the slit to pull on the wall, but that hadn't worked. And for the last five minutes, he had been pounding on the wall without making a dent. Unbelievable! Here was the lad who, at the age of twelve, had decimated a five-foot thick wall surrounding Veresah. The wall in front of Laura was no more than five inches thick. So why wasn't he able to demolish it? *What if no one can get me out except Dience?* She knew Lucifer was unable to free her. They were like matter and anti–matter to each other. If they touched, the universe would cease to exist.

Diana passed a sandwich through the slit to Laura as she said, "No more pounding. That obviously isn't working. There has to be another way to free Mom." She tipped an open bottle of water up and let the liquid run down the wall. Nothing happened. "That doesn't work. Guess water only returns *altered* metals back to their natural state. These rock walls are in their natural state. Manus, do you have any ideas?"

The High Priest shrugged. "Tis conjured. Dark magic *must* hold it together."

Raonull looked down at his hands as he flexed them. "Then why the hell did Kathryn say I had to come on this rescue mission?"

Kathryn, deep in thought, poked her bottom lip out.

"No use hacking at it with our swords if tis conjured," Paul said as he and Michael crossed blades in mock battle. Both men were extremely bored. The rescue of Laura was supposed to be an epic event, to be written down in the annals of history, and they were supposed to be the featured warriors responsible for her liberation. So far, all they had done was find her and direct others to her location.

Douglas stepped up to the wall. He had been more than happy, at first, to let Raonull hammer away at it. Having experienced Raonull's brute strength personally, Douglas had thought Laura's wall would be down in seconds. Now that everyone was standing around looking lost, he figured he'd take a shot at the wall. What could it hurt?

With the sorcerer's book tucked under one arm, Douglas stretched out his hand until his fingers touched the wall. They tingled and he jerked them back. Surreptitiously, he looked around. Everyone was in a huddle trying to come up with a solution – with the exception of Paul and Michael who were still hacking away at each other. Good! Cautiously, he extended his hand again. This time he felt a hum of power before his fingers even made contact with the wall. "Guys?" he called hesitantly. Everyone ignored him. "Hey, everyone!" All conversation ceased, and Douglas felt their eyes trained on him.

Diana gasped. "Can everyone see what I'm seeing?"

Manus and Morrigan nodded and in stereo said, "Power."

"Douglas, touch the wall," Diana commanded. "What do you feel?"

Douglas licked his lips. "It tingles."

Morrigan hissed, "Look at the book."

Douglas lifted the book away from his side and gasped, "It's shimmering."

"Open it," Kathryn urged. "Take your hand off the wall, and open the book. See what it does."

Douglas sank into a cross-legged posture and let the book fall open on his knees. "Oh, my God!" He looked up at the rest of them, his face beaming. "I can do it. I can dissolve the wall! The book doesn't like dark magic. It wants to destroy it."

"Then do so, boy," Vaaron insisted.

Douglas looked down at the book, and his brows drew together. "I need time. It's not a wave your hand and it's done kind of thing, but I *can* dissolve the binding of the rocks. We'll still have to move the loose rocks and sand out of the way once the dark magic is gone."

Raonull flexed his biceps. "I knew Grandma would need me."

"He's coming!"

Everyone looked down the tunnel. Ella, flying at top speed, and panting heavily, crashed into Raonull and wrapped her arms about his neck. Raonull stood his ground as he caught her. "Catch your breath, Ella. Here, take a sip of water."

Ella pushed the water bottle away from her lips. "He's coming. He'll be here within minutes." She pushed the water bottle away, again, as Raonull tried again to get her to take a sip. "Stop that! You don't get it. Lucifer is coming! We have fifteen minutes tops."

Paul and Michael stopped clashing their blades together and grinned with delight.

"Bloody hell," Vaaron muttered. "Lass, how many come with him?"

Ella gulped down a breath of air. "I saw him from far away. I didn't want him to see me. I could tell there's only one dragon." She grinned. "I never knew how fast I could fly, until tonight. Dragons are slow."

Vaaron nodded thoughtfully. David moved up to his side and said, "We have to protect Douglas at all costs until he has Mom free from the wall."

"My thoughts exactly," Vaaron concurred. "Paul and Michael, I want you on the Earth side of the portal. You will be our first line of defence. Diana and Morrigan, you will stay here and guard Douglas. Kathryn, I want you here with Douglas, too. Raonull, Manus, David, and I will protect the Anandrian side of the portal. Ella..."

"I'll stay with Raonull," Ella declared.

Vaaron shook his head. "You should stay here with your cousin."

Ella stomped her foot. "I will stay with Raonull. We may need a hasty retreat, and if we have to move all these boulders once Douglas dissolves the dark magic, Ray will have to be in great shape."

Vaaron's brow rose. "And how do you propose to keep Raonull in great shape?"

Ella fluttered her wings. "Where he goes, so do my wings."

Vaaron chuckled. "They are very pretty, and I'm sure they can move you about quickly, but I don't see how they can help Ray..."

Kathryn whipped out her dagger and threw it at Raonull. Ella snapped out a wing, and the dagger bounced off harmlessly.

"Jesus!" Raonull exclaimed. "What if Ella hadn't caught that, Kath?"

Kathryn's lip lifted in a lopsided grin. "Grandma's here. She would have made you all better." She turned to face Vaaron.

"Close your mouth, Grandpa. Ella has a few surprises. I'd leave her with Ray."

Vaaron's eyes sparkled with amusement. "Yes, I can see why Ray might benefit from having his own personal fairy."

Laura snapped her fingers drawing everyone's attention. "The standing stones somehow augment Lucifer's powers. They are the reason why the portal remains open even though Lucifer isn't present. I heard Dience and Gary talking about the ring of stones when they drove me north."

"Got it! Need to get to the standing stones." Raonull said as he turned and sped down the tunnel on the heels of Paul and Michael. Ella fluttered her wings and took off, too.

David and Manus each grabbed onto one of Vaaron's forearms and started pulling him towards the portal. "No more talk, Dad," David said. "Lucifer will beat us to the portal if we hang around Mom any longer."

The three men rounded a corner in the tunnel and were just in time to see Raonull leave the stairs on the wall to go out the top of the portal. Ella was flying right beside him. Manus saw worry in Vaaron's eyes as he followed their progress. "Your grandson will be fine. He is one of the finest warriors Anandria has. With the exception of David and Jeff, he has more training than most. And his extraordinary strength gives him an edge no one can equal – plus, he has a fairy!"

All three men grinned at that last statement and readied themselves for combat. David loosened his sword and dagger, checking that they slid out of their sheaths with ease, while Manus and Vaaron drew their weapons and tested the weight of them in their hands. David still preferred martial arts over weapons, but he wasn't foolish enough to go into battle without backup weapons. Whereas, Manus and Vaaron were more comfortable wielding conventional weapons, even though they were well versed in David's fighting style.

Raonull and Ella topped the rim of the portal, and Mandy poked her head out from behind her boulder. "What's happening?"

Raonull motioned for her to go back into hiding as he hissed, "Lucifer's coming, and Mom's still not free. Douglas is working on that."

Mandy ducked behind the boulder. Her heart raced, and she began to pant. Her hands moved to cup her protruding abdomen. She was even larger than before. *Is magic speeding my pregnancy on?* Her hand landed on Jeff's arm, and she squeezed digging her nails into his leathery skin. "I can't go back. I won't go back. Lucifer must never know I carry his child. Help me, Jeff."

Jeff nodded, and removed her hand from his arm. He stood and held out his hand. "Come," he commanded.

"Where?"

"Trust me."

Mandy took his hand. He pulled her to her feet and began walking away. When rocks made it difficult for her to move with her growing girth, Jeff picked her up and carried her. Soon they stood within a stand of evergreens. Mandy's eyes widened when she realized he was heading for the camouflaged dragons. "We're leaving?"

A curt nod was all she got. Jeff walked up to a dragon and said, "Lower your wing." The beast stared at him for a moment, but finally complied. "Northwest," Jeff commanded once they were mounted on its back. The dragon burst through the evergreens and took to the skies.

Mandy loved the feel of Jeff's hard body behind her. "Where are we going?"

Jeff's raspy voice whispered in her ear making her shiver. "Many times, you have told me about the small town where you were born – the place where your mother came from. It seems isolated enough."

Mandy twisted about in his arms. "We'll never make it there before sunrise. Northern British Columbia is a long way away."

Jeff smiled down at her. "True. We fly until close to dawn. As morning approaches, we'll find a barn, or another structure large enough to house our dragon. Vaaron said he used to carry a tarpaulin-type cloth before the towns and cities of Anandria had built dragon shelters. If need be, we might have to raid a Canadian Tire Store." Jeff chuckled. He could imagine the reaction of some small town hardware store owner if *he* walked into the store. "I will keep you safe Mandy, never doubt that."

Mandy sighed and laid her head against his shoulder. If anyone could do it, Jeff could. *I wonder what the people of Chetwynd will think about a single mom coming to town on a dragon with a gargoyle in tow...*

54

Lucifer narrowed his eyes. All his dragons were in Toronto. Only a skeleton crew of gargoyles guarded his new Lair. But, if he wasn't mistaken, the disappearing dot on the night's horizon was a dragon. *How is that possible? If it isn't mine that means...*

No, it was out of the question. Anandrian warriors could not have found his new Lair. Maybe what he had seen was an eagle, caught away from its nest after the sun had set. Lucifer chuckled. He was on edge, and his imagination was getting the better of him. He felt Dience squirm. Hades hated movement on his back when he was flying. "What's wrong?" Lucifer growled.

Dience looked up at the angelic-looking man sitting behind him. He pointed towards the horizon. "That looked to be a dragon, Master."

Hell, it's not my imagination. Perhaps someone from Anandria had come looking for Amanda at the cottage. But that didn't make sense either. The sun had just gone down. They would have arrived no sooner than he – unless they had chanced the cloud cover and had made a run *before* the sun had set. Lucifer grunted. That had to be it! They'd come. They'd seen. She was not there. *Unless that had been her escaping...* He fought the urge to alter course and pursue the other dragon. Damn blood magic! It had him constantly battling a raging lust for Amanda.

Focus!

"Hades, when we arrive, set us down just inside the portal."

Hades looked back in acknowledgement.

Suddenly, Hades floundered in midair. An atmospheric disturbance bounced them around. Hades squeaked – which to a normal person sounded like a ferocious scream. Lucifer and Dience barely stayed on his back. Lucifer managed to slip a hand under a glistening black scale and secure a death grip on the beast. The other hand, he twisted into Dience's tunic. "Steady," Lucifer barked as he realized what he was feeling was a great disturbance in his portal's magic. What the hell was happening? "Hades, faster!"

The old dragon fought to fly in a direct line, cutting across tracks of forest and small lakes until the ring of standing stones became visible in the distance. Lucifer sucked in a shocked breath. The ring was not complete! One stone lay toppled into the centre of the portal and another was about to join it. "Raonull," he hissed as he urged Hades downward. To Hades he yelled, "Land outside the ring."

Hades bounced in midair again when the second stone toppled into the portal. The amplification of magic, and homing properties of the ring, were diminishing with every felled stone. Raonull had to be stopped.

Lucifer's rising rage caused black clouds to coalesce overhead and blot out the moon. Sheet lightning flickered followed by ominous rumblings overhead. Below, the scene appeared as if lit by a strobe light. Streaks of lightning burst out of the clouds and rain added to the macabre picture.

Lucifer's lips formed a grotesque smile. Raonull had slipped! It had happened when he had begun loosening the third of thirteen stones. Now his feet were dangling into the portal – but his hands remained glued to the third stone.

Thud!

The ground trembled under Hades' weight – this was no stealth landing, this was war! Lucifer's smile widened. "Dience, get Laura and take her to the hearth in the dining hall. Secure her to the manacles that dangle inside the hearth. I will look after our strong friend, here, and then we will..."

Lucifer gasped as he walked down Hades wing. A warm glow rose up out of the portal and, damn, a fairy was lifting Raonull back to solid ground.

A streak of lightning arrowed down – its path directly in line with the fairy and Raonull. The lightning exploded. *Damn, it's run into fairy magic* – and the lightning's energy sprayed outward like a fireworks display. Lucifer frowned. A damn fairy was in the mix. He hadn't seen one for centuries. *They were tricky little buggers.*

55

Raonull shook his head. He had been dazed by the boom that accompanied the lightning strike. It took a minute for him to realize he was being lifted up to solid ground. "Ella? You should be with Kathryn."

She smiled sweetly as she lowered his feet to the ground. It was amazing how much weight she could support now that she understood her flying capabilities to a greater degree. "If I'd done that, you'd be toast," she replied smugly.

They both jerked and turned at the sound of metal clashing. Paul and Michael had slipped out of the brush and had engaged Lucifer and Dience the moment the pair had stepped off their dragon's wing. Their blades were a blur, their footwork amazing on the rocky ground. Raonull shouted, "Don't kill him, Mike. He's the demon Dience!"

Michael's blade faltered.

Dience lunged and sliced Michael's thigh open.

Stunned by the demon's success, Michael gripped his blade tighter and began a systematic attack on Dience. A nip here, a cut there – despite his new, pronounced limp. Michael needed the little blighter to suffer, and from the look of horror on Dience's face, he was accomplishing the job quite successfully.

Raonull looked back at Ella. "I have to finish toppling the stones. Keep watch, hon."

Ella nodded. A noise drew her attention down into the portal. Manus and David were climbing the steps to the surface. Vaaron had disappeared back down the tunnel to where Laura was entombed.

"Give you a hand, son?" David said to Raonull as he emerged through the portal and stepped onto Earth. "Looks like Michael and Paul have Lucifer and Dience engaged, so we can get to work."

"That'd be great, Dad," Raonull gritted through his teeth as he leaned against the third standing stone. It toppled easily. The rain accompanying Lucifer's lightning had helped to soften the ground. "If you and Manus both work on the next stone..." Raonull grunted as he leaned against another stone. It wobbled slightly. Raonull eased up and glared at the stone. His fingers curled into a fist and he slammed it as hard as he could. The stone gave way cracking at its base with a loud snap. It fell into the open portal. He shook his hand. Skin was missing, but it wasn't something his grandma couldn't fix. Four stones down!

A weird wind began to funnel into the portal towards Anandria. Raonull felt an urge to follow it. He realized a lot of magic was accompanying the wind. *Magic was being sucked back into Anandria!*

A dragon roar was the only warning Raonull had that Rusty was bursting out of the evergreens. *What's my dragon doing?* Rusty flew high, weaving erratically as he missed bolts of lightning.

Raonull held his breath. Rusty began to dive straight for Dience, and Dience had no idea the beast was coming. Raonull's breath gushed out when Michael backed off at the last second letting Rusty's talons latch onto Dience's shoulders and snatch him off the ground. Dragon screams answered Rusty's cry of triumph, and the grove of evergreens exploded when the rest of the dragons joined Rusty in the night sky. Dience's pitiful shrieks, whether from fear or pain, were all that could be heard as Rusty and his escort squadron of dragons disappeared over the hilltop.

Lucifer glared at the pair of southern warriors. Both were careful not to make eye contact with him. *Damn! So much for compulsion...* Lucifer's mind worked furiously. More dragons meant more Anandrian warriors. *Maybe not out here, but through the portal.* Even if he defeated these fools and stopped Raonull and his kin from destroying the portal, there was no way he could free Laura. Sure, he could undo Dience's magic, but he couldn't get close enough to Laura without their powers colliding and annihilating the universe.

He needed Dience! *Not happening.*

"Hades!" Lucifer roared. He needed to leave *now.* Yes, Laura would probably die trapped within the rock of his Lair, but she would be reincarnated. He should have years to complete his domination over the people of Earth. Perhaps, he'd have centuries with her out of the way. It depended upon the length of time before she was reincarnated.

Another standing stone tumbled into the portal. Manus and David had managed that one together. Lucifer felt his rage soar. Creating this magnificent ring had drained him – he was still weak, magically speaking, and needed time to recover.

A bolt of lightning hit the platform of rock that acted as the base for the standing stones. Rocks blasted apart and were flung into the air. Six of the monoliths teetered and began a slow tumble into the portal. There were only three stones left standing. Lucifer felt magic draining away from Earth. *Shit!* But, then again, it wouldn't *all* leave. The tear between the dimensions remained unresolved, Lucifer thought. Only the enhancement of the magic he had created with the standing stones, and the activation of his portal, would be affected. Aye, let them destroy his portal. He could admit defeat – this time.

Thunder and lightning quieted with his decision. More pressing matters called now that Laura's soul was safe from his touch. Good riddance to her – *for now.* If he was lucky, he wouldn't deal with her soul for at least another century.

Lucifer lunged at Paul in a lightning fast series of strikes. The warrior tried to match him, but Lucifer hit him on the arm and cut tendons. Paul's sword clattered to the ground. *Damn it, the one who had engaged Dience is hobbling over.*

Lucifer decided to cut his losses. He ran up Hades wing. If he stayed any longer, all the stones would be down, and the rest of the warriors would be on top of him. He reached Hades' back and checked to make sure Michael wasn't trying to mount Hades as well. But what he saw gave him pause.

Michael and Paul had joined Raonull, David, and Manus in the destruction of his beautiful ring of standing stones. Raonull smashed over one of the three remaining stones, David and Manus had another teetering precariously, and Michael and Paul had their backs up against the final stone, inching it over as their legs pushed in a repetitive pulsing pattern.

"Hades, get out of here, now!" Lucifer roared.

The old dragon beat his wings. Wind swirled lifting twigs and dirt off the ground. His talons scraped the rocks as they took off. He had to fight the current of magic that was rushing back into Anandria.

David and Manus tumbled the second rock into the portal. Lucifer could hear the men cry out encouragement as they joined Paul and Michael with the last stone. He glanced down. With five powerful men pressing on the final stone, it collapsed into the portal. All thirteen stones met at the bottom of the portal in an apex that funnelled magic back into Anandria in a tempest so powerful, it latched onto anything Anandrian that was nearby, and drew it in...

56

Sweat broke out on Douglas's brow. He was on his knees with the book clutched tightly in one hand. The other hand traced patterns over the conjured rock wall Laura was stuck behind. He tried to ignore the sounds of battle coming down the tunnel – it sounded, and felt, like the bloody cave was collapsing. He closed his eyes and gave his head a shake. "Block it out," he whispered. "Concentrate." His eyes opened and he continued to move his fingers over the wall.

Kathryn sent goosebumps down his neck when she breathed into his ear, "Oh my God! It's working."

Vaaron careened around the corner of the tunnel panting heavily, "Lucifer is here."

Douglas felt his stomach clench. He couldn't be distracted now – not when the pattern he was tracing over the wall had started to glow a bright golden colour. He moved his hand back to the centre of the wall and pushed in with his fingers. They sank into the rock like it was a pound of butter. He set the book on the ground, careful to keep it open where he could see it. His free hand pushed into the wall beside his first hand, and he began pulling them apart. His eyes widened when he read the book's next instruction. Skeptically, he pursed his lips and began to pull air into his lungs.

An oily blackness swirled out of the small hole his hands held open. It twisted through the air and arrowed into his mouth. Everyone was horrified when he collapsed on top of his book. Kathryn fell to her knees and cradled his head in her lap. "Douglas! Oh, Douglas…"

"Bloody hell," Vaaron yelled startling them all. "Look at the bloody wall."

Even Kathryn looked up and gasped. No longer was the wall unnaturally smooth and solid. Now, it stood like a sand castle, with individual grains of sand and stone visible. Vaaron shoved one hand into it and watched as part of the wall slid in a mini avalanche to the floor. "Dig!" Vaaron commanded. Muffled grunts came from behind the wall of sand and stone. Then the sounds stopped abruptly. The slit Laura had communicated through had collapsed. "Dig!" Vaaron roared when his mind heard Laura's terrified thoughts. She was having difficulty breathing and moving.

Diana and Morrigan dove in next to Vaaron. Kathryn hauled an unconscious Douglas further away so he wouldn't be buried alive, too. Sand and stones flew as everyone dug.

Morrigan nearly jumped out of her skin when a hand broke through from the other side hitting her in the face. "Got her," Morrigan claimed as she clasped Laura's hand and pulled. Diana and Vaaron dug furiously on either side of Laura's hand. Morrigan kept constant pressure on Laura's limb, pulling gently. More and more of Laura's arm came through. "Guys?" Morrigan gasped. "Her hand just went limp. She's in trouble. We have to get her out *now.*"

"I know. Her thoughts just cut off." Vaaron thrust his arms deeply into the sand that kept cascading down. He felt cloth and latched on. Without worrying about hurting Laura, he pulled with all his might — she could heal herself afterwards if he caused any damage. The sand gave way as he pulled. Then he felt Diana's hand brush up against his, assisting. The next thing he knew, he was on his ass clutching his limp wife in his arms. Morrigan and Diana smiled foolishly down at him.

Everyone was covered in sand. Vaaron tipped Laura's head back. *Damn sand is in her eyes, up her nose, and dribbling out of her mouth. She is still suffocating!*

Diana lifted her mom out of her dad's arms, set her on the floor, tipped her head back, and swept a finger through her mom's mouth. Her training as a lifeguard, when she had been a teen, was paying off. She lowered her mouth and gave a puff of air.

Laura convulsed in Diana's arms and began throwing up. Sand spewed out of her mouth followed by the sandwich and water they had passed to her earlier. She coughed and heaved some more. Finally, her breath evened out. Her hands rubbed her eyes and when she lowered them she blinked red eyes at her family. Sand rimmed her mouth.

"Don't talk, love," Vaaron said on his knees next to her.

Wise man. But I have one thing I must say. She crossed her arms over her chest. "Heal thyself," she whispered. A white glow shimmered over her body. She convulsed until she heaved again, spewing the last grains of sand out of her body. As the glow diminished, she wiped an arm across her mouth. "I never want to be buried alive ever again," she said vehemently. "It's almost as bad as being tied to a stake with flames licking at your feet." Her eyes swept over her hovering family members. "Thank you!" Then her eyes stopped on Kathryn who was imploring Douglas to wake up. "Here, let me," Laura said as she moved over to them.

"Wait!" Vaaron barked. "'Twas dark magic the Druid absorbed. I saw him suck it into his body. 'Twould harm you, Laura, if you tried to heal him."

Laura flinched. She'd had more than enough dealings with dark magic. If there was another way to help the Druid, she would prefer that option.

Douglas's eyes fluttered open. "Kath," he whispered as he lifted a hand and stroked her cheek. "Feel sick..."

Kathryn nodded. Douglas's skin was pale and slightly green, making her think of the *Wicked Witch of the West* in the *Wizard of Oz*. "Dark magic sickens you. Can you expel it from your body?"

"Don't know how," Douglas gasped.

Morrigan scooped up the sorcerer's book. "Would this help?" She held the open book up.

Douglas ran tired eyes over the page. "It says the magic must be purified by pouring it into a pure vessel." His eyes looked up from the book at the worried crowd gathered around him. "I have no idea what that means."

Kathryn sat quietly with his head in her lap as the others threw out wild suggestions. Finally, she said, "Let me try something." She leaned over Douglas. Her lips hovered over his. She felt a pull.

"What are you doing, Kath?" His head began to lift off her lap through no effort on his part.

"I'm testing the strength of my name," she whispered a second before she touched her lips to his. Her kiss deepened and she carefully began to suck.

Morrigan slapped Diana on the shoulder. "Jesus! Would you look at that?"

Douglas's green pallor rapidly faded. Kathryn's hair began to float about her head, and everyone saw a murky green energy leave the ends of her hair and dissipate into the air. Kathryn pulled away. Everyone gasped as the last of the dark magic pulled out of Douglas's body and arrowed into her mouth. A final burst of energy puffed out her hair before it floated down to lie flat against her head.

"What did you do?" Douglas asked as he sat up under his own steam and wrapped Kathryn in his arms.

"My name means, pure. I was the vessel that was needed to purify the dark magic inside you."

Douglas shuddered. "Thank you, Kath." He pulled her into a hard hug. "Are you sure you're all right?"

"Yeah, I am now." She turned her head and placed a soft kiss on his cheek. "Thanks for saving my grandma."

Vaaron cleared his throat. "If the lad is fine, we need to assist the others..." A quake hit the tunnel and everyone instinctively covered their ears and tried to stay on their feet. A cloud of dust whooshed into the tunnel. "Bloody hell!" Vaaron roared as he took off down the tunnel with his sword in hand.

57

"Move!" Lucifer roared. He bashed his heels against Hades' scaly hide.

Hades beat his wings hard, but the return of magic into Anandria was rapid and swift, enhanced by the inverted apex formed at the bottom of the toppled standing stones. Just as they had amplified magic, so too did they work in reverse, siphoning power back into Anandria at an alarming rate.

"Blast it, Hades! Get out of here!" Lucifer glanced down. They were hovering. Then they began to lose ground. "Goddamn it! Fight ye wicked old beast!"

Hades let out a panicked scream. His wings gave out to fatigue, and he surrendered to the relentless pull of the returning magic.

"No!" Lucifer roared as they spiralled over the portal. Beneath them, Lucifer saw Ella get picked up by the magic and pulled into the portal. Her wings flapped uncontrollably. Raonull grabbed onto her leg as she fell, but he, too, was dragged along. Paul and Michael rolled off the portal's ledge and latched on to nearby trees. The trees bent nearly in two, but they kept the southern warriors anchored on Earth.

Small rocks and stones crumbled into the portal. Lucifer wrapped his arms securely about Hades long neck. They were going down. There was no stopping the return of magic to

Anandria. Lucifer's dark magic imbued in the stones was dissipating rapidly as the portal imploded.

He squeezed his eyes shut.

This was going to hurt. He would survive, immortal that he was, but he would not come out unscathed...

58

❦

Ella and Raonull hit the bottom of the portal hard. Ella couldn't catch her breath, but Raonull had the presence of mind to roll with her when dirt and rocks started falling – besides, there was one massive dragon heading their way! They slipped through a gap between two of the stones and fell a bit further to spill out on the floor of the Lair.

"Oomph!" Ella cried as what little wind she had sucked in was knocked out of her again.

Vaaron whipped around the corner of a tunnel followed swiftly by Diana and Morrigan. They skidded to a halt. Gale force winds buffeted them as magic returned to Anandria. Stones and rubble were being sucked through the standing stones to litter the floor of the Lair. *"Where's David and Manus?"* Morrigan shrieked in her amplified goddess voice, making the tunnels shake.

"Here, Morrigan!" David bellowed as he and Manus stepped through another gap in the downward pointing stones. They were covered in dirt and both had scrapes and cuts marring their skin. "You can turn off the goddess volume. We're all right."

Lucifer's dragon hit seconds later, and instinctively everyone flinched and covered their heads. Morrigan's amplified voice was nothing in comparison to the quake the impact of the dragon caused. Walls cracked and fine silt showered down coating everything. Then a deathly silence fell. The portal was plugged. And somewhere buried in the rubble were Lucifer and his dragon. A final, wild breeze lifted everyone's hair and whipped it about dispersing the silt that covered them.

The men lifted their swords. They waited with growing anticipation for Lucifer to squeeze through the debris – but there was nothing. Neither he, nor his dragon, stirred under the tonnes of rock that filled the portal. But they knew no matter how crushed his body, or how much he bled, Lucifer would still live. He was immortal. But his dragon...? Perhaps Hades was dead...

"Diana!" Douglas yelled as he arrived on the scene with Kathryn and Laura following behind. "Diana, join with Kathryn and Laura."

Diana lowered her sword. "What?"

Douglas nodded towards the collapsed portal, stopped next to Diana, and held out his glowing sorcerer's book. Excitement lit his face. "We can separate the dimensions – the tear can be healed. It's all in here." He swept an arm about Laura and pulled her up to one of the inverted standing stones. "Stand here." He grabbed Diana and pushed until she was standing next to her mother. "That's right, mother, daughter..." He looked about and held out his hand to Kathryn. "And granddaughter." He grinned with satisfaction as he pulled Kathryn next to Diana. "There we go. Three generations of the most powerful females in Anandria standing shoulder to shoulder. Now, ladies, place your hands on one of the standing stones, so that Laura's right hand touches Diana's left and Diana's right touches Kathryn's left – forming a conduction line for magic from one generation to the next." He dropped the book off to the side and placed his hands on Kathryn's shoulders. "Life mates should rest their hands, like so, on their partners – as a natural boost."

Kathryn looked over her shoulder at Douglas, one brow arched in question.

He nodded and smiled. "I am yours, Kathryn."

She shivered as his hot breath brushed against her neck. If she answered him in kind, they would be legally wed in Anandria. She smiled. *Yeah, he's a keeper.* "I am yours, Douglas." Her eyes twinkled. *Douglas probably has no idea we are now wed.*

"Good," Douglas grunted as Vaaron moved up behind Laura, and Manus joined Diana. He nodded at Ella and Raonull. "I know you two belong together. Hold hands and stand behind Manus and Diana. Ella, you're close enough that I want one of your wings to curl about Vaaron and Laura. Ray, stretch out your arm and clasp my shoulder – we'll make a living circle. It will all help."

"Now what?" Laura asked from the front of the huddle where she was touching the stone with both hands.

"On a count of three, in unison, we will all say, heal thyself. One, two, three..."

"Heal thyself," they chorused together.

Brilliant light blinded the group. A violent explosion threw them back to land in a heap. Poor little Ella ended up on the bottom of the pile, but they were all in one piece thanks to her fairy magic. Grinning from ear-to-ear, Ella watched as a final piece of rock bounced off her invisible fairy shield.

"Glad you had the sense to shield us," Raonull said as he helped her to her feet.

Ella giggled. "I didn't. My wings were out, and I guess the shield automatically kicked in."

Douglas retrieved his book and brushed it off. He scanned its open pages and nodded with satisfaction. "The deed is done. We've healed the tear between the dimensions. Lucifer is buried inside the collapsed portal – probably why we experienced that violent explosion. Lucifer will not be leaving Anandria with his powers intact anytime in the near future."

Vaaron eyed the solid rock that was once an open portal. "Lucifer will have to dig his way out. That could take a long time, depending upon his injuries."

A shrill dragon cry echoed out of a tunnel off to their right. "Daisy!" Kathryn cried. "Daisy, we're here." Everyone heard scrabbling talons as Daisy picked up her pace. She let loose a roar of excitement when she burst into their area of the Lair. "Daisy, did you find the way out?"

Daisy extended her wing, and waited for Kathryn to mount. "Grandma, I think you and Grandpa should be the first to leave. Grandpa, take Grandma somewhere safe. Then send more dragons back for us. If, for some reason, Lucifer finds a way to free himself in the next couple of hours from the sealed portal, we don't want him going for Grandma again."

Vaaron bussed Kathryn on the cheek. "Lovely child. Your grandmother needs her rest. But I want everyone to follow Daisy to the exit. There are probably dragons already on the way. Debra's bees will be leading the beasts to the area."

Kathryn watched everyone fall in behind Daisy as the dragon shuffled back into the tunnels of the Lair. She jumped when she felt fingers tangle in hers. "Oh!" She bit her lip and smiled up at Douglas. For a moment she had zoned out. And thanks to the Sight, she now knew it would be more than just a few days before Lucifer would threaten Anandria again. He was immortal... He would survive... But it would take him a long time to recover...

Raonull looked back over his shoulder at Douglas with a smirk on his face.

"What?" Douglas demanded.

"Welcome to the family, cousin-in-law."

"What?" Douglas sputtered.

"You heard me. You married my cousin back there. Everyone heard you declare yourself to her, and she responded in kind. That's how Anandrian marriages happen."

Ella squealed and turned about to face Kathryn. "We're related!"

Kathryn grinned and nodded before she turned her blue eyes on Raonull. "What about you, Ray?"

"Me?"

Ella's wings thwacked out, and she fluttered them, rising off the ground until she manoeuvred to a spot hovering in front of Raonull's face. "I'll start, strong man, so there'll be no mistaking my intentions." She poked him in the chest with her fingernail.

"Ow!" he protested. His arms shot out and wrapped about Ella's waist. He pulled her in close, despite her flapping wings. "Even with your annoying pokes, I want you in my life, Ella Donella. For some unknown reason, it's my desire to spend the rest of my days with a fairy."

"We heard that," Morrigan shot over her shoulder.

Raonull rolled his eyes. "Of course you did, Mom. You're the Goddess of War. Your hearing is extremely acute." His Aunt Diana sniggered. "And you, too, Aunt Di, Deity of the Hunt. Christ, a man can't catch a break in this family."

Ella poked him in the chest again, and Raonull winced. "Don't you want to hear what I have to say, strong man? Hmm?"

"If he doesn't, we want to hear if you are foolish enough to invite my son into your life," Morrigan said on a chuckle.

Ella sighed. "Too late, Morrigan. He's already entrenched in my heart." She sighed. "He saved me from the in between place, and cared for me..."

"Bloody hell, woman, are you going to say the words?" Raonull groused. Ella still dangled in his arms. Her elfin grin and twinkling green eyes enchanted Raonull.

"Is that any way to entice a girl to share the rest of her life with you?" Scrunching her nose, she aimed her finger one more time at his chest and grinned as he opened his mouth in protest.

"Ella..." Raonull warned.

"Okay, okay. Raonull, despite your foul moods, and short temper, I would be delighted to tie my life to yours." She giggled and dipped her head to kiss the tip of his nose. Then her whole demeanor changed and she grew serious. Her hands cupped his cheeks as she directed his gaze to meet hers. "Raonull, I would be honoured to share my life with you. I want to laugh, fight, and grow old together." She sighed. "I don't know how I fell for you so quickly." Raonull squeezed her in a hug until she squeaked. "Careful strong man."

"Always," he replied softly. "And for the record, Ella, it's well known that Anandrians fall hard and fast when they meet the one they are to be with." He nodded to the two couples ahead of them. "Just ask my mom and Aunt Diana – both child brides."

"Ha!" Kathryn said from behind. "Aunt Morrigan is almost as old as Grandma..."

59

Mandy brushed hair from her face as they flew through the night. They had slept in a barn curled up on bales of hay. Jeff had slept next to her, spooning her throughout the day. His hard body had kept her warm. Their only unfortunate incident had happened when the farmer had come out to the barn before sunrise. His terrified cows had been mooing, so he had arrived with a shotgun in hand – probably thinking some predator, like a coyote, was lurking about – not a dragon.

The man hadn't a chance. In one bite, the dragon had downed the man and spit out the gun. Then the terrified cows were next. There were only four of them, and from the dragon's reaction, they had been tasty. Mandy still remembered the deep belch the dragon had released before falling asleep.

Jeff sat behind her as they flew. Absently, she picked at the skin on his arm. She had been feeling kind of weird since they had left cottage country behind. She wasn't sure what was bothering her, but she was feeling off and listless. Perhaps it was the pregnancy. But Jeff was feeling off, too.

During the day, she had felt restless while lying in the hay. It was then that she'd noticed Jeff's black leathery skin was cracking and peeling off. Patches of pink skin lay underneath, and when she had tried picking at it, he had brushed her away irritably, muttering, "Go to sleep."

She looked down at the arm wrapped about her waist. The forearm was almost human looking. There were only a few patches of black skin clinging to it. And his hand... Mandy jerked. He had four human fingers! Only his thumb was encased in black with a talon on the end. He was changing! She checked out his other hand that clung to one of the dragon's scales. It still had a full complement of talons.

"Jeff, you're changing," she yelled over the wind that whistled past them.

"I know."

Mandy twisted about, startled by his familiar *human* voice. Patches of black skin hung off his cheeks, and one eye was a chocolate brown. There was a bit of black hair peeking out at his temple.

"You have a streak of grey in your hair," Jeff murmured into her ear.

Mandy's hand whipped up to her wildly lashing hair. She grabbed handfuls lifting the strands in front of her face. Sure enough, there was a patch of grey on the left side of her temple. "What's happening?"

Jeff's mouth next to her ear whispered, "It seems the magic is disappearing."

Mandy felt alarm rip through her body. All she could think about was her new found beauty vanishing. She shivered. Jeff's hot breath still tickled her ear. Disappearing magic would explain Jeff's slow return to humanity. She cringed away from Jeff's hard body sitting behind her.

"What's the matter, Mandy? Afraid you're losing a slave?"

Epilogue

Vaaron groaned as he got into bed. "I am getting old," he grumbled to Laura.

Laura was propped up against her pillows with a book lying in her lap. Her hand reached for his to tangle their fingers together. "We're not *that* old, Vaaron."

"We are grandparents! Tis time we enjoyed our latter years." He rolled towards her and claimed her mouth in a long, deep kiss.

Laura eventually pushed him away with a gentle chuckle. "You don't kiss like a grandpa."

Vaaron wiggled his eyebrows. "There are other *things* I do not do like a grandfather, either."

Laura laughed with delight. "I know. But Vaaron, I am worried."

"Why, love?"

"I'm tiring more easily when I transform gargoyles. I have to keep taking breaks, or putting off transforming some until the next day if there are more than six. I used to be able to do at least twenty in a day. And what if Lucifer suddenly turns up? Then what?"

Vaaron placed a finger over her lips. "We'll not talk of him. From what Aisling and Kathryn have said, we will not be seeing the Dark Lord for a while. And when he does make an appearance, 'twill not be our battle." He ran a finger down Laura's nose. "You have fulfilled your destiny, love."

"How?"

"You returned to Anandria, subdued the evil that was flourishing here, and finally repaired the tear between the dimensions. No one could ask more of you."

"But what if...?"

"Nay, I will not hear more, what ifs. If you are tired, we will send the bloody gargoyles through your portal to Earth. There, their magic will dissipate, and they will return to their human forms just as those did that were left on Earth when Lucifer's portal closed."

Laura sighed. "True. I still find it hard to believe that so many of those that were gargoyles have declined our offer to let them use my portal to return to Anandria."

Vaaron tweaked her nose. "I remember a young woman who once wanted to go back to Earth and forget about Lucifer."

Laura's colour deepened. "I know I didn't make the best impression when you found me. But I did come around. Now, I can't imagine abandoning the people of Anandria to Lucifer's evil."

Vaaron nodded. "And that, love, is why some of those who were gargoyles do not want to return to Anandria. For a time, they were evil. I believe all they want now, is to live out the rest of their lives in peace with no fear of being recaptured by Lucifer."

"I can see that. But, getting back on topic, the people of Earth are still trying to cope with the changes Anandrian's have brought. I don't want to mess them up by sending more gargoyles through. I'll change them slowly, but surely." She reached over to the night table and picked up a vial of Kimberly's shrinking potion. "I just wish this would still work on Earth. I'd love to bring our dragons home."

Vaaron grinned. "Raonull likes having Rusty on Earth. He cannot use his strength there anymore, but at least he gets to go flying – and the Earth armies have been co-operating, leaving our green-eyed dragons be." He squeezed Laura's hand. "'Twas a wonderful idea you had to wrap colourful bandanas about our dragons' necks to show they are friendly. David told me that most of Lucifer's beasts have been destroyed, and the few remaining ones have fled to other corners of Earth." He frowned. "I do not like what we have heard about Toronto, though. When our warriors fought against Lucifer's forces, many great buildings were destroyed. Our dragons, and Lucifer's, crashed into them in the heat of battle. Elfare says that the downtown core is a wasteland."

Laura felt her eyes begin to tear up. The topic of Toronto immediately made her think of Mandy and Jeff. She rolled away from Vaaron with the pretense of putting her book on the night table, but her thoughts betrayed her.

"We will find Mandy. Jeff is with her. He will take care of her."

Laura sniffed. "I worry."

"We all do, love." Vaaron tipped her chin up and looked into her teary eyes. "But for now, relish what we have. Anandria is at peace, Raonull and Ella have decided to stay in this dimension. I understand they are just about ready to leave on their trip north. Ella is determined to find more fairies who can tell her about her fairy powers." Vaaron chuckled. "Raonull is dreading that knowledge." Vaaron was gratified to see Laura's lips tip up at the thought of Raonull bowing down to his tiny wife.

But Laura knew Ella was really searching for more knowledge in anticipation of the day when Lucifer would reappear in their lives. "I just wish Kathryn and Douglas were able to spend more time with us."

"Now, Laura, you know tis impossible."

"I know, I know." Laura snuggled up to Vaaron and tucked her head under his chin. "I still find it hard to believe that that old oak in the backyard of the Professor's house, is now home to the golden book that opens all the continental portals, and the portal in Moyen." Her fingers ran through Vaaron's chest hairs. "I understand why the book has to remain on Earth, only to be released if another breach is made by Lucifer. I mean, if Lucifer ever got his hands on it..." Laura shivered.

"Agreed." Vaaron gave her a squeeze and tried to ignore her fingers trailing across his chest. She was driving him mad. "I am simply grateful that the tree in the Professor's yard was an oak, since their roots always tap into vestiges of magic. It keeps Kathryn and Douglas close to your portal. And speaking of Douglas, he has become quite an adept Druid. One day he will pass on his knowledge to his son."

"Or daughter," Laura interjected.

"Aye, or daughter. He, and generations after him, will keep the golden book, our key to the portals, safe."

"Vaaron?"

"Yes, love?"

"What will happen when we die?"

"We will be reborn and find each other again. We are soul mates, destined to carry on the fight against evil throughout eternity."

"But we will have to grow into our powers?"

"Aye, and Lucifer will grow stronger while we do so. Tis the natural order of things. Good, must grow strong to balance out ever present evil." He gave her a squeeze. "Others will fight the fight until we are strong again. Our time is almost past in this lifetime. I only pray that we are granted, what Earthlings call, our golden years, where we can relax and enjoy each other before the cycle begins again."

Laura opened her mouth to speak, but Vaaron rolled bringing her beneath him. "Tis time we start relaxing, love. I wish to be well rested by the time we get to our next life." He lowered his head and caught her lower lip between his teeth before he kissed her. He sighed and turned on his side spooning her. "Sleep, love. I know you are tired."

Laura pushed him away, and he *let* her, his brow raised in surprise. "I don't think we want to be too relaxed, yet," Laura claimed. "There's a little yellow dress in the wardrobe, and I still fit into it..." Laura watched with satisfaction as her husband jumped out of bed with a loud guffaw, ripped open the wardrobe, scooped up the garment in question, and tossed it on the bed where she lay ogling his bare behind.

Laura sprang out of the bed, the yellow dress clutched in her hand, and headed for the exceedingly brilliant shower Vaaron had constructed. She smiled when she heard, "Bloody hell," come from behind her naked backside.

She would worry about the future later. She pulled up the stretchy spandex dress. Perhaps, tomorrow would bring answers about what had happened to Mandy and Jeff. Perhaps for the rest of this lifetime she would never have to deal with Lucifer again. Perhaps...

"Gotcha!" Vaaron crowed.

*In Anandria, the meaning of a name can enhance one's power.
Below are some of the significant players:*

Laura and Lauren = Laurel, which stands for peace, victory, health and prosperity. In real life Laura is my eldest daughter.

Vaaron = A fictitious name created by my late husband.

Anandria = I discovered this word in a medical dictionary and thought it sounded exotic enough for a magical dimension. Its true meaning has nothing to do with my stories.

Mandy (Amanda) = Worthy of God, lovable. This name was randomly chosen for Laura's best friend. I did not know the meaning of the name when I started, but the meaning will come into play later on.

Dience = I needed a demon name and began looking at parts of words for different sounding names. Dience came from the word *obedience*.

Morrigan = A war goddess, chosen specifically for this character.

Lucifer = Guess what other names are applicable...?

Jeff = Peaceful gift, divine peace, God's peace. I needed a name for the double date chapter, so I ran names of friends through my head and landed on Jeff.

Trymian = Encourages. I felt this name was excellent for the older general who mentors young warriors.

Elfare = A totally fictitious name.

Maleficent = When I picture dragons, they look like the one in Disney's animated *Sleeping Beauty*. Besides, she was Lucifer's dragon...

Apona = Embracing. A Hawaiian name. I was looking for something unique and fresh, so what better than a word from my favourite vacation spot?

Audrey = Noble strength, strong. This name is perfect for a woman who runs a castle. In real life, she's my mom.

Moira = Bitter. Needed for foreshadowing in Book 2.

Dr. Greenwood = A tribute to my real life doctor who helped my family through tough times. I wanted to acknowledge him by including him in the story.

Diana = Divine One, Moon Goddess, Deity of the Hunt. In real life, she is my youngest daughter.

David = Beloved One. In real life, he was my husband – *my* beloved one, and missed deeply.

Debra = Bee. What does one do with a meaning like this, except give the character powers over bees? In real life, Debra is my niece.

Kimberly = From the wood of the royal forest. Another tough name, but I gave her an affinity for plants. In real life, Kimberly is my niece.

Barbara = Stranger, or foreigner. My relatives have difficult names to incorporate, but I eventually found a role for Barb as a dwarf (rarely seen in southern Anandria). In real life, Barbara is my sister-in-law.

Gary = Carries spears. I gave Gary a contemporary role as a Private Investigator. I figured if he were an Anandrian, he would be great at hitting what he aimed at with a spear. So, as an undercover P. I. anything he pointed at with his camera he could shoot with excellent results. In real life, he's my brother.

Hades = Unseen, or dark god of the underworld. I needed a dragon to replace Maleficent in Lucifer's world. Hades seemed like a very sinister name that Lucifer would appreciate.

Ella = Beautiful fairy. In real life, this is my mother's middle name.

Donella = Dark-haired elfin girl. It seemed perfect for Ella's last name.

Douglas = Dark stranger, or dweller by the dark stream. In real life this is my father's name.

Adair = From the dark oak tree ford. Since I was making Douglas a Druid, and Druid's are noted for using oak trees, I used this as his last name.

Daisy = The day's eye. A perfect name for a dragon that is small and has a sunny disposition. In real life Daisy is my 75 pound mutt, who loves to be loved – she is also the runt of her litter.

Kathryn = Pure. In real life this is me! Am I pure? Hmm...

Raonull = Mighty One. Perfect for a character that I wanted to have herculean strength.

And, at the last minute, I had to add in two names, as both Laura and Diana got married before I finished writing the third book. So, introducing two new warriors and drinking buddies...

Paul = Humble. Paul is Laura's husband in real life. And in real life, he is truly humble...?

Michael = A gift from God. Michael is Diana's husband in real life — and she thinks he is!

CPSIA information can be obtained at www.ICGtesting.com
Printed in the USA
LVOW06s0341180116

470535LV00006B/212/P

9 781460 262214